WILLIAM SCHLICHTER

# NO ROOM IN HELL

THE GOOD, THE BAD, AND THE UNDEAD

LIVONIA, MICHIGAN

NO ROOM IN HELL:
THE GOOD, THE BAD, AND THE UNDEAD



Published by Umbra
an imprint of BHC Press

Library of Congress Control Number:
2016954063

ISBN-13: 978-1-946006-51-6
ISBN-10: 1-946006-51-3

Visit the author at:
www.bhcpress.com

Also available in eBook

Cover design, interior book design, and eBook design
by Blue Harvest Creative
www.blueharvestcreative.com

# ALSO BY

WILLIAM SCHLICHTER

## NO ROOM IN HELL

400 Miles to Graceland

## THE SILVER DRAGON CHRONICLES

Enter the Sandmen

The Dark Side

**WHEN THERE'S NO ROOM IN HELL,**
**THE DEAD WILL WALK THE EARTH.**

GEORGE A. ROMERO

# CHAPTER ONE

KAME BOWLIN HURLS the tiny brunette from his truck cab. She bounces twice across the grass. Before she recovers, he laces his fingers into her hair, dragging her to her feet. In the sunlight Kame notes how young she is, but after cupping her left breast, her age loses its distraction. He yanks her by her hair, pulling clumps of it free as he leads her inside the farmhouse.

The barrel of a Barrett M82 sniper rifle inches through the splintered board of a barn loft wall. It focuses in on the second burly unwashed savage as he throws a second girl to the ground. Amid her protests, he rips her garments from her teen body.

The rifle scope magnifies the brutality inflicted on the flailing girl in the grass.

She screams.

He cuts her leg muscle in the lower calf, ending any shot she had at a track career. He slashes at her remaining tattered clothes with no care if he cuts her as he tears the rags for access. Her screams turn to whimpers as he enters her. Submission becomes her only plea to him not to kill her once he's satisfied.

The crosshairs in the scope match up to the center of his bobbing head. The crackle of a shot doesn't stop the violent moments of the remaining man in the truck, even though it is thunderously louder than any weapon the three men carry. In the truck cab, the third girl has her jeans yanked down to her knees and she beats her attacker's shoulder with her fists. Her futile resistance only seems to arouse him further as he climbs on top of her. He seems to be having issues with removing his own pants in the confined space.

The crosshairs focus on him.

The girl's scrawny fingers claw at her attacker's face.

He punches her then continues struggling with his belt. It won't unclasp. Angered by this, he takes it out on the girl with a second punch.

The trigger finger eases back.

The attacker slides from the truck.

The sniper in the barn halts the trigger pull before wasting a round and revealing his location. Surely a second shot would attract the man in the farmhouse.

The attacker drops his pants. He reaches into the truck and jerks off the girl's boots, and yanks her jeans off completely.

She no longer kicks at him. The two punches must have been more than she could take. As small as she is, a third hit might kill her if the second one hasn't done her in.

Her attacker crawls back into the cab. As he mounts the motionless girl, a bullet tears open the side of his head, spraying the back windshield glass with chunks of brain the instant before it shatters from the traveling bullet. The attacker's useless skull isn't even a hiccup for the projectile at such close range.

Seconds later a set of sturdy black combat boots peek from the opening leading into the hayloft of the barn. A heavy duster overcoat obscures the sniper's bulky frame as he swings down. He hangs for a second, allowing his body to stretch as close to the dirt as possible before dropping. On the ground, it takes him a moment to move. Once he's sure nothing's physically wrong, he hobbles forward, limping the first few steps until his left leg seems to correct itself into a normal stride. His slightly uneven gait leaves him as the stiffness from lying in the barn works itself out of his leg muscles. He slings the rifle over his shoulder before flipping his coat behind the weapons on his hips. Choices of pistols line his gun belt. He reaches behind the shiny .357 revolver on his right hip to pull a Beretta obscured behind it. He marches straight from the barn.

No need for concealment. Constant screams from inside the farmhouse mean the third attacker remains too preoccupied with his victim to have noticed the two thunderous shots.

The man kicks over the first vagrant. The 50 caliber round did its job too well. The man has no face and neither does the girl. The second attacker's body pins the second girl in the truck cab. The only movement is her chest heaving with breath. He must be too heavy for her to push off or too wide to shove off her in the cramped cab.

The tortured screams from inside the farmhouse claw at the sniper's stomach. Staring at the girl in the truck cab, he decides he'll come back to check on her. He cowboys up and marches boldly to the farmhouse, shifting his stride at the porch to a stealthy shanty. He crouches down to peek through the diamond-shaped window in the door, and grips his Beretta with two hands. No Dirty Harry, one-hand, badass, gunslinger moment right now. He crouches lower and slides inside, professional in his tactics.

Two shots ring from the farmhouse. A minute passes and the sniper steps out, taking each step to the grass with slow reflection. Regrettably, what he saw inside disturbed even his calm demeanor. He pushes the bile creeping up his throat back into his stomach.

His somber trek to the truck takes an eternity. The trauma imposed by the third man on the girl surpasses even his experiences in carnage. He yanks the dead man from the cab and lets him fall to the ground in a disheveled heap. The teen's chest heaves in shallow breaths as she gulps for air through a swelling face, thankful the pressure's off her. Blood from scratches decorate her inner thighs. He looks down at the dead attacker. His lack of underpants reveals even death won't stop male priapism. He just couldn't get it out fast enough to abuse her.

She raises her head, and witnesses her would-be savior rummaging through the dead men's pockets, confiscating anything of value.

He returns to the truck cab.

As he marches in her direction, she cries without sound and stares wide-eyed at the man in the sable duster coat. She tugs and yanks at her shirt tails in a feeble attempt to cover or protect herself. Even without penetration she has been traumatized from the assault.

He grabs her pants, pulling the legs so they are no longer inside out.

"I won't hurt you," he says, handing her the jeans.

It takes her a few long minutes to consider reaching out for them; like a wild dog snapping at a bone. She snatches them, bunching them up against her chest like a squirrel protecting its stash of nuts. Using her feet, she shoves herself against the far door, away from his reach.

He sets her shoes on the seat. "I meant it. I've no desire to harm you."

"My f-f-f-friends," she stammers.

"Sorry." He knows nothing else to say.

Tears flow down her face and soak the top of her shirt.

"I've done what I can for them." He fishes in his combat vest pocket.

"Are you military?" She dries some of her tears on her pants.

"No. Hardly any soldiers left. The government turned them loose too late to do any good." He tosses several small sealed packets at her. "Alcohol pads. Clean out those scrapes. Stupid animal mauled you with his dirty fingers. You can't afford an infection."

She snatches up the pads before opening her legs—presenting herself. "Take me with you. You do…whatever to me...just, please don't leave me here."

The thought of enjoying her unshaven and juicy young body sends a deep tingle through him. But it lasts only a second. A natural reaction to an attractive sexual offer, but one he has no intention of accepting. He knows the poor girl's beyond confused. No one assaulted as she was would offer themselves for pleasure minutes later. Water collects on her purpling forehead, but not the glistening of nervous pleasure sweat to attract a mate. Her wetness stinks of fear. She must offer, hoping willingness on her part might be less painful if he were to take her.

He sets his sniper rifle on the hood of the truck.

"Come here." He waves his hands in an inviting, fluttering motion.

She skitters toward him.

He closes her legs before tearing open an alcohol pad. He proceeds to clean the scratches like a father would his two-year-old daughter's cut.

"I don't force myself onto young girls."

"I'm 22."

"I don't rape women, or little girls who lie about their age." He presses the alcohol pad hard against her thigh, scraping out any foreign debris. The scratches look as clean as possible. "You keep sanitary as you are able. Let's see if we can find you a sandwich." He picks her up like she weighs nothing.

She lets free a tiny glint of smile. With her arms tight around his neck, he slides her into her pants. She buttons them herself as he walks around to the back of the truck, drawing the .357 before opening the hatch.

"Do you have a name?"

Squeakily, she responds, "Emily."

He tugs at a box in the truck bed. It slides out too easily to have anything in it.

"How did you end up here, Em?" He pulls out a second empty box. This one has a faded FEMA label.

She ties her shoes. "There was a refugee camp. It was controlled by military and the government sent supplies, then the soldiers thinned out. Civilian contractors, for lack of a better name, have been taking over search and rescue patrols, or so they said. These packs of guys would patrol the tents claiming to locate people—missing family members—and had orders to reunite to them. The biggest group was led by the Bowlin brothers. Kame Bowlin took Sophie into the farmhouse." Emily shifts toward the house.

"Did you know the other girls?"

"Only from around the camp." She approaches the back of the truck. She halts when she sees the .357 instinctively rise toward her.

He holsters the gun and pulls a duffle bag from the back of the truck.

Emily knows his gun movement is more instinctual than a direct threat against her. She's seen a few people get shot in the camp because they're all too jumpy. She takes a step back.

She spots the second attacker and her companion both missing their faces. Months in the camp have yet to harden her to death, only teaching her how to cry without noise. Tears roll down her cheeks.

He yanks a backpack from the truck bed and pulls out canned soup and MREs. "When did you last eat?"

"We were stopping to eat, or so they said." Emily's eyes won't leave the girl's faceless body. "Did it hurt?"

"The bullet leaves the body before the brain processes the hit." He keeps his explanation sterile.

"Couldn't you have saved her?" she pleads.

The man marches over and yanks the dead attacker off the girl. A knife flops into the grass. "He cut her throat. After he started fucking her. It causes the muscles to constrict as she bleeds out. What I did was quick, stopped her from drowning in her own blood as he enjoyed her becoming a vice."

Emily begins to gag. She coughs up bile. Her stomach, as much as it heaves, has nothing to puke up.

He takes a water bottle scrounged from the backpack and hands it to her. "Don't go in the farmhouse."

Emily takes a sip, but immediately coughs up the water. "The other one do the same to her?"

"I don't know if he was going to rape her. He derived his pleasure from other things."

"Oh *god.*" Emily coughs.

"I doubt he cares."

He grabs Emily and throws her behind the truck and lands nearly on top of her.

She tries to squirm out from under him. Fear grips her preventing her from punching at him. Her throbbing face a reminder of what happens if she struggles. Maybe this man wants to do more than rape her.

He pins her down and clamps his hand over her mouth.

Her eyes scream betrayal. Why let her get dressed and care for her if he wanted to assault her?

He slides his coat off and unzips his combat vest.

She hears it.

The squeak of worn brakes. Another vehicle has arrived.

She remembers to breathe, knowing he has kept his word about not hurting her.

Three doors open and slam shut followed by the crackle of bullets loading into gun chambers.

Emily squeezes her thighs together to hold in the sudden urge to pee.

He pushes himself off her. He leaps to his feet, favoring his left leg. He raises his hands in the air and steps out from behind the truck.

Emily only sees her savior. For a man with a bad leg, his upper body has no issues.

Male voices scream for him to keep his hands up and to slowly remove his gun belt. The gleaming .357 on his right hip sparkles at her through the many grooves cut into the leather holster. The powerful eight-inch barrel hangs from the bottom of the holster. Her eyes are drawn to its display. His right hand moves to grip, not the magnum, but the automatic Beretta sheathed just behind it. This new gun slides free of its holster with the click of the safety going off. Nine shots ring out, five before her fingers reach her ears.

Bodies smack against the vehicle and then fall to the ground. Emily hops to her feet, but crouches low, slowly raising her head to peek around the truck.

Three men, all in miss-matched military fatigues, lay dead on the ground, each with two shots in the chest and one in the center of the forehead. Only one was able to clear his weapon from its holster before death.

Her savior approaches the truck. "Stay down." He draws the magnum. Walking around the Jeep the strangers arrived in, he opens the back door, gun poised to shoot.

Nothing.

Only three men. The fourth seat has a sack instead of a passenger. He pulls it out and hears the dull thud of full tin cans.

"So much food."

He ejects the clip of his Beretta and begins to add bullets. "Always keep your weapon fully loaded."

"What—"

"They were going to have fun with your friends and sell you for a bag of food. Your dead girlfriends may have suffered but you, you would've been the camp plaything for weeks before they let you starve to death."

She collapses to her knees in a disheveled heap. The reality of what just transpired sinks in. Without him, her last few days of life would have been the most horrid she could imagine.

He holsters his loaded gun in order to search the new men. He takes everything useful from them and stuffs it into the back of the Jeep.

Emily stares, watching him remove boots, and any useful clothing not soaked in blood. He wraps a nice white camo jacket around her shoulders. It's padded for winter wear and still has the dead man's warmth. She should hate it, but it gives her comfort. She drops to her knees then slides against the truck tire, scrutinizing his purposeful movements. He drops granola bars into her lap before siphoning the gas from the first truck to fill the Jeep. He loads his sniper rifle into the front seat and rechecks each man for a final sweep of useful items, ignoring the dead man in the farmhouse.

Once satisfied they are stripped clean of useful items, he yanks Emily to her feet. She wobbles a bit but stands on her own. He helps her put her arms in the sleeves like dressing a two-year-old. He wraps a belt around her waist with a pistol holster attached to it. He waves a pistol in front of her face.

"Ten shots with one in the chamber. Safety on..." is all she hears of his explanation.

He practically carries her to the Jeep, places her inside, and buckles her seat belt. He even wipes a crumb of food from the corner of her mouth. He returns to the barn, retrieving a black bag and small gas can. He tosses the duffle bag into the Jeep before emptying the gas can on a hay bale. He chucks the bale inside the house. He strikes a road flare and throws it in after. The house erupts in flames.

"Are you leaving me?" she screams, waking from a trance.

"Look, little girl, you need to hold it down. Those gun shots will attract the biters. Not to mention the fire." He leaves her again.

It takes him what seems like forever to exit the smaller outbuilding. He carries a pair of bolt cutters and a corn knife.

"I needed some bolt cutters and I figured a farm had some."

"You seem so prepared."

"I try to travel light." He stretches open the skin around her eyes to gaze at her pupils. "You're in shock." He puts her tiny feet on the dashboard and reclines the seat as far back as it goes.

"You know where there's safety?"

"I know a lot of things." He winks at her before turning the Jeep key.

He nudges the Jeep against the tree. The slight bump jars Emily awake.

"You hit the tree."

"I meant to. I've found most people will figure a Jeep wrecked against a tree is useless. They won't bother with it."

"Why don't we just drive wherever you are going?" She pokes at the swollen spot above her left eye.

"I don't want to lug all these supplies around, and I don't want to attract any unwanted guests where I'm going."

"How long have you been doing this?"

"You ask a lot of questions." He disembarks from the vehicle.

"Should I come with you?"

"If you want to stay alive." He marches into the tree line.

Emily jerks at the seat belt buckle, nearly falling out of the Jeep to chase after him. "You were going to leave me. What if I had just taken the Jeep full of food?"

He jingles the keys. "I doubt a socialite girl learned to hotwire a car."

She struggles to keep up with the near limping man who appears to be just under the age of her father. "What makes you think I'm some kind of preppy girl?"

"When I put your shoes on you, you had painted your toenails. I've my doubts a girl bent on survival has the time for a pedicure."

"I like to look nice. It's the one luxury I got in the camp."

"Lot of time for dating where you sleep?"

"You put me in the truck the way my dad used to tuck me in at night. Why are you being such a cartwheeling douche-goblin to me now?"

"Think about it. Nice won't keep you alive."

He grabs her by the jacket and pulls her down to the ground. After the last time, she decides to trust him at the moment and remains perfectly still. He produces small binoculars from his coat. After a moment he hands them to her and points. Emily glances across a field with them. A warehouse sits hidden among trees.

"The place looks new. If the grass were mowed."

"People are stupid. They panic. Imagine the sheer number of people killed rushing to get to Bass Pro when they first realized Grandma was a slobbering dunderhead. I bet thousands ran there knowing they could get a gun."

"I take it not you." She hands back his binoculars.

"I'd a few guns in my closet, so no, not me." He scans the area around the warehouse. "Next, people ran to Walmart and looted the place. More killings, more car wrecks. More chaos. People's brains returned to Neanderthals. Anyone who could remain calm and retain thoughts made it through the first night."

"I was part of an organized evacuation."

"Not many were lucky like you."

"So, what is this place?" Emily asks.

"Kids today. You don't understand how anything arrives on the store shelves." He exerts mild effort to reach a hobbled stance.

Emily wants to ask about his leg but doesn't. "Seems like all your knowledge is an advantage for me right now."

"It does." He gives her the corn knife. "Use this first. The less noise the better."

She grips the machete with both hands, unsure how to handle the weapon even with a practice swing.

She stays on his heels as they cross the field to the warehouse. "So how does stuff get to the shelves?"

"Products are shipped into a central location, unloaded from one truck or train and loaded onto new trucks to be sent to the individual stores. Everything stores need to restock their shelves is shipped to a warehouse before it is sent out to individual stores."

"So this place has food?"

"Some. It's a distribution center for non-perishables. Food would mostly be shipped directly."

"What did you used to do, work in a grocery store?"

"It was a summer job once during high school. This place's off the interstate, so most people don't know about it. The doors are all still secure." He flips the lock on a cargo bay door.

"So you went after bolt cutters and stumbled onto me."

"Yeah...I'm sorry I couldn't save your friends."

"Nobody can save anybody." A tear rolls down her cheek.

He snips the padlock, waving her back before dropping the bolt cutters. Emily raises the corn knife. Gun drawn, he swings open the door.

Nothing. No gross undead smell. The place is clean, clear and dark. He hands her a pen light. "Stay behind me."

"There's no stink."

"A good sign. Doesn't mean the night watchman didn't die in his sealed office. I didn't reach Eldorado to get bit."

"Eldorado?"

"God, you kids can't survive without Google." He rolls his eyes. "When the Spanish conquistadors invaded the American continents they slaughtered thousands in search of a fabled city of pure gold."

"This's Walmart, not a gold city. I don't get it."

Debating if he should continue, he explains, "It was a metaphor for lost treasure."

The wheel turns for Emily as she recalls and English class lesson. "Oh, I get it. You were comparing two things using like or as."

He flashes the light over sealed boxes of products, scanning for anything useful. "A simile."

"Oh. What's *hiss* and *buzz*, you know, where words sound like what they mean?"

"Onomatopoeia." He cuts open a box and jerks out two duffle bags. "Here." He shoves one at her. "You're going to have to carry back some supplies."

"Carry to where?"

"The hundred plus miles back to my camp."

"A hundred miles!"

"A little more actually." He cuts open a box and pockets some small vials.

"Do we have to walk?"

"Some of it."

"No way. The military base's closer."

"Something like forty miles. But you'll never go back there."

"Why not?"

"The best reason, you said Bowlin had brothers, and if he doesn't return some of them will..."

"Will what?"

"I don't know, but you'll wish you were dead long before they kill you."

# CHAPTER TWO

COLONEL WILLIAM B. Travis jogs the freshly spread gravel along the newly constructed chain link fence. Running at his age keeps his joints from stiffening. It seems these last seven months have aged him twenty years on top of twenty more for having a teenage daughter.

Tattered designer clothes dangle from what was once a woman on the outside of the security fence. Rotten flesh hangs from her bones as chunks of meat have been bitten away from her arms. She must have been beautiful before death. She shambles at the fence wanting to satisfy a hunger for those still living. She hisses at Travis as he jogs by.

No one in history has had to deal with an enemy like this. The Infected are the perfect soldiers; they never tire, never sleep, and never stop. Hell, those rotting corpses don't need pay or time off and don't bat an eye when their fellow comrades fall in the line of duty. Blow one up and it still doesn't stop them.

Perfect soldiers.

They do need to eat—their only motivation.

Speculation from Army Command is the undead are the by-product of an engineered virus and introduced as a weapon.

The colonel believes the plague wasn't engineered by someone's military. Reports state it is spread worldwide. So, who initiated this war and how did they plan to win?

Infected gather along the fence. They must smell what's beyond. Warm living flesh—a lot of it. The hunger instinct never wavers from the primordial lizard brain at the base of the skull. Hearing seems to function as well. Scary cataract-glazed eyes prevent vison, and yet they track the living. Even on fire they just keep going: ever in search of satisfying their hunger.

Ratatatatatatat!

The colonel unsnaps the securing strap on his sidearm and runs toward the M16 fire. His training kicks in because no sane person would race toward the sound of rapidly dispensing bullets.

A group of soldiers spray Infected with more bullets.

"Attention!" The men, without hesitation, snap into formation awaiting the colonel's inspection. "What the hell's going on?" Travis demands.

A sergeant steps forward. "We've been ordered to expend this ammo, sir."

"Expend my ammo, sergeant?"

"Yes, sir. Lieutenant Browns couldn't fit these boxes on his truck. He ordered us to expend these rounds."

The colonel scowls. "Sergeant, when he ordered you to do this, did he give you specific instructions?"

"To eliminate any Infected at this end of the base, sir."

The colonel jerks the M16 from the sergeant's hands. "He didn't order you to waste it. He ordered you to use it." The colonel spins around, raises the rifle to his shoulder, and squeezes off five rounds. Each bullet splatters open the skull of an Infected on the other side of the fence.

"Don't waste my ammo, son. I want each of these bullets in the skull of one of those Vectors. We don't have spare ammo to waste. No one will be making any more bullets for a long time. I won't have this again or you five will be on permanent Infected burn detail. Clear?"

"Sir, yes, sir!" They cadence in unison.

The colonel ejects the empty clip, and takes a full one from the sergeant before slinging the weapon over his shoulder and jogging on.

They don't have extra ammo. Maybe he shouldn't have said they wouldn't be getting any more. After nine months the men should know not to waste a single bullet. Half a clip to an Infected's chest does nothing. Hell, many weapons are designed to disfigure not kill. Sending a human soldier home with missing limbs costs willing governments valuable resources to care of the wounded. The disfigured warriors promenading among the civilian populace makes a war unpopular, a tactic employed when both sides have the ability for compassion. Here, these things just keep crawling—forever hungry.

The field he jogs was to be a new tent city for the growing number of civilians still surviving. There should be a lot more people alive but the damn media sent too many to rescue stations already overrun in those first few days. Early energy broadcasts should've sent them here to the Fort.

The civilian numbers arriving overwhelmed the previous base commander. After two months he lost it—ate a grenade. He had to make sure he didn't come back as one of those things. Travis wonders if he had been the smart one.

He has to maintain control of this base, though. Keep his only daughter safe and secure. The only reason he keeps going.

Hannah trudges through the growing muck around the tent city. The refugee shelters remind her more of a third-world slum than a military base in the middle of Midwest America. She saw such a camp once in Africa. Her father had to tour such a place once with a Bush president. She was young. She remembers the plane ride and the little girl at the camp—the one near death, a walking skeleton. The men dragged her away when she begged for food. Loud pops happened after. She knows now they shot her. They shot a lot of people.

Bush sent troops home.

She tries to blend with those stationed in this part of the camp, but she has hot showers where she sleeps. These people have brief and cold running shower water. Her blonde hair hangs in a single ponytail. She had splashed it with some mud to appear dirtier. These people won't trust someone who's too clean looking. Dried blood from a bullet hole decorates her sleeve. The oversized jacket serves another purpose: to hide her budding fifteen-year-old chest.

Hannah didn't understand and had no capacity to help the little skeleton African girl, but the people here she does understand. She knows how to help, even if some of them have forgotten what it's like to be human. Maybe they haven't forgotten. Maybe this is how people are—violent, heartless and selfish. People seem to have been only a few Happy Meals away from reverting back into the savage creatures who crawled from the primal ooze a few hundred thousand years ago. People are savage and that is abundantly clear here.

The base commander before her father built a new gate at this end of the post. Her father pulled back troop patrols to secure what he said would be more safe room for people arriving soon. What he won't admit to her is his substantially shrinking number of troops. He gave clearance for several groups described only as local toothless hillbillies to leave the camp and patrol for survivors. They bring back a few, but mostly they bring back looted supplies. The Bowlin brothers use those supplies to fund a black market. They've even taken away a few people, claiming in another camp their family members survive. She knows of no other camps, but no one wants to believe everyone they once knew has died.

The Bowlin brothers have a circle of tents and a personal team of non-thinking guards easily paid off with foodstuffs, or worse, flesh. A young mother begs the oldest brother for some baby formula even though the camp has already given her rations for her newborn.

Hannah has seen the stacks of formula Washington sent, and she's even handed some out at first until she realized simply handing out food was not enough. She had to do more to help survivors.

She eases closer. The mother explains her baby daddy traded, no, gambled the formula in a card game and lost. Now she has a starving child. He warns there will be a price. The mother agrees.

Kade Bowlin leads the mother into his tent.

Hannah should be too young to fully know what's about to happen but she's not. She knows. The real question is how depraved a sexual act will this mother have to perform in order to feed her baby.

Even with her own slight urges of wanting a boy to explore parts of her body with his hands, Hannah knows consensual pleasure isn't what Kade extracts as a price from women needing food. She pushes the sexual thoughts from her mind. She'll make sure the Bowlin brothers pay for such violations.

The colonel reaches the end of the new fences. Few Infected have gathered here. He jogs up to a group of cargo trucks. Lieutenant Browns snaps to attention at the colonel's approach.

"As you were." The soldiers complete their task of loading cargo trucks. "You give those jokers extra ammo to expend?"

"Yes, sir."

"Next time, you tell them one bullet per each Infected."

"Sorry, sir. We just couldn't fit—"

"I don't want any explanations. We don't have ammo to waste."

"No, sir."

"SITREP!" the colonel demands.

"These trucks are all loaded with the equipment you ordered. The bunker has been hidden and the cement truck's ready to seal it, sir."

"Good."

"Sir, I've got to know. Why don't we just train a few hundred civilians to use these weapons?"

"When you and your men get back inside the fence you're all ordered to get on the next supply chopper. Washington wants to debrief men who have been in the field. Your group has had the most patrols."

"True, sir, but—"

"Those weapons are for resupply."

"Washington's found a way to beat back the Vectors?" Browns asks.

"Lieutenant, you'll be debriefed and filled in on the Pentagon's plan. I just know fuel has become an issue, so resupplying any large troop movements once the retake begins will be difficult."

"I understand, sir."

The colonel turns without another word. *No. No, you don't, son, but I've my orders. You don't even get 'a need to know' pass. I doubt you'd follow orders if you knew what Washington was planning.*

Hannah drags a sandbag off the bottom of a tent wall. The seam between the base and the side has torn. She uses the tear to crawl inside and slides past stacks of boxes all marked FEMA.

She knows these supplies were not issued by the military. The Bowlin brothers must have found it while out hunting for survivors. Her father was foolish to have trusted these men. He may not want to risk the soldiers, but at what cost? It's their job to protect civilians.

Hannah reaches into a box and removes FEMA-labeled beans. Burly, hairy arms lock around her like a vice as a shit-smelling hand clamps over her mouth.

"What do we have here?"

She jerks once in an attempt to escape. Her accoster bear hugs her so tight she loses a breath.

"Now, now, pretty, can't have you going anywhere." He carries her like she weighs nothing into the command tent of Kade Bowlin.

Hannah closes her eyes.

"Get the fuck out! Shitfurbrains!" Kade chucks an empty wine bottle at the burly man, barely missing him.

Hannah feels herself being spun around and the door flap brushes the side of her head. The scene in front of her is etched permanently into her memory. Kade Bowlin has the young mother bent over the table with her jeans around her ankles. She has the look of holding back screaming in pain as if Kade had been doing something with the bottle before he tossed it.

What was he doing to her? Hannah forces the image from her thoughts.

Kade storms from the tent. "What the fuck's wrong with you?" He slaps the man on the side of the head.

"Sorry, boss. Caught her in the tent stores, stealing beans."

"I wasn't stealing," Hannah protests, "I was gathering evidence."

Kade hands the woman her baby formula. She hurries away, limping. "Need anymore, you come see me." He turns his attention back to Hannah. "Evidence of what?"

"Evidence you aren't disclosing all supplies you find when you go on patrol."

"Disclosing. Such a big word for such a little girl."

"I won't debase myself by using your depraved language. Tell this shit-smelling sheep fucker to put me down."

Kade laughs. "Sheep fucker. He would if he hasn't." He shoves his face into hers, glaring into her eyes. "If I were your father I'd wash your nasty mouth out with some soap."

"Touch me and my father will send in every last piece of military hardware this base has to hunt you down."

Kade realizes who this girl is. He grabs her by the wrist and drags her behind him.

"Where're you taking me?"

"To chat with the colonel about a young lady who needs her ass beaten."

# CHAPTER THREE

DETECTIVE HYUN SU Rho hangs out the window, locking his feet against the sill so he doesn't plummet five stories to his death. Twin extension cords rain from the roof. He catches them and pulls them inside. He plugs them into surge bar protectors, and tediously connects the spaghetti stream of cables to the computer tower on the desk.

Police detective Marcus Danziger races down the stairs from the roof, hurrying to the computer.

Hyun Su presses the power button. The machine whirs to life.

"Why is the machine so loud?" Danziger asks.

"I doubt you will attract any DKs. We're too high up."

"Damn thing sounds like a jackhammer. They always sound this loud?" Danziger plugs his right ear with his trigger finger.

"It's not loud at all. You just haven't heard a computer in months," Hyun Su assures him. "Other than the constant moans of the undead, there's no ambient noise floating around." The monitor flashes to the operations screen. Hyun Su types in commands. "Too bad we can't power the full server."

"The solar panel will barely power the captain's machine. At least he used his computer to keep backup files."

"Good for us." Danziger dangles a flash drive before Hyun Su. "Before he died he said plug this into his computer. The password: *crimeleadstoprison1*."

Hyun Su types. The drive opens to a screen of a few dozen folders. He has case files on dozens of unsolved cases. Hyun Su opens one and reads. "The Murphen case. He has evidence the stepson did it."

"Hey, don't waste power. Open the case files on the Blonde Teen Slasher." Danziger drags a printer over to the desk, plugs it in, and loads paper into the tray.

Hyun Su reads what appears on the screen. "Why weren't we given this information? Why did he keep it from us?"

"He had to sequester it or it was his personal theories on these cases we couldn't use without direct evidence. What he knew and what he could prove are two different things." Danziger slams shut the paper tray.

"He had an unnamed suspect we were never given to investigate."

"Print it."

"It's two hundred and eighty pages."

"Print it!"

Hyun Su strikes the key. A low hum begins as the pages stream out.

Danziger grabs the first few pages scanning the information. "After the killer took my daughter, the captain forbid me any access to this case. I heard he had a possible suspect."

"You'd have beaten a confession out of him."

"Any father would. He assaulted my little girl. He deserves no trial."

"Due process would have assured he stayed in prison," Hyun Su says.

The power snaps off. The printer dies in mid-release of paper. Danziger jerks out the half-printed page and rifles through the stack.

"Damn!"

"Should we rewire the solar panel?" Hyun Su asks as an offer to assist his friend.

"No need." Danziger drops all but one piece of paper. "A list of the addresses of possible suspects. There wasn't enough hard evidence to request search warrants, but these people were always persons of interest for the chief."

Hyun Su glances at the list. "Not a problem anymore."

Danziger nods at his partner. Detective Hyun Su leans against the opposite side of the door frame of the rat-infested apartment and returns the nod. Hyun Su kicks in the door. Danziger zips in low, taking cover behind a couch. He rises up, scanning the room with his weapon ready to fire. Hyun Su hangs back.

"Clear."

Hyun Su eases inside with his gun ready. Danziger motions for him to move right toward the kitchen while he goes left to what should be the bedrooms. They split up.

Danziger kicks a chair as he exits a bedroom. He throws a shoe box onto the couch. Hundreds of Polaroid pictures scatter over the cushions.

"Damn." Hyun Su grabs a picture. "Wrong apartment." He drops the scantily clad image of a prepubescent girl. "Fucking child molester."

"Yeah. This was a sick fuck, but not the sick mother fucker who took my daughter."

"We'll find him."

"There are two more possible locations." Danziger holsters his weapon. He storms into the kitchen and tears open drawers. He dumps trash on the couch, flips open his Zippo and lights the end of a roll of paper towels.

"Danz, you know I'm behind you no matter what. Bastard did... your little girl...I want him dead, too."

"Just get to your *but,* Hyun Su." He drops the flaming paper towels onto the pictures.

"I want to leave with the caravan taking off for Fort Leonard Wood. I want out of this city."

"Then we have two more locations to quickly search."

The couch erupts in flames.

"Those addresses are overrun by the DKs," Hyun Su protests. "It's suicide to go there."

"I've got to check each location before we join those going to Fort Wood. I've got to at least leave with a name or some information allowing me to track him down."

Pawing at a chain-link fence, a small dishwater blonde screeches in the low moaning howl typical of the DKs. Hyun Su tugs at Danziger's arm. He won't budge. More corpses gather and rattle the fence.

"Few more DKs and the fence will go."

"Look at her, Hyun Su." Danziger pulls his partner by the shoulder, directing his eyes.

"Just another naked lame brain."

"No. Look at her. She was a teen, blonde."

Hyun Su does more than glance at the once human. "She could've been fifteen."

Danziger crouches down on his hamstrings. Despite the shriveling graying skin, Danziger can tell her inner thighs were bruised. Non-lethal cuts decorate her body.

"She's one of his victims."

"Agreed." Hyun Su rises back to his feet. "I doubt she made it from the other side of town to here. Could mean he was once in this area."

"He's still alive and still hunting."

"The building you want to search…" Hyun Su points across a stream of undead. "We'll never get across this street."

"They're slow. We can outrun them."

"Danziger. Not a hundred DKs."

"We've got to get over there. This dead girl's proof he's here."

"It proves he killed a girl after the plague. He could be far gone. We don't know how long she's been dead."

More undead push against the fence, hungry for the two cops.

"When the first few DKs were brought in, the coroner said it was impossible to predict when they died. Even having known they were only dead a day or two at most. She's not evidence he—"

"He killed my little girl!"

Hyun Su shoves Danziger against the dumpster. It rattles. The corpses spit and moan-howl with excitement. Regaining his footing, Danziger takes a step forward pushing Hyun Su back with just his body.

"Your daughter won't get justice if they eat you!" One of the poles snaps at the base. The corpses moan-howl, pushing forward. "The fence falls and some of these guys will find their way to the caravan. We'll be the cause of dozens of deaths if you don't give up your dick."

Danziger glances at the walls of the buildings they stand between. "What the hell are you talking about, Hyun Su?"

"You know the story about the whale. The peg leg captain was so obsessed with destroying it, that it killed his entire crew for nothing."

Danziger jumps up and grabs the ladder of a fire escape. He pulls it down. "We go up. And I'm not Ahab."

"You sure?" Hyun Su grips the rung of the ladder.

"He lost sight of his goal and put his crew at risk. I put nobody at risk but myself."

"What am I, chicken chow mein?"

Danziger jams a cinder block against the door to keep their only escape route from slamming shut.

Hyun Su stands on the edge of the building staring to the west. "I'm going to miss the view." Across the city, past streets filled with the undead, stands the towering St. Louis Arch gleaming over the skyline. "How long do you think it will last now there's no one to take care of it?"

"This will only be the end of the human race if we let it."

"We've got to make it through this with our humanity."

"We've got to weed out the evils of the old world first," Danziger snaps. His partner shames him with a look. "Okay, you're correct. I do have to stop chasing my whale."

"No. Never. The man needs to die for killing all those girls, but not at the cost of your life. We should leave with the caravan and re-examine how to search for this guy. If he's not dead we'll have to go where there are people to get new victims."

"Okay, but we're here. If I leave the city now we'll have no idea who this guy is. Knowing his address means nothing without his identity." Danziger points to a side street. "Looks clear. These old factory buildings were being converted to loft apartments. They've been mostly abandoned."

"And if this building isn't where he was hiding?"

Danziger doesn't answer as he climbs down the roof ladder.

"I'm guessing this has to be his door."

"An electronic combination lock. Why would anyone need security in an abandoned building?"

Hyun Su tugs on the door handle. "I thought when the power went down these locks released to prevent being trapped during a fire?"

Danziger marches back down the corridor. "I don't know anything about them." He smashes open the emergency glass of fire equipment and yanks out an axe. "I found a key."

Hyun Su steps back—gun ready.

Danziger swings.

The metal rings.

The reverberations, many at a slightly higher tone than living humans hear, echo throughout the building. A DK milling about the doors of the warehouse jerks its head at the noise. Two more quick zings of sound pull it toward the door. It moan-howls and shuffles toward the clear ringing.

On Danziger's seventh swing, the axe shatters the lock. Swing number eight sinks the axe into the bolt lock tearing it from the frame. Number nine sends what remains of the lock tumbling across the floor. Danziger pushes the door open slowly. Hyun Su raises his gun.

DKs gather in what was being remodeled as a lobby to the coming loft apartments. The ringing has ceased but not before it attracted half a dozen corpses to stagger up the stairs. Their moan-howls draw more undead inside.

Danziger, gun at the ready, circles around a table where straps have been bolted in order to secure a person supine to the table. He smells blood.

"I would say this could be our guy." Hyun Su flips the latch on a cabinet. He jumps back as dozens of medical instruments and other cutting tools rain toward him. Hyun Su trips over a chair and swipes his pant leg against a hacksaw.

Danziger pulls him out of the way of the rest of the falling tools, but not before blood pools at Hyun Su's foot.

"I thought spring-loaded booby traps were only in the movies?"

Danziger flings open drawers until he finds some towels. He rips the cloth to make a bandage. "How bad is it?"

"I doubt I'll get time off for being wounded in the line of duty. Hurts like a mother fucker."

Danziger yanks another towel and under it a photo album hides. He forgets all about his bleeding partner. Each page of the homemade book has 8x10 portrait photos of young girls between fourteen and sixteen. Some look professional, others look staged. All look dead.

"Danziger. I'm bleeding over here."

Danziger flips faster through the book. He flings it across the apartment with a barbaric war cry. His daughter's picture hangs torn in his hand. Danziger's knees buckle.

He slumps.

Through his tear-welling eyes, the wavering image of DKs fill the apartment doorway. "Two on the right!"

Hyun Su spins around at the growing moan-howls. Danziger fires. The DK to the left drops. Hyun Su ends the existence of the two on the right.

More DKs flood through.

# CHAPTER FOUR

EMILY STARES AT an actual paper map her savior has spread across the hood. His .357 holds down one corner of the paper while the Beretta secures another corner and the gun from his left hip, a Smith and Wesson M&P, secures a third corner.

Emily's confident he has another firearm on his gun belt he hasn't drawn. Her boredom gets the best of her and she reaches for the shiny Taurus. He slaps her hand away.

"Ouch." She rubs the swollen red flesh.

He never stops examining the map, taking a compass from his vest pocket.

"I just wanted to look at it."

"It's not a toy."

"I know." She keeps rubbing the back of her hand where it stings. "What are you trying to do?"

"Determine how to get back home."

"You drove us down a dead end road."

"I know."

Emily glances again. The front truck tires stop right on the edge of the brown dirt where the road meets the grass. "Just use the GPS."

A quick laugh rolls from the bottom of his gut. "Look, little girl, GPS doesn't work anymore. I don't know how your generation's going to survive the end of the world without your cell phones."

"So you already said. And I can live without my cell, and my hair dryer, and I bet I can live without tampons."

She grabs his full attention. "You bleeding now?!"

"As if."

"They smell blood. You even think you're going to start, you let me know."

"Gross. I never even told my dad."

"Fine. But you tell me."

"And something else. GPS still works. It's a satellite navigation system. These dead people aren't flying spaceships crashing into satellites, so if you have a car charger I can use my phone."

"You're forgetting something."

"What?"

"You need service to operate your phone. Even if these towers work you haven't paid your bill in months. The computers controlling the phones will have automatically shut down your service since you didn't pay."

Emily's face melts.

"Actually, pretty good reasoning, though. There may be hope for you yet," he complements.

She finds herself able to smile.

"A car with GPS should still work, but let me show you how to read a map."

"I don't understand what you're doing."

"Teaching you how to read a map."

"No. Why'd you turn down this dead end road?"

"We're going to walk overland. It's faster and maybe safer than the main roads. The biters seem to congregate along it. Then again, so do living people."

"I know I shouldn't trust people after...but not everyone has to be evil."

"No. But telling which people are trustworthy now is not the same as it was before."

"Will you teach me?"

"I'm still learning myself. I've put together a camp of people I trust. We're building—rather, rebuilding, a life."

"Is it safe?"

"So far, but we've rules, and we still need items to survive. It's my job to find what we need."

"Not even you can carry enough items from the warehouse by yourself to be any use."

"Nope. We get back I'll bring a team to raid the distribution center. Hunting alone for supplies puts fewer people at risk. I would bring a crew of at least ten."

"And if you'd gotten there and the place was empty…they could have died on the mission for nothing. Sometimes you speak like you were in the military," she deduces.

"They wouldn't take me. I've got a bum leg, but usually I walk it off."

"So why park this truck in the middle of nowhere?"

"I've set up, let's say, stations, where I've stashed supplies I need to survive outside my camp. With no cars on the road anymore I don't find it effective to drive around in one vehicle. It draws attention."

"You keep saying. Those people in the camps are just trying to survive."

"You forgetting about the ones who nearly raped you?"

"No, but only a few of them. Most are just hungry and scared."

"The people safe in secure camps can afford to be a little nicer than someone out here. Meet someone who's been scavenging for food for days and doesn't know how to hunt—see how nice they are."

Emily bites her bottom lip. She appreciated the full safety the refugee camp offered even with its overcrowding. But maybe she should have learned more about how to be safe outside the fence.

"Out here, if someone finds one of my stashes of food or a gassed up truck I just have to walk a little farther down the road, but I know where I have more stashed. I'm not stashing this piece of junk, but I wanted to explore this road and see where it leads. If we cut across country here," he drags his finger along the map, "we will reach a truck I stashed. We take it along some back roads and work our way to my camp."

"This must have taken a while to set up."

"Each time I go out I've got to go farther and farther to find supplies, but at the same time we're becoming more self-sufficient. Soon supply runs will be a novelty." He folds the map and slides it inside its waterproof sleeve. "You ready for this?"

"I think." She flips the bag over her shoulder.

He pulls the large bag of food from the truck, removing a can of peaches and stuffing it under the seat.

"You sound so sure about being self-sufficient."

"We'll have to give up certain material items, but yeah, I think it will work." He picks up his magnum and checks the chamber before holstering the weapon.

"Why do you do that?"

"Don't want to be caught with an empty chamber."

"But you haven't used that gun. You use this one." She points to the Beretta.

"I will fire this one. It has eight shots and I keep it super shiny. It distracts people. They are too busy watching this hand-cannon to pay attention to what I'm doing. They figure I will pull it and not the hidden Beretta I have holstered behind it." He picks up the Beretta. "I like this gun. It's lighter, easier to pull and accurate." He ejects the clips. He counts ten rounds and one in the chamber. "This one's my favorite, sixteen shots, Smith and Wesson M&P. Everyone says it has a kick. I don't feel it."

"Why not pull it since it has more bullets?"

"Tried. I draw the Beretta faster, and speed, even against the biters, is essential. So I keep it as a backup on the left hip. It also provides a distraction. They don't know which side I'm drawing from. It provides an extra half-second and keeps me alive."

Emily smiles. "If thirty-five bullets can't keep you alive then you're in trouble."

"You've got to get them out of the holster first, and not miss."

Emily drops the bag and falls against a tree. "How do you do this?" she whines, breathless.

"I've been walking for months. It actually helps strengthen the muscles. It's been easier to find free time to walk since I haven't had to work to earn money for the electric bill."

"I got to rest," Emily pants.

"Soon."

Snap.

He spins at the sound, hand on the gun. A biter shambles from the trees. He snags Emily's corn knife and embeds it in the biter's skull.

Emily jumps to her feet, still breathless, with new energy to flee.

The blade rings with a ku-chunk as it tears out of the skull. He spins around. "Don't scream."

"I won't scream." She unhooks the bag from her shoulder. "But we'd better run." She points.

He turns. Dozens of biters crash through the tree line. They snap and moan-howl as they race toward them. He draws his gun, then the whiff of rotten flesh drifts on the breeze blowing upwind from the attacking corpses.

"What are you waiting for, shoot!"

"Running might be better." He chucks his bag of supplies onto hers, grabs Emily's arm mustering up his fastest possible pace. The undead won't bother the packs.

"You have more bullets than—" Emily's cut off as dozens of undead tear through branches.

"Not now!" No matter how great of a shot he is, no matter how many thousand rounds spent in practice, even if he had a bandoleer of high capacity clips, the growing number of undead would overwhelm him long before he could expend thirty-five shells. Still, a half-crippled thinking man should be able to outrun the faltering corpses.

"Where do we run?"

"Anywhere but here!"

Emily races ahead of him. Her glance back to check on his progress causes her to miss the upcoming wooden fence. Emily flips over the top sprawling into the lush grass.

He leaps the fence landing next to her. He grunts, ignoring the pain of his landing and scoops Emily off the ground, only needing one arm to lift her to her feet.

She doesn't know what happened to his leg, but she's sure he shouldn't have leapt a fence. The trees open into a forgotten yard surrounding a fancy log cabin.

Emily races for the porch. She tugs on the doorknob. It won't open. "Someone's boarded up all the windows." Panic washes over Emily until she spots her savior remaining perfectly calm.

He throws his coat behind his hips as he spins around, drawing both his pistols. He fires one gun and then the other. Chunks of skull, brain and coagulated blood fountain from each biter.

Someone boarded up the windows. Someone could be inside the cabin. Emily bangs on the door hoping someone will let her in. She holds back the urge to scream, her cries would attract the attention of more biters than the noise of rapid firing guns.

Emily steps to the edge of the porch. "I can't get in!"

The door flies open. A couple of hands grab Emily and drag her inside.

"Help!" Emily panics.

A man steps out holding a shotgun. "Hurry! Get inside."

Emily's savior leaps onto the porch, empting the last five M&P rounds, demonstrating his skill by not missing. The guy with the shotgun races inside, followed by the man still shooting at the biters. The door slams behind them. Emily's savior has an empty gun in each hand, leaving him with no way to draw his magnum. If the man with the shotgun turns out to be a threat, he will have no other option but to pistol whip him.

He sizes up the situation, and decides to give their rescuers the benefit of friendship, raising the M&P to show the open slide.

The man with the shotgun holds it at an angle revealing he doesn't know how to use it.

He bets the shotgun has only one round loaded into it—maybe. The way the man handles it, it seems a little light to have five shells loaded. The problem with testing theories is one round of buck shot covers a lot of territory.

"Thanks for letting us in."

"It was God's will."

A small woman unclasps Emily's arm. "It was God brought you to us."

Emily notices the waxing of her savior's face. In the small amount of time she's known him, she'd bet he follows no religious path, but she keeps this thought to herself.

"God led you to us," the shotgun wielder adds.

"We can discuss who brought who where and how, but first, let's put away some guns."

"Sorry." He lowers the shotgun. "It's not loaded. I found it here. I'm Joshua."

Before Joshua introduces the other two men, the small woman says, like a mantra, "God brought us here."

"What were you doing when you were led here?" He asks.

"We've been following His word."

He slips the empty clip into his pocket and eases another one in the M&P. He holsters the weapon without releasing the side. "God talks to you?"

"Through one of his prophets," she says as she holds up a hand crank radio. "We were following his broadcasts when the tire on our van blew."

"I didn't want to change it on the blacktop," Joshua adds.

"Smart."

Joshua explains, "We rolled in here when the wave of the punished drove us into the house. The owner had saw fit to barricade the home before he went home to God."

"The punished?" Emily asks.

Her savior's eyes snap at her like a father about to ground her for a month.

"Yes, child, the punished. God promised to rid the world of sinners. The soulless never to reach His glory." The woman lifts her arms to praise His glory.

Scrapes, like a dog at the door, turn to pounding as more and more biters climb onto the porch. He draws his Beretta and jams in a fresh clip.

"It's okay, mister. God will protect you, just as He has been protecting us."

A boarded window collapses in from the weight of three biters. Before those undead recover more biters crawl in on top of them, filling the window.

"Where's God now?"

"Don't blaspheme," Joshua snaps at him.

"You're not one of the faithful. God's sending them in here after you because you are not worthy in His eyes," the woman says, her accusatory index finger shakes at him in disdain.

"I don't have time for this shit. Em, get upstairs!" he snaps.

Emily moves to the stairs. The woman holds out her arm as a gate stop. "Sweetie, the punished are only here for those faithless. You don't have to follow him," she points at Emily's rescuer, "if you believe in Him." She points up.

More biters crawl through the window. Emily's savior pushes past the two unnamed men. Joshua raises the shotgun, and finds the Beretta within an inch of his temple. "Yours is empty. Mine's not."

Joshua lowers the shotgun and steps back.

"Em, get the fuck upstairs."

Emily bolts for the stairs. Joshua swings the shotgun like a club. Biters spill through the door. The shotgun connects with his bicep. He staggers back. Moments of intense decision must take place in a tenth of a second. His mind fights back the surging pain of his left arm. He feels the capillaries bursting and the bruise forming. He counted at least seven biters entering the door. As he focuses on not thinking of the pain, counting biters and avoiding the zealots, he notices a long handled axe leaning against the fireplace.

The seven biters...he's sure hitting four will trip up the remainder. He's not sure he wants to kill the living. Weighing the situation, he considers. *Right now these people are misguided. No one has given a reason for the rise of the dead. God forsaking us is as good an explanation as any. The axe is the key to an escape plan, not a foolproof one, maybe even a completely stupid one, but it will keep the living alive.*

He pops a biter and kicks the closest servant of God just as Emily reaches the stairs. He shoves the woman after her. His smoking gun burns the end of Joshua's nose. "Move," he orders. The four religious fanatics dart for the stairs.

Bam. Bam. Bam.

Two biters fall. The third bullet splinters the shoulder. Not a miss, but not effective on the undead, either. The second the two biters fall the third moves into their position.

He grabs the axe in his left hand and backs up the stairs. Two more biters drop from head shots. He holsters the Beretta. The axe digs into the wood.

The stairs act as a bottleneck, allowing no more than two biters to approach at a time. He splinters the wood, rendering the bottom step useless. He has seen some corpses still use tools, rocks to smash, one even held onto a gun even though it was essentially just a loaded club. He hopes they don't have enough of a brain stem left to figure out how to climb over a few broken steps. He jerks the axe from a biter's head and drives it into the next wooden plank.

"Look out!" He turns in time to use the axe to block the shotgun—turned club. Glancing past Joshua, he spots Emily, struggling to free herself from the other man's grasp.

*So much for sparing these poor, misguided people.*

The shotgun flies at him again. Readjusting his footing to block the blow means using a step he just smashed through.

# CHAPTER FIVE

KADE DRAGS HANNAH by her arm to the gate of the base headquarters.

"Corporal, get Colonel Travis," he demands.

Hannah has given up struggling against his iron grip. She has no doubt Kade has more strength than she could ever gain. She contemplates screaming, drawing attention to him, but decides this may harm her case with her father. It's childish. He clearly won't hurt her, especially not in front of the soldiers. The soldiers would beat him down good. Later he'd just take it out on some poor mother trying to feed her baby.

She forces away the image of Kade behind the bent over woman and the wine bottle. The way the poor woman limped away. There's only one thing he could have been doing with it. She coughs up bile as her stomach twists in a knot. Hannah feels the hard jerk as he drags her through the gate.

"Good morning." Her father, sweating from his morning run, greets Kade, not even questioning why Kade has a hold of his only daughter.

"Colonel, I think we should discuss this...in private." He flings Hannah at her father.

"Acceptable." Travis grabs Hannah to steady her.

She bites her tongue. She wants to protest and scream, 'just shoot this ugly bastard,' but reason works better on her father. She has no tactical advantage here. This man must be shot before he violates another woman.

Hannah plops on the leather couch in her dad's office. Travis sits at his desk. Kade remains on his feet uneasily glancing at the rifle the colonel places on his desk.

"Sit," he offers.

Kade glances at the chair but he keeps on his feet. The simple invite's not enough for him to give up the high ground; a strategic power play on his part he believes makes him the big man in the room.

An illusion, Hannah knows, if her father keeps to his normal tactics.

Travis slides open a desk drawer and pulls out a bottle of scotch along with two glasses. He pours the brown liquor, corks the bottle, picks up a glass and sniffs the fragrance. He soaks in the aroma, but does not drink.

Travis waves his hand offering the chair again. "Please, join me in a drink."

Kade snatches the glass, and falls back into the chair. He gulps the shot, an insulting gesture if the colonel lets it get to him. A pure waste of the expensive liquor and possibly last to be made. But at least they have reached a level playing field. Hannah smells the testosterone in the room.

Travis savors the liquor's bouquet before sipping his drink. "You just dragged my daughter across the camp. I need a reason not to shoot you like a dog."

Bold on Daddy's part.

Kade backs down and moves like a knight on the chessboard. "We had a deal. You're precious little girl was caught stealing from my tent."

Hannah upsets the board. "I was not stealing! Dad, he was raping a woman with a wine bottle."

"Sit down and remain quiet." Travis keeps his eyes on Kade.

Kade keeps one eye on the weapon. Hannah falls back on the couch in a pout.

"One of my men caught her taking food from my tent. He brought her to me. I brought her to you, unharmed. None of my men have raped any woman in this compound."

An accurate statement, by Kade's definition only. Hannah knows her father's face. He believes no rapes have been committed behind the fence.

Kade smiles. Speaking the truth works. He gains nothing with a lie. The woman willingly participated, even if it was forced upon her by circumstance. What Hannah understands and her father realizes is Kade's choice of *in this compound.*

Thoughts race through Travis's mind. *How many women has Kade rescued who never reached the military base because he assaulted them in the wilderness and left them dead so they couldn't report on him?*

Her father's attention turns to her. "Hannah, what were you doing on the refugee side of the base?"

"I was passing out food. Helping people. The Bowlin brothers run a black market. He trades items to needy mothers for depraved sexual acts."

"We've a deal," Kade spouts his constant defense.

Travis leans forward in his chair—a debating attack posture. "We *had* a deal. Since the growing number of refugees, I've needed more of my soldiers to keep order on the base. You were to patrol the area and bring in survivors. Anything you found on the patrols you could keep or trade."

"He has food. The tent was full of FEMA boxes."

Hannah's words jab at Kade. He avoids the urge to stare daggers at her. Better to focus on the colonel and the rifle.

"We found an overturned FEMA semi. Under our deal..."

Hannah doesn't understand what deal they had, or why Kade admitted to the food so freely. Something else has to be going on. Her father would never let a man like Kade run loose.

"Trading a few cans of soup you find out there is one thing, but entire stocks of emergency food go beyond our deal."

"My men took the risk to recover it."

"Then you keep a few boxes. The rest will be circulated into the rations for the base. We've a lot of mouths to feed. And even you only want to deal with the right amount of hungry people."

Fire lights Kade's eyes at the colonel's threat.

Hannah protests, "What about the black market and the woman—"

"Quiet, Hannah," her father snaps. "The black market's a necessary evil. It needs to exist to bring hope. People still cling to items they had before the apocalypse. Items they don't need now and won't keep them alive. But when they have them, they feel better and it helps keep people safe. I don't approve of trading for sex, but if it's not forced, it becomes a choice."

Hannah's anger prevents her seeing how painful it was for her father to make such a statement. "Such a male's answer. She had no choice! She traded her body for baby formula."

Colonel Travis's full attention turns back on Kade. "All babies get more than enough rations."

"Then why'd she have to trade?" Hannah's question eats at her.

"Maybe she likes what I do to her."

Hannah feels the bile crawl into her throat.

"Kade!" The dam bursts on Travis' anger.

Hannah's never heard her father speak in such a tone before.

"I don't take nothin' from children. The black market isn't your problem. I provide a service, get a little ass for me and my men, but we remain on the level. We've a deal. I honor my deals. But maybe you should investigate the growing gambling dens. Give you a better picture on how women lost their government-issued formula."

From her father's widening eyes Hannah knows the existences of the gambling dens are news to him.

Soldiers simultaneously burst into three tents near the Bowlin brother's part of the camp. Kade witnesses the dragging of card players and other clear deviants from each tent. Several scantily clad women are also shoved down into the mud, their hands zip-tied together. The entire action seems to last for an hour but only transpires over sixty-seven seconds.

Kade's dwindling black market profits due to these high stakes poker games caused concern among his brothers. The cards were becoming popular as a means to earn quick supplies. Confronting the practitioners would result in a turf war costing Kade his station within the camp. People were betting everything they had left in the world to win what they needed to survive. Only most were losing. A few would win big to attract others, but no one beats the house, just ask anyone attending Gamblers Anonymous. Kade even endorsed some of the games, at first, getting a small kickback. He had left that part out when he explained to the colonel what he knew.

Kade grins even as soldiers carry the white FEMA boxes from his tent. With the elimination of his competition he just boosted his own cache.

"They left us twelve boxes," Hector whispers.

"More than we need to continue our trade along with our other supplies. We make another run and get more. The tractor trailer was still half full. This time we just don't bring in as much, and maybe find a place outside the fence to stash the rest."

"You know best, boss."

"The colonel has done more for us today to increase our situation than you know. Consider those few food boxes as an investment."

Hector clearly doesn't understand why Kade finds this arrangement acceptable. He's merely blind muscle. Every organization needs unquestioning muscle.

The colonel lights up a stogie.

"Dad, do you have to smoke in here? This Humvee has no windows to open," Hannah whines.

Travis ignores her. He glares out the window at his soldiers cleaning up the poker games. They carry the spoils from cheating people out of what little they have and load them onto the back of a cargo truck.

He had decided on the punishment for any non-essential personnel involved in this, now as Travis puffs his Cuban cigar, he determines how to live with it.

One of the men controlling the gambling den makes part of the decision easier. He draws twin machine pistols and fires with the intent of not being taken alive. Bullets pelt the cargo trucks and soldiers and civilians dive for cover.

More than one soldier gets the brilliant idea to stop this counterattack at the same moment. Travis sees the train wreck about to happen, unable to do anything. No one thought through what will change so many lives in the next five seconds. Even with all the training in the world no one is competent enough to deal with how the apocalypse has changed reality. No one was trained for this.

Quick on their feet, soldiers pop up, flipping their M4 carbines to full auto and clamping down on the trigger. The twitching dance of a hundred bullets impaling a single person happens in two seconds. The next two seconds expand the damage. The man was surrounded by other living people and the soldiers, no thought was given to the bullets tearing through or missing their target completely. Collateral damage—the military's actable term for civilians lost in a military operation. Soldiers directly across from each other dance with the impact. Wild shots strike civilians. People die.

Only now, after the end of the world, people don't stay dead.

# CHAPTER SIX

DANZIGER JAMS THE fire axe to secure the door from the DKs filling the apartment.

"Danz, I'm bleeding, bad." Hyun Su props his leg up on the bed while he lies on his back on the floor.

Danziger rips a sheet and wraps it around Hyun Su's leg wound. The baby blue material mushrooms with red. He ties a second strip of cloth around the first.

"Tie a tourniquet."

"If I do, you won't be walking long. I can't carry you out of here." Danziger grips Hyun Su's hand, pulling him to his feet.

Fingers claw at the door. The frequent scrapes give way to a shoving and pounding of hungry DKs.

"What's your exit strategy?"

"I was hoping you had one." Danziger yanks on the window sill.

The door buckets against the axe.

"Those DKs are the most aggressive I've seen."

"They haven't had a steady food supply in a while. Hunger drives them." Danziger smashes open the window.

Noise sends the DKs into a frenzy. The door gives under the thrashing of bumping bodies.

Danziger helps Hyun Su out the window onto the fire escape.

The axe flies from the door, skittering across the floor. Danziger races for it. Half a dozen undead shove past each other attempting to enter. He reaches for the axe before the DKs trample over it, but stops when he hears Hyun Su shout.

"Danziger!"

He whips his head around. Hyun Su points to an end table. A fallen picture frame rests. He doesn't hesitate. He trusts his partner and grabs the frame, leaving the axe, and jumps to the window sill. Hyun Su works his way down the metal steps. Danziger pauses to look at the framed image. He smashes the frame on the rail and stuffs the photograph of a man with an older woman into his pocket.

He slides down the stair rail, catching up with Hyun Su. "Better be him in the picture. The axe would help get us out of this."

"If you don't know what your whale looks like then this was all for nothing. I can't die for nothing. It's bad for my Chi."

"I thought Chi was a Chinese belief?"

"Your point?"

"You're Korean."

"Most white people can't tell the difference." Hyun Su drops from the ladder. Clotted blood splatters on the asphalt like a smashed ketchup packet. He limps out of Danziger's way.

"I don't think race matters anymore. All the living are food for the dead." Danziger grabs Hyun Su's arm and acts as a crutch to help his friend hobble along.

DKs fall from the fire escape, splattering in heaps of broken flesh. One lands on its head. The second's legs crunch into goo, but the upper torso drags itself after the two detectives.

"We better move." Danziger steps up his pace, half-pulling Hyun Su with him.

"I don't think I can climb the ladder."

"We'll find another way out of here."

"Not before the white whale gets me." Hyun Su drags his knee on his next step.

"You better stop now."

"Stop what, Danz?"

"Thinking about giving up. We won't die today."

More DKs drop from the fire escape. Bent on eating they leap to their disfigurement. They break arms, legs, backs—slowing them down. A few smash their skulls and they twitch for a moment then cease to function.

A large male DK drops from the rail landing on its feet. It bursts into a full run, moan-howling as it barrels into Danziger. The detective and his partner smack into the ground from the tackle. Danziger feels the air forced from his lungs as his chest deflates on impact with the pavement. Normally he would take a minute to recover his breathing, but the DK won't rest. The monster has already moved closer in order to sink its teeth into Danziger's pink skin.

Light-headed from blood loss, Hyun Su flails his arm, slapping the beast. A living person would be taken aback by such a desperate move but the undead takes no notice. The swift moving DK clamps down on Hyun Su's hand. Before completing the bite, Danziger wedges his pistol between the rotting teeth. The bullet sprays coagulated blood through the opposite cheek. He moves his hand and squeezes the trigger again. This time the bullet rips through at an angle. The shell rides around the skull ricocheting. The third shot after another quick twist of the gun and the DK's brains splay out the back of its skull.

Danziger shoves the inanimate creature off them. The other damaged DKs pick up the pace toward the two detectives.

"I've never seen one move so fast."

Danziger tugs Hyun Su to his feet. "He had a thick skull. I've heard you can live after a shot to the head, but he took two."

"You're going to have to leave me, Danz. I'm too weak."

"What, you want me to let them eat you while I escape? I don't abandon my partner." He pulls down a fire escape ladder. "We get to the top we can rest all you want."

Hyun Su falls over. Danziger drags him away from the edge.

"Danz, help me to the wall over there."

"This isn't some fucking goodbye moment."

"I'm afraid it is." He raises his hand and shows the cuts from the DK's teeth. "He got me, brother."

Danziger raises his gun. The barrel shakes in his hand.

"I can do it," Hyun Su offers, pulling he own gun from his belt.

"No. I can't watch my partner blow his brains out."

"I can't watch your hand shake. You might miss." Hyun Su props himself up against the wall. He stares out at the skyline, taking in the view of the Gateway Arch overlooking the ravaged city. "You ever been up inside?"

"Yeah, a couple of times."

"I've lived here my whole life and I never once went inside. How do you live some place so long and not visit the most majestic of human creations? My regret, Danziger. Do me a favor, don't die with any regrets. Don't let the white whale consume you." After a moment, Hyun Su hands Danziger his gun and two full clips. "I don't think I can do it after all."

Danziger sucks in a deep breath before he reaches for the gun. "It's the least I can do, my friend."

"Wait until I turn? I just want to enjoy the view. I want my final memory to be one of human accomplishment."

Danziger plops down next to Hyun Su. He pulls the photograph from his pocket and flips it over. Scribbled on the back: 'Levin with Mom,' and a date. A name and an image. It's more than he had before. With it he might finally locate his daughter's murderer. Hyun Su's head falls against Danziger's shoulder, snapping him from his thoughts of vengeance.

He nudges his shoulder. "Hey, you awake?"

No answer.

Hyun Su's chest fails to rise.

Danziger slides out from under his partner. He folds the picture and stuffs it deep into his pocket. Hyun Su's body lies lifeless on the rooftop. Danziger gets to his feet, stepping back from his friend.

Hyun Su's eyes flash open in a glazed cataract stare.

Danziger ends his closest friend's existence.

# CHAPTER SEVEN

LEFT WITH NO real choice, Emily's rescuer allows the shotgun to impact his shoulder, sending him slamming into the wall. Despite his muscle bulk, a seemingly high pain tolerance and being able to take a hit like a linebacker at full speed, this hurts. No amount of preparation makes a difference when someone swings a steel pipe at full speed. Luckily, being as tall as he is, his shoulder takes the brunt of the impact. He's sure his head was the intended target and would have been taken clean off.

The last thing he wants to do is kill the living. With the growing number of biters at his heels, he could use these people's help to survive. But somehow people never look past their petty beliefs and realize they have to work together to face this new world.

He flicks his left wrist. A blade the length of his forearm extends from under his coat sleeve. He jams the shotgun wielder in the gut before he swings again. As Joshua slumps to his knees, the shotgun loosens in his hands. Emily's savior wrenches it free from his attacker and dumps the still-alive acolyte to the bottom floor. The biters scramble to this fresh meal.

He sinks the axe into the step and marches up to the second floor. The woman screams and runs to a bedroom. The other acolyte feels the blade slash across his chest. Emily squirrels out of the way. The screams of one acolyte are replaced by the thump of the second one impacting the floor. He twists something against his arm through the coat sleeve. The blade drops to the floor.

"Fornicators!" the word echoes from the bedroom.

He moves fast. Emily stays on his heels.

The woman screams and damns the young naked couple now shamed on the bed.

"You defile yourselves out of wedlock and bring sin to our group. You're the reason the punished have brought the evil to us. Sin must be cleansed from the world." She raises the .22 pistol Emily had on her waist and fires twice at the young man. The girl and Emily scream. Her savior clubs the woman with the butt of the shotgun. She slumps to the floor. The gun bounces across the floor.

"How many are in your group?" he asks the naked woman on the bed.

Her eyes never leave the dead man who was just inside her.

"Look, I want nothing to do with their Bible thumping. But there's safety in numbers and..." the girl tries to explain.

"How many?" he demands.

"Six of us."

Emily plugs her ears with her fingers, but the shot has already damaged a frequency of her hearing. She slumps to one knee her brain ringing with microphone feedback whines. He holds his smoking .357. Nothing remains of the face of the fourth man as he collapses to the floor, the axe in his hand.

Her savior kicks the .22 at Emily.

"Keep her covered."

He takes the axe and dumps two bodies to distract the biters.

"Should I let her get dressed?" Emily asks on behalf of the girl. She feels her discomfort, imagining if she were naked with a gun pointed at her she'd want to at least cover herself.

"No."

Emily keeps the gun level, but says nothing as the girl draws the sheet around her. She figures he'd at least let her cover herself. After all, he saved her from those crazed rapists.

The axe smashing wood echoes blearily audible over the growing moan-howls of the feeding biters.

He comes back in, sweat covering his face. "They won't get up here."

"How do we get out?"

"Let's worry about it later." He pushes her hands down lowering the pistol aimed at the nude girl.

"What about her?"

"I've a name you know," protests the nude girl. "Bella."

He looks at the quivering naked woman. "Do you have to use the bathroom?"

"Yes," Bella stammers, staring toward one of the doors. "We flush this one." She points to the door next to the closet.

His gaze clearly questions her believability. "How? This building has no power to run the pumps."

"There was a hand pump out back. We found buckets and filled them and the tub. We'd all use the toilet and then flush. It's been so nice to go indoors."

"Good plan. Go use it, but leave the door open."

He keeps one eye on Bella as she uses the toilet.

"Why are you being so mean to her?" Emily speculates her savior has some form of bipolar disorder. He protected Emily from being raped but now she finds him unreasonably gruff toward this helpless woman.

"Emily, we don't know her."

"She wasn't one who attacked us."

Bella stands before them in a hunched begging stance. "I want some clothes."

"No." He pulls a zip tie from his coat. "Lay on the bed in the position you want to sleep in."

Bella does without question. He binds her wrists to the bed. "Em, cover her up." He drags the body of her dead lover from the room.

He dumps the body over the rail and watches as it crashes onto the biters who continue munching at the other corpse.

Emily marches after him. "I don't understand. She's a helpless woman, and I was a helpless woman this morning and you treated me so much better."

"This morning you were a helpless little girl and not part of a group trying to kill me. Now we sleep in this room and tomorrow we'll see about all three of us escaping this place. Bella stays tied up until I feel trust."

Emily pouts and stomps back into the bedroom. He moves a heavy oak chest of drawers toward the door.

Emily pauses. "Wait. I want one of the buckets of water. I want to wash my cuts."

He opens the door for her.

Emily struggles to carry the five gallon bucket down the hall without splashing water on herself. She half drags the bucket. She slips a small folding pocket knife from her jacket and tosses it on the woman.

Bella smiles at Emily.

Emily plops the bucket on the floor of the other bedroom. Water splashes her jeans. He tilts the dresser, sealing them in the room. No way could anyone push open the door without first making a lot of noise.

Emily strips to her underclothes.

He unclasps his gun belt and drops it on the table beside the bed. She was right. He had another gun secured behind his back.

"Why so many guns?"

"I like breathing." He kicks off his boots with well-worn soles.

"You don't have to be so mean."

"It keeps me alive."

Emily parades around the room in her panties and form-fitting tee. Normally she would hide herself under a blanket before she allowed such an older man to see her almost buck naked; however, he's treated her with respect instead of as a piece of meat. She finds a wash cloth and uses the cold water to dab at the cuts. Her thighs have turned purple from the attack. She almost asks him to inspect the cuts but his eyes avoid her. She smiles, not wanting to ruin the gentlemanly behavior he exhibits toward her in his own way.

Averting his eyes from Emily takes more willpower than expected. He would never force himself on any woman, or in her case, a little girl. But her attractive figure still brings on distracting human urges. Urges that in the face of danger would cost lives if she were to become bitten and he loved her too much to end her. Too many people had died because they couldn't shoot a loved one returned from the dead. One mistake he won't make. The M&P rests near his right hand. He closes his eyes. "After you feel clean, run an alcohol pad over those cuts again and sleep in the chair."

Pop. Pop. Pop.

He jerks from his slumber, gun in hand. The moonlight illuminates enough of the room for him to witness Emily fall from the chair.

"What?!"

"Low caliber weapon. Most likely a .22 pistol."

Two more pops echo and then a woman screams.

He pushes the chest of drawers away from the door. The moon's illumination keeps shadows dancing in the hall. A biter fumbles around the stair landing. He eases into the other bedroom. The sheets are empty except the zip tie he snags from the bed. The broken end feels cut. The constant moan-howl of biters emanates from the open window. He eases through to peek out. The biters have gathered below a tree. They tear at Bella's flesh.

He hears Emily's bare feet squeak the floor behind him. He spins around, grabbing her and pulling her face against his chest to prevent her from the view outside the window.

"I wouldn't. Spare yourself when you can."

Emily jerks away from him, and glances out the window. "My fault." She flings herself at him burying her face against him again. "I let her go." He feels her budding hard nipples dig into his chest. He pushes her to arm's length removing her perky breasts from his body.

"Bella made her choice."

"She was scared of you. You could've been nice to her."

Staring into her green eyes he asks, "Where did she get the gun?"

"What?" Emily wipes away a tear and lowers her face, not wanting to cry in front of him.

"She had a gun." He takes Emily's chin in his hand glaring into her eyes. "Did you give it to her?"

"No. Just a penknife to cut the zip tie. I swear."

"They had a shotgun with no shells and needed to protect themselves. She had a loaded gun she kept hidden, even from her traveling companions. I wouldn't shed many tears for her. She doesn't rate high on the trust factor."

He leaves Emily to her thoughts, wanting to return to a comfortable sleep, a luxury he rarely gets scavenging for supplies.

She races after him. "How did she get down?"

"A thought-provoking question." He drops the chest of drawers against the door. "She used the tree next to the window."

"Then we can use it to get down." Emily beams with excitement.

"You, maybe, not me. And remember, she didn't get far."

"She fired a gun. Noise attracts them."

"You're catching on, Em." He closes his eyes and rests his hand near the M&P again.

"It's getting cold. Can I cuddle next to you?"

He never opens his eyes. "There's a quilt. It will provide plenty of warmth."

"Do you not like me?"

"Go to sleep, Em."

Emily's toes touch the floor. "I'm there," she whispers.

He releases her hands. "Stay put. There could be a straggler or two still in the house." He hands her the shotgun before sitting on the stair step he'd left intact. He eases himself off the ledge until he stretches out his full body, dangling just a few inches off the floor. He drops.

He signals her to move. Emily avoids the blood stains as she steps into the kitchen.

The acolytes left a small mess of empty tin cans on the table. He checks the high cabinets while Emily scrounges through the lower ones. They find expired food and no pots or pans worth lugging around.

He heads through a laundry room clearly added on to the back of the cabin. Up on a top shelf, where only an NBA player could view without a step stool, rests a box of shotgun shells. He grabs them and loads the gun.

"How did they miss those?" she asks.

"Got to be tall."

He jerks the hand pump up and down until water belches out of the spout. Emily scoops water into her hands and drinks. He slides his canteen under the spout to fill it.

The hand-cranked noise would barely scare small animals away, but the growing numbers of walking dead seem to come at the slightest twinge of sound.

Nothing staggers from the tree line.

"Where did they all go?" Emily keeps her voice low.

"Not sure. Something else must have attracted their attention in the middle of the night." He constantly scans the tree line, unconvinced the biters are all gone.

"More interesting than us?" she asks.

"You didn't snore loud enough for them to hear."

"I don't snore."

"Keep telling yourself that." He flashes her a grin before returning to glance at the ground. "I guess the woman drew the biters outside when she fired the gun and after they finished eating her they meandered away at some new sound or smell."

The blood-stained grass has the outline of what was once a person. He snags the .22 from the wet ground and wipes it as dry as possible before dropping it into his backpack.

"Are you just going to leave all the food we gathered?" Emily bounds across the yard.

"Easy, little girl. We don't want to just run over there."

She stops short. "You don't think these things are smart enough to hide in the trees and wait for us?"

"If they develop a thought process we could be in real trouble." He slings the bag he took from the distribution center over his shoulder. "We can reach this used car lot I know by noon and drive until we run out of gas."

"You said it was a hundred miles."

"So if we drive awhile, we can cut out twenty or thirty miles we'd have to walk and we'll be much closer."

"I don't know if I can do this."

"Your bag too heavy, Em?"

"Being outside the fence. With no protection. I've never had to deal with—"

"Life without a phone app?"

"You're such a dick," she quips.

"I'm going to keep you alive."

"You don't have to be a douchebag about it."

"Pick your orifice."

"You're trying to confuse me."

"What an easy job, confusing teenagers."

"I know sarcasm, just tell me which direction to walk."

He points. "Walk through there, keep your senses alert."

# CHAPTER EIGHT

TRAVIS CRUSHES OUT his cigar.

"Stay here!" he snaps at Hannah as he draws his pistol before leaping from the Humvee.

"Hold your fire!"

The soldiers remove their fingers from the trigger but keep their M4 carbines trained on the Infected as the undead stagger to their feet. The moan-howls send many people into a panic. They flee the area, looting whatever contraband they find. Two dead soldiers shamble toward Travis.

"Stand your ground, and hold your fire." He levels his gun.

Bam. Bam.

The two shots strike the exact center of each corpse's forehead. He pops two Infected civilians. Travis marches up to each of the fallen and shoots the skulls of the dead who have not yet reanimated. "Get these bodies to the burn facility." Two soldiers sling their rifles, pull on latex gloves, and remove the bodies.

"Clear these tents." He knows the civilians remaining are part of the criminal element of camp. His voice booms preventing any misinterpretations in the new law. "This gambling for supplies ends now. You want to *trade* your personal property I won't stop, monitor, or discourage it. Criminal activities exploiting the weak will be harshly dealt with." Travis keeps his orders as vague as possible, but truly dealing with this situation should have been addressed by a professional speech writer. "Get this cleaned up." The soldiers move faster than before.

"Take me back to the headquarters." Travis climbs into the Humvee.

"All you're going to do is shut down the gambling and threaten?" Hannah screams at her father.

"Hannah, this's not the time or place."

"This's the perfect time, Dad. You need to take Kade out."

"You should feel lucky you're my daughter. I wouldn't have a discussion with anyone else of lower rank about my decisions."

"I want to protect these people."

"And you think I don't, but you lack a larger understanding. The people here are going to trade what they have for what they want. We can't stop or police. We take out Kade and three more take his place. I've some control with the devil I know. Not as much as I'd like, but enough to protect most of the people here."

"You should protect them all."

"We can't. The world has changed. We're going to have to start to choose who's worth protecting."

Hannah finds herself without a comeback. Shock overcomes her as she realizes the pressure her father has been placed under. "Dad, is there something you're not telling me?"

"You need to stay closer to headquarters. You want to help people, keep passing out foodstuffs to the refugees."

Hannah realizes something's terribly wrong, and her father won't say within earshot of his soldiers. She keeps the subject on the Bowlins. "Kade's hurting people. You should've arrested him."

"No one's reported him. If he's raping women, none have come forward to report him. I need witnesses to do anything."

"You have to stop him. The next poor woman could be me."

"I won't let anything happen to you. I'll make sure you're protected."

The Humvee pulls up to headquarters. A private rushes out to open the door.

"Make sure my daughter's escorted inside and she stays there until I get back."

"Dad," she protests.

"Don't make me have you confined to quarters."

"So, I want to help people less fortunate and I'm being sent to my room." Hannah moves her foot in order to crawl out.

"You're fifteen and as headstrong as your mother, but you're still my daughter."

"I still want to protect these people, Dad. Someone has to."

"I'm protecting these people. You may not like how I have to do it, or my inability to share classified information with you to explain why I make some of the choices I do, but rest assured I want to save lives. As many as I can."

"When you let criminals walk free, I don't think I'll ever understand." Hannah hops from the Humvee. A string of her blonde hair catches in the frame. She pulls the snag free and races inside the building.

Travis steps out. Part of him wants to chase after his little girl and assure her everything will be all right, but he knows nothing will kill the monsters under her bed. She will just have to become a good little soldier and live in the new world.

"Corporal Jameson," he calls to the young soldier at the gate.

"Yes, Colonel."

"I'm reassigning you. If my daughter leaves this part of the compound I want you to escort her and keep her from the refugee side of the base. When I get back I'll place some female guards on her as well."

"Sir." He salutes.

"Colonel Travis."

Travis turns at the voice of a PFC who is running toward him with a sealed folder. *Like there's another colonel on this base,* he wants to scream at the man for stating the obvious. "Report, Private."

"I've been ordered to deliver this, sir." He snaps to attention.

Travis returns the salute. He breaks the seal on the envelope. He slides out the paper and reads the first few lines. "Who else has seen this?"

"Lieutenant Haze handed me the sealed envelope personally."

"We have new orders from Washington. Assemble my command staff."

# CHAPTER NINE

DANZIGER CUPS THE photo of Levin in the palm of his hand. He now knows the face of his daughter's murderer and will find him. He leans into the window of the last truck on the caravan line. None of the men inside look like Levin. He moves on to the next vehicle, a van loaded heavy with supplies. As Danziger reaches the seventh vehicle in line, a man dressed like he's traveling on an African Safari steps in his path.

"You're scaring people."

"I've got to find this man." Danziger jams his arm at the man in a talk-to-the-hand gesture. "Seen him?" He displays the photograph cupped in his palm.

"We're all looking for lost relatives. I understand if you want to find him before we leave the city."

"I've got to find him before you move these people on."

"You're not going to get through all these cars before we have the highway cleared and the caravan starts moving."

"Then hold the caravan."

"It's a hundred miles to the military base, and the undead have been spilling out of the city. They're running out of things to eat. We do this now or we won't be able to save as many lives as we have leaving right now."

"Then get out of my way. I'm going to check as many of these vehicles before you move out. I have to find him." Danziger wants to scream for the murderer of his daughter but he knows tipping his hand will only cause Levin to rabbit.

"I'm going to insist you stop this irrational action."

"It's not irrational." Danziger figures it better to let these people think he's crazed in his search for a lost relative instead of a serial killer.

"I know it's rough. We all want to know about our missing family members, but let's get out of the city. The military's cataloging everyone who enters their refugee center. After we arrive we'll check the list and find whoever it is you're searching for."

Danziger knows if Levin makes it to the military base he won't give his real name, and without working computers there's no way to confirm his true identity. Three men circle him. Danziger knows they mean to flank him. He changes his tactic, "I'm a police officer. I've got to find this man."

"Your badge doesn't mean nothing now," the burly black man with a gang tattoo spouts. He sucks in his gut to tower even more over Danziger than he already does.

Danziger slides the photo into his back pocket, and then rubs the three-day growth of hairs on his chin with his right thumb and forefinger. He contemplates asking a question but decides the former rules for a cop have gone to the same place as his need for requiring a search warrant. He clips the butt of his pistol against the cheek of the black man.

His lip begins to turn purple as it swells. "You gonna pay for that."

"We're not going to inflict violence on one another." The man ready for the African Safari draws a revolver. "We've seen enough death. We have to stick together to reach safety."

Danziger raises his arms in a non-threatening manner. "I'm not giving up my gun."

"Just back up away from the caravan. When we get rollin' we'll get you a spot on a truck, but you have to stop scaring these people."

Danziger backs up, keeping an eye on the big black man. The man in the safari outfit waves the black man on. He marches with Danziger away from the caravan to where piles of trash and wrecked vehicles are being used to dam the interstate. A few men, mostly in deer hunting camo, keep vigil next to a fire.

"Curtis," the bearded one calls to the safari dressed man, "caravan not left yet?"

"Interstates' still clogged. They want to get more cars cleared before rolling out," Curtis says.

"Movin' cars makes a lot of noise. These jelly-brained bastards love noise." The bearded man eyes Danziger. He notes the man has no supplies other than extra gun clips in his front pocket.

"You guys still want to remain?" Curtis asks. "We've got a few cars with empty seats."

"Some should direct any stragglers toward the fort," the bearded man offers.

"The US military will be kicking ass and taking names. They'll take our country back."

Danziger almost laughs at Curtis' statement, but he thinks better of it. He needs to get back to searching the caravan. Besides, if the military has taken no action in nine months, he doubts the good 'ol USA will be flag waving by July fourth.

"Someone needs to be here to clean up," Curtis agrees.

"You've got a lot of women and children with you. They need to be taken to safety and food."

"We'll get them there. Watch this guy until we're ready to move out. He's pretty distraught looking for a family member. Scare'n a lot of people. When we roll out, let him rejoin us."

"We can't afford to leave the living behind."

Danziger decides it's better to just go along for now. With so much chaos, giving these guys the slip and moving back to the caravan wouldn't be difficult for a man of his training.

"I'm Tom," says the burly man who hands Danziger a tin cup. "It's hot, and it's brown and it has been filtered through beans, but I'm not sure it can legally be called coffee anymore."

Danziger nods. "Thanks."

"I won't pretend to understand how you feel. I know how I feel about losing my wife. If I thought there was a chance she was in the caravan, I'd tear apart every car looking, too."

"How do you know she's not?" Danziger asks.

"'Cause after she got bit, I...Cherish means a lot of things."

Danziger knows this guy had to carry out her execution. Such information might work in his favor. He slips the picture from his hand. "I'm not looking for my family. My daughter was..." he employs a dramatic pause, "murdered before the world ended." He passes the picture to Tom.

"Terrible." He glances at the picture in a counterfeit of a look.

"She was kidnapped and tortured by this guy."

Tom takes a second harder look at the image. He soaks in the details of the man's facial features. "Are you sure it was this guy?"

"I was a cop. I was investigating his multiple killings until he took my daughter. Now there're no rules about being too close to a case. I'll finish finding him."

"There are no courts, either. You won't see him go to prison."

"There's only one kind of justice left for him." Danziger pats the handle of his holstered gun.

"I'd most likely do the same. Hey, James, c'mere." The camo dressed but clean shaven man snags the picture Tom is holding up.

"How do you know he survived this?" Tom asks.

"My partner and I found a recent victim," Danziger fudges. He has no idea how recently the last victim died. "And where he cut these poor teenagers up before he raped them."

"Sick fuck." James stares at the photo as if to burn this guy's face into his brain.

"Partner?"

"Said I was a cop. He didn't make it. We found where he was killing these young girls, but it was surrounded by DKs," Danziger adds to inspire theses guy to help him.

"And you'll kill this guy if you find him?"

"The world ended and I saw proof he's still killing little girls. The way things have become, who will notice one more walking dead girl? He'll never stop taking victims now."

James gives back the picture. "We've seen him. He was loading suitcases onto a bus with the caravan. Real nice feller."

"He would be. He instills trust. Trust traps his victims." Danziger hops to his feet.

Tom raises his arm in a stopping motion. "We can't let you go yet."

James clarifies, "Yeah. They shot the last guy who was harassing people in the caravan."

"I have to find him."

"We'll help you, but he ain't going anywhere yet, so just relax. Have a cup of filtered shit." He swills the liquid in the cup. "At least it's wet."

Danziger's mind wrestles with the reality that these two men are correct. He'll never stop Levin if he's shot by those protecting the caravan. Yet his brain screams about being so close to his daughter's killer. He must do something now.

"Do whatever you do to remain calm in high stress situations. They train you to be composed in cop school," Tom reminds him.

"You seem to know a lot about it."

"I was a fireman. You don't rush into a burning building half-cocked. Not losing my head has kept me alive for the last nine months. Most people dying today no longer keep it on the level. James, take Howie and patrol down by the caravan. You see the guy, come back and tell us where he is. Don't talk to him."

"Howie's busy with those religious nuts. They're talking about heading south to some church claiming God will protect the righteous from those afflicted by God's wrath. If you're free of sin and have been accepted into God's book, the DKs can't harm you."

"Going to get him killed for sure. I got to stay here with...?"

"Marcus Danziger," he responds.

"Danziger here. I don't trust he'll stay put if I go look for this killer."

"I'll stay."

"I wouldn't if I were in your spot. I want you to get him, but I know the man you punched, Tyrrell. He's just looking for payback. Most of St. Louis gang members were a lot closer to wannabes than the hardcore bangers. Not him. He's got prison tats. I'd say he's killed a few people even if he hasn't served time for it."

Danziger wants to kick himself. As a cop he should have seen all this but believing Levin was in the caravan put blinders on him. He killed Hyun Su with his blinders. His best friend tried to explain with his last words. The whale didn't kill Ahab, the blinders he had for the whale did. If he had kept a more open mind and didn't focus solely on the whale Ahab could have killed the whale, had his revenge and survived with his crew intact.

"Hunting for this serial killer has made me a fool."

"God, man, he killed your little girl. I'd do nothing but hunt him, too."

"How long before this caravan ships out for the military base?"

"They keep hitting snags. Every time they move a few miles forward they find a massive car pileup along the interstate. Takes days to clear."

"From what I saw, the crashes seem to have happened in clusters." James wraps a nylon rope around a sports bottle. "So they clear away one cluster of cars and they hit another one."

"They've got to contend with a lot of undead in each car and a lot of undead stragglers surrounding the road."

"What should be about a three-hour drive could take days."

"And there's no place to drag the damaged cars. People drove on the shoulders and then the medium and into the service road. In a few places I bet thirty cars wide block the path."

"It's not safe."

"The caravan ain't going anywhere soon."

"Understand why most of the people not wanting to head to Fort Leonard Wood stay to guard this location. We're a group. There's no organization hierarchy but we've protection in numbers, I guess. It's a fall back point. The hotel has been secured if we need to evacuate, but all the supplies are now in the caravan."

Danziger recognizes, "You're not protecting the rear. You just realize what a death trap the interstate is."

"I don't know where I want to go," Tom admits. "The city's not safe with some two million of those dead things alone. I think some more have filtered from across the river, too."

"The Mississippi?"

"Correct."

"May not be a problem for you much longer," James adds. "The guy who sounds like Gambit from the X-Men said the military blew some bridges up in the south to stop the flow of the DKs from one side of the river to another."

*Why would they cut off the ability for military ground forces from coming...?* Danziger shuts the only answer out of his mind.

"These people want to go to the military base at Fort Wood. Some got it into their heads the government has ordered a firebombing of major cities to eliminate vast numbers of undead, and then it's just a matter of time and mopping up small pockets of undead."

"Seems drastic."

"It makes sense on some level, but everyone passing through here has a different story or theory on what has happened, what's going on, or what will happen. Nobody knows and we don't know if we even still have a government."

"Now, Tom, we've seen those helicopters heading in the direction of the fort. They've cargo supply crates attached. Somebody's sending them supplies."

"You're correct, there's a lot of speculation from everyone." Danziger turns the conversation back to the information he needs to know. "How long's the caravan?"

"About three miles of cars."

"The guy in the Safari jacket, he guard the convoy's whole length?" Danziger asks.

"I don't think so," James says.

"So if I jogged around I could come out and restart my search at the front?"

"I'd hike way around, because any movement in the tree line's likely to invite a bullet."

"People are trigger happy," James agrees.

"Okay, so I walk way around."

"You take off in any direction other than the caravan and I'd have no cause to stop you," Tom says.

James offers, "We could escort him north, make sure he doesn't do anything foolish."

"Take Howie with us. Before more religious talk gets him killed."

"I didn't know you weren't a believer," James seems shocked.

"I prayed every time I went into and out of a burning building, but those true believers are more dangerous than the DKs. Guys like him remind me of the late night TV evangelists who pilfer the life savings of little old ladies."

"He seems more like David Koresh who burnt up those kids in Texas." James fumes.

"You don't like his snake oil?" Danziger says.

"You're passing around the Kool-Aid, too, Danziger, but I prefer your brand to his," Tom clarifies.

# CHAPTER TEN

EMILY STARES OUT the truck window. Despite being April and trees budding with new leaves, the world seems crueler than it should be.

"I haven't seen an abandoned vehicle for a few miles."

"I've kept this part of the road clean." Not entirely the truth. It wasn't just him.

"Why this truck? It rattles. Makes my butt hurt. I like the first one we had. And you already had it loaded with supplies. It still had gas. We didn't need to switch."

"We've several of this model in the compound. They need one for parts. So I'll let my mechanic decide which ones to use and which ones to scrap. The first truck we were in will remain in place for when I need it again."

Shocked, Emily asks, "You have a mechanic?"

"I've rescued lots of people. Most I've taken back with me are necessary to keep the camp functioning."

"So you've tried to restore some of how it used to be."

"No. The way it used to be doesn't work as long as the dead keep coming back to life. There are necessary rule changes for society in order to survive in this brave new world."

"You think they might stop?"

"Figuring out what causes the reanimation has not been my priority but someone might find a way to stop them. I wonder why they don't rot faster. The winter cold and the heat should have deteriorated them more."

After pausing for a moment to think, she blurts out, "What has to change?"

"I guess I should explain how it is if you live under my house, and I do give you the choice of wanting to live there."

"It's not a choice."

"Well, it beats the alternative. And I do mean *I* have built a colony of survivors. I've rescued just about all of them myself and we work together to maintain a comfortable and safe lifestyle, but it's not easy. We have rules and stiff penalties if they are not followed, because I'll be damned if I'll tolerate a jail and wasted food resources on someone while the rest of us work to feed ourselves."

"So you enforce capital punishment for crimes."

"We don't have a lot of crime; people are too busy working to commit offences. First rule, the biters are no longer people. Second, after proper training and certification everyone must carry a sidearm."

"Even little kids?"

"Everyone, once trained. We're trying to keep to above age ten, but you must carry, too. No matter how safe the fence is, we do everything to keep the undead out. If you get hospitalized for a major injury, they'll handcuff you to the bed because no telling when a biter could reanimate."

"Everyone with a gun, a little like *Tombstone*, but reasonable."

"Everyone works or they don't eat."

"Explains why you don't have need for a jail. You don't have food to waste on someone to just sit in a cage. Why not just make them work?"

"Takes six people, minimum, to guard one person in a jail for three shifts. No way. Those six individuals guard the fence. Keep everyone safe from dozens of undead. Which is more important than running a jail."

"You don't work, you don't eat." Emily wonders, "No school?"

"We're working on an education program. Actually, we do have a library. We hold town meetings and discuss a lot of instructive concerns. We're leaning toward instituting an apprenticeship program. Pass on the skills necessary to survive. But I want the little children to be able to read. We won't return to the dark ages and illiteracy."

"So, I'll have to get a job."

"We'll find you something you're suited to."

"I'm fifteen." Nine months ago fifteen meant being told to stay away from boys and dreaming of a princess prom dress. Work was not in her vocabulary.

"You're right, we've no need for someone who can text and paint her nails at the same time. Not a viable skill in the apocalypse."

Annoyed with his constant badgering of what he thought were her generation's habits, she ignores him and asks, "What will I have to do?"

"Most likely if you don't have an aptitude for some specific skill we'll start you out on the farms."

"You have farms?"

"The goal's to become self-sufficient behind the fence. We grow crops and raise livestock so people don't have to go outside the fence. That's what I do. I risk my life. I gather supplies, or in the case of when we met, I scouted a location for supplies. I'll then take a team back to gather necessities from the distribution center, because we know it's still stocked. I keep my people out of harm's way."

"What happens if you don't come back?"

"Someone else will have to deal with supply runs if it happens."

The brakes squeak as he slows the truck.

Emily questions his stop at the red sign. She wonders if it is out of habit until she realizes the road fails to continue across the highway. Impeded by cargo containers dropped from trailers to create a barrier along the road. They must be at the secure entrance to his colony. Sandbags, sheets of metal and cut up car parts make machine gun nests on top of the trailers. Men with high-powered rifles stand guard. Along the actual blacktop road runs chain length fence. Heavy metal gates have cattle panels over the chain link wrapped in barbed wire. Rebar poles ground into spikes set at levels to puncture tires if they try and crash the gate. Higher ones spear the undead as well as strings of razor wire to prevent encroachment by anyone unwanted. The cargo containers end where chain length fence creates a dog run in both directions along the road.

Having lived in the military base Emily expected a small fenced in farm. "How big is your camp?"

"We've fenced in a good chunk. About twenty miles north of this road to the river, including part of a national forest. Cattle won't graze much and no corn grows in the trees, but it serves other purposes."

The entry post reminds Emily of some kind of Nazi Mad Max compound. Even the well-organized pattern of guards seems ridiculous with their hodgepodge of uniform attire. The truck draws their attention and they keep their weapons ready.

"You don't have any girls guarding."

"Not on this shift. We've a few. One girl shoots better than me."

Emily imagines witnessing better shooting than her time with him and doubts many are faster and more accurate than her savior.

"Prove yourself a crack shot during your training and you'll have guard duty instead of slopping hogs."

"Motivation to learn to shoot well."

He turns the engine off. "Stay in the truck." He slides out, his hands held away from his guns.

"That you, boss?" one of the guards asks.

Emily eyes the man asking the question. He holds what looks to be a credit card long ways at the bottom. He releases the card and pinches his fingers before it slides all the way through, flips the card over and does this again and again.

"Open the gate. I've got a house guest."

"An invited one, I hope."

"A new hog slopper."

The man nods at someone else who pulls a lever. The gate swings open. The men lower their rifles.

He drives the truck inside.

"Why does he play with that card like that?"

"The morning of the end of the world he put one hundred dollars on a prepaid card to use and never got a chance to spend it."

"Oh," Emily says.

"Some people just can't let go of the old world."

Metal spikes decorate the gate in the center of the entrance sally port.

He jams the truck into park removing the keys. "You're not going to like this next part, but trust me. I find it the best way to stay safe inside the fence."

He reaches across her and pulls the gun from her holster before exiting. Emily slides out her side. She keeps her eyes on what he does next.

A hatch cut into the cargo container opens. A hand reaches out and unlocks a chain length window cut into the cage they are now in. He slides the shotgun, box of shells and Emily's pistol through the portal into the cargo container. "Those should all be good. Wasn't hunting for weapons, but we'll take all we can find."

"All good, boss," a voice praises from inside.

He takes the pistol he recovered from the grass and sets it on the shelf. "This one was left in the dew and blood."

"We'll make sure it's disposed of." The arms inside open a plastic baggie marked repair. "Looks good enough for parts."

Extreme recycling will become the new way of life for a while. Broken items will have to be sorted for parts. The way his grandfather grew up in The Great Depression. Everything was recycled and reused until it crumbled into dust. And even then he figures they would find a use for the dust. The age of the disposable society has passed since nothing new will be manufactured for a long time. No longer can society afford living in a disposable culture. Clothes will be worn to rags, the rags used until they become squares on a patchwork quilt.

He's glad his grandmother never lived to see this brave new world. He wishes he had learned her skill with a needle before she passed. She made beautiful quilts. One still exists in his home. If he ever gets a chance to return, he will retrieve it. Spring may be approaching but the next winter will require quilts to survive.

"I'm going to do this first." He steps into the next cage and closes the door separating them. A metal rod about four inches in diameter shoots across the gate preventing him from returning through or Emily from entering the cage to join him.

"This is rule four, and we make no exceptions." He unclasps his gun belt first before shedding his garments. He tosses his clothes and items through another window in the cargo trailer. One of guards folds them up for him. Once bare skinned he holds his arms up level with his shoulders, turns around with his palms facing up. Although curious she averts her eyes from his groin. Easier than she thought possible since the scar running down his left leg draws her attention. It must be the reason he limps.

"All clear, boss." He steps through to the next cage where he's allowed to redress.

"The bar slides back into the cargo container.

"Your turn, missy," the guard calls to her.

Reluctantly, Emily steps into the next cage. The sliding bar zings, sealing her fate. Her heart beats in her chest. Stripping before these strange men causes a bead of sweat to form on her forehead. She understands they are just looking for bites and their glances will be quick since she has none, but after the attack she's not sure she wants anyone other than her savior to gaze at her nakedness. He saw past her most vulnerable moments. She trusts him more than she'll ever trust anyone else.

He snaps his pants button. "They're looking for bites. We can't have anyone sneak in who might be bitten, die, and kill us in our sleep. It's happened at a few home-grown refugee camps. No one gets in who is bit."

She slides out of her coat.

"I guess try and think about it like changing in the locker room."

"They only let girls in the girl's locker room."

"You ain't got nothing we haven't already seen."

He admonishes the guard, "You're not helping."

"Sorry, boss."

"Get out of here." He scolds the man on the other side of the bars.

"But the rules state we have to make sure she has no bites."

"I know the rules. I made them." He exits the cage pushing the guard out of Emily's view.

"Go ahead, Emily, pass your clothes through here and when you're nude spin like I did. Austin up there will visually examine you, but only him and me." He points up.

She strips quickly, embarrassed the way she was in middle school gym when she was the only girl in a training bra, stuffing her clothes through the porthole. She holds her palms up and twirls.

Austin keeps his eyes on her. Purple skin marks her face and legs. "What's on her leg?"

"It's bruised from a human attacker. No bites. I cleaned it myself."

"I give her the clear." Austin's words cause the gates to be opened. Emily rushes in and grabs her coat. She hides in it as she dresses.

He pulls his boots on. He snaps his eyes away from watching Emily dress. He has seen her exposed and completely vulnerable already, having rescued her from an attempted rape. Austin, at least, is smart enough to understand what he meant by her thigh bruises without having to spell it out to him adding additional embarrassment to Emily. She must feel even further traumatized by being forced to strip naked before strangers and have her body inspected. He has no understanding of how Emily must feel right now. Despite the lack of physical penetration, the man still brutalized her and the feeling of being powerless to stop this guy from ripping off her pants and tearing open her legs had to be just as bad, if not worse, than actual penetration.

Knowing a low percentage of women reported rape before the end of the world he understands why. They have to go through the original forced event, and then have to be gawked at by evidence collectors and forced to relive the experience again and again with cops, lawyers and the judge. Having it happen once and forcing it from their minds after the body heals must be what those women attempt to do and has to be a part of the reason why. The women who did take it to court have an unparalleled courage.

She's cute, young. Even if she's too young, it has been a while since he has been with a woman. He had foregone carnal pleasures for a while. Emily has offered herself to him, but she's confused, and as nice as it is for a woman to want him, he has to know she's not just spreading herself in a prostituting gesture in order to be protected. He will protect her the way he protects all those in his camp.

In his conscious avoidance of watching Emily, he neglected to notice the small group gathering around the immediate inside of the gate area. A flaw he'd need to correct. If he weren't inside his compound it could mean his death and it could end this flimsy community held together with the Scotch tape and bubblegum he provides. He has worked too hard to start this place and those who have joined him even harder to keep it. If they are to survive then they must be ever vigilant. And the modesty of a teenager has lost priority.

Emily finishes dressing before he swings open the door to the inside of the compound. "You going to be okay?" He asks her softly.

"You've seen me naked, so it wasn't as bad as I first felt." Her feet hop out of the cage. "Somehow I feel safer in here than I did at the military base."

"Well, that's a start."

He adjusts his gun on his hip before joining the gathering crowd. "Always nice to have such a warm welcome home."

A Native American, near seven foot tall, with raven hair braided with a feather embraces Emily's rescuer. He has two red lines painted on his cheeks—a Sioux Indian battle tradition. Even without them he looks scarier than shit to those who don't know him. There's a gleaming silver tomahawk dangling from his belt. Emily eases next to her savior, putting him between her and the towering hatchet-wielding giant. Keeping her eyes from meeting the Sioux, she glances at the midriffs of each person gathered. All are armed with pistols, even the few that carry rifles have a handgun on their hip. It brings her back to the reality of how brutal life is even with the protection of the fence. There are too many biters, too many lumbering dead not to have a gun.

"Wanikiya is my second in command. He runs the compound when I go out to gather supplies or search for survivors, with the skills to keep the hot water operational."

Emily knows she heard incorrectly. Hot water—something she would willingly whore herself out for after nine months of sponge baths and no pressure cold water showers.

She feels his remark should have been taken as a joke but this crowd, a mixture of workers, display faces of concern, anguish, and disappointment.

Emily keeps her eyes on his hands. They go nowhere near his guns. He brings these people items to add to their coffers, so their disappointment isn't with their leader. He reminds her of a good Roman general with his sharing of the spoils ensuring his reign as sovereign over his people. He doesn't give her the kind of vibe of a conquering hero, not having much experience with asshole champions other than her classmates winning state her freshman year. He could have brought back three times as many supplies if he were applying for Caesar.

He notes Emily hiding behind him. This group's unknown to her and could feel imposing. What he does to keep this community alive is important, but what he won't admit is it's kind of a cheat. The end of the world reduced what's necessary to live, and jobs become more manual labor intensive than working in the vegetable gardens. Scavenging the ruins of civilization is a far less menial task than tending to spring tomatoes.

This gathering isn't about him. Something bad must have happened while he's been foraging. Wanikiya nods in greeting at Emily.

What has now become instinct causes his hand to brush over the Beretta behind his .357, just in case. His quick evaluation of the situation reveals that at least five of them would have bullets in them before they could fire at him. Who knows, a lucky shot could be all he gets. He doubts even with his speed an expenditure of all sixteen rounds is possible against targets capable of shooting back.

He shakes thoughts from his mind. These people aren't here for a coup. They have elected to have basic laws keeping them alive in here. The question becomes, what happened behind the fence while he was in the wilderness to bring them in such force?

"Once again, you're welcome, sir," Wanikiya's barreled voice greets him.

He still expects the voice of Tonto with a what-do-you-mean-we-paleface drawl. Wanikiya has no such accent. In fact, his English is of someone highly educated. The Sioux man has become his trusted friend since the world ended, but he doubts Wanikiya was his given birth name before the undead walked. George or Bob or Frank is more likely. Wanikiya speaks little of his life before the end. Most people are better off not to. Despite the community and the trust grown here, there are those who would wish to destroy it, and using a person's past effectively could work against them.

Several men unload the truck brought through the gate system.

"The spirit god smiled on you once again," Wanikiya compliments.

"Some ammo this time, couple of renegades were considering using Emily for sport. And they had an arsenal. She's a good choice for the farm."

Their code for no useful skills. At least not in this world. Two CPAs, a lawyer, and a business executive for a dot com company all shovel pig shit now. Their old world skills don't translate well to the apocalypse. People forget how capable they physically are when it comes to picking up a shovel or learning to shoot. Those who hit what they aim at work the wall as guards. Poor shots work in labor. One day the workforce at the camp will outnumber the guards but not until the geeks stop rising.

"Always good to be back, but this can't be a social greeting."

"No," Doctor Baker addresses him. His nurse, Kayla, keeps an arm on seventeen-year-old Samantha.

Sam hangs her head so her long dirty blonde hair covers her eyes. Her clothes are too big for her skinny frame. Nothing in his imagination reveals how this scarecrow of a girl could have possibly done something worthy of an armed escort.

He notes Sam has no gun. She was slated to be instructed while he was gone. He found her along with two others sleeping in a school bus some two weeks ago. They had no skills, but working cattle and throwing hay bales is quickly taught.

Two men escort Kyle from the guard tower at the end of cargo containers. There are three, maybe four, Kyles living in the compound. This one's 22. Most likely a pothead, at best, but he was with a group with two EMTs. He couldn't have passed them up. He could hardly reject one person on a feeling and convince the others to accompany him. Besides, Kyle could use a shovel.

He thought Kyle wasn't on farm detail. He was on new fence patrol to expand the compound. Whatever happened was between these two. He has an idea, but hopes he's wrong. The world has fallen apart outside the fence. Inside civilization, at least the best version of it, will remain as long as he breathes. Kyle's been handcuffed behind his back and has a black eye.

He feels Kyle's stomach as if he were seven months pregnant. Kyle's eyes scream *what are you doing, homo?,* but he keeps quiet.

Nothing's broken. They didn't beat him, he speculates, at least not beyond the eye.

Wanikiya begins, "Kyle skipped his work detail."

They must deal with loafing swiftly. There'll be no slackers fed, and they don't need his approval to punish laziness. Kyle's guilty of something grander.

"If he was still on building fence detail then he had to be checked in at the gate."

He confirms procedure was followed with a simple glance from Wanikiya.

"Sam also missed her shift," Wanikiya continues, "and was found asleep in the barn. She claims Kyle assaulted her."

"Rape will not be tolerated in this community," he stresses. "Accusations of rape won't be tolerated, either. This crime's serious and requires swift action if we are to remain a community."

Emily witnessed firsthand how he dealt with rapists.

Dr. Baker offers, "Physically, she shows the trauma of forced intercourse."

"Are you sure?" he asks.

Emily watches the man who saved her violate Sam's personal space as he lifts her chin gently and peers into her eyes. Emily feels sick at the taunt he gives Sam next.

"Maybe she likes it rough. Some girls get off on a hardcore slap then a solid fucking." He never averts his eyes from hers.

Emily observed him being harsh and mean to her as his way of toughening her up, but he was never this way about the rape. He's treating Sam like she asked for it. Emily understands from staring into her eyes that this girl did anything but ask to be violated.

Her eyes, the windows to the soul, reveal she didn't ask for this. Now the humiliation he's subjecting her to is just as horrible as Kyle pinning her to the straw-covered floor and thrusting himself repeatedly inside her, and making her tell him to moan she wanted more.

Emily spots truth in Sam's eyes and realizes her rescuer recognizes the truth.

But his knowing and confirming it are not the same. "He get off forcing you to beg to be violated?"

"What the hell, dude, you can't ask her stuff like that!" Kyle protests.

Sam's eyes well with the memory—the pain. She fights hard within herself not to cry. She won't shed any more tears because of Kyle.

He hates to make Sam feel worse, but he has to know. He has to be sure, because what will transpire in the next few minutes will be done to keep his community safe. This trial will reveal that to have heaven there must be a devil.

"Tell me what happened, Sam." Comfort consumes his voice.

"Kyle..." her pause is long. "He followed me into the barn. He'd been asking me to be his girlfriend for a few days. Said if we were a couple, we could request a house once the new area he was helping to fence in was completed, and maybe I could be assigned to a new task. He knew I don't like feeding pigs. I told him I wasn't interested. I didn't want a boyfriend." She holds in her tears. "I watched the last one be eaten by those biters."

"What happened in the barn?"

Emily sees a caring man in her rescuer. More so than he wants to let on.

"He wouldn't leave me alone. He made me. Made me touch him. Then..." She collapses under her own weight. Kayla helps her to sit on the ground. Sam cries, scrunching into a fetal ball.

"Dude, you going to let her railroad me with this display of little girl crying?"

He holds up one finger which stops Wanikiya from striking Kyle.

"I'd have to say without more lab equipment the vaginal tears were from forced entry."

"Don't I get a say? I have rights," Kyle protests.

"Under what system? It's survival of the fittest now," Barlock snaps. The linebacker guard holding Kyle would pound the kid if he could.

"Not here. Not behind this fence. We've a community here, and the rules we have keep us from becoming like out there. Anyone who doesn't want to live by these rules, pack a single bag and step outside the fence right now. I will have order. This is my house."

Stern and angry, but not yelling, he reminds Kyle of this, and since everyone here's alive because of him, Emily notes they all agree.

He keeps his concerned tone and asks, "Kyle, what happened to your eye?"

"When they arrested me I got hit."

"No other beating?"

"They wanted to."

"You resist the cuffs?"

"You're damn right, dude."

He ignores the eye. He should praise his men for only the one hit, not an unreasonable action in an apprehension. The kid should be thankful they didn't beat him.

"Well, I've always the notion you're innocent until evidence to the contrary is presented."

Kyle jumps to his defense, "She wanted it. She begged me. When she got in trouble for missing her shift she said I forced her."

"Plausible."

He glances at Wanikiya for his contribution to the event.

"We found her asleep in the barn. Discipline was going to be administered—a few days reduced rations, but she was naked, bleeding, and her clothes were torn."

"Menstrual flow?"

Emily finds the question strange even after he asked her about her own monthly. She used to watch *Matlock* with her grandmother and he never asked witnesses such questions.

The doctor shakes his head no.

"Kyle, did you rape Sam?"

"She wanted it."

"Stand her up."

The nurse, along with a guard, hold Sam on her feet.

He looks at Sam, "You understand the seriousness of this?"

She nods.

"I've a zero tolerance for this. Penalty will be swift and severe. So, I ask you, one last time, did Kyle, this boy standing right here." He grips her chin with a firm hold and twists her face at Kyle. "Look at him. Did he rape you?"

Seconds.

Maybe a minute passes and she blurts, "Yes."

He snap turns on his heel facing Kyle. "Does anyone have any evidence, anything to show Kyle's innocence?"

He nods at a guard by the watchtower. He disappears into the building.

"No one. This is a man's life here and the life of our community."

"She wanted me!"

Emily notes the swift and speedy trial is nothing like *Matlock*, but it's effective and the boy has been given his chance. Whatever happens she feels safe here with the man who saved her.

The guard from the tower wheels out an acetylene torch and carries a butcher knife.

"What are you going to do?" Kyle struggles against his escort.

They tighten their grip.

The pop of the acetylene igniting makes some of the group jump.

The guard heats the metal cleaver to red.

"Strip him." He pulls on a leather work glove from his duster coat pocket and takes the white hot cleaver.

Wanikiya wraps his fingers into Kyle's hair and shoves him against a stump before pulling his body back. Kyle's junk sprawls onto the stump.

"I won't tolerate rape in this community. Doc?"

"She was forcibly entered. I have no doubt," Dr. Baker confirms.

"The evidence has been reviewed. Convicted rapist..."

Kyle screams and the putrid smell of cooking meat and singed hair sickens the group. Wanikiya allows Kyle to collapse to the ground. A smoldering nub replaces his penis.

Emily turns her head. She hears the cleaver sink into the stump. The annual rings blacken from the heat.

"Dr. Baker, when you feel Sam capable of returning to her duties, release her. Wanikiya, Kyle's now assigned to protection duty outside the fence. The rest of you pass along the penalty for forcible rape. We won't give in to what's going on outside our community. Our newest member, Emily, was being attacked by rapists when I found her. It won't happen here. We keep our humanity."

Emily wishes he hadn't shared her attack with these strangers.

"I'll see he's found a new duty. What about the new girl?" Wanikiya asks.

"I'm going to introduce her to Dar. Send someone to get her later."

The group returns to their duties all queasy from what they witnessed. Dr. Baker remains.

"Doc, he doesn't need your attention. They'll take care of him at the outer guard station."

"The area of shipping crates, about a half mile past the east end of the compound. You have no medics there," Dr. Baker protests.

"Kyle will continue to serve in the protection of his compound, but he'll never set a foot back inside."

"You sealed his urethra. He will be unable to urinate."

"Take care of your patient, Doc. Make sure Sam heals, and after she's processed, check Emily over. Most of her trauma is mental, but she was attacked, too."

"Processed?" Doesn't sound pleasant. Emily contemplates but the doctor asks first.

"Are all criminal penalties this severe?"

"You're free to leave any time, Doc, if you don't like it. But the dead don't distinguish between people who maintain morals of the old world and those who don't. Neither will most of the survivors out there. This's the only place we're not meat for the grinder, and at first, at least for now, punishment must be harsh and swift. There will be no rapes within these walls."

Emily notes the farmhouse was once elegant, but due to neglect it has slipped into disrepair. The dilapidated building structure remains stout despite shutters falling off the windows. The twelve foot high fence surrounding the home, small yard, and garden area make it invitingly safe.

"Do you reinforce all your buildings with a second row of fence?" Emily asks.

"This was the colony's first home. We secured this building and lived in it for a while until we could build the larger fence and take over other buildings and secure the area. I keep it as living quarters. We moved our headquarters to an elementary school. It works as a community building. The school's the only place big enough to hold our Sunday meetings now."

"Church?"

"More like town hall."

A young boy about Emily's age, maybe a year younger, eyes them suspiciously from the front porch. Emily's eyes meet with his. He's not eyeing them, he's staring at her with distrust.

"Manners, Dartagnan," he snaps at the boy. The tone feels harsh. Nothing like the way he just spoke to Sam.

Dartagnan peels himself from the column. "Not time to plant yet." He shakes his head longer than necessary.

*Retarded?* Emily wonders. No, he doesn't look special. He appears normal, except decorating his left arm are six watches, each of a different color.

"When?"

"Next full moon. I'll plant the garden." He gets excited as they cross the threshold of the chain length fence. "Did you bring?"

"I've told you, I won't be able to find you gifts every time I go out."

Dartagnan frowns. He seems to throw a temper tantrum with just his eyes.

"Say 'hi' to Emily."

Dartagnan's face screams in refusal.

"Dartagnan," he snaps.

"Hi. Emily."

"What do you say?"

Dartagnan's face returns to a resounding *no* expression.

"Dartagnan."

"Welcome to my home. Would you like to come in?"

"Thank you. I would." Emily almost curtseys to the young boy. "Is he your son?"

"Just how old do you think I am?" He snaps at her. "He's a kid I found."

"He has no gun," Emily notes.

"Qualified to carry has one exception. He can close the fence and lock it if he needs to. Dartagnan's a *special* case."

"So he slops hogs?" she asks.

"No." He pulls out a cloth bag and hands it to the boy.

Dartagnan unwraps it in slow motion. His face lights up at the model paint vials. "No red."

"Dartagnan," he snaps.

The boy responds to this. "Sorry. Thank you for what you could find."

"And," his tone works like a switch.

"I appreciate what you find since there are no more stores."

He races inside, calling out, "I still need brown."

He recognizes the question growing within Emily. "I won't be nice or do any coddling of the boy. He responds better to my harsh tone. Like he respects it or needs it. His mommy babied him. I've run across plenty of normal people who never lasted as long as he did after the undead shattered his customary routine mom set for him. He had to adjust, and those kinds of kids don't adjust."

"What's wrong with him?"

"Nothing as far as I'm concerned. In the old world my job would have labeled him autistic, I think. But he controls his pee, so he can function on his own."

"The watches?"

"He keeps his own schedule now, but it's healthy."

"You said everyone works."

"The young Dartagnan is quite possibly the hardest worker within our camp."

Emily follows him into the house. The once living/dining room space has been converted into a group of tables for a scale model of the camp being built on top of them. Dartagnan has already opened the vials and is running the brush over a building.

"He works on this. And every building, every tree, matches real life."

An open toolbox full of tape measures rests on a chair. Emily doesn't ask but wonders how this job is essential to survival in the apocalypse.

"What he does, and this's where his real gifts come into play, is to calculate what we need to keep us alive. How many cattle we need. How much land and feed we need for the cattle. His mind is some kind of mathematical calculator. I bring in a new person such as yourself and he tells me what I need to feed and clothe you. Before I arrived with those boxes of shells he knew the exact number of bullets inside the fence."

He turns on the fluorescent bulbs suspended over the model, allowing Dartagnan to work in better light.

"You have electricity." Emily hasn't seen a non-generator powered light in months.

"The Salt River was dammed for hydroelectric power. We have lights for as long as the dam holds and the river flows. We keep the dam closely maintained and the entry gate at the dam ends heavily fortified."

"People would storm this place just for the power."

"They would fight to get in, ultimately destroying what they covet and then none of us would have anything. We still have to do a lot of the labor by hand. Gas is in short supply and vehicles won't run forever. I've never seen a battery-powered tractor. We need to get this place up and growing food so after processed foodstuff has expired we won't need much from the outside."

"So Dartagnan's job is to math all this out."

"He determines what we need and what I must find."

"And the model?"

"Somehow it keeps his mind focused."

The right side of the model ends or begins with the house they stand in and the growing colony expands to the left and remains unfinished.

Emily walks around the model. "Why don't you want to expand this way?"

"The best answer, some twenty-five miles that way, is the Mississippi river. Give or take a few miles. Without human interference the river will flood. We shouldn't have a problem from flooding this far inland. Besides, strategically, this location is where to build a wall." He points to a growing stack of cargo trailers being built into a cliff side along the river north of the farmhouse.

"Wall will keep all biters out." Dartagnan smiles.

"Current fortifications do refocus a bit more against a siege mentality. We expand inward as we need to, and recapture homes, farms, and soon even a clinic, but in no way will we be able to return to life the way it was before."

Emily looks somewhat confused at his plans.

"Eventually I hope to reduce the number of guards, adding to our workforce, but for now safety is priority. If we aren't secure then it doesn't matter how well our tomatoes grow.

Dartagnan scribbles on a legal pad. He uses a ruler edge to tear the perforations perfectly straight. "Here are the things you're going to need."

He takes the paper and reads down the list. "Most of the items should be in the distribution center." He hesitates at the last item. "Why so many?"

"The girl. The vet assistant. The small animal trained girl. She doesn't think many cows are pregnant. Without new births to replenish the herd, their resources to our food supply will severely diminish.

"Can we feed this many cattle?" He asks, before mumbling, "If it's possible to find this many in one location." The biters have scattered whole herds if they haven't eaten them.

"The new fence expansion will open more grass to graze. The exact area I can measure after the fence is up since I am not allowed on the outside to measure. I can determine how much grass we need once I measure. You can cut down some of these trees."

"That's a national forest. We only cut down the dead ones for firewood. Plus that ground is too rocky to farm, and there are deer."

Dartagnan's face flushes. Somehow the advent of deer upsets him. "I haven't calculated for deer. Could throw all my numbers out of balance. Must keep the camp resources in balance. Humans never keep balance." Dartagnan shakes from anxiety.

"Dartagnan, do you want to have to go to the chair?"

"No."

"Then calm down. We can guestimate the number of deer if I get some of those motion cameras for tracking."

"Okay."

He looks at Emily. "That's why we're in this mess. The human race has always been unable to balance itself with nature."

Dartagnan returns to painting.

"Okay. I'll get the cattle, and we'll get more grass to feed them."

"How?"

"You let me worry about that."

# CHAPTER ELEVEN

SOLDIERS LOAD GENERATORS and water pumps into cargo trucks. Travis surveys the engineers as they scoop out wet mud from the bottom of the pond. The material adds to the bank wall creating a much deeper pit. Dump trucks back up to the empty pond. They pour in burnable materials. Soldiers stack shrouded bodies like cordwood among the garbage. When the garbage becomes covered by the unmoving dead more dump trucks scatter broken wooden furniture and other broken boards on top of them. A chemical truck sprays used motor oil over the wood.

Travis's fist crumples the side of the envelope he holds.

*Choice: noun—an act of selecting or making a decision when faced with two or more possibilities.* On paper such an easily defined word. The reality of this becomes grander as he stands before the growing number of weak and defenseless people filling his base.

"Colonel."

"You should return to base command, George," Travis suggests. "All this noise will attract them."

"I won't abandon my commanding officer, Colonel." The major stands next to his friend.

"I will make it an order."

"I will follow my orders, but I won't change what has to be completed here."

Bulldozers scoop out more dirt to expand the far side of the pit.

"Just following orders didn't work at Nuremberg," George proposes.

"We won't face a Nuremberg. In the end there won't be anyone left to put us on trial for what we are about to do here."

"We'll persevere and defeat this," George assures his commanding officer.

"Not this enemy. Not one constantly gaining soldiers as our forces deplete." Confident, Travis states, "We won't come back from this."

Personal transport carriers pour from the base. "Washington authorized this?" George asks in disbelief.

"Everyone who's ill, not expected to recover, all kidney dialysis cases, any in a coma, and other medical conditions requiring hospital care or constant monitoring are to be the first."

George chimes in with his strongest argument first, "Hitler did the same thing with mental patients and homosexuals."

Travis snaps, "You think I don't know history? I told you, if you can't do this you're dismissed. Nothing will change the fact that all these people are walking dead already. There'll be no more medicine manufactured. In a few days they'll die and convert to the enemy. Traitors without a choice but to seek flesh. They'll bite and convert more followers. As our resources dwindle we must select who we protect."

George understands the burden of following command decisions. This is the first time in his career he's ever felt it necessary to question an order and before he follows it he has to be sure.

"No commander should have to order the execution of Down syndrome children. Old men should be allowed to pass away peacefully in their sleep." The cargo trucks unload ancient and sick civilians. Most have to be helped from the truck. Several with Down syndrome, and scraggily women with small children climb out. Two more cargo trucks bring even more sickly dregs.

"It is your duty to refuse to follow any unlawful orders, sir." George challenges the colonel.

"The Uniform Code of Military Justice Article Ninety-Two makes my duty clear. What we're presented with was never speculated in the Constitution. We defend against all enemies, foreign or domestic."

"It also clearly says no person should be deprived of life, liberty or property, without due process of law. These poor souls are not yet the enemy."

"There's the rub. They soon will be. In one of those trucks are five people with dialysis issues and in the next load of supplies there won't be medicine or machines left. They will die. They will become the enemy. They don't get a choice."

"Colonel, I'll follow whatever orders you give, as long as you believe in them. If you have a doubt, don't do this."

"I wanted to reread the entire manual, not just the parts on following orders and even the Constitution itself, but I've reread the signed orders and they do support the Constitution. This has to be done as a first line of defense. The crime perhaps lies in the fact it has taken nine months to give these orders. How many people died because those with terminal diseases weren't eliminated immediately?" Travis gives George no chance to answer. "The growth of an undefeatable enemy is predictable and has an intimidating, unstoppable force. We don't have the soldiers to protect all these people. We won't have the supplies to feed all these people. Then we'll be facing two enemies. We'll have to shoot more innocent people."

George releases the greater danger plaguing the survivors. "They're cutting more than just kidney meds."

"Rations and some other medicines. I'm having the medical staff preparing a manifest of who will die without pills. They'll be a part of the next group we dispose of. I've been examining essential personnel to rebuild after the apocalypse is over."

"Who do you choose to feed to keep humanity alive?"

"Civilization, or something like it. Humanity dies when we march people into graves and shoot them in the head."

The soldiers march the ragged worn huddled masses into the pond turned mass grave. The sick helpless people have nowhere to run. Machine gun fire tears through them. The screams are quick. No one has time to plead for redemption.

"There will be no turning back now."

"I never had a doubt. There's no other solution."

Hannah slides the bedroom window up and leans out. The drop from the second floor looks to be about twelve feet. If she dangles her body as far as it stretches her drop becomes about seven feet from her toes to the ground. The lower floors are now barred as a precautionary measure. She straddles the sill as someone bangs on her door.

"Hannah. You okay in there?" Corporal Nick Jameson calls from the other side of the door.

"I'm fine, corporal... Just changing!" She hopes to keep him from barging in. Had her father been able to immediately assign a female detail to her she doubts she'd be changing clothes alone. But whatever orders were sent from Washington took precedence over carrying out his duties as a father.

Hannah knows she shouldn't look down. She should just swing her other leg out, drop away from the building, catch the ledge with her hands and descend to the ground. She glances at the grass. Her brain shoots warnings throughout her body causing a freeze in her muscle movements. She hesitates. Fear of falling consumes her. She imagines slipping. The landing of her flattened body on the ground. The force of her ribs pushing up inside her chest cavity, air forced from her lungs through her mouth and nose along with splatters of blood. She feels the tug of gravity, not from below, but from the side as she falls onto her bed. Corporal Jameson pins her down.

"What the hell are you doing?" he demands.

"Someone has to help those refuges," Hannah says.

"I've orders to keep you here."

"If I scream right now, what do you think your punishment will be?" Hannah threatens.

The corporal realizes the door's shut and to a passerby, it looks as if he's sitting on top of a struggling underage girl. Her screams would at minimum banish him to the stockade. He jerks back to his feet on the floor, clasping her by the wrists.

"I can't let you leave Headquarters."

"You could accompany me. The colonel wants you to protect me." She bats an innocent eye.

"Not what he meant," Jameson snaps.

She relaxes her fist and he releases her wrists.

"He may have put a stop to the gambling, but the Bowlin brothers are still operating a sex ring. There're too many poor girls being violated. I want to show my dad more evidence. So he will kick them out."

"Not a good idea. Kade won't be as nice to you a second time."

Something in Hannah's brain matures. She flails her fists on his chest forcing him to catch her arms and draw her closer to prevent her punches.

"What's wrong with you?" He shoves her back to the bed effectively pinning her against him to prevent more cuffs.

She reaches up with her lips and touches his. Caught off guard Jameson doesn't move allowing Hannah to slide her tongue into his mouth. He jerks his head away upon the tingling feeling of the poorly executed kiss. *Even when it's bad it's still good,* his platoon buddies' voices echo in his head. *Get Some!* Her lack of experience becomes evident with the lousy pass of tongue and reminds Jameson she's just a little girl.

Hannah shifts to her innocent mode. "What did I do wrong?"

His eyes lock with hers. "You're just a kid."

"I'm fifteen, and you're what, nineteen, twenty?"

"Back end of eighteen."

"If we were in high school right now lots of seniors date freshmen."

"They do for one reason, only."

Hannah slides her hand down his muscular chest toward his belt. "If you help me I'll suck on you."

He moves himself back to regain his composure. "I doubt you know how."

"It's like licking an ice cream cone." Her hand falls to the bulge in his pants. "You just tell me how you like it." Hannah sounds like an experienced madam.

Jameson forces himself away from her. "I don't know how I'd like it."

Hannah props herself up on her elbows. "You've never had a woman do that to you?"

"You've never performed that before either," he retorts like a kid on the playground.

"Yeah, but I'm fifteen. You're a United States soldier."

Embarrassed, Nick admits, "I've never screwed a girl."

"No way." She holds in a giggle. "Never?"

He looks ready to cry. "It's embarrassing. I'd never live it down if the guys in my barracks found out."

Hannah blurts out, "But you are so hot."

"Wish the girls I went to high school with thought so. They thought I was their best friend."

Hannah knows what it means to have jammed him into the friend zone. He would never get anywhere with them because he was too nice, and too nice was not the kind of guy any high school girl wants to date. "Well, they were wrong. And now you get to have some special girl and not some cheerleading slut."

"Where exactly am I going to meet a special girl?"

"We're still out here. Actually the choices of special should be a lot greater because the dumb ones have been eaten."

He cracks a smile. "I can't let you go back to the refugee's side of the base. And there's no way I'll allow touching between us."

"We could talk here for a while. Tell me about those dumb girls and why they thought you were locked into the friend zone."

"Why do you want to hear about that?"

"I like knowing people. You better open the door first. Or you *will* see the inside of a stockade," Hannah warns.

Jameson sprints to the door swinging it wide, fumbling with a book to prop it open.

The four-by-four slams to a halt before impacting an over turned semitrailer. Two armed men stroll on what's now the side turned roof. Three more men load boxes into the back of a bronco.

Kade hops from the four-by-four. "Hold up, Kale."

"What the fuck, bro." He flips his t-shirt over his sweating head.

"The colonel raided our stash."

"I'll kill the mother fucker."

"Hold up. In the process he took out the gambling ring. We now operate with impunity."

"Fuck, bro, I hate when you use big words."

"If you'd have stayed out of juvie, you'd have gotten a better education."

"None of that matters now. Hell, what I learned in prison works out here better now than any fucking school shit."

"How much do you have loaded?"

"About half the bronco," Kale brags.

"Should be enough. Too much and the good colonel will confiscate it."

"I'm goin' to have to gut that fucker."

"Before you do I've some plans with his daughter," Kade sneers. "Might even let him watch." Embracing their own diseased perversions—they laugh.

"Kade." The driver of the four-by-four keeps one hand on his holstered gun as he approaches.

"What now, Hale?"

"Something's bugging me."

"I told you to stay away from those girls with stinky slits. There's going to be no more cream to cure that burning." Kale laughs harder at his own joke.

"Ignore the primate. What's bothering you?"

"This's basically a one-lane black top. It's not a road for semi-trucks at all."

Kade glances both ways up and down the road. "Dumb ass driver got lost. More than likely he wasn't local. Panicked with all the undead."

"I guess." Hale knows better than to openly disagree with a Bowlin brother, but he doesn't adjust his tone.

Kade's anger swells as he realizes Hale disagrees with his assessment. "Spit it out or I'll beat it out of you."

"The truck jackknifed going the wrong direction."

"You know he ain't wrong." Kale rubs the shaggy patch of hair growth only on his chin.

"He must have gotten lost. FEMA's job was to give supplies to people who needed it during an emergency."

"They did a bang up job in New Orleans."

Kale ignores the retort. "Or so the government says. They do lie. And if not they're incompetent. A lot of people died from Katrina and from FEMA's fuckup. " Kale now takes more of an interest in the cab of the over-turned truck.

"If the driver wasn't lost then why else would he be out here in the middle of deer shit junction? Dumb redneck."

"My daddy fucked your mom." Kale kicks the windshield glass.

"You came out of my dad's testicles," Kade gives Hale a 'you're getting your ass kicked later for bringing this up' look.

The glass shatters into thousands of shards. Kale sticks his head inside. "No fucking GPS."

"Could have flown out when the trailer jackknifed."

"If I'm right in my thinking, the kid gets some extra pussy. We'll trade some food; get him a virgin so his tiny dick feels how tight a girl can be."

"You know I don't like leaving the base this long. We've too much at stake for one of us not to be there. Kame's been gone way too long."

"Fine, but chew on this. This lane ends at a dairy farm. It was shut down when we were kids. Before we used to throw hay for the other farms along this road."

"So?" Kade says.

"I found this truck because we were scouting barns for secondary locations to store supplies. I never made it to the dairy farm."

"There are thousands of barns and abandoned and foreclosed-on farms in the four county area alone."

"I bet they ain't got fully loaded FEMA trucks heading toward them," Kale says.

"Fine, take the four-by-four and go check it out. I'm going back to camp with the supplies."

"No. You've got drive it. If some dumb soldier-boy notices we switched vehicles they'll think we're plotting something." Kale points out.

"I hate when your thoughts aren't completely stupid."

Kade leans comfortably over the metal gate.

Hale keeps his finger next to the trigger of his rifle. "They all look like Will Smith from that *Men in Black* movie. Down to the ray bans."

"Amazing they've stayed on all this time. I count fifteen."

The government-suited undead mill around the barnyard, trapped by the metal pole fences. They take no notice of the newly arrived truck.

"They've never left the yard."

"They don't remember how to open a gate, dumbass."

Hale levels the rifle.

"Save your bullets."

A once agent staggers at them. Kade draws his hunting knife, slamming it onto the creature's skull as his other hand slips into the coat to draw the Glock. "They should all be armed."

"So we get some guns and a barn large enough for a couple of semi-trucks."

"But we don't know if any tractor trailers made it here." Kade sets the Glock on the hood of the truck.

Hale shoulders his rifle and unsheathes his long bladed knife. His stabbing of the undead sends the body crashing against the gate. The rattle invites the remaining corpses.

"I didn't get the gun."

"Don't panic." Kade slices through another Infected. The top of the skull sails through the air landing before another Infected. "Someone else shot at this guy."

"How can you tell when they were shot?" He stabs an Infected through the eye.

Kade hesitates unsure how to explain. "The blood."

"It's all a dried gooey mess."

"No the blood spilling from an Infected's more coagulated. Pay more attention to what's going on around you."

"It's hard."

"There're no more short buses, kid. You don't get a do over or extra time." Kade spears another Infected.

Sixteen identical Glocks rest all in two rows across the hood. Hale drags a body away from the gate.

"Make a burn pile somewhere in a field. Let's keep them out of the yards."

The slamming of a screen door sends Kade spinning around, a Glock in each hand. Hale fumbles with the sling on his shoulder unable to get his rifle into firing position.

On the porch a female agent aims her Glock at Kade. "State your name and purpose here."

Kade shifts to his business tone. "We're looking for supplies."

"Stop fucking with that rifle, mister." Hale halts and fumbles his hands into the air.

"Under US law I have standing orders to shoot looters."

"We're not looters." Kade lets both guns dangle on his fingers as he raises his hands.

A second agent cocks a shotgun.

"What do we do?" Hale whispers.

"You do nothing." Kade takes a step toward the farmhouse and purposely places the fence post between himself and the direct line of fire.

"Stay where you are," she calls out.

"Look, we don't want trouble."

A third agent side steps past her and keeps his gun on Kade. "You killed them?"

"You got to smash their brain. You three been locked in that farmhouse the last nine months?"

"Has it been that long?" She lowers her gun, but only by inches.

"We'll just get in our car and go."

"You two look well fed." The first male agent notices.

"We're stationed at the military base. They still get government supplies."

"Lies," she screams at them. "You two were never soldiers."

"True enough. Civilian contractors. We search for supplies and survivors and return them to Fort Wood. We earn a little extra food. Don't have a lot of need for greenbacks these days."

The second male says something under his breath. Hale spots an Infected agent staggering from the edge of the farmhouse.

"Shut up, Hale." Kade's harsh whisper scares him.

She steps down from the porch followed by the second agent. "Put your guns down and back away from the truck," she orders. "Once we check the vehicle you'll drive us to this military base."

"Sounds like a plan."

The dead agent sinks its rotten teeth into the neck of the second male. His screams send the other two into a panic. The shotgun wielding agent fires. The buckshot tears open his companion's chest. The undead agent snarls at the loss of his meal. She spins around and fires into the chest of the undead.

Kade flips the gun handles back into his closing palms with a maneuver any trick shooting performer would envy. He fires on the run smashing open the skull of the male agent. He pops the Infected in the brain. She turns back, but before raising her gun he punches her jaw with the full weight of the gun in his swing. Kade kills the chest less agent for good measure.

"Makes twenty," Kade calculates. He jerks the handcuff from her belt. "Still following regulations. Stupid bitch." He cuffs her hands to the column holding up the porch roof.

"Let's check each of these buildings. Make sure there aren't any more Feds. Hale pulls the barn door open. Nothing. Bays for unloading semi-trucks remain empty.

"Must have been the first truck."

"It's not a total loss. Perfect location for a fall back point when Fort Wood falls."

"The fort isn't going anywhere."

"Hale, haven't you noticed our little business has picked up?"

"I just get to stand guard, eat well and fuck some girls."

"Enjoy, because the food drops have become further apart. The one reason we've been doing so well. The food's not lasting. Soon there won't be enough and this place will be perfect for us to hold out." Kade orders, "Burn those Infected, pack up the guns. I'm going to have a chat with our prisoner." He drags the struggling woman inside the farmhouse.

Hale hears the click of the door lock.

Kade slams her onto the kitchen table.

"I'm a federal agent," she protests.

"There's no more government, sweetheart. And even if there was, no one will ever find out what I'm going to do to you. After I've satisfied my urges, I put a bullet in your brain and burn your body. Just like thousands of others. It's the perfect crime." He cuffs each of her ankles to the table legs. Kade rifles through the drawers, drawing a butcher knife.

"The nice thing about this is I don't have to restrain myself on you like I have to with those girls at the base." He slides the knife through the fabric of her jacket. He grips each edge of the tear and yanks. The ripping material scares her into screams.

"I haven't cut you yet."

"You don't have to do this. I'll do whatever you want. Please let me go."

"You'll do whatever I want."

She jerks, struggling at her bonds.

"This is what I want." Kade caresses her left shoulder. "Such soft, supple skin with a nice muscular build. I like a woman who takes care of herself." He brushes his chapped lips over her shoulder. "You excite me." He exhales an exasperated breath.

With the knife tip, he drills into the center of her deltoid muscle. Blood mushrooms from the hole. She screams. As the knife twists deeper, the agent stops her struggle.

# CHAPTER TWELVE

DANZIGER SIPS FROM his makeshift canteen.

"Make it last. Clean water's gotten pretty scarce," Tom warns.

The line of abandoned cars stretches north to the horizon across both lanes.

"How long before we turn west?" Danziger asks.

"Three, four miles."

"We should head back. I want to talk with those church people more before they head south," Howie whines.

"Howie, you need to stay away from those fanatics." James pulls a plastic water bottle from an open car window. He slides the empty bottle in his pocket.

"They make a good point. Surviving has to be a part of God's chosen plan. We've seen some hairy stuff." *Hairy*, Howie's term for all they have survived since the apocalypse. "God has to be looking out for us."

"My partner had a vasectomy and married a woman who had her tubes tied. She ended up getting pregnant with his baby. They called her their little miracle. Made Miracle her middle name. The odds of her conception had to be greater than winning the lottery. The God you speak of, you think protects His chosen. I can't imagine a more chosen person than that little girl."

"She had to be important to God's plan," Howie agrees.

"I put a bullet into that eight-year-old girl's skull after we found her eating her mother's flesh."

Dumbstruck, Howie remains silent.

"I don't know if God watches over us or not, but he has no plan."

Tom pauses at the end of each vehicle, looking to his right or left before he steps past the space between the abandoned cars as if he's sure something will jump out and grab him. A likely scenario, but the undead won't crouch in wait, at least not in a planned manner, and there won't be anyone living waiting in ambush. Not on this part of the highway; there's nothing of value here.

"Someone should syphon the gas from these cars," James considers. He peeks into each car he passes. Most are so crammed full of personal possessions it would take hours to inspect each one for any useful item.

"People are stupid." He taps the roof of a car with a flat screen television filling the backseat. "They rescued their HD TV. Bet they left a cupboard full of canned goods."

"This's why we should follow those religious people. They're giving up all earthy goods."

"Howie, you need to consider what they are preaching. What if they don't consider you worthy?"

"I'm alive. I haven't been bitten. According to them I've God's blessing."

"According to the group you met they're going to join a larger group. You don't know what the larger group finds worthy. You get there and they may not let you in.

"God left this place a long time ago," Danziger adds.

Tom continues, "No god would punish all the decaying children I've seen since this started. They committed no sins, and the only invisible force keeping you alive is blind stupid luck. You want to pray, you go right ahead. You ask God for help and wait for him to come. The only lightning bolt to save you from a DK will fall from the shotgun you carry."

"Harsh, man." James shakes his head.

"So's this new world."

Trapped among the vacant cars an armored personnel carrier calls to Danziger. He hurries past Tom.

"Hold your pace, officer. We're not alone on this interstate."

Danziger hops into the back of the military truck. Mostly picked over and left empty he discovers a flak jacket in a storage bin. He slips it on. It's too snug to secure, but provides some protection, especially his back. He grabs a pack and feels heft—grenades.

"Find anything useful?" Tom calls from guarding the rear entrance. He waves to James who swings open the cab door.

"No. The soldiers took everything they could carry."

"All the military vehicles we've searched are empty," James calls out, also finding nothing. "Still can't get over those people packing their big screen."

Danziger drops an empty canteen into the backpack. "If I do find anything useful I can at least carry easier."

"Too bad the flak jacket doesn't fit. I saw a DK bite a guy wearing one, never made it to the skin."

"It will work for now." Repeating thunder crackles in the distance.

"Sounds like machine gun fire." James flattens himself against the personnel carrier before scanning for the source.

"Noise means there are DKs around, or there will be."

"I'll take point." Danziger flings one strap of the pack on his shoulder and races toward the shots.

"We don't have to do this. We don't have to help this guy," Howie points out.

"No, you don't. None of you have to risk anything for me," Danziger agrees.

Tom fails to respond. He runs to the inner concrete barrier dividing the north and south bound lanes. "Stay along this wall." He inches forward.

Danziger follows suit, pistol drawn.

"Go, Howie," James orders. "I'll take rear." The foursome eases up the road toward the gunfire.

"Why are we heading toward the expenditure of bullets?" Howie asks.

"Someone needs help," Tom reasons.

Lights sparkle on the overpass as it comes into view. A hoard of Infected crawl over a growing number of corpses as soldiers unload clip after clip into the never-ending mass of rotten flesh. The firing slows as soldiers cease in order to change out the barrels of their guns.

"They're going to be overrun." Danziger unslings the backpack.

"I'm not sure how." Tom views the penciling soldiers through the scope of his rifle.

"They are about to be overrun. The Infected just keep climbing on top of each other to reach them." Despite the lack of speed, the sheer numbers of undead swarm the overpass.

"We pull back and save ourselves," James offers.

"Can't do that."

"We may have to. We don't have near the ammo they have and once they stop firing the DKs will turn on us," Tom points out.

Danziger pulls out a grenade from the backpack. "What kinds of damage will this do?"

Tom glares at the cop for lying about not finding anything, but realizes it was not meant as a deception. Weapons are the key to survival.

"You'll draw them toward us for sure," James says. "They like loud noise."

"They do. How many do you have?" Tom asks.

Danziger fumbles through the bag. "Ten, maybe."

"Anyone got a good throwing arm?" Tom asks.

"Grenades aren't a killing explosive. They are more for maiming. Won't stop the undead. Blow off a leg, they still keep crawling toward food," Howie points out.

"We don't use the grenades to attack the DKs. We use them to explode the gas tanks of the cars under the undead pile."

"Good idea, but couldn't that set off a chain reaction to all these cars?"

The machine gun fire slows as the moan-howls get louder.

"Fire break." Tom punctures the gas tank of the nearest car. Gas floods out. "No gas, no secondary explosions."

Danziger gives everyone two grenades.

Tom punctures the next car's tank and moves onto the third. "When I say, pull the pin and throw. Try and aim for the back of the car and then run back about five cars." He slams his knife into another car. He hopes without gas these cars won't explode. The machine gun fire dissipates. The screaming moan-howls of the DKs replace the rattling fire.

"Now!" Tom hollers tossing his two grenades and diving into the ditch. Danziger throws his two before diving over the median wall. Howie and James throw and run from the punctured cars. Rapid explosions replace more explosions. Chunks of car, twisted metal and flaming suitcases of clothes rain down on the interstate.

Forced to dive for cover from the shower of flames, the soldiers stop shooting. The undead hoard swarms through the fire as if none of the cars are burning. The fires destroy a few Infected, but most just emerge fully engulfed in flames. They shamble forward, burning. Searching for prey to satisfy their hunger. Danziger props his arms over the median barrier and takes aim. He pops an Infected. It goes down tripping two engulfed corpses behind it.

Tom pulls himself from the ditch. He runs. The pile of lifeless bodies the Infected scale to reach the soldiers on the overpass blazes in flames. The corpses spill into burning rings of fire. The soldiers line the guard rail and turn sniper. They pick off shambling cadavers as they stagger toward Howie and James.

"Tom, move to the divider. Get into the southbound lane!" Danziger pops another DK. He takes aim before squeezing the trigger again. He must make every shot count.

Tom skirts between the vehicles, zig-zagging back a car and over a car to reach the concrete median, avoiding the undead.

"Before we all crawl over this wall, what do we want to do?"

"I say we join the soldiers," Danziger chooses.

"I vote the soldiers," Howie agrees, handing his shotgun to Danziger flipping himself onto the median and over the wall.

"Head to the off-ramp," Tom points out. "Before the DKs. The fire's not stopping them."

"Not until the brain cooks, and that takes time," Danziger adds.

"Let's just move. Those soldiers won't cover us forever." James throws himself up onto the concrete median.

The foursome hoofs it toward the southbound on-ramp. Rifle in hand, Tom returns to his bob and weave pattern, Howie on his heels.

The soldiers cease their fire into the herd. They let the Infected on fire just burn, none of them capable of scuttling over the median to reach the overpass.

Danziger keeps his pace to a jog. The other three sweat in their heavy camo coats.

They reach the edge of the overpass. A female soldier swings her rifle over the edge pointing directly at Danziger. "Halt or I shoot!"

Danziger throws his hands in the air. "We're on your side." Howl-moans of DKs screech from the flames.

"Our side? You dumbass! Explosion will draw every Infected from here to the river."

Danziger hadn't realized. He just wanted to save the soldiers.

"Look, lady, if you're right then we need to get out of here," Tom spits and pants from his run.

"There's no *we*, civi."

"You're not here to protect civilians?" James falls into shock as his disillusionment of the military sinks in.

"If you're not here to help civilians then what are you here for?" Danziger's not sure he wants the reply.

"Not here to answer to you," she snaps. She wears no rank or other identifying patches on her uniform.

"One thing's for sure, we're more likely to survive if we all work together." Tom reaches the top of the off-ramp.

A few soldiers shoot at DKs. The rest inspect their gear and repack supplies to compensate for a dead soldier.

"You aren't qualified to assist us." She snaps the dog tags from the dead man's neck. "Evident from your debacle with the grenades."

"You're a reconnaissance team. We're natives of this city. We can assist and you're a man short," Tom offers.

As she checks the dead soldier's pocket and removes his last letter to his family, the man bolts up. Before he sinks his teeth into the girl, Tom fires.

"What the fuck!" She points her pistol at Tom's head. The soldiers support her by swinging their weapons at Tom.

"Wait. Wait! *Wait*!" Danziger lowers his own gun to the pavement. "He turned."

"You better start fucking explaining," she demands.

"Was he bitten by one of the DKs?" Tom lowers his rifle.

"We know those corpses didn't shoot him," Howie attempts to help.

Tom snaps his friend a 'shut the hell up' stare.

"How do you think what you call 'the Infected' grow in number?" Tom keeps his voice at a reasonable tone.

"Our briefing didn't contain said information." She lowers her pistol.

"Again, I want to offer our help."

The tall soldier nods at her.

"We're not here to recon the bridges."

"What?" Danziger grabs his pistol.

"Teams have been dropped into the city to blow holes in the bridges to prevent the flow of these monsters in and out of the city. We've been instructed to destroy all the river bridges."

"Trapping the living."

"Not the entire bridge. Just enough of a gap preventing the Infected from crossing. Later a bridge layer tank seals the gap." She seems confident with this explanation.

"You're ten miles from the nearest bridge," James points out.

"Our chopper experienced engine trouble. The pilot set down here then took off. We saw him land over there, but no smoke from a crash."

"We thought that area was heavily infested," Tom admits.

"Not since your explosion drew them this way."

"We'd better get moving before more DKs come here. They love noise."

"What bridge was your team assigned?" Tom asks

"I-70 Bridge over the Missouri River." She slings her bag over her shoulder and hands the fallen soldiers Colt 9mm SMG to Danziger. "You look like you need a weapon."

"The Blanchette Bridge—still a good ways down the road." James points north.

"We were going to turn on Highway 64 and head west," Tom explains. "We're trying to help Danziger here."

"Why's this civi so important?" She gives him one extra clip. "All I can spare."

"I was a cop in pursuit of the Blonde Teen Slasher. He's taken refuge in the caravan heading toward Fort Wood."

"Then why the hell didn't you arrest him?" She waves her soldiers to move. They scout down the on-ramp.

"The men guarding the caravan ran me off. We are circumventing them."

"I suggest you get moving before more Infected crawl this way."

"Don't you soldiers still need a guide?"

"We'll follow this highway." She jogs after her team.

"What if you have to abandon it?"

"We're Marines. We'll improvise and overcome."

"James, you and Howie guide them. I'll help Danziger find this killer."

"Tom, I don't think we should split up."

"Howie, if they are blowing the bridges it's because the military's working on a counter strike to take back the city. With two swift moving rivers at their backs they'll take back our country. And you run faster than me. Go."

Howie and James follow the female Marine.

Danziger inspects his new rifle. "You believe they plan to take back St. Louis?"

"Why else would they blow only part of the bridges?"

Danziger doesn't want to accept a military abandonment. Besides blowing the Blanchette Bridge would only make sense if they were going to clear the city as a beachhead to take back the west side of the river.

"You don't have to come with me. Assist your friends with the bridges."

"No, you need to get to this caravan. If you don't, no one will even know this killer's still at large."

# CHAPTER THIRTEEN

CHAD SLAPS THE side of a plastic bucket. "Come get it!" he howls.

The semi-truck cattle trailer backs through the gate over the cattle guard into the field. The air brakes hiss. Men scamper out. One man bounds up the ladder to the roof of the trailer while two more open the back. A second semi-truck without a trailer, and a suburban park along the road. Men with rifles hop out securing the area. They move with experience, but not like battle-hardened soldiers. A second four door Jeep stops and Emily's savior gets out, pulling on his black duster coat.

"We're secure, boss," Linzell reports.

"Keep an eye out. The biters like to keep to the interstate and this place's off the beaten path, but there are lots of cattle. We still don't understand what attracts the biters."

"I thought it was noise."

"Sound draws them big time, but who knows what else still works in reptilian brains." He doubts science will be anything more than educated guesses when it comes to the undead.

"Chad's sure making a lot of noise."

"They'll come to the bucket. I bet those cattle haven't had corn feed in a while."

"You know a lot about farming, boss?" Linzell detects a hint of experience in the man next to him.

"I know some, but we've real experts back at the camp. People who wanted to grow up and become farmers. We'll just bag'm and tag'm."

"Wish the vet we had knew something."

"She does, she was just trained in small animal care. It's better than nothing. Besides, Linzell, you don't exactly strike me as a farm boy yourself. You seem to lack a distinctive farmer's tan."

Linzell laughs from his gut. "White people, still find ways to make racist jokes, even after the world ends."

"It's our one skill—oppressing the minorities."

Linzell stops laughing. "The only minority any more's the living."

A Black Angus cow pokes its head from the tree line. Chad shakes the bucket sloshing the grain around inside.

"It certainly changes the 'us versus them' mentality." The glint of metal in the sunlight catches his eye. Two more cattle amble from the trees. Chad sloshes the bucket. They trot toward the sound of shuffling grain.

"Linzell," he whispers, "circle wide and come up behind where those cows came out of the trees." He nods his head in the direction he wants the young man to head.

"You spot something, boss?"

"Not a biter, the cattle are too calm." He mouths the words, barely moving his lips to give his order. Linzell follows the instructions.

"About twenty so far, boss." Chad beams.

Emily's savior joins Chad as more cattle burst from the woods.

"The trailer holds sixty."

"I heard Dartagnan's numbers..."

"I trust the kid's figures completely, but computations don't take all variables into account. They aren't always black and white answers."

"But too many cattle will eat all the grass and then die. So why take more than we can feed?" The heifers trot at Chad's shaking bucket. He steps backward slowly toward the trailer.

One cow walks among the trotting herd.

"Dartagnan doesn't take into consideration outside factors, like we're here now and can get cattle. We'll need more in a few months and we may not be able to find—" His .357 leaps into his hand level with the double barrel shotgun of an overall clad farmer.

"Damn you're fast, boy."

Chad drops the bucket. "Where the fuck did old MacDonald come from?" The cattle attack the spilt grain.

"Get the bucket and get these heifers on the truck," he instructs Chad.

"We still shoot cattle rustlers in this state." the farmer shifts his barrel to Chad.

"You're not going to shoot and you should have kept your gun on me."

The farmer slides the barrel end back at him. "Happy now?"

"Can't let you shoot my crew."

"Can't let you steal my livelihood," the farmer responds.

"You want to explain to me how this is still your livelihood, and leave out the part about how your daddy's granddaddy built this farm with his bare hands."

"You're a smartass cattle thief."

The men securing the trailer and road take aim with their rifles.

"We've got you dead to rights," Chad brags.

"Shut up, Chad."

"Maybe so, but I've got you. Your group looks like it would fall apart without their leader."

"They might." He never breaks from his calm demeanor.

"Just shoot him," Chad panics.

"Shut-up, Chad. Scatter gun will hit you too, if loaded with buckshot."

"You're too calm. This's not the first loaded gun shoved at you," the farmer deduces.

"Only way to be with a gun in your face." He places his finger on the hammer and squeezes the magnum's trigger enough to decock the gun. "I tell you what, I'll offer you a proposal."

Two teenage boys, both with rifles, shove Linzell from the tree line. "Dad! We got one."

"Seems like you wanted to offer me a proposal." The farmer feels he now has the upper hand with a human as a bargaining chip.

The thought flashes through his mind he should just have shot the glint of metal when he first spotted it and prevented all of this. The cattle would have scattered, but they could be rounded up again. Just taking what they need to survive should be enough justification for killing this man. He has an entire group to protect and provide for. What's one more dead farmer in a world of the walking dead.

"I want to offer you my proposal."

"I'm listening." The farmer keeps his gun aimed.

"I take you, and your family, along with the cattle, back to our community."

"Not much of an offer. We've only seen a few of those rot-bags around here."

"You'll see more as they run out of food in the city. So far they tend to cling to the interstate. People are still stupid enough to travel along them. These cows will attract hungry undead soon enough."

"I've killed a few more rot-bags lately than at first."

"Sixty cows fit in our trailer. Your experience won't go without merit."

The farmer lowers the shotgun. "What about my family?"

The two stout farm boys bring Linzell to their dad.

"Pack them up." He waves to his crew and they lower their rifles. "We've a fenced in compound, but we have a few non-negotiable rules."

"What are they?"

"After properly trained, everyone carries. You seem to understand the need for a gun. Everyone works, or they don't eat. I bet the only thing changing for you is the location."

"Nothing unreasonable so far."

"A few other minor things, we're a little short on housing right now so you'll bunk in a community building until we have you a new farmhouse, but since you come with the cattle, I'll accelerate you into a family house."

"I've goats, too."

"You a trailer to haul them?" he asks.

"Yep."

"What are we going to do with goats?" Chad asks.

"Milk and cheese."

"From goats?" Chad's face melts in disgust.

"You'll get used to the taste," he snaps at the kid.

The farmer drops the shotgun to his side and offers his hand in friendship.

"I'll take you at your word."

He holsters his magnum and returns the firm grip. "My camp could use a few more farmers."

"It seems like it."

A woman in well-worn overalls carries buckets to the truck.

A young girl carries a baby goat. "Why do we have to move, Mom?"

"We're going someplace safer," she assures the little girl.

Emily's rescuer places a box in the back of a dually truck attached to a gooseneck trailer. "We've built a wall to keep biters out." He takes another box from Linzell. "You're lucky you get to pack and bring the things that are important to you. Most people I help don't get the option to bring their pets."

"This isn't my pet." The little girl runs back to the house.

"You're not good at consoling children." The mother scowls.

"I used to be, but now all that 'Jimmy broke up with Suzy to date Jenny all before lunch' garbage seems to pale compared to dealing with biters." The mother gives him the buckets and runs after her daughter.

"Cynical much?" Linzell adds.

"Linzell, my friend, it keeps me alive." He pats the young man's shoulder. "Go back with these people and have Wanikiya set them up. Since they are responsible for the goats, they need a farmhouse as soon as we have one."

"I thought we went on seniority? I was hoping to move out of the bunkhouse," Linzell whines.

"Seniority's about the fairest method, but exceptions are necessary when feasible. The engineer I saved to help run the hydro plant. We got him a house quick."

"So expertise trumps seniority?"

"Experience adds to seniority, as it should."

"You're the boss, boss. But shouldn't you send someone else? Those boys got the jump on me. We had some words."

"I want it to be you. I want no hard feelings between any of us. You escorting them shows you understand why they took you captive. I know not everyone will like each other, but one thing we have to do is live together without needless conflict."

"I don't think those boys like me."

"Because you're black?"

"I felt the redneck vibe a bit," Linzell says.

"All the more reason to become friendly."

"You pulled me from a flipped car and I was cut so bad, no one else believed I wasn't bit."

"I'd a car accident once. Lot of blood, no bites."

"Did I ever thank you, boss?" Linzell asks.

"Just make sure these people make it to their new home safe. All the thanks I need."

The semi-truck backs the trailer into the loading bay of the distribution center.

"We could've used Linzell," John says.

"Better he shows those people he understands why they took his gun. After all, I was going to shoot that farmer."

"You were?"

"John, I'm ready to shoot anyone who pulls a gun on me. He had provocation: we were stealing his cattle, but we've lost the option of hesitation and double thinking." He glances over John's shoulder, past the semi to the tree line.

"You see something, boss?"

"We're being watched from the trees." He grabs John's arm to prevent him from spinning around.

"Watched? Biters don't watch." His hand shifts toward his gun.

"Could be some group of raiders, but I think it's scared survivors, not smart enough to find bolt cutters."

"What do you want to do?"

"Load the truck with the supplies we need, and if there's room, whatever else is useful. Maybe a baby crib or two. I'll stand guard out here."

"You expecting, boss?"

Laughter punctuates his team.

"It will happen one day. We'll need lots of baby stuff."

"There's another semi over there. Trailers empty. We could load it. I could drive it back," John offers.

"Cuts our security detail down. You won't have a shotgun rider."

"You'll ride shotgun."

"I'm not going back this trip. I've got a new area to explore. Dar's list had a few more items on it. I want to locate them quickly. Once Dartagnan calculates the new people and cattle, I'll have a whole new list of supplies to gather."

"How does such a brain work inside such a…" John holds back his original word and inserts, "kid?"

"Be glad he survived. Dar's calculations allow us to flourish. I figure when a brain's over powerful in one area other areas don't function as well."

"I guess, boss," John agrees. "Two trucks mean even more supplies. Get every bit of useable food cleared out." He lowers his voice, "Besides, those survivors may break into this place once we go and leave nothing for later."

"If you get the second semi started, load it. Try not to bring anything expired, and if you find some more model kits, pack them, too. I'm going to make sure those aren't raiders." He pulls a M1903 Springfield rifle from the semi. He checks the chamber before marching off the parking lot.

Smoke fizzles from a dying fire. He moves his hand close to the coals until he feels warmth. In every Western movie he's ever seen the tracker's action tells him just how long ago the fire was built. In real life, however, it gives him no real idea except that a living person used it recently, but long enough ago they let it burn down without adding more dry wood. A course of behavior spanning hours giving him no useful time frame as to when people were last here.

He keeps the Springfield rifle ready. The smell of overcooked meat hangs around the camp. Dangling from a spit are bits of flesh. A ragged tent remains zipped up. Some tattered clothes lay strewn about the ground, and a meat cleaver rests next to the fire pit.

He knows they are hiding in the brush. The smell of rank unwashed people hangs in the air over cooking meat odor. He tries to ignore the stench as easily as he pretends to ignore those hidden in the weeds. He has smelt cooking flesh once before, and he hopes he's wrong this time. Civilization hadn't fallen far enough into savagery in the past nine months for people to have turned on one another like this, at least he hopes not.

They pitched this camp less than a half mile from the distribution center, which contained ample canned goods, and yet they didn't even try to enter it. There weren't any marks on the door from someone trying to beat their way inside. Even in the panic to flee the biters, had people become so stupid they forgot how to scrounge for bolt cutters to remove the locks of a building? The homes of the town on the other side of the interstate should still have some supplies. Stale potato chips have to be preferable to this.

These people learned not to move with living around, but they must not realize they stink and not to hide downwind of prey. Freezing in place is no defense against the biters, so he wonders what other groups they've had to cloak themselves from. They've nothing of value and he wouldn't take from them if they did. This group of three isn't brash enough to attack his team. He figures leaving them alone is his best option. Part of him wants to kill them, put them out of their misery before they decide to feast again. Better to take the supplies and leave without attacking other living people. Part of him wants to fire into the brush just to startle them, but why attract the dead with a rifle shot? The semi-trucks make enough noise.

He backs from the camp not wanting to tempt them with his backside as a target.

"Abe, is there still food inside?"

Abe answers, "Quite a bit. We could fill another couple of trailers if we had someone to drive them."

"I'm sure our two semis will attract enough attention, but I'll scout this place again."

He packs a duffle bag full of food cans.

"We're ready to move out, boss."

"I'm not going back with you. I've a new area to scout."

"A lot of cans to carry," Abe points out.

"I'm leaving this for the people who were watching us from the trees. I don't know how they are surviving or why they haven't figured out how to find bolt cutters, but from the look of their camp they need food."

"Generous."

"Well, our group comes first, but since there's so much, let's share the wealth and help others." He adds, "If it's feasible to our own existence."

"It sort of destroys the charity of it."

"Charity no longer exists." He slings the bag of cans over his shoulder. "Put my rifle back in the truck, and have a safe journey home, Abe."

He drops the duffle bag next to the fire pit. The smell of the hidden people remains strong. He backs away from the camp with his hand on his magnum. Housing for a community of four thousand residents offers a plethora of supplies. Even if people took all the food with them they won't have packed every tool. These people hidden in the grass have taken on strange behavior or maybe they just couldn't handle losing their iPhones.

Smash.

The decorative pane of glass shatters. He reaches inside and twists open the dead bolt.

Funny how people remembered to lock their doors when the evacuation orders were given. Even after Katrina people have trust in the government organizing rescues. It seemed everyone forgot about the New Orleans disaster fuckup at the Superdome. And the government knew Katrina was coming, they had time to prepare. This diseased carnage of carnivorous corpses was over night. No time, no warning, and people marched to their deaths in the name of rescue. People packed too much or not enough. And what they did pack wasn't necessities.

A kid in his twenties mills around the mailbox. He's been dead for a while. Shooting him would attract attention and he's not worth a blade right now. Besides, his stench masks other smells. For good or bad, the kid exists for the moment.

The glass breaking draws the teen biter's attention. Now he should just end the biter. Save him the time later. Or the possibility that this creature could attempt to jump him at the wrong moment. Kill them all should be a rule he implements back at his camp. He finds no guilt in it, but others may not be as cold, especially when a biter reminds them of a loved one.

*Kershunk.*

The bowie knife severs the brain from the spinal column. This thing was one of the dumber ones. He unzips the kid's backpack. Compact discs spill out. Not only did he pack useless items, he took out-of-date tech. An MP3 would have given him more room to carry food, and the batteries last longer. Nothing useful. A can of tuna. Tuna turns his stomach. He pockets the tin. Someone will eat it. It won't be wasted, but he'd have to be near death desperate before it's him.

Luckily, his compound and scavenging skills afford him the option to be a smidge picky. Finicky won't last. There'll come a day when grasshoppers will taste good and he'll be thankful for them, but not today.

He locks the dead bolt behind him just in case. The house has no dead fragrance. The living room has collected some dust, but the home was immaculate before the apocalypse. The cabinets have canned goods. He munches on stale Krispy Rice. It's palatable. He knows better than to open the fridge. Regular kitchen utensils fill the drawers. He pockets the matches. The garage has what he was hoping for—a car. Simple sedan. Nothing special, economical. The garage also has an assortment of tools but again, nothing special. He pops the car trunk. Clean, looks unused. Tossing in a couple of extension cords, a tree saw, and hand axe, he sees nothing else worth looting.

He'll have to set up a new travel truck since he didn't return one to his last hidden location when he was with Emily. He doesn't even want his own people to know his routes. Trust's not an issue, or maybe it is. But he hasn't lasted nine months by being reckless. Homes contain so much useless material items and yet a plethora of goods to maintain life. He finds blankets and a quilt in a closet and what he hoped for—.22 ammo, a box of five hundred and fifty rounds, unopened. Everyone wants high-powered rifles to kill biters, but a .22 gets the job done and is the most common American weapon. The ammo's cheap and sold in large volumes. A round will take care of a corpse and he now has a lot of rounds. He chucks the clothes, shoes and linen into a pile on the floor. No gun. At least not hidden in the usual places.

They must have taken it with them.

The dresser has nothing but undershorts. The nightstand, the most logical place to hide a gun, is next on his list to be rummaged. The drawer has a few cheap romance novels and some lube about as kinky as this lady got. He reaches into the drawer, fishes round and a CLICK releases the top. He slides it over and reveals a hidden drawer. Rings, a diamond pendant and a .22 Ruger rest there. He pops the clip. Ten shots. It will do. He bags the rings.

Sadly, some people still find the metal valuable. He has traded gold for food. Wondering what the fool trading thought he was going to buy with it. Maybe one day the world will be restored to some order and gold will retain purchasing power, but for now it is useless weight. Unless he encounters another fool who wants something shiny. He'd trade all those rings for another clip of ammo if he could.

More blankets and a Ziploc bag of pills drop into the car trunk. He tosses in some more baggies. They do keep everything fresh and, more importantly, dry. Fresh is good. Dry is better. He slams the trunk shut.

The key turns.

Nothing.

Even being secure in the garage the battery died. He pops the hood and attaches the portable jumpstart he carries to the positive and negative connectors on the battery. He cranks the starter. The engine whines. He makes a pass through the garage again. So many tools, but none useful enough to lug the some hundred miles back to his camp or the forty he must go first and then back. He'll cut some of those down by going across country, making this trip a kind of triangle and throwing off anyone who might attempt to follow. A well provisioned loner invites attack.

The car roars. He lets it run, repacking his jumpstart. It's worth lugging around, and even if it's not good for quick escapes, it certainly saves on some shoe leather. He plugs the charging cable into the cigarette lighter. A little over half a tank; even by taking side roads he will have gas to spare.

He finds it hard to imagine traveling between thirty and forty miles an hour may actually be too fast even on this empty two-lane blacktop. It beats walking and should be enough time to stop if someone has abandoned a car on the road. But he knows this sort of third back road into what was once the city of Rolla. From Rolla it's a mere twenty miles to the military base. Only he's not sure of any third roads leading from Rolla and the interstate remains clogged with abandoned cars. The service roads aren't much better. He'll get to Rolla, and find a place to examine his map. At least he'll have covered the last eight miles in fifteen minutes whereas the next twenty could take two days.

The airbag slaps him in the face.

# CHAPTER FOURTEEN

"FATTY!"

"Fatty!"

"God you're so fat."

"How'd you ever outrun the zombies? You heifer."

"Fatty. Fatty."

The five men constantly berate Sarah.

In tears, she tries to run from them, but they surround and block her from getting away.

"God, you smell. Can't you fit into the showers?"

"The biters smell better than her."

The men keep tormenting the heavy girl.

Their words bring pain. One grabs the MRE in her hands. "She don't need this. There're starving children in here."

"She can live off her blubber." He slaps her stomach.

They laugh at her jiggling flesh. More tears burst from Sarah's eyes. Snot bubbles form in her nose as her face reddens.

Kani Bowlin munches on her ration as one of the men grabs her ass and shakes the cheek, forcing the flab to bounce. The men laugh.

"She ain't so bad. Look at this cushion. You could bounce on her pretty good and never touch the bed."

"Just don't let her roll over on you. She'd crush you," Kani says. They laugh.

"Bet no man's ever tried to ride this heifer."

Sarah pukes the little bit of her ration she was able to eat.

"Gag a little more and maybe a man will want to hump you." Kani hands off the MRE to another of the abusers.

"I've got something to make her gag." Her abuser fumbles with his crotch. More abuses bombard her. They pass the MRE among themselves.

Sarah feels abdominal pain tear at her. Hunger grips her. She hasn't eaten in twenty hours. The abuse, the depth of the pain of the new world is no better than the old. Ostracized, she runs to the new fence. Panting, she shoves her finger through the wire mesh, inviting the few Infected not yet picked off by the soldiers to bite her. She'll show those boys. She'll end it. She'll bring them into the hell she has been driven to her whole life.

"Don't. Don't do it."

Sarah turns to the young voice.

Hannah pleads with her. A soldier poised behind her keeps a hand on the top of his sidearm. If she's bitten, he'd shoot her and she'd never get a chance to have revenge on those boys.

"I don't know how bad it is for you, but ending this way..."

Sarah chokes on the thought of choosing to become a walking corpse. "You just don't know. You just don't know how bad it is in here."

"I know I can help. I know I want to help." This may be it for Hannah, someone her father won't protest her protecting.

Hannah takes Sarah's other hand. She feels the warm touch of someone who still cares. Someone with love. Someone who has yet to fully understand the cruelty of the world touches Sarah, giving her hope.

Hannah pulls Sarah's fingers back from the fence.

"Come back with me and let's get you cleaned up."

Uncomfortable, Sarah sits on a real bed wrapped in nothing but a small towel with the top of her buxom chest about to burst out of it. She has seen this building from a distance. It was built to house unmarried troops, allowing some of the base housing to become quarters for the refugees. Sarah doubts anyone was prepared for the number of people who would flee here. The original compound design was a few buildings with minimal amenities. None of the refugees, even the five Bowlin brothers, have hot showers like the soldiers are accommodated. They seem well fed. But then again, they have to stay sharp to protect them.

Hannah brings in a shirt.

"This's as large as I could find. I'm having your clothes washed. Didn't you have a change?"

"No." Sarah forces herself to make small talk with the teen girl. "I barely escaped when my family turned," she cries.

"I'm sorry. I forget so many have lost people close to them. I still have my dad." Forbidden to help the woman she wanted, Hannah decides to help Sarah by getting her away from Bowlin abuses.

"You're lucky. And lucky to be so thin. The emergency supplies don't cater to heavy people."

"My father's been transferring some of the more sick and infirmed people out of the base. I could see if they need help taking care of them."

"I'm not a nurse."

"No, but you don't need medical training to help feed and change these people."

"Kinda gross, but I'll do it."

"I'll talk to my dad. Maybe he'll see how bad the Bowlin brothers are if he hears it from you."

"You left the safety of Headquarters again. Damn it, Hannah! After I flog your escort… Do I need to put you in the brig?"

"No, Dad. I just want to help people."

"You need to stay safe." Travis balls his right hand.

"Is my safety more important than all these other people?"

"Yes, damn it. You're my daughter and your safety comes first."

Hannah appreciates how much her father cares about her. Travis wishes to tell her he will take care of this. He wants to, but there's a larger picture. Protecting her is spiraling out of his control as his orders reveal how the government has nearly collapsed and each helicopter in supply drop may be their last. He can't explain to her that the next parade of refugees banging at the gate should be turned away.

*Damn it, Hannah, we can't feed everyone. Damn it. I can't save everyone. Damn!* He wishes he could scream.

The violation of a few women should send him into public outrage, but the black market actually helps maintain some control as Kade's providing some items he no longer has to ration. Problems remain. People don't need shaving razors, but they think they can't live without such an item. Kade trades razors, making him important. Any more action against Kade could cause riots. He hasn't the troops to prevent disturbances. He barely has enough now to patrol the fences. Travis stopped ordering soldiers to gather survivors.

"I'll do whatever I have to in order to protect my only child." Travis wants to do more to protect her. Instead of wasting energy pumping life into something unable to be revived. He should be gathering his best soldiers and supplies staking out a defensible area to wait out the end of civilization. He should be devoting himself to solely protecting Hannah.

"Shutting down the black market is not a viable option. People need the distraction until Washington sends in more supplies."

"Just kick the Bowlin brothers out."

"The five of them have quite a following. Gun play would ensue costing a lot of people their lives. And costing me valuable soldiers I need to protect the base. Washington has recalled over half my troops in the last few weeks. Living soldiers are more important than the violation of a few women."

"Rape isn't right."

"A few brutalized women are better than a few hundred dead ones. This conversation's non-negotiable."

"I'm not one of your soldiers."

"Hannah, the only reason you're not in the brig—"

"Dad, this isn't right."

"I don't like removing the rights of individuals, but we have to face what is important for the good of all of us."

He wants to tell her the war has an end. They'll all return to their homes, and after some mass funeral pyres life will be as it was, but reality has proven otherwise. It wouldn't be a lie. The war would be over soon, but it will be America's last war and there won't be anyone left to record how mom and apple pie couldn't defeat walking corpses. No, better for her to be mad at him than to tell her he'd put a bullet in her temple before this camp succumbs to evil and she becomes a poor underage girl sucking cock for scraps of bread.

"Do as I tell you. Stay away from the refugee camps. In fact, go back to our apartment and pack an emergency travel bag."

Before she questions the orders, Hannah realizes her father has his way of sending a coded message. He's no longer capable of protecting her, let alone so many others in the camp. She thinks back to all her exploring. At first they built a fence and erected portable buildings, much in the way a child would build with Legos. Then, as the undead army grew, more people flooded in and a tent city arose. A second fence line was erected as were more and more tents. The place burst with people. It would only take one getting in who was bitten and there would be no place left for anyone to run. Her father instructing her to pack a bag meant this place wouldn't be safe for much longer, but where could he be sending all those people from the hospital?

"Father."

"No, Hannah. Just do it. Forget about the Bowlins."

Being the resident local survivalists, the Bowlin brothers assume the place of the military patrols outside the fence in the last few weeks. Hannah spied them leave the camp and returning with foraged supplies and small groups of refugees, but only when it suited them.

She plays her last card. "Kame made a run off base and took three girls with him. They claimed they had found their families in another camp..."

Travis wants to interrupt her with the information that there are no other camps, but clearly confirming her suspicions would cause her to insist further about removing the brothers from the camp. So he just listens.

"They haven't come back yet, but the last time they took a woman with them she didn't come back either," Hannah continues.

So much, so many to take care of shouldn't be an excuse to allow such tragedy to occur under his nose. Protecting people is his mandate, and clearly Travis has failed, but the question now remains, what is the greater good for the group? Individuality may be lost. Is the molestations of a few girls worth losing the lives of ten thousand? Before the outbreak the answer should have been yes, but now...now the rules have changed and he must protect humanity even over his own daughter.

"How do you know this?" Travis asks.

"I've been talking to people."

"Hearsay's not evidence."

"Ask Sarah, the girl I want you to help. She saw them leave," Hannah says.

"Trading food for sex may not be the most moral act, but kidnapping these girls...will stop."

Before Hannah gets excited about this, he adds, "I'll have to have absolute proof."

"Just send some troops out. Kill them when they're off base. No one will know."

"I won't put my men at risk. It's not just a raid on Kade men, it's the Infected. They are growing in number."

"Why hasn't the government evacuated the civilians?"

"Hannah, I'm not allowed to explain..." Travis pauses, then makes a quick decision. "There's no place to evacuate to."

# CHAPTER FIFTEEN

JIM SLAMS ON the brakes. The U-Haul trailer jars forward inching the truck onward with the momentum, sending his passengers against the dash.

"What the fuck, dude!" Rabia slaps Jim's arm. "I thought you could drive, white boy?" Horns howl.

"Fuck. This's not New York rush hour, fuckers." He climbs out the window. "Stop honking, fuckers!" He slides back into his seat. "Did everyone forget that those things are attracted by noise?"

"Too late, Jim." Ed spots why they stopped.

Now the milling mass of walking corpses along the interstate has shifted and become a wave of rotting flesh streaming toward the truck.

With car after car barely pushed aside to crawl down the interstate, there's no place to turn around.

No time run.

In reality, nowhere to run.

Rabia jerks the slide on her pistol. "Get us out of here white-boy."

Jim slams the truck into gear. "Hold on to your potatoes." He presses down with both feet, one on the brake the other on the gas. The back tires whirl to life sending up white rubber smoke. Drawing the undead directly to him. He releases the brake and the truck propels forward at breakneck speed. Running over once-people with a dull smacking thud. The bodies accumulate, jerking the truck up and down as if it was going over dozens of speed bumps.

Jim attempts to steer, but a tangled corpse in the wheel wells sends the right fender into an abandoned Honda. The rice burner skids against the concrete barrier and bounces off, slamming back into the truck's passenger door crumpling it permanently shut. Ed feels the door bruise his thigh. Rabia's gun ejects from her hand and bounces around the floor before sliding under the seat.

Jim fights to keep the truck steady, but he refuses to un-mash the gas petal. Two more cars spin away from the truck's superior metal frame, but the modern metal cannot match the 1960-something Plymouth Buick tank metal. They impact. Rabia feels the kiss of glass on her forehead. She slumps into her seat. Before all goes black, she witnesses the windshield crack in a spider web.

Danziger drops behind the blue mailbox, gun in hand. Blood mushrooms from Tom's shoulder. A DK shambles down the middle of the street.

"How bad is it?"

Tom rubs the wound. "Feels like it just scraped the skin. Burns like a mother." Tom slaps a feminine hygiene pad on the bleeding skin. "Don't say nothing. And from now on we can't walk down the middle of the street."

Danziger asks, "Did you see where the shot came from?"

"The upper window of that drugstore, I think."

"Makes sense. Good location for supplies. They must figure we're going to raid them."

"We mean you no harm. We're just passing through. If you'd shot the DK we'd have just moved on." The corpse moan-howls the only response. "We don't want anything you have. We've nothing of value to even trade." A lie. He knows the guns they carry are better currency than any greenbacks. "We just want to get to the caravan leaving for the military base."

The growls lumber closer. Danziger peeks at the building. The local drugstore provides cover for his assailant. The drugstore would have been well stocked with supplies. The building appears secure, but a poor choice of a hiding location. Anyone in need of anything in this neighborhood would start there in a search.

"Just shoot!" Tom screams.

"I have sixty-four bullets in this rifle. We're going to need them."

"We need to find a couple of machetes," Tom suggests.

The corpse lumbers toward them.

"He sure don't move quickly."

"Some don't. Most seem broken."

"But in a group of them they'll bring you down like a pack of lions."

"Lion groups are called prides," Danziger corrects Tom before calling back out to the drugstore. "Just shoot the dead thing and we'll move on."

Tom swings his rifle around. "I'm going to have to shoot it."

"We'll still have to outrun whoever's in the upstairs window."

"I shoot the meat-bag, you run. Better covering position from those buildings across the street."

Bam.

The DK falls to the ground. A smoking rifle barrel draws back inside one of the drugstore windows.

"Take a step toward this building and you get the same," a deep voice calls from the window.

Danziger puts a sterile gauze pad on Tom's torn skin from the bullet graze. "It's not bad, but infection is a greater worry. How far do you think we are from the caravan?"

"Cutting across people's backyards I'd say about two miles, but if we keep moving at an angle it could be longer, but still way past the end." Tom circles his shoulder to evaluate his range of motion. "Unless it's rolled out already."

"We better get moving."

Aleydis finds herself falling.

The nearly two-foot drop takes forever as she is jarred from the bus seat. As she tries to right herself the bus continues to shake. Kelly, a stringy blonde about her age steadies herself, "You have to get up. We got to go."

"Shouldn't we wait for the shaking to stop first?"

"It's not an earthquake." The short middle-aged man leans over the seat and offers his hand to pull her up.

"What's going on?" Aleydis struggles to get back to the seat, but the violent shaking keeps her on the floor.

"The rotters. We have to go." He offers his hand to her again.

"Take it," Kelly screams at her while stuffing a blanket into a satchel.

Aleydis lets the man get her out of the seat.

"Grab your bag and let's go." He pulls the handle on the emergency escape hatch in the roof. "Up you go." He stuffs Kelly through the hole.

Aleydis reluctantly steps back from him. The front doors smash open and rotters lumber inside. She jumps up, grabbing the hatch. The man shoves her through. He climbs on the seat. A rotter reaches for him. He jabs a screwdriver into its eye, shoving the brute back onto the next monster in line. Those few seconds of the dead rotter falling onto the other allows him to crawl out the hatch.

The undead shoving and pushing against the bus don't notice the trio. Thousands of walking corpses surround the bus, caravan, and interstate. Aleydis screams. Both Kelly and the man clamp hands over her mouth. The bus shakes. The DKs jump and claw reaching for a finger hold in order to pull themselves up.

The man lets go of Aleydis and turns counter clockwise slowly, taking in his entire surroundings. People jump from their vehicles still dragging their possessions. They run into the woods drawing many of the DKs after them. He witnesses stupid decisions as people drag bags of clothes and other worldly goods, slowing their escape. Many hold on to their luggage, even as the undead drag them to the ground and eat their flesh.

The bus violently rocks. The DKs hunger for the three people on top.

"Okay, girls. How far can you jump?"

"Jump where?" Kelly seems calmer than Aleydis.

"Truck bed." He points. "The rotters are going to tip this bus."

"Wrong way. Everyone's running the other way."

"They ran the wrong direction. Trust me."

Given a lack of choice, Kelly leaps from the bus. The boxes in the truck bed cushion most of her landing.

"You have to go," he yells at Aleydis.

Fear keeps her frozen on the rocking bus.

Kelly scrambles to the roof of the truck cab and waves for Aleydis to jump. She knows better than to yell, and the rotters around the truck have failed to notice her. They keep shambling to the shaking bus.

Two cars down a man jackrabbits from a car. He jumps over one car trunk avoiding grabbing corpses. Kelly prays he reaches the divided median where the dead thin out enough to avoid them. Aleydis wants to cheer him on. The man on the bus with her spins her around so she doesn't see the jackrabbiting teen slide over the roof of a car and into the waiting arms of a dozen undead.

"You have to jump." He half shoves her from the bus.

Aleydis screams all the way to the truck bed. He follows her pulling her from the boxes before the rotters turn and grab them. He pushes Aleydis to the cab roof before grabbing a crutch from a pile of personal possessions. He smashes the nearest rotter in the face.

"Where do we run now?" Panic creeps into Kelly's voice. The girl has nerve, but even she won't take much more of this.

He slams the crutch into another rotter before joining the girls on the roof. "We run for those trees." He points.

"Those monsters are coming from that direction. Everyone's running the other way."

"Exactly. The ones coming from the north out of those woods have thinned out because they are heading south. Leaving fewer rotters to deal with. Unfortunately, they'll be chasing those poor souls running south." He points back across the interstate.

The bus smashes to its side drawing more DKs to the crushing metal noise.

"We go now." He drops from the roof.

Kelly shoves Aleydis from the cab into the man's arms. He sets her on the ground feeling wet on his hand. The man realizes Aleydis has an abdominal wound from the crimson fluid dripping through his fingers.

They run through the monster's grabbing arms racing through the cleared ground between the interstate and the tree line. He stops. The girls pause.

"Keep running!"

The girls sprint faster, weaving between the thinning herds. He grabs the handle of a machete sunk into the shoulder of a rotter. He has to kick the creature in the chest to yank the blade free. Once he has the weapon he races after the girls.

They reach the tree line. The rotters have thinned. Three turn to pursue them. Kelly runs right into a rotter. The man sinks the machete into its skull.

"We keep moving through the woods. Don't stop."

"Who are you?" Kelly asks her savior, falling against a tree sucking in deep breaths.

"Don't stop," he scolds them.

"I don't know who you are." Blood blooms through Aleydis' shirt.

"I'm a guy trying to stay alive. Call me Jack, if it gets you to run." Levin smiles at his joke.

Aleydis huffs in deep breaths. "Something in one of those boxes was sharp."

"We've got to get clear of this herd before we fix your wound."

They race off into the woods.

"Suburbia." Tom kicks a deflated beach ball into the green water of a backyard pool.

Danziger fiddles with the latch on the gate. "The thing's rusted shut."

"Use the butt of the rifle," Tom suggests.

Danziger raises the weapon to drive the butt like a hammer against the lock when the creak of a swing forces his muscles to freeze. Danziger waves Tom to be quiet. Tom becomes a statue, but not before he raises his rifle. Danziger points over the fence to the yard next to the one they are in. Tom side-steps in that direction. Danziger crunches some dead bushes to peek over the fence.

A dead girl in a ruined pink dress swings in the back yard. She turns her head and hisses at Danziger. She pumps her legs to swing again.

"You ever see one behave like that?"

"It's not swinging, detective. Look at her hands."

Danziger notes her wrists have been duct taped to the chains to prevent escape. "Someone couldn't deal with their precious little girl turning."

"Should we kill it?"

"I think we should tread lightly. I've heard stories of people who keep loved ones chained and feed them parts of the living because they can't bear to let them go."

Danziger won't pass judgment on such people. He has no idea how he'd behave if it had been his little girl who'd been bitten. He just knows what he will do to her murderer.

"How do you want to handle this? I've got to bust the gate lock."

"Let's avoid the noise and go around the other way, or at least a few houses down."

"Safety first."

"You want to find your daughter's killer then we don't need unnecessary risks. The world's full of new killers, and not just the DKs."

"You're going to keep me alive through this aren't you, Tom?" Just like Hyun Su did for most of their partnership on the force.

"I'm not sure how you've made it all these months." Tom tries the back door.

"I had this Asian good luck charm."

"It must have worked well."

"It did until I lost it."

Locked.

He heads out the back gate into the alley. "Me and the guys, we held out at the fire station till they closed off that section of town, then we took off just outside the city and holed up in a few houses with some others. Our food ran out so we came back into

St. Louis. Took up as guards to protect those who gathered as they planned the caravan to the military base. It paid in food."

"I heard about the group maintaining a western wall. We still operated as police for a few months, but as more people turned..."

"The city fell apart."

"We stayed police as long as we could. The city plummeted into chaos block by block. We stole a solar generator and used it to pull up the police files on my daughter's killer. I couldn't let him get away."

"Leading you to the caravan."

"The only place he could be. And you saw him."

"Yeah. He was helping a lot with the teens. Some of them lost parents; he worked like a counselor. He was helping people with their emotional states. Something no one got to focus on while just surviving. I think he prevented quite a few people from ending it."

"The more people stay alive the better."

"Sound advice." The ker-chunk of two shotguns being cocked force Tom and Danziger to spin around.

A half dozen people hold weapons on them.

"No one's crazy enough blaring car horns!" Honorably discharged Sergeant Mike Hammerstein jumps from the back of the Jeep. He brings up the rear of this rolling buffet. Unslinging his M16, he taps the trunk of the car in front of him and waves his hand in a 'knock it the fuck off' signal. He moves to the next car tapping the roof.

"Stop with the horn," Mike orders.

"Fuck you, GI Joe."

Mike thought the BDU camo pants would be best when he realized the world had gone to shit. They were comfortable and actually afforded some protection. The nylon fibers woven into it are difficult to bite through. He bought them at some retail shop, not sure they were ever military issue.

Now his gun. He wishes it were military issue. He bought it when he got back from Kuwait. Knowing how to convert the semi-auto weapon into a fully functioning machine gun would be ideal for today, but he had once believed in the law, so he kept the weapon as it was purchased. Too bad his trigger finger isn't what it used to be. The horns die down and the thumps of a car crash echo down the line. As terrifying as hearing metal twist, snap, and pop like crumpling paper, the next echo causes Mike to lose a splash of urine.

The growling choir of undead fills the air. Even with the number in the city none of them sounded as loud. A few people run screaming past Mike. He has no idea where they think they are going. He crawls into the back of a truck, climbing over the tied down supplies. He stands on the cab, rifle in hand.

Smoke pours from the lead truck. More people abandon their vehicles. Mike loses the rest of his bladder as he stops counting what must be a hundred thousand undead shambling across the interstate before him.

# CHAPTER SIXTEEN

EMILY STRUGGLES TO carry a single steel post from the truck bed. Rad scoops it from both her hands with one of his as if it were a toothpick. The muscle bound guy twirls the bar like a baton and stabs it into the ground. He drops the cylindrical driver over the post. A few slams of the post driver and the metal sinks deep into the soft earth.

"We'll have this goat pen up in no time."

Emily's arms shake as she picks up another post. "I don't think I'm much help."

"Nonsense. We'll get you stronger. Twelve hours a day, every day working like this and you'll pack on the pounds."

"My poor hands won't take that."

"They'll get tough, too." He takes the post from her and sticks it in the ground. "I tell you what, I'll make sure you get the first glass of goat milk since you helped build these pens."

"Yuck."

"There can be no more 'yucks,' young lady." Behind her in military fatigues stands an older man with a grandfather face. He introduces himself. "Chief Petty Officer Simon, US Navy retired. Small Arms Marksmanship Instructor."

"I'm Emily." Her blistered fingers feel crushed under the grip of his hand.

"Well, Emily, you ready to find out how well you shoot?"

"I guess."

Sensing her reluctance, Rad asks, "They told you there were certain rules here?"

She nods in affirmation. "You guys work fast."

"We need to know how everyone shoots. Then we'll get you a job, if building fence isn't where you belong."

Grateful to stop moving the heavy posts, she pulls off the gloves from her blistered hands, "Where do we shoot?"

Collecting along the fence, as thick as summer locusts, biters snarl and moan-howl. They grab and yank at the wire. Wind chimes on spinning weathervanes clink together frenzying the biters. The dog run reaches an end here with a secured gate that continues on past a cargo container with only a single fence. Installed inside the fence is a pit of steel fence posts driven to snag anything propelling itself into the compound. On the other side of the trench, a third cargo container rests across the top of the two containers forming an H. It would only take the moving of one of the bottom containers by a few inches to send the top one crashing to the ground effectively blocking entrance into the camp.

A few tables stand at the end of the cargo containers. Steel posts mark distance to the fence but she's not sure how far apart they are. Simon lays a box of bullets, full clips, ear plugs, shooting glasses, and finally a pistol from a gun case, in front of her. "Safety's our first rule. You ever fire a gun before?"

"Does the Playstation count?"

"No."

"Is this your job here?" Emily asks. Despite all the bullying the man who saved her from the marauders gave her about being a teen girl, she wants to understand what she has to do to survive in her new life.

"I train, instruct, and evaluate everyone for firearms use. I also maintain the armory which involves keeping track of all weapons inside our camp. Recently we recovered a gunsmith, and I assist him in the cleaning and repair of any new weapons, but we'll discuss how to clean your gun and keep it clean if you pass training."

"So this is what you do to get to eat?"

"Nobody go over the rules with you?"

"It was a lot to soak in."

"Your shooting ability determines a lot here. We put great shooters on guard duty and the best shooters on wall at the entrance or on field duty with those working outside the fence. Essential skills are assigned next, people where we need a skilled worker or someone able to learn on the job are placed next. Finally, the last group we call the farm, but that's our code for ditch digger. Bet it makes you wish you'd have paid more attention in school."

"I was only a sophomore," Emily defends herself. "Rad seems smart. Better than just a fence builder."

"He is, but we haven't much need for a commercial artist. Smart people don't have the skills to survive without computers."

"You sound like our leader."

"I don't know what our leader used to do. He's clearly educated, but no stranger to labor jobs. The kind of person we need to make this new society work." Simon never drops his military demeanor.

Emily makes a mental note to ask her savior what he used to do for a living.

Simon snatches the gun from the table as he explains, "This's a .22. Your targets will be actual biters."

"You want me to shoot those people?"

"They're not people anymore and you must be able to protect yourself and everyone else in this camp from them. No warning shots. You take them out."

"So how do I use the gun?"

"Point that end at what you want to kill."

Emily raises the pistol. She jerks the trigger. Miss.

"Squeeze the trigger. During practice you've all the time you need. Aim, squeeze. Don't jerk. Ease your finger back."

Emily closes her eyes before moving her trigger finger. The gun jerks. The bullet pings against the cargo trailer. The biters moan-howl at the noise.

"You can't be scared of the gun." Simon draws his own weapon.

Bang. Bang. Bang. The deafening thunder tears through the skulls of three biters. "Don't fear your weapon. It's a tool." Simon adds, "And the only thing keeping you alive."

Emily takes a seat on the bench attached to the cafeteria table. Two boys and a girl, all older than her but closer in age than everyone else eating, join her.

"You must be the new fish."

"Great way to introduce yourself, Luke," the girl scolds. "We're not in prison."

"We got to try something to call the new people."

"Calling me a fish is a sure fire way to make sure I'll take no interest in you, and given the limited number of people surviving these days, it would suck to be the last guy on earth without a date." Emily may not be strong or shoot well, but she hasn't lost her skill at berating boys.

"You need cream for that one, bro?"

"For what?" Luke asks.

"She burnt you good," the girl laughs. "I'm Juliann. How long you been here?"

"I was brought in two days ago. I had to stay in the infirmary."

"Did they handcuff you to the bed?"

"No." Emily's not sure if she should be offended or scared by such a question. "The doctor's name was Baker, not Gary."

"The last person they brought in and kept in the infirmary for the first few days they kept handcuffed. He had some scratches that were *suspicious*."

"That's just a rumor," Juliann barks.

"Beats the other one—they just shoot you at the gate if they think you've been bitten."

Emily drives her fork into the casserole piece on her tray. "This stuff better than school food?"

"Somewhat. Wanikiya is a way better chef than a leader, but still cooking for all these people, it can be worse sometimes."

"Food is food, Kyle. I didn't eat for five days. If Wanikiya cooks I'll enjoy it."

"Have you had your gun training yet?"

"Leave the poor girl alone," Juliann scolds.

"This's the only time we get to talk. I want to know what's going on in the world."

"I want to know if Simon tried to teach you with that bent .22."

"Bent?" Emily had wondered why, even after she kept her eyes open to shoot, she couldn't hit a biter.

"It's a test."

Simon takes a seat. "That it is. It's my way of weeding out people who don't know weapons. You'll get another chance to prove yourself."

Shocked by this, Emily stares angrily at Simon.

"So did our fearless leader find you?"

"I don't want to talk about it."

"You don't have to," Juliann defends her.

"Without the Internet new people will be the only way we get news," Luke says.

Emily understands the need to know. "I was pretty sheltered to what was going on. I didn't know it was as bad as what I saw on my way here."

"Lucky."

Simon stops shoveling in his meal long enough to say, "Kyle, don't punish the girl because she hasn't faced the terrible darkness befallen this country."

"I just want to know." Kyle grabs his tray and leaves the table.

"Forgive him. Kyle got separated from his family. He doesn't know what happened to them."

"We've all lost people."

"Most of us know what happened to them." Simon returns his empty tray to the dishwasher counter.

"Any warnings about other tests?" Emily asks.

"They'll assess what kind of skills you have. No one around here will tell you it's possible to grow up to be president anymore."

"Especially if you are good at digging ditches," Luke adds.

Simon returns to the table. "Let Emily finish. I need to retest her this afternoon. Nothing has changed outside the fence. With each new person we rescue we learn the world gets worst."

"Always the optimist, Simon." Luke swallows his last bite. "Not everyone out there surviving is the devil incarnate."

"Nine months of avoiding being eaten changes people."

"You'll get used to this place." Juliann smiles at her. "It's the safest place I've seen." She speaks as if her life was worse before the world fell to the apocalypse.

"You've been in this building before?"

"I spend a few days in the classroom you converted into a hospital."

"It works great for a community building. Food, hospital, armory, bunkhouse for those who have not yet been assigned homes. Eventually we might turn some of the rooms back into classrooms.

"School."

"Yet to be determined." He points at the wall.

A section of a mural full of children of every ethnicity has been partially painted over by the rules. A title, "Rules of Acheron," hangs over a motto, "we depend on each other."

> Rule #1: Biters are not people. Infected will be executed immediately.
> Rule #2: All citizens, once properly certified, will carry arms.
> Rule #3: Everyone works: Everyone Eats.
> Rule #4: Punishment of violations will be severest as to the crime.
> Rule #5: Protection of the Compound circumvents all other rules.

Scrawled underneath is sublimation about new rules being added or amended based on the camp's need and adopted in town meetings.

"It's still a work-in-progress."

"The last rule kind of blankets everything," Emily notes.

"You saw what they did to that Kyle kid?"

"He raped a girl."

"The evidence indicated so. At our next meeting we may have to add specific crimes and punishments. Mostly people get docked food rations. Cuts down on a lot of petty issues because people don't want to miss a meal."

"What kind of crimes are people committing?"

"A few people get caught slacking off. Right now there's a lot of labor work and not enough people to do it. As we grow that should get better. Creating rules to survive in this world will be full of trial and error. It's not just enough to survive. We have to create a new way of life."

"I'm ready to learn to shoot. And figure out what I'm best at besides hauling around metal poles."

"Best kind of attitude to have around here." Simon turns his head so she doesn't see his smile.

*Bam. Bam. Bam.*

Biter heads blow open from the bullets. A few get shot in the chest, but with each pull of the trigger Emily strikes an undead.

She drops the clip from the smoking pistol and places both on the table.

"You're getting better. One more clip without a miss and I'll certify you to carry."

"I'm still not getting that many head shots."

"You're not missing either. Head shots are the most difficult to make. The movies make them look easy, but it's not. You ever notice on the news when they show a prisoner being escorted to court and how he wears a bullet resistant vest?"

She nods.

"If head shots were so easy then why don't they armor his face as well?"

Emily comprehends. She loads the gun, releases the slide, and aims before squeezing the trigger. Each round impacts a biter. Three slump finally dead. She places the empty gun and clip on the table.

"Nicely done. Not a miss and three kills. Good enough to carry. Not good enough for even light guard duty."

"So it's back to building fences?"

"It's an honorable job." Simon packs up his shooting supplies. "You don't need a high caliber gun. I've got a small .22 perfect for you back at the community center."

"It's too early for supper to return there."

"We'll find Wanikiya and see if they've come up with an actual job assignment for you. We'll take the long way back. I'll show you more of the compound. You'll work a full day tomorrow. You've earned a meal tonight."

Simon places the case in the back of the Jeep. "We'll skip the main entrance where it intersects this road with J highway. So far we've been expanding west using the road as an eastern border."

"Why there?" Emily desires understanding of her new home, realizing she never knew the geography of the military base.

"Besides boarding on a national forest, which limited the number of biter encounters at first, Highway J goes across the Clearance Cannon Dam."

"So there's a big lake as your northern border, which acts as natural protection."

"Smart, but also the dam's a hydroelectric plant."

"That's why we have lights." She beams.

"We've a gate entrance there, too, but we keep it closed off with a tank. Not much north of the dam population wise."

"That has to take a lot of guards."

"One reason why everyone who's unable to shoot with high accuracy or hasn't another skill works the farm jobs. It only takes a few to tend cattle, but a lot to patrol the fences."

"I guess we'll always need guards now."

"As we take over more farmland we grow more of our own food and rely less on scavenged food. We're resigned to keep our human growth in line with our food production so we maintain a livable colony."

Emily replays Simon's words in her head. "Wait. You mean you aren't letting just anyone inside the fence?"

"Our leader's not out there collecting refugees. He's collecting people necessary to survive in this colony."

"It doesn't matter how you restate it. You'd leave some poor helpless woman, who spent her life on welfare, outside the fence to be eaten if she had no viable skill inside this place, over someone who could rebuild a generator," Emily huffs in anger. "Why did he even bring me here?"

"I never reason why," Simon concludes. "He must've seen something in you."

# CHAPTER SEVENTEEN

HE LEANS BACK from the deployed airbag covered now in the bloody outline of his face. The multiple spider web splinters of shattered glass cloud his vision. Not sure what he hit. Stiff from hours of not moving he forces his arm muscles to flex. His head swims with pain and he notes the faint odor of gas.

Leaking gas, the other new currency of the world, dripping, wasted onto the ground. He moves but his body keeps him in the chair. He pulls on the door handle. It won't budge. He yanks the handle. No progress. He wraps his fingers into his pants material using as a level to pick his left leg up and prop it against the door. Jerking back he slams his boot sending the door flying open.

Growls.

His guns are under his right side. He slides the M&P from its left thigh holster transferring it to his steady right hand. The growls turn to barks. This accident didn't attract biters, but man's best friend. The car hood pops and contorts as a pit bull walks across it. The dog snarls and slobbers. He hears the shuttering of padded paws on the asphalt. A few dogs move past the open door into his line of sight.

No wolves. All domestic dogs, or at least they were domestic nine months ago. Now they have banned together returning to natural pack instincts. The pit bull has assumed command and must be the strongest, largest most vicious of the dogs or he would not be allowed to rule.

Biters scattered most of the wild game. The one reason they fenced in the national forest as part of the camp over houses and fields—deer meat.

He knows a lot of the cattle and other farm animals have been eaten. So these once pets have turned on their masters to fulfill their basic needs.

Every movie he's ever watched insisted creatures form hierarchy packs. If the pecking order's broken the animals will scatter needing to reestablish a leader before they resume an attack. If true, this would give him plenty of time to escape. He wonders how factual this is, especially when it comes to being hungry. Will the need to eat outweigh the need to have a ruler?

He raises his M&P toward the pit bull. The cracked glass hinders his ability to draw a clear bead on the animal's forehead. He needs a single clean shot. Just in case. After all, he could bark a kill order before he dies and the frenzy of attacking dogs could negate them realizing they have no leader before they kill him, or at least mangle him before he forces them to retreat. Just how wild have these canines reverted? Will they fear the thunder boom he unleashes?

The bullet exits the windshield and smashes through the left eye of the beast. The dog rolls from the hood in yelping whimpers.

He forces his body to deal with the pain in order to escape the car. The dogs look to their fallen pack leader, and then their fear of man overwhelms their hunger. They race for the woods. He fires into the trees twice to ensure the mutts continue to run from him.

He slumps against the car. In the center of the road remains what's left of a riding lawn mower.

"Who the hell parks a lawn mower in the center of the road?" He squeezes off another round, striking the mower before falling back against the car. His body betrays him as he becomes numb from the impact of the crash. He slides down the side of the car to the ground.

Don't pass out. Don't pass out.

He picks himself up from the asphalt. “So much for not passing out.”

The sun hangs low in the western sky. The dogs scattered, and blind luck kept any undead from finding him while he slept.

“I don’t want to be out here in the dark. I must have hit my head. I’m talking to myself, out loud no less.” He uses the door as a crutch to stand on unsteady feet. “No choice but to move. Can’t stay exposed like this. Even if dogs were my only problem.”

The dead pit bull has cooked in the heat of the afternoon sun. Part of him thinks the death smell may have protected him from any passing biters.

“Think. No visible houses.” He staggers to the trunk and pulls out a couple of the blankets. “Can’t walk down the road in the dark.”

He shuffles forward.

“This can’t be good. From a distance I look like one of those things.” He reaches down and touches the gun holster on his left hip. The bottom leg strap feels like a needle jabbed into him. He runs his finger over the cracked plastic buckle. He must have hit the steering wheel and bruised it.

“That’s tender. I must’ve hit my head. I can’t stop talking to myself.”

“Maybe you should stop talking to yourself and pay more attention to what’s going on.”

He hobbles around at the voice.

A ratty pair of mud-covered twenty-somethings approach him. One draws back a compound bow.

Pain shoots through him as the quick turn reveals new places he must be bruised.

“I told you no one would be ‘specking a mower in the road.”

“It was a great plan, Sis.”

He bites the corner of his lip to prevent screaming from the needles stabbing everywhere he impacted in the crash.

“I’ll tell you an even better plan. You two turn and walk away while you can still breathe.” Flexing his right hand in order to draw cramps his shoulder.

"Listen, gramps."

"I'm not that old."

"Open your coat slow," demands the kid with the bow.

He pulls open his coat. The male's eyes go right for the shiny barrel of the .375.

"Look! He's got a big one."

The kid's arms shake from keeping tension on the bow. He lets his arm slide in an inch, weakening the bows draw. "Use two fingers to pull it out."

"You saw that on some cop show, didn't you?"

"Just pull it out with two fingers, gramps."

"It's too heavy for just two fingers."

"I don't want you to put your hand on it." He thinks about it for a moment. "Sis, you get it."

The girl darts across the asphalt reaching for the gun. Putting herself between her brother and the man who jerks her arm and spins her around as a shield to catch the brother's arrow. She screams as the shaft sinks into her flesh.

With no warning he snaps the sister's neck.

The mud-covered boy stares down the barrel of the magnum before he's able to notch another arrow.

"You like my gun?"

"You fucking killed my sister," the mud-covered boy howls.

"I'm going to kill you and then find someplace to sleep like a baby."

The kid drops the bow and runs. He raises the magnum.

The kid disappears into the trees.

"You must have been feeling lucky." He lowers the gun and staggers down the road.

*Don't pass out with your shoes on. That's good advice but I'm going to have to. I should be more worried about a concussion.*

He uses the banister to pull himself up step by step to reach the upper stairs. He feels safer on the second floor. Many biters have a hard time climbing stairs and a stairwell is a natural bottleneck.

Only one or two dead can get up the stairs at a time and they're not smart enough to do anything but climb.

His head swims again.

He takes the first bedroom sealing the door with an overturned dresser just like he did when he escorted Emily. Anything trying to get in will make enough noise to wake him.

He should have checked the room first, made sure the closet was empty but he'll just shoot a biter.

Empty. No monsters under the bed either. He falls face first into the pillow his boots on his feet.

Sleep.

Dreamless because he passed out.

The sun shines in.

He cracks his eyes enough to know it's the next day, or at least daylight. He could have slept longer. At least he woke up and not as a biter. He closes his eyes. He knows he's had a greater head injury before, but maybe he hit his head just right this time. Kicking his boots off he goes to sleep.

*He slams the car into park. The small SUV jolts to a stop in the center of the highway.*

*Streaking across the sky are the fiery flames of a meteor.*

*The highway becomes a makeshift parking lot as he and dozens of others get out of their cars to witness the flaming boulder. He steps out of the still running vehicle and watches the streaking meteor flame across the sky. It crashes into the ground hard enough to create a ground quake. He grabs the door of his SUV to keep from being bucked to the asphalt. Black smoke billows from behind the trees.*

*Sirens blare.*

*Fire trucks race by as if they had been following the burning object. The force of their speed sends him back against his SUV. None of the fire trucks are painted with the name of a town or county. They disappear, sirens wailing.*

*He climbs back into the vehicle, flipping the radio to a news station.*

*"Early reports air traffic control stations have shut down across the country leaving thousands of people stranded in planes with no guidance to landing fields will not be confirmed or denied by the FFA."*

*"Sixteen confirmed plane crashes have occurred within the last hour. Authorities are urging everyone to return to their homes and clear all major highways. Due to the number of planes still in the air if interstates aren't cleared within the next thirty minutes the National Guard will be forced to move off all cars."*

*He presses the phone button on the steering wheel. "Daughter," he commands.*

*The phone rings and a plucky teen voice answers. Before she can say more than, 'hi, Daddy,' he grills her.*

*"Where's your sister?"*

*"Practice."*

*"And your mother?" 'Your mother' sounds more like 'fucking bitch.'*

*"I don't know, Dad."*

*"Then you turn on the news and stay home no matter what."*

*"I saw the news, it's on the cable channels as well."*

*The last time he saw cable channels interrupted for news events the Twin Towers fell.*

*"Dad, you know Mom doesn't deal well with emergencies. Come get us."*

*"I'm an hour from my house and four from you. They're closing the roads. By the time I take all the back roads to get to you this will all be over."*

*"Daddy, just come get us."*

*"Daddy, just come get us."*

*"Daddy, just come get us."*

*"Daddy."*

*"Daddy!"*

*"DADDY!"*

His eyes flash open. Sweat covers his forehead. He hears pawing at the door as if a cat is trying to get in. He draws his Beretta.

The pawing continues and doesn't stop when he drags the dresser away from the door. He flings the door open, pistol level. Nothing there. Damn crawlers. He lowers the gun to shoot whatever undead slinks across the floor and spots the calico cat bounding into the room.

Damn cat.

He escapes the room before it rubs up against his legs. He takes the stairs with caution. The cat's a clear indication no biters are around, but he never lets his guard down.

The farmhouse sits off the road in the midday sun. His muscles ache and stiffen from the crash, but nothing more than a few swollen contusions decorate his body. He throws a quilt over a barbed wire fence and heaves his left leg over. He'll cut across the fields to reach the city of Rolla. Once there he'll acquire a new car. Something new. They seem to start better. Old farm trucks might be more reliable, but after nine months in dormancy, they're a bitch to start. It will have to be from a dealership with these new microchipped starters.

With luck he won't find too many biters until he reaches the city. They may have migrated closer to the military base as well. Cats, dogs, even cattle, have adapted to not making noise to avoid attracting them. Humans with their higher brain functions never seem to understand.

Movies always show abandoned modern cities—Old West ghost towns have a different look—as trash filled. Papers blow in the wind, garbage cans overturned, cars abandoned, maybe a body or two in the street. Not here. This place remains pristine, like on a Sunday morning right before everyone gets up for church, and he figures everyone in this part of the state gets up to attend church. Not a single broken window or even a lone biter wandering. There seems to be a distinct lack of cars, as if everyone has a garage. The city doesn't even feel abandoned, but asleep. A lot of towns have doors smashed open and people's possessions strewn about the lawns. At first, it was televisions and computers, but when power faded it became clothes and canned goods. Some places have a rotten food smell. For lack of a better explanation. Not here. Later if he has time he'll re-scout this place. It has a Kmart and a Walmart and a few other major stores possibly with supplies intact. With a major college campus as well with dorm rooms full of Ramen Noodles, those things never seem to expire, and even if they do, no one really notices a difference in taste.

For easy math purposes, this city is thirty miles from the military base. Could everyone here have immediately just followed the evacuation orders? As close as they were, maybe they figured they could just go back home if they had to. Of course, as close to the base as they are, they could have been evacuated in an orderly fashion quickly where places further away fell to pandemonium.

He reaches a car lot and considers a truck. Next door a bicycle shop calls to him. If not for a thirty-mile trip those would be nice to explore the town on. No noise. Better yet he recalls a motorcycle place a few blocks down. Even going slow weaving in and out of traffic on the interstate he could be there before dark.

The real killer in the apocalypse might be the boredom. Sure, every now and then an undead corpse tries to eat you, maybe on a good day an army of biters bang at your door and occasionally a few desperate people attack, but most days it's just a lot of nothing. How did primitive man just hunt for a living? After they killed a deer to feed the tribe, what did they do with their time? Maybe the Pyramids were built out of boredom. 'Hey, let's fuck with future generations and build a massive stone temple in such a way no one can figure out how or why we did it.' Somebody did the same thing in the 1970s when they invented the Rubik's cube.

He knows better than to let his mind wander too far. The cars parked on the highway may have enough room for the Harley to pass between so far, but infinity welcomes careless drivers.

The road from the interstate has been cleared of all debris. Plumes of black smoke billow from the southwest. He tastes the smoke on the wind. The military must be cremating the bodies of the undead. Soldiers load trucks with useless burnable items from the businesses.

Those men on guard take note of him, but don't attempt to stop him.

He slows at a new forward checkpoint constructed out of sandbags and concrete barriers at what used to be a civilian-friendly entrance to Fort Wood.

The corporal in charge of this new gate signals for him to cut his engine.

He complies.

"If you wish to take up as a refugee in the Fort, you are going to have to surrender all weapons."

"I work for the colonel. I'm one of his contracted scouts."

Uneasy trigger fingers have soldiers attached to them. "Then you have the proper paperwork."

"I'm going to slowly reach into my pocket, okay?" He waits until the corporal agrees before sliding his hand under his duster overcoat, behind his back and below his gun belt to reach his rear jean pocket.

The soldiers don't raise the weapons but they are quick to clink their machine guns in a manner that reminds a person they are fully loaded.

His arm moves even slower as he hands over the note.

The corporal reads it—twice. "I need to call and confirm this."

"It says as much." He drops the kickstand and leans back on the Harley. "I'll wait."

He slips off his coat. Even the military boys seem impressed with hardware around his waist. He unzips the tactical vest, before reaching down to unclasp the tie straps on his left leg holster before unhooking his gun belt. He lays the line of handguns across the top of his folded coat. Removing the vest requires more effort than he realized. The stiff Kevlar padding had kept his insides in place.

His arms slip from the vest. His legs give way in a wobble. The corporal catches him.

"You okay, sir?"

"Just a bit woozy."

A private unslings his rifle.

"I'm not bit," he assures them. "I crashed a car."

"Sorry, sir. You must report, under guard, to the infirmary."

He pulls another gun hidden in his boot. "I might need some help." He drops the gun on his coat."

"That's a lot of weight in guns."

"Not so much. I'd carry one of those M60s if I could."

"Nice, I bet you'd handle one easily by yourself because it's going to take a few of us to move you."

Colonel Travis waves his hand. The medics leave the room.

"This isn't the hospital on the base."

"My soldiers almost had to carry you in."

"It's all contusions. Had a little fender bender on the way in."

"Bet it takes forever for your insurance to pay off," Travis jokingly says, but still keeps his CO tone.

"Try finding a bank willing to cash a check these days." He laughs to himself.

"Your hidden camp still safe?"

"Didn't the soldier report back?" He adjusts himself in bed to sit up more.

"What soldier?"

"Two trips ago, some kid followed me. He was in uniform. I lost him, but he should've been able to backtrack to base and return to report in. Hell, I left him close to the road."

"I never sent anyone to follow you. I don't want to know where you hide. Your continued success ensures I've a place to send my daughter."

"I take it even the greatest army on the planet can't defeat these things?"

"By the time the government figured out killing the dead was the key to survival it was already too late. Once it started those who survived had to be willing to bludgeon, smash, or shoot even the closest of loved ones." Knowing he couldn't do that to his own daughter, how could he expect anyone to do the same? "People just couldn't do it. It was too hard to shoot Mom, smash in children's heads, shred husbands and wives. Those able to defend themselves stayed where they were, the others were able to escape to refugee camps."

"People fled so fast to safe zones many stores were left fully stocked."

"You've seen a lot more out there than I have. You're a highly intelligent man, why didn't you evacuate to a refugee camp?" Travis wonders.

"I made a promise to save someone."

Travis guesses he failed, but not having first moved heaven and earth to achieve it.

"I reached a refugee camp. I guess the government took little interest in the smaller safe centers it first directed people to evacuate to. By the time I got there...it was nothing more than a crater infested with biters."

"Doesn't mean they didn't escape, or even make it to a different—"

"I know."

His response explains everything to Travis. The colonel won't ask again.

"The civilian government has fallen. We're to retreat to a single rally point. The last executive order given was to withdraw all able bodied military forces and convert the United States into a military dictatorship, until this crisis has been abated."

"Part of me wants to be outraged. Not just the shredding of the Constitution, but the abandonment of a few million civilians with no possibility of rescue."

"We'd never be having this conversation if you were a soldier," Travis confirms.

"Why are we talking?"

"I've my orders and I will carry them out without question."

"They don't include your daughter," he deduces.

"No."

"Colonel, I need a master welder."

"Always right to the point with you."

"I'm not your friend. And I guess we don't have a lot of time."

"You're in no condition to travel with her now. You pass out beyond the fence and you'll both be eaten."

"I'll travel with a few others now, and when I return I need things." He handed over Dar's list.

"I don't have a lot of time. Every supply run the government makes they pull out troops."

"I'll be back in a week."

Travis calculates how much time he has. "Is it secure?"

"I won't tell you about it."

"You're correct. I don't want to know where you're hiding. I need my daughter to be safe. This place? With DC's fall, I don't know how many more supply runs we'll get, and when the food stops the riots starts."

"My home is safe. I could use a few soldiers, only ones that are absolutely loyal to you and will follow me. I don't bring just anyone into my group."

"But you'll take my daughter."

"We've a rule. You work or you don't eat."

Travis opens the door. "Corporal."

The soldier hands the colonel a clipboard. Travis glances at the clipboard. He flips through the yellow pages. "I've three civilian welders listed as their primary occupation. I'll have them brought to my office. See if you like them. You already took a great nurse.

"That she is. Do the welders have families?"

"One has a son. Another a wife and daughter."

"Any engineers on your list?"

"I'll give you one of mine. He will follow my last order to the letter, but you'll have to take another non-military person."

He knows he won't like this. It's probably some damn lawyer. "Who?"

"My daughter keeps trying to save everyone from the rats infesting the base. We've a heavy set girl who I need out of the camp before she's killed." Travis leaves out he may have to send her to her death if she doesn't go.

"Any skills?"

"Typist is on the official register."

Better than a lawyer. "Such a useful skill in a world populated by reanimated corpses." He wants to let out a deep cleansing breath but the steering wheel's kiss prevents him from sucking in too much air. "I'm going to need a quick trip to your armory and everything on that list."

"This will take trucks."

"And a hummer." He swings his legs out of the bed. "I always wanted one of those. I'd like it in black."

"We're going to have to abandon a lot of equipment. I'd rather it go to protecting my daughter than be scattered among the rabble overrunning the base."

"The success of my colony functions on no useless baggage. Everyone works. Everyone pulls their weight or they don't eat. You tell her she may have to muck the hog stalls to earn her dinner, and if she agrees I'll make room for her."

"Affirmative."

"I'll inspect the welders and when I return I need that hummer loaded with...well, load it with what you would pack to protect your daughter."

"You don't want much."

"When this place disintegrates into the madness you're talking about, you're going to have to use bullets on living people. Ammo I'll need for the biters. You do the math."

"Brock, how long have you been a welder?"

"Twelve years professionally. I learned before and again in high school, so close to seventeen maybe. I even started a course in underwater welding, but the SCUBA part didn't sit so well with me."

Not much need for divers in Missouri. "I want to offer you a job."

Brock laughs. "In this economy?"

"Well, before you answer. It's a long exposed trek to my camp. With your skills you would make us more secure. We have a few rules, one is you don't work you don't eat. So we'll find something for your wife to do to earn her keep."

"I have a nine-year-old."

"She can spread grain to the chickens. We haven't worked out school yet."

"You want me to drag my child and wife out of the safety of this base for the unknown?"

"Safe's a relative term. I need a welder. There're three on the colonel's jobs list. You do what you want, but my camp has more to offer than here. And, yes, it's a long, dangerous walk, and everyone humps it with a supply pack. Age appropriate, of course."

"I don't see any appeal to leaving the base. My family's safe here."

"Your choice. Have them send in the next candidate."

Brock turns to go then asks, "You're not going to keep persuading me?"

"I don't have time, besides even you should've noticed that the MREs aren't as plentiful."

"Do you know why?"

"If I tell you, then those soldiers outside won't let you return to your family."

"A little cryptic isn't it?"

"Cryptic doesn't begin to cover my week."

Kade leans over the hood of his truck. "LJ, you ever see Colonel Travis personally escort anyone to the front gate?"

"Nope. Seems to me he avoids the civs."

Colonel Travis escorts a man in a black duster coat to the gate. Travis gives him a black field pack. Already gathered at the entrance, Sarah, a man in fatuities, and a man with a woman and small child.

"Is that the fat girl? The one Kani was courting?" Kade asks.

"That's her, and with a full pack of supplies. She won't walk too fast with those cankles."

"They all have full packs. Only the soldier has a rifle." Kade pounds out a beat on the hood. "Hale, get a truck ready to go to the farm?"

"We're loaded. Some of the boys wanted to know if we're going to recruit any females to reside there."

"I guess we need to. I'll get us the right kind. You find Kani and have him put a recon team together. Go out the back gate and swing around. I want to know why the colonel has taken a personal interest in this group, and is sending them out without a vehicle.

"Sure thing, Kade."

"And tell him to keep it on the DL. I've a feeling more than a few packs of supplies could be at stake here."

# CHAPTER EIGHTEEN

DANZIGER CEASES HIS struggle against the ropes securing him in the chair. Two men carry a portable generator down the stairs into the dark basement. Their arrival activates the eight DKs secured behind a wooden-framed cage built at the far end.

Tom keeps his voice low and calm. "Why don't you let us go? There's no reason to keep us. We won't tell anyone you're here. We've our own family to reach."

They fire up a generator, hooking it to a battery recharger. The humming generator attracts the DKs like a dinner bell. They scratch at their wooden cage, reaching for nourishment.

The scraggly bearded one removes a battery from a circular saw and locks it into the charging unit. The light under the battery flashes red. He approaches the wooden cage and grips the hand of what was once a woman. He holds it lovingly. Danziger spots their matching wedding rings.

He has to pull his hand away as she attempts to maul him. "They'll find a cure, baby, and then you'll get out of here."

"There's no cure. They are dead."

"The dead don't walk. The army calls them Infected. Means there must be someone developing a cure."

Tom keeps his calm voice over Danziger's antagonizing of the man. "We've seen the military. They destroy anyone bitten."

"You'd say anything." He turns to the other man who helped with the generator. "Charles, how long 'til we feed them?"

"Once that battery turns green. We're good to go in a few hours."

A dead little girl sticks her head out of the slot built into the wooden cage for the insertion of chopped body parts.

"You'll all get fed, soon."

The pair head upstairs. Once the door closes Danziger jumps, moving his chair. The red charging light flashes in the corner of his eye. "How long do you think we have?"

"Not long. I think the carbon monoxide from the lack of ventilation in the basement will kill us before they cut us up."

DKs claw their stockade.

"Why not just hack us up with an axe?"

"Danziger, why the hell do you have to analyze so much? From where I'm sitting I don't think they cut us all up at once. There are bandages and surgical tools on that table."

"They cut off a limb or two and make us last. They think they are feeding family."

"I'm just guessing they don't get a lot of people through the suburbs to keep these things well fed," Tom speculates.

"I'm open for suggestions." Danziger watches the flashing light flicker red faster with each flash.

"Can you pick the handcuffs?"

"If I'd something to use."

"There's a dental pick on the tray of medical tools. They must have raided a dentist office."

"That would work. How do we get to it?" The tools rest outside of Danziger's field of vision.

"Move your chair so you face my side."

Danziger jumps. The heavy metal-framed patio chair doesn't allow for much movement. He huffs for air by the time he gets the chair turned to face Tom's side. "Now what?"

"Break my arm."

"You're serious."

"I didn't say I liked this plan, but unless you got something better."

"It's going to hurt."

Tom nods.

"No screaming."

Tom nods. He bites the lapel of his jacket.

Danziger kicks the arm. He kicks it again. *How many kicks will it take to snap the humerus?* He kicks again.

"You're going to have to kick harder. It's going to hurt, but if you don't do it, you're going to kick me to death."

Danziger kicks again.

"If you don't kick me hard enough then we need a new—"

*Snap*! Danziger sends Tom to the floor.

Tom quivers, biting his lip. "Oh, that hurts."

"You gotta move."

Tom slides out of the chair. Danziger watches his friend worm across the floor until he's free of the chair and able to stagger to his feet. "I changed my mind. This was a bad idea." He shuffles to the tray of utensils and cups the dental pick in his hand. He carries it to Danziger.

Danziger fiddles with the pick until he gets it into the tiny keyhole. "We used to do stuff like this to the rookies. There was this one girl she did this in like five seconds."

Click. Danziger slips his free arm through the ropes. He unties the series of knots they secured him with. Once free of the rope he twists around the chair and works on freeing his other wrist. "Give any thought to getting out of the basement?"

"We just kill the fucking DKs. If we don't escape, at least we put an end to what these people are doing."

Danziger rubs his free wrist. "Maybe we fix your arm."

He grabs a crowbar from the table and uses it to spear a DK fishing its arms out of the feeding hole. The soft flesh crunches as it falls to the ground.

"You could free me first."

"Don't you ever watch horror movies? I free you and they come back down the stairs before I do this." He drives the crowbar into another of the undead. He avoids the little girl and destroys the brain in what was once someone's grandmother.

Danziger steps back from the cage. The litt
out the food hole.

"If you can't finish the girl, free me. I will
little girl reminds Danziger too much of his dau

"There's still the one taped to the swing."

"Let her go. Free me." Tom winces from the pain.

Danziger works the dental pick into the cuff keyhole. Tom releases his breath as the pressure on his broken arm relaxes. "We're going to have to set the bone."

"There's plenty of wood to use as a splint down here."

Tom snatches the crowbar and stabs the little girl. "Not here. I couldn't hold in the scream."

The stairwell door opens. Tom waves Danziger to the shadows. He hides next to the stairs and once the first pair of feet passes by he jabs the crowbar up to trip the second person.

The man lets out a wail and collapses onto the first person. Danziger clubs the first person with the battery-less skill saw.

"Help! They've escaped."

Tom smashes him in the head.

"*Help*!"

This time Tom sinks the crowbar into the man's skull. Sounds of scuffling feet on the upstairs floor echo above them.

"There's no other way out of here."

Danziger motions for Tom to guard the stairs while he whirls around the basement. A lot of hand tools and buckets are in clear view, heavy items to turn into makeshift clubs if those upstairs come down without guns. He knows that's wishful thinking. He tears the lid off a plastic tote and spills Christmas decorations. He dumps a second tote full of Christmas.

Scuffling chairs and furniture moving echoes over the floor, either that or they have unleashed a buffalo herd into the house. Danziger guesses they are panicking, but not panicked enough to come down the stairs one at a time. Instead, they sound as if they are creating a barricade to fend them off when they do attempt to exit the basement.

Danziger dumps a cardboard box full of old recipes. He tears the side of the next box open revealing a stack of *National Geographic* magazines stored away.

"How crazy do you want to get?" Tom whispers.

"We go up there, as is, we're dead." Danziger sends a metal shelf clattering to the floor.

That crash sends more scurrying around upstairs. Guns cock.

Danziger kicks at the spilled content on the floor. Nothing useful. Nothing to be used as a weapon or even to help him once he does escape. He shakes his head at Tom now at a loss for an escape plan.

"How important are all these dead people to you down here?" Tom calls out.

"Don't hurt our momma," a woman calls out. Other voices tell the woman to hush.

Tom and Danziger both glance at the pile of dead bodies.

Tom mouths at Danziger—burn them.

That's so crazy it might just save them. Danziger shoves the papers through the food hole and as much of the Christmas decorations that will burn. He pulls down another shelf full of boxes. The contents spill. Stacks of vinyl records scatter. Behind that shelf is a hidden window.

Tom leaves his guard position to pull open the window. Planted bushes keep the outside hidden as well. Danziger boosts Tom up before he smashes the glass of several Christmas lights. He wraps the broken lights in tissue papers. He strings them through the documents before plunging them into the generator.

Sparks flash.

The dry papers flame quickly.

Danziger kicks over the generator before he climbs out the window. Gas splashes from the tank. Tom crouches under a window. The house rattles from the generator exploding. It was bigger than Danziger expected. The fireball subsides quickly. Danziger wonders if he still has eyebrows.

Tom finds his moment and bolts from the house. Danziger follows, stopping only for the second it takes to land on the other side of the fence. Tom races between the houses across the street. Danziger knows they will need the supplies those people took. He wants to go back for them. They'll be distracted with the fire. He could recover the packs, and maybe their weapons among other things.

"Come on, detective," Tom calls out in his loudest whisper. He holds his left arm against his chest to keep it immobile while he runs.

Danziger punches his own open palm, and lets out a frustrated breath, before he barrels after Tom.

# CHAPTER NINETEEN

"COME ON YOU rat bastard!" The skinny male screams at the shambling corpse. He backs up a dirt-covered ramp toward the top of a cargo trailer.

Simon shuts off the Jeep motor to prevent attention being drawn to him.

In the metal forest ranger watch tower a bulky muscular man keeps a hunting rifle on the biter. It shuffles forward slower than most corpses, but it remains persistent in its pursuit of lunch. The skinny male reaches the top of the ramp, turns, and leaps over a hatch cut into the roof. He stands on the other side waiting. The biter stumbles forward occupied with food, not aware enough to notice the hole. It falls. The moan-howls of a few dozen biters pierce the air.

Simon starts his Jeep and pulls alongside the cargo containers. "How many do you have full now?"

"We have three we've sealed. We may need another container soon." The thin man jumps down from the ramp.

"You still have four to fill." Simon takes a cooler from the back of his vehicle.

"I've put eight in this one this morning. We've been seeing a spike in biters."

"There have been quite a few hanging around the west fence line. You boys should do something about them."

"Use your target range." The muscle bound man along with three more men all decked out in prison tattoos line up before Simon. One drags an empty cooler.

"It's not our job," the skinny man balks.

"That's not our deal with the boss." The muscular man makes the rifle he carries look like a toy cork gun.

"I thought you were to capture the biters, Grayson?" Simon inquires.

"Let's be clear, Simon. We five have an arrangement with the boss and it only pertains to the biters on this side of the colony. Check your fence, there ain't a single biter this side."

"The side that doesn't need protecting."

"Because we protecting it." The skinny man-ape slaps his chest.

Simon's sure he flashes some street gang sign he fails to comprehend.

Tony takes the cooler from Simon. "We protect this end. We stay out of the colony. We capture biters. We eat well. We follow the same rules as you, only we live outside the fence at this time."

"Pretty good deal for five men found chained on a prison bus."

Grayson clamps his hand on Terry. "Simon, you trying to start something? We live up to our end. We know why we aren't allowed inside, but we keep you safe."

"I should respect what you boys do, but you're all criminals."

"I bet we ain't the only murderers inside your camp," Terry squeals.

"In the old world we were accused of such corruptions." Grayson has a calm Jedi demeanor. "How many people have you killed since the world ended?"

"They're already dead."

"Not the biters. People. You haven't shot anyone living to stay alive?"

"It's a blurred line, old man. I killed a man," Tony beams with pride. "But that was before."

"Kill anyone since?" Grayson asks.

"Not that weren't dead already," Tony boasts.

"I know the boss has killed the living since the end. And he keeps you safe so don't come out here and start shit with us, Simon."

He glances at each of the five men in the eyes. "Without perimeter defense we'd never be able to sleep at night."

"Is that your way of apologizing?" Terry spits.

"Nobody else would do this job," Tony adds.

"That *innocent* kid raped that poor girl. Now he's here." Grayson pats the cargo container. "At least with the five of us you know what you got to deal with. We all killed who we wanted dead. You don't know about anyone else you bring inside."

Simon puts the empty cooler in his Jeep. "Being left chained in a prison bus to die leaves no questions as to your past. Too bad not everyone comes with such a résumé."

Simon gets back in the Jeep. "I had the cooks add an extra pie for you." He drives off.

The four look to Grayson for an answer.

"Test us? I guess he knows now how loyal we are to our word."

"Why'd he do that? We do everything the boss wants," Tony defends.

"He wanted to know if we'd leave our post," Terry ponders.

"Simon looks for weak links in the chain of defense. Today, he doesn't consider us a weak link. Now he has to deal with the biters growing on the other side of the camp."

"How do you know they're growing?"

"People have fled the cities and this place is where the food is."

Luke plops down across from Emily at the cafeteria table. "How you doing, girl?" He uses his 'God's gift to all women' tone.

Juliann and Kyle fill the spaces next to her.

"Hope you don't mind us joining you again." Juliann smiles.

"There are no assigned seats." Emily notices there are few open seats in the cafeteria. "Even with this room so crowded, dinner doesn't feel rushed."

"Other than guards and a couple farm hands no one has a night shift job, so we can enjoy each other's company a bit more."

"We're starting to get a little more leisure time in the evening."

"People are able to relax because it's safe here."

"Speaking of relaxing, how did you get such a cushy job?"

"You hit on me at every meal, and now you know you're just being a jerk. Even with limited dating choices you don't stand much of a chance of winning a girlfriend."

"Scoring all those touchdowns aren't so impressive anymore. Girls want guys who protect them, bring home food and not be an asshole."

"Back to caveman time. Luke, you should fit right in," Juliann quips.

"Well, roses and selfie pics are out for dating ritual."

"So I should just roll up my dress and open my legs because we haven't got a movie theater?" Emily asks.

Juliann drops her fork into her mashed potatoes.

"What's wrong?" Kyle asks.

"I'm never going on a date again." Juliann's eyes water.

"There are plenty of guys that want to date you."

"No. I'll never go to another football game, go shoe shopping, Skype. None of that will ever happen again."

"We'll get those things back," Kyle says in an attempt to convince himself as much as her.

"I think I liked it better when you failed at flirting than this depressing conversation," Emily says.

"Then who'd you fuck to get assigned to the library?"

"You know, if food wasn't so precious I'd smack this tray across your face. For your information, they worked me on the farm first and I don't shoot well enough to be a guard."

"Let it go, Luke," Kyle snaps. "We find a lot of stuff in the houses and someone has to organize it. You wanted a greener world. No more throwing things away, and if she has to sort books and DVDs so we have something to do during our leisure time, then it's important."

"How do you figure?"

"Because they wouldn't give her that kind of job unless it was. Boredom can be just as damaging to a group as a bite."

"Bad shot or not, she could stand behind the fence with a gun."

"I trust Wanikiya and our fearless leader. I certainly don't want to go out there and hunt for supplies so if he says I need to stand behind the fence and jump up and down to eat I will do it."

"What do you know about him?" Emily asks.

"He found me with a small group," Juliann says.

"I hid with a family who worked for the dam at the power plant. Haven't really seen much, but he recovered them and now I build fences." Kyle adds, "But I sleep in safety."

"I didn't get much rest either before I was found. We were kind of a large group at this ambulance station. Two EMTs were trying to protect people. He swooped in like Captain fucking America and shot so many biters so fast. I know when he's back from a run I sleep like a baby."

"That's how he found you. Everyone here tell those stories. What about him? What do you know, besides he's a crack shot? How'd he get the limp?" Emily wonders.

"You came in the main gate with him. Didn't you see the scar when he stripped?" Juliann asks.

"He has a scar. Maybe it's the reason he limps, but how did he get it?"

"I don't even think Wanikiya knows. He had it before they started this community. I know that much."

"I've heard rumors. He's really smart. He just knows things. Medical, farming, Shakespeare…"

"Not mechanical. That pump worker taught him how to jump-start and hotwire older cars."

"But he learned fast and after one time of being shown."

"I just want to know about him." Emily sucks her lip over her bottom teeth to disguise her smile.

"She likes him."

"He saved her life. I bet half the women in this colony crush on him for that."

"He doesn't chase after any of them."

"I wouldn't date him," Juliann explains. "He spends more time outside the fence than in. One day he may not come back, and knowing every time he went out he could die, I'd go crazy."

"You didn't say how he found you?" Luke asked.

"He saved me...It was bad. Way worse than any biter attack." Emily drops her head. In the old world she'd spend years in therapy to deal with the attack. Now she must just get over it.

"I guess we were lucky to be rescued so early. New people who come in keep talking about how much worse it is out there."

"The world we knew does not exist anymore." Luke slaps his chest, "Me be strong man, must protect tiny woman."

Emily laughs, "You keep working on that."

Juliann joins her in her giggle.

Wanikiya cleans his hands on a dish towel before grabbing the radio in the cradle above the station where he was cutting onions. "Wanikiya here?"

Both women preparing food glance disgustedly at the wireless receiver.

"We've a situation at the gate," the voice crackles over the speaker.

"I'll be there."

"There's always a situation at the gate," the older redhead says as she washes tomatoes in the sink. "Running this place is a full-time job in itself."

"It's impossible for you to feed everyone and keep running off to put out fires around the camp. Not with our leader gone all the time." The dark-skinned Nina fails to hold back her frustrations.

"He does spend a lot of time outside the fence salvaging what we need to sustain ourselves. It just feels like he's gone all the time."

"Maybe he should just relinquish the camp to you, and we elect a second in command, and keep doing what he does." She places the tomatoes on a towel to dry.

"Mary Kate, don't speak that way."

"Do I miss where we voted out free speech?"

"No."

"Then the Constitution still applies in here until it doesn't."

"Administrative duties sometimes fill up whole days; others I've nothing to do. Besides, I like to cook," Wanikiya adds.

"If we keep growing it will become a full-time job. Town hall meetings are great for small numbers and small issues."

"You want to run for alderman when the time comes?"

"I just don't want your world famous omelets we're eating for breakfast to be my last meal, because we should have a full-time leader instead of a cook."

Wanikiya hangs his apron on a hook by the door. "Mary Kate, I'd be happier just being the cook. Sometimes I don't want to make the kinds of decisions the leader of this new world has to make." He wraps his gun belt around his waist and clasps the buckle into place.

"I think we should blow it up or burn it down," Barlock points to the small white house down the highway.

Wanikiya looks at each window of the house through the rifle scope. "No burning. Fire gets out of control and we'll burn half the woods and maybe the colony."

"We could take a team out and demolish it."

The Sioux nods. "Scavenge anything useful, anything burnable we cut up for the fireplaces. We should eliminate all port of calls around the camp. It's not the first time we've had to run someone out of there." He lowers the rifle. "Did you get a number in this group?"

"We don't know. Austin was doing a random sweep with the telescope when he spotted one."

"I guess we should invite them in," Wanikiya says.

"We don't know them. What if they are a scout party for raiders?"

"If they are, they are poor scouts for being seen, and expert spies should have never taken up in a house a block from our front gate. Good spies would hide in a place we wouldn't watch," Wanikiya says.

"You know a lot about scouting."

"My father taught me how to track."

"Did he teach you how to sneak outside the gate without any one of them knowing?"

Wanikiya contemplates the need of a second entrance on this side of the compound, but occupying it would take more people they don't have. "We should just take a truck. Be friendly."

"And just let them in?"

"We'll explain to them they must be willing to work in order to eat. Our first order of business after we get them inside the fence will be to tear down a house."

Wanikiya climbs down from the top of the cargo trailer. A guard calls out that people are leaving the house.

"How many?" Wanikiya asks.

"Nine, maybe. They've piled into the back of an El Camino and are in transit."

The car halts before the fence. The guards keep their rifles ready.

A woman stands up from the bed. "We seek sanctuary."

Wanikiya calls out, "We are prepared to offer you refuge, but you must be willing to follow the rules of our community."

"We already follow God's path, and are willing to accept the rules of sanctuary."

Barlock tugs at Wanikiya's arm and whispers, "I don't like the way they keep referring to this place as sanctuary. There were some crazed fanatics who thought God caused the undead to rise from the grave to punish the sinners."

"I've heard those stories, too, but we don't turn people away based on their faith, even if it's convoluted." Wanikiya hollers, "Before we let you in you must understand everyone here works for their room and board."

"We're willing to do our part," the woman calls out. The whisper murmur of agreement among the group confirms her answer.

Wanikiya steps from behind the cargo container into view of the sally port. "We'll let you into our gate system. You need to surrender all weapons and submit to physical inspection."

"We agree," the woman calls out.

"Open the outer gate," Wanikiya orders.

The truck pulls into the first airlock.

"Disembark from the truck, place any weapons inside the window in the container. Then step forward and remove all clothing."

She wraps her hands around the bars of the inner gate. "Why must you gaze upon our nakedness? It is a sin in eyes of the Lord."

"And it would be a worse sin to let one of you in here who was bitten," Barlock warns.

"We're all faithful; only those full of sin in his eyes would be bitten."

"Then we won't let you in. It's non-negotiable." Wanikiya stands firm.

One of the men gets out of the El Camino. He whispers in her ear. "Test of our faith," the woman says back to him as if she questions his response. She removes her coat. "We shall pass all tests to prove we are faithful."

The others disembark from the vehicle and disrobe. One man removes his shirt and has a festering mass of flesh near his belt line.

"Suspicious infection!" calls out one of the guards sending the others into frenzy. The survivors draw handguns in response.

"Everyone calm down." Wanikiya unlocks the door built into the gate into the first empty airlock. "We need to check out his wound and make sure it's not a bite."

"God would not turn any of us into one of his wraiths. The faithful won't suffer his wrath."

"Then you need to move on. We'll open the gate and you can continue along your way."

"No! We must be admitted to sanctuary."

"There is no sanctuary for those who won't follow our rules."

"We follow God's law." she points her revolver directly at Wanikiya's face.

"We won't risk the safety of everyone inside unless we know for sure your man isn't infected."

"We must be let in," she demands.

Wanikiya feels himself being yanked backward. Barlock drags him through the gate. The woman fires. The survivors open fire with her. The gate guards assume defensive positions.

"We need your order, Wanikiya," Barlock demands.

"We don't let possible infected people into this compound."

"Then give the order. The men won't fire unless you order," Barlock confirms.

"Those people will run out of ammo the way they are firing at nothing."

"Not before they shoot one of us! Wanikiya, give the order."

"Light them up," Wanikiya reluctantly commands.

Barlock clicks his radio. "Light them up."

The gate guard's immediate response sends a halo of bullets into the nine people. Bodies riddled with holes flop and contort long dead before they fall to the ground.

"Cease fire! Cease fire," Barlock orders and the guards fall back into position.

"Outfit a team to go in there in tactical gear to clean out the bodies," Wanikiya orders.

"Tactical gear?"

"I don't want anyone hurt."

"We got two wounded guards. Looks like nothing life threatening. I called the EMTs.

"Good. Get tactical gear. Don't go in there without it.

Sporting latex gloves, Dr. Baker cuts the pants of the man with the festering wound.

"Was it a bite?" Barlock asks.

"Yes, but maybe not from a human mouth, looks more like an animal bite."

"They drew weapons over a possible animal bite, why not just say so?" Barlock wonders.

"Maybe they thought we wouldn't listen," Wanikiya speculates.

"Maybe they were crazy." Barlock plops a cardboard box on the tailgate. He pulls out a leather bound book. "Their supplies consisted mostly of these."

Wanikiya runs his gloved finger over the golden inlaid cross on the cover. "How many?"

"Over fifty."

"A lot of space they could have used to hold more water or food."

"I could see carrying one or even each person having their own, but why so many extras?"

"They must have thought it would protect them."

"Not the book, Him. And no matter what you believe, this time will test the faith of all humankind."

"What do we do with them? Some have blood all over them."

"Take the bloody copies and burn them with each of their bodies. The good ones...go in the library."

Emily scatters DVD cases on a table. She stacks each film into general categories.

Wanikiya carries in a box, "Where do I set these?"

"What's in it?"

"Books."

"By the counter over there. I'm out of room. This was a small school library."

"Use the empty classroom next door."

"No shelves."

"After we expand into the subdivision I'll make sure you get shelves."

"This job's a lot harder than it looks. With the security of the fence people have some free time to read and watch a few movies, and as soon as I get stuff shelved it's gone." She grabs a DVD from the table. "Do you think they'll make any more movies?"

"I think one day the world we knew will return somewhat to what we once knew, but not completely. People will make movies again, write books, surf the Internet, but you may have grandchildren before it happens again."

"There something else bothering you, Wanikiya?"

"I had to give orders today...the kind of orders I don't like to give."

"Was it to keep the colony safe?" Emily asks.

"Yes it was."

"Then it wasn't the wrong choice. Nothing keeping us safe is the wrong choice." Emily opens the box of Bibles. "Are you still collecting the wish list for the camp?"

"Anytime someone needs something we're unable to make ourselves or a job arises requiring a certain skill set, I add it to the needed supply list."

"Then I have someone we should add to our list." Emily smiles.

# CHAPTER TWENTY

EMILY'S SAVIOR PULLS on the doors to the In Quick/Out Fast convenience store. Someone chained the doors together from the inside.

"It will be dark soon." Major Ellsberg keeps his back to the building and sweeps the parking lot with his rifle.

Little Olivia kneels at the door, cups her hands around her eyes, and peeks in. "Those coolers still have water bottles in them."

"Why has no one bothered this place?" Brock asks.

"We just have to get inside without busting open the front doors." He steps away from the door to examine the building.

Karley peers in. "How do we get in?"

"Smaller window: we bust it." He points to the glass high in the wall. "Major, you think you can drop inside and open the emergency fire door in the back to let us in?"

Agitated, Brock says, "You didn't answer my question."

"I found stores looted with even the shelves gone and the same kind of store across the street left untouched. I've no idea why. This place sits off the interstate, and with the road signs down unless you lived here you may not know this place exists. Why would anyone come down this road?"

Karley jumps his case. "Then why'd you bring us this way?"

"That's easy, hon." Brock puts his hand on her shoulder. "He's avoiding people, living or otherwise."

"I'll fit, but if all you want is the back door open we could drop Olivia in there. She's the perfect size."

"No way." Karley scoops up her daughter. "Why not just smash the glass and bust the chain?"

"Because I want to sleep in this building tonight despite the rotten burrito smell. We bust a window and we may not know if we smell the dead or just bad food. I'm not sending a nine-year-old in there."

"Then I'll do it," Brock volunteers.

"I'll do it." The major slings his rifle. "How about a boost?"

He steps under the window making a cradle with his fingers laced together and with little effort hoists the major up by his boot.

Ellsberg draws his knife to use the butt as a hammer. The glass rains onto a potato chip bag display. He knocks loose any last chunks of the non-shatter glass.

"Watch for biters," he calls out as the major's boot leaves his hands. "Just in case."

"Thanks for not sending in Olivia." Karley holds her daughter tight.

"Until properly trained on a firearm, I won't risk her or anyone. I just can't drop down from a high window."

"I noticed you limp, but I thought it was from your car accident."

"A long ago accident. The car crash aggravated it."

Major Ellsberg rattles the chained doors, but they won't open. He waves for them to head around the building.

The group moves around the building.

"Sarah, you've been quiet," he notes.

"I don't have anything to add. But I never thought I'd feel safer outside the military fence."

"Brock, hold this door open. Major, you and I will re-sweep this place. Every corner."

Ellsberg nods. After satisfied the building's a safe bed for the night he gives instructions to them. "The toilets have water. We'll add more from all the bottles we can't carry or even use the power drinks. But don't just flush until we leave if possible."

"It will mask the smell of dried hot dogs and stale pizza.

"Smells good. It's been months since I've smelt anything hanging in the air that wasn't road kill," Brock says.

He stuffs protein and breakfast bars into a bag. "And I'm guessing most of us haven't had soda and sugar-filled candy in months, so go easy or you'll get sick."

Brock picks up a liquor bottle.

"Drink the water and stuff your packs with as much as you can carry." He pulls down two whiskey bottles and slides them in his bag. "And no liquor."

"You're taking whiskey."

"My medical staff uses it to sterilize their equipment."

Karley questions him, "You've a medical staff, and where we are going you need a welder?"

"We're going someplace safe. Safer than the refugee camp."

"How do you know?" Karley asks.

"I've built it."

"And that makes it safe?"

He gives her a 'don't fuckin' doubt me, woman' look. "So far, but everyone I've invited in has to do their part. It's not a democracy anymore. It's working together to survive. Now curl up in the corner and get some sleep."

"Brock, what did you get us into?" She slams a fist into her husband's arm.

"Away from a place where women were being abused," Sarah speaks up.

"I never saw anyone being abused."

"You were in the housing section of the base. A lot of bad stuff was happening in the tent city," Ellsberg begins. "As far as the base being safe, it was an illusion. There were too many people let inside. It's a week, maybe two, from collapse. There's not enough food."

"Why didn't you tell us?" Karley demands.

"And cause a panic? Even more people would be hurt," he adds. "I want people who are willing to make our community work, not go because they are afraid."

"But they were sending the infirmed out of the base. They were relocating the sick. I saw the trucks."

Major Ellsberg gives the only answer, "There was no place to send them."

Once everyone's asleep he sneaks out the fire door and climbs the ladder to the roof. The stars seem brighter. With a few months of less pollution the sky seems clearer.

Lightning bugs dance in the field.

He closes his eyes.

Jolted awake by the thudding crash of a fender against a gas pump, he grips his weapon. Emily's savior hopes the people inside the store have enough sense to remain quiet. Especially Karley.

"Push it over."

"Won't it explode?" the driver hangs his head out the cab window.

The guy yelling at him slaps him with his ball cap. "No, dumb fuck. But you got to push the pump over to reach the gizmos to manually pump gas into the truck."

"Can't you just flip the switch inside the store?"

*No, don't go inside.* He sets his weapon down and dries the wetness of his palm on his pants. The morning dew has collected on him.

"You need electricity."

"You're making too much noise. The munchers move faster at night."

"A myth," the guy wearing the ball cap says.

"What do you know about it?" The driver taunts.

"You two, knock it off. Faster at night or not, noise attracts them." Kani completes his inspection of the store's perimeter.

"Hey." the fourth man pulls on the store doors. "These things are chained from the inside."

"Means the food's still in there."

"Bet we'd get a lot of sweet ass for chocolate bars." He pulls the winch cable to the doors, fishing it around the handles.

"We get some pretty sweet ass as is. Those two sisters the other night." The men laugh.

He doesn't want to imagine since he saw what guys like this did to Emily and her companions.

"Yeah, the small one didn't like it in the ass, but she took it like a champ." The man with the ball cap sneers.

"She was hungry, fuckhead."

"For my fat cock."

"Why you always got to fuck them in the ass? You faggy or what?" Kani ribs him.

"Those dirty little whores. Only place to fuck 'em is in the ass."

He draws his M&P pistol.

Sarah slides across the floor to peer out the door. Ellsberg grabs the top of her pants in an attempt to pull her back, but he lacks the strength to move her bulk. He waves for Brock to move his family back. They slide across the floor toward the bathroom.

The major wonders where his new leader has disappeared to and if he heard these guys why he didn't warn them before he vanished. The man has been on his own a lot, maybe he just didn't think to wake them. Still, now should he act or should he wait and see what the marauders plan to do about the store.

Sarah spots Kani before the grinding winch gears scare her back. The stress on the doors sends an eerie screech throughout the building until a hinge pops. Olivia covers her ears. The high pitched tear of metal catches the attention of aimless biters in the fields. Now with a direction they shamble with investigatory hunger.

A second hinge snaps. One of the men hollers. The other stops the winch. Liquid soaks the first's stomach.

"What the hell!"

"The hinge piece must have shot out like a bullet." Kani grabs some dirty towels from the truck bed to staunch the blood flow.

"Doubtful, you morons." The man in the duster points both guns at the remaining three men.

Hollywood would have viewers believe this cool drawdown moment with a gun in each hand creates the perfect action sequence. Not in reality. No one can aim and fire and hit targets with two different weapons at the same time. But he wonders if these idiots know.

Before they draw on him, he fires. Three bullets tear apart the biggest guy. The next barrage of lead sends the already wounded one into spasms. Red-stained mucus spews from his facial orifices until he gags on his own fluids. The third man takes a bullet, but ducks onto the floorboard of the truck. The fourth disappears.

He holsters the Beretta and draws the .357.

Brock's family takes up residence in the concrete walled bathroom. Ellsberg jerks his finger in a demanding motion for Sarah to join them. She vehemently shakes her head no. She wants to help. Somehow knowing he took a welder and soldier out of the camp makes her feel so small she must prove her worth to this group and not be just another fat girl. She has nothing on the surface to offer this place he's built. Moreover, she wants her shot at these men. Their torment and abuse must be repaid. Ellsberg flips his rifle to fully auto and takes up an ambush position for anyone entering through the front doors.

Kani works his way to the back of the bronco. The driver slides out the passenger side of the truck. He pulls a machine gun from the back seat. The canopy over the pumps prevents anyone on the roof from seeing him hand the weapon to Kani.

Noise now has the attention of a few dozen biters within a mile radius. The undead scuffle forward their moan-howls form an echoing hum attracting even more undead to the convenience store.

Kani dips out from under the pump island canopy spraying bullets at the rooftop. The duster clad attacker has fled. Kani swoops around and jumps into the cab. "Put it in gear and drive, Jimmy!"

Jimmy slams the gearshift and peels backward from under the canopy. The doors fly from their frame and smash into the canopy support poles. The Bronco jolts to an instant stop now anchored to the building.

This gives the man in the duster coat a second of advantage. He glances from the corner of the store front. Five, six, seven rounds smash into the windshield.

Jimmy's head turns into a spray of red mist. Kani falls from the cab with two shots in each clavicle. The man in the duster coat kicks the machine gun from Kani's reach.

"Who the hell are you?" Kani pleads.

He dumps the cylinder of empty shell casing. Eight plinks echo on the pavement. He slides a clean bullet into each chamber making sure they clink into place in his magnum. The sound torments Kani as he knows his death approaches.

Sarah runs from the store. Ellsberg follows sweeping his rifle ready to fire. She kicks the first attacker she reaches, although he is already dead. "These men tormented me."

"Don't waste your energy. Just put a bullet in their heads." He jams the cylinder into place.

"What?" Confused, Sarah halts her next kick.

He blows the head off a corpse scuffling from the road before handing the smoking gun to Sarah. He grabs the machine gun and a belt of clips from the back seat. "Put a bullet into each of their skulls before they try and eat you and be satisfied. We're about to have company."

Undead scamper from the tree lines. Sarah shoots the first man. She's pretty sure he's already dead but she has to be sure.

"Where's Brock and his family?" He reloads the machine gun.

"Bathrooms. They are solid concrete walls," Ellsberg adds.

"Good location. We should take up position in the other one. Wait out the corpses until morning. Once they eat these guys maybe they'll stop looking for us."

Sarah shoots another one. "This one's a Bowlin. His brother runs the black market at the fort."

Kani sobs. "Come on, Sarah." He backs toward the doors. Major Ellsberg follows suit. More and more undead scuffle toward them.

Sarah points the gun at Kani's face. "He's still alive."

"Leave him to be eaten or finish him. We got to get inside."

"Please don't, please. Help me. Help me and I'll get you all the food your fat ass could want," Kani pleads.

"You really think I want food. You misguided redneck."

"Then fuck you, you fat bitch. I'll fuck'n ride—"

She scatters his brains over the pavement.

# CHAPTER TWENTY-ONE

"FIVE...SIX... SEVEN." Kade glares through binoculars. "Pake, how many supply choppers flew in last time?"

The dirty coated man flips through a palm-sized notepad. "There were twelve."

"And the time before?"

"Twenty. Most weeks it was twenty."

"We've been gifted down to seven choppers of food to feed more people than were here last week. This could be the end of government handouts. From now on we trade only for useful items. No more jewelry. Ammo will get the best trade. Guns, knives, fuel, and blankets are next. Tell the boys no more sex for food. I want the far tent packed and squared away on the truck. As soon as it's full, take it out to the farm," Kade orders.

"Right away."

"When this goes south, it's going to be bad. I want most of our camp off the base."

Pake stuffs his notebook in his coat. "Kade, you got a guess on how long before it falls?"

"I'd guess people have squirreled enough food away for about a week, if they were smart. Those not rationing won't get their bellies too full on seven cargo choppers. It takes about five to stock the military stores. The soldiers won't go hungry."

"They'll have some supplies stored."

"Not enough to appease the mob if next week there are only seven or less choppers." Kade contemplates this for a moment. "If we could find more survivors I'd bring them in and let their numbers really bust this place up. It's going to fall."

"But it's safe and we're making a better living now than before the plague started. I sure get laid a lot more."

"No one's going to haul you off to jail for solicitation. I want a chance at the armory. We've got a good place to hole up, but some heavy weapons would make it secure."

Two helicopters drop their cargo and land. Kade watches them take off through his binoculars. They are fully loaded with soldiers. He attempts to count them. Two more choppers land and take on military passengers. Nearly fifty soldiers march onto each chopper.

"Pake, we may not have a week."

Colonel Travis takes the sealed envelope from a soldier who salutes and returns to his H-92 Troop Transport Helicopter. Forty-four soldiers race for the seats on each aircraft.

"One hundred and thirty-two men will cut into our defensive position, Colonel."

"We drop all patrols and no more burn detail. We've eliminated most of the infirm already. We'll have another a week with fewer troops. Anyone who's been watching will have noticed troops leaving for a few weeks."

"Permission to speak freely, Colonel?"

"No more advice on how we should stay and help. There's no way to feed these people, and when the food stops we will have the Infected and the hungry to fight. Our best bet remains in pulling all military forces back to a staging point and retaking the country. Survivors will be acclimated."

"It's a massive purge of the weak, infirm, aged and unwanted."

"History dictates the strong will survive making the future of the human race greater. Maybe this's God's plan to keep us marching forward. He said he'd destroy the world again, but not with flood. The dead walking the earth..."

"He didn't ask anyone to build an ark first."

"The animals aren't threatened with this plague the way they were with flood waters. This eradication's strictly about humanity."

Travis tears the seal on the envelope. He reads the single piece of paper inside. "How well do you know your military history, George?"

"Not as well as I should, and I doubt history books have anything relevant on facing an army of the undead."

"All battles have relevance, but a Roman commander Manius Manilius besieged Carthage in 149 BC, and took two years to overrun the city in which they fortified every building. It was such a hard earned victory they plowed over the city and sowed it with salt to render it unlivable."

"Why destroy your spoils?"

"I won't discuss the lack of evidence the Romans actually practiced this, because we are now expected to salt our fields."

"Colonel?"

"Bring in the demolition team and wire the hospital and all motor pools. If it's a military building, wire it."

"Abandoning these people is one thing, but to eliminate all useful support buildings when we're gone is nothing but murder."

"We've surpassed the rules of murder in this new world. Now get me the demolition team."

# CHAPTER TWENTY-TWO

A TREE BRANCH splinters over the skull of a DK. The now brain dead creature collapses before Tom drops the useless wood to the ground. Danziger tosses him a new branch, making sure Tom catches it with his good arm.

"We need to find some real weapons."

"As long as we don't run into too many, this will do, and it's noiseless." Tom swings the branch. He chokes up on the limb for a better balance to his thrust. "The rifle you lost would have been anything but quiet."

"We need shelter for the night. I grew up here and had no idea there was so much forest this close to the city."

"A lot of people fought to keep these areas from being developed. Most people in the city have everything at their disposal so they don't have a reason to venture outside the border. But those who live near the city have to venture in and know within a few miles of the city the landscape turns back into farmland." Pain shoots up Tom's arm. He winces, refusing to whine in pain.

"Fewer DKs then?"

They reach the edge of ground torn asunder by the dragging and tramping of hundreds of pairs of feet. All plant life and foliage has been scraped to dirt. Ragged trees remain without a single branch until five foot up each trunk.

"What did this?"

"More undead than I imagined. Thousands."

"You said the caravan was this way." For the first time panic hiccups in Danziger's tone. He felt little concern about not having supplies knowing they would reach the caravan's path and they had plenty of extra. Tom knew people in the trucks who would help them. Maybe even someone who could properly set the broken bone in his arm.

Thousands of undead tromping toward all those people. They knew they would face DKs but none of them suspected the number would spill into the thousands. Even in the cordoned off blocks of city streets, he saw no more than a few hundred at one time.

"How do you want to proceed?" Danziger asks.

"Looks like we have three choices: we turn back and die at the hands of those survivors or we move forward and run into a herd of thousands and die."

"You said three choices."

"Detective, I figure we just die. I only have one arm. No shelter will protect us from a few thousand dead. Even if you had your fancy rifle and used every bullet to kill one, fifty or so undead wouldn't put a dent in the wave of monsters that chewed through here."

Danziger marches after the herd. "We move to the caravan. They had a lot of guns, and if everyone could shoot fifty DKs, it would put a dent."

"Do you know why I didn't go with them? What was more appealing than a large group going to a military base for protection? Why didn't my friends and I escape a city we knew was populated with a few thousand, for sure? The road had to be safer, right?"

"I want my daughter's killer. I didn't think about you."

"Brutal honesty. We need that in this new world. You hang onto it more than the hate you have for the murderer of your daughter and you might just survive this."

"So why didn't you go?" Danziger asks.

"Those running the caravan were dumb fucks. The nut job in the safari khakis thought he was a big game hunter. Maybe I knew so much noise would attract all the DKs. Babies crying, loud motors, hell, just the number of people talking would bring more dead than I've seen together. No, I knew that trip was a death sentence."

"Then why help me find a way to reach them?"

"Something to do, I guess. I don't have anything to do anymore. Any goal I had for my life: add to my mutual funds, advance my career, meet a woman on eHarmony...that's over."

"I still have my daughter's killer to find. He's not some undead creature, he's still a breathing monster and I will put him down."

"Then what?"

Danziger takes a long time to answer. "Try and survive...I guess."

"Not much of a plan. Just survive."

"It's what we were doing before. Just surviving. Going through the paces of living paycheck to paycheck just eking out a meager life."

"You see no difference now?"

"You don't have to come with me. I'll find this guy."

"I want to know what we are going to do after we kill him."

"We know the military's planning on retaking the country. We meet up with their advanced forces."

"I'm too old to enlist."

"I doubt age will be an issue in the war."

The trees break into an open field stretching to the divided highway. Cars gridlock all the lanes. A few DKs mill around. Stragglers separated from the massive heard tearing up the ground on the other side of the highway. The nightmare of bodies of the dead and the mangled remains of those eaten by them litter everywhere.

Danziger creeps up to the half-eaten body of a man and unhooks his fingers from the automatic rifle he held. Spent shell casings crunch under foot. The ejection port remains open, revealing a dry weapon. Danziger fumbles through the guy's pockets for an extra unspent magazine. He fails to find one.

Tom exchanges his branch for what looks to be a bloodstained fireplace poker. Danziger keeps the rifle, figuring the metal frame makes a better club than the branch he held. He follows Tom to the road.

"Would you know if any of these trucks would have medical supplies?"

"Some do," Tom admits.

Doors to most of the caravan cars remain flung open. More half-eaten bodies clutter the asphalt. For as many expended shell casings on the ground, Danziger figures there should be a lot more DK corpses.

Panic fire.

These idiots didn't aim they just fired blindly, and attracted more undead to them. Had they kept calm and chosen each target, they could have survived this or at least thinned the herd, allowing others to escape.

Tom ignores the cars. Danziger figured they'd gather supplies from them since these people just fled leaving everything. He runs after Tom, pausing at a Jeep to trade his rifle for a double barrel shotgun. He cracks the breach revealing two unspent shells.

Catching up to Tom, Danziger finds him ransacking a Jeep. He pulls boxes out of the back uncovering the folded down seats.

Keeping his voice low he says, "I helped pack this Jeep. The head ramrods wanted a few cars with just supplies in case of a breakdown there would be extra food and water." He flips the now cleared seat up. "And extra guns." On the floorboard rests a stack of rifles and several gun belts.

"We clear out the back, take turns sleeping and find the trail of any survivors. We keep quiet, there aren't enough DKs to bother us."

"You don't think your killer survived this attack?"

"People ran. They left everything behind and ran. He's out there. He's too smart not to be."

"Then he's good enough to still be alive in the morning." Tom hands him a can of beans. "We pack what we need and find his trail. After we rest."

"There will be a lot of trails to distinguish from with dozens of people having fled the caravan."

"The thought crossed my mind. Killers need victims?"

"Usually how it works."

"After panic leaves those running away, they'll gather back into groups for security."

"You think he will join with others."

"Best way to grab a victim."

"Maybe he grabs some lone girl separated when everyone ran?"

"Then we eliminate those suspects from those groups gathered back together."

The herd tore up so much of the landscape that Danziger's unable to find any distinguishable trace of where living people fled and the dead followed.

"This's nothing like tracking a deer."

Tom keeps his rifle ready. He kneels along the destroyed ground his arm secure in a taut sling. "There're shoe prints of someone running. The DKs drag and shuffle their feet. A living runner has a stride. They ran and the herd followed."

A few dead half-eaten bodies litter the highway.

"I doubt this herd grew in numbers. So many undead devoured most of what could have reanimated."

"What side of the highway are we on?" Danziger asks.

"South."

Danziger travels to the north. The area between the asphalt and the tree line has no freshly attacked bodies. A few DKs are scattered about with bullet holes in the skull. A few people defended themselves before they fell or ran.

The ground becomes less destroyed by trampling feet. He finds three sets of footprints, two smaller feet and one of a booted man over the top of the shambling steps. Or at least someone wearing male boots. He has seen forensics determine the weight of a person through how deep the impression sinks into the dirt. He figures it's a heavier person so it's most likely a man.

"Tom, if you were in fear for your life, would you run toward danger?"

"Soldiers are trained to run toward gunfire, which is the stupid direction if you ask me."

"So are cops." Danziger follows the footprints. They seem to be willing companions. "From what I've seen of these monsters they suffer from a mob mentality. They get moving in large groups it's hard to make them break rank."

"I concur." Tom drops to his hams, rests the rifle against his leg, and feels the boot print in the soil.

Danziger keeps with the trail to the tree line. A DK with a smashed skull lies there. "So someone who kept their faculties during the attack might have realized the safest direction to run was back the way the herd came."

"These prints were made after the majority of the dead shambled through. I still would check to the south first. You're putting a lot on one set of tracks. Even if they travel in the smart direction."

"This guy's smart," Danziger reiterates.

# CHAPTER TWENTY-THREE

FALLEN TREES CREATE a defensible clearing.

"Looks like a good spot for lunch." He drops his pack. "When you sit, sit in a circle, backs together, so you can watch all around as you eat."

"Why couldn't we just take a car, or at least walk along the road?" Karley whines. "My shoes weren't designed for hiking."

"Cutting overland through fields and forests has to be faster," Sarah deduces.

"It's only faster if we know where we're going." Karley wails, unable to hide her fear of being off the military base.

"The biters stay close to the roads. Not much food in the woods." He understands these people have been within the safety of walls, but they need to halt whining. "Ellsberg, you up for a scout? We'll let these people rest."

"You're going to leave us?" Olivia panics. Karley grabs her before she runs to the man in the sable duster.

"No, I'm just going to check out what's ahead. Make sure it's safe."

"Don't go too far. My mommy's really scared," Olivia projects her fears.

"Olivia," Karley scolds, despite the truth of her words.

He lets out a small laugh. "I'll be right back, little one. You protect your mother."

Ellsberg tromps through tall grass. "I didn't want to say anything in front of the others—"

He cuts him off, "You're not happy I left you all sleeping in the convenience store."

"You're damn right. I went along with this as a favor to Colonel Travis. He and I go way back. I told him I'd make sure your camp was secure enough to protect his daughter."

"What about your own family?"

"What about yours?"

"Fair enough," he changes the subject. "There are a lot of old farms off the main roads. I ran into a family who had no idea the corpses had risen. They made about one trip a month into town. So we do need to be careful when crossing the land in case someone thinks we're poachers or undead."

"I haven't had to deal much with the Infected. I was working on a new refugee camp when orders came in to remove troops."

"You're going to leave a lot of people unprotected."

"I didn't see you volunteering to take on more survivors," Ellsberg says.

"I've accepted a more realist view of the situation. Without using the algebra I learned in school and forgot. I've X amount of food to feed Y amount of people. I won't support more than can be fed."

"Sounds Utopic."

"Could be, Major."

"So why were you on the roof?" Ellsberg probes.

He holds back an answer until he thinks of something almost truthful. "Trouble sleeping, just felt like I needed to stand guard."

"Next time, wake me. Let me know you're gone. I don't want to shoot you by mistake."

"Can do."

The trees open to a field stretching to a forgotten farmhouse. What has to be a marriage of three beauties lying on beach towels sunning themselves causes him to rub his eyes. Before he asks, Ellsberg drops to one knee to hide in the grass.

He controls his fall to lie down. "My knee doesn't work right." He removes binoculars from his duster. "So you see them, too."

"Four living, breathing women."

"Four?" He raises the binoculars to his face.

"There's one on the porch." Major Ellsberg peers through his rifle scope inspecting the house. "More people who don't know the world ended?"

"It's early spring. Quite a chill in the air to be sunbathing." He scans the porch. A jacket clad man rocks in a chair sipping from a glass. He strokes the hair of a fourth woman poised next to him like a loyal hunting dog down to the chain and collar around her neck. "The one on the porch is chained like a prisoner."

"I think they are prisoners of one sick fuck." Ellsberg lowers his rifle. "Look at the hands of the sunbathing women."

"They chained, too?" He swings the binoculars around until he finds one of the bikini clad women. He follows the arch of her back to her shoulder and down the line of her arm past her breast until, "Oh my god. He's cut off their hands."

Ellsberg flips his safety off.

He grabs the major's forearm pulling him into the grass.

"What the hell are you doing? I'll take him out from here."

"We don't know how many friends he has. There could be five more guys in the house."

"Point taken. How do you want to handle this?" The major seems to want a second assessment more than a command.

"I wanted to cut through this track of properties to get to another road so we can pick up transportation on the other side. If we go around we run the risk of being caught in the open for the night. Lot of dangers in the dark."

"I won't leave those poor women like this," Ellsberg says.

"Then we need to scout the house and figure out how to help them."

"I'll take the tree line and come around from behind the house."

"No. Sneak back to the group and keep them safe. I'll scout the house. If there's more than I can handle, I'll get you because we'll need a plan."

"I should go along. If you get into trouble we've no idea where to go from here."

"Trust me. This is what I do." He flashes his cocky smile.

"You get them cleaned up for dinner, and make sure Elle's extra clean," the jacketed man on the porch speaks softly to her, unhooking the collar chain.

Tears stream down the chubby brunette's face. Elle knows what's in store for her.

Observing from the edge of the tall grass, he watches the man go inside the house leaving the four women unsupervised. He visually searches the farm grounds for another watchman. Something has to keep the girls from running.

They march to the springhouse. No one guards them, unless the man has a high-powered rifle and a scope located in one of the windows. He wonders if the women have developed Stockholm syndrome, or worse, it's impossible to run away without hands.

Three handless girls allow the woman with hands to wash them in the freezing well spring water. She runs a wash cloth over them gently like a mother caring for a baby.

*This guy has a supply of fresh water. He extorts pounds of flesh from them, now what do they eat?* He wants to sneak to the springhouse and ask the girls how many people hold them prisoner, but if they do suffer from Stockholm syndrome, they'd report him. He eases back up the grass line parallel with the house. He finds no signs of more than just the one man, unless someone else remains quiet. The lack of hands prevents resistance.

He feels sorry for the poor women as they march back to the house.

*Why doesn't she run?*

The one with hands could race from the springhouse keeping it between her and any rifle. Using the binoculars, he confirms what he feared—her feet. She's been burnt. Small burn scars on her legs and feet, but enough to make running painful. She's forced to care for the other girls. The back of her legs sport whelp and whip marks, bruises and scars from beatings.

Raising the question, how does the jacketed man feed these women?

He saved Emily. He will help them, but how do they survive in a world no longer tolerant of the handicapped? He should just leave. Gather his people and travel on. Forget this place. Too much of some useless chivalric code tears at him—defend the helpless.

He has killed and selfishly saved only certain people to keep his camp functioning in order to exist in this apocalyptic world. Why doesn't he just leave these poor souls to their fate? Ellsberg might try and rescue them, and he needs the engineer. He has more reasons to abandon them. They're unable to work without two hands. There are no more amputee rehab facilities. They'll be a burden. Need constant care and drain food resources with no way to contribute back.

*Leave them!*

No question, he should just forget about this place.

No. No matter what...no matter the justification of any innovative rules necessary to survive in this new world, he won't sleep at night knowing he has left these women to suffer under torture. Even if he marches in there and puts a bullet in each of their skulls, he won't leave them to be abused any longer.

His watch takes forever to click five minutes past the time the women paraded into the house. If someone had been observing them out the window, they should have taken up a new preoccupation with the girls inside.

Stealth has never been his strong suit. He's too big of a man to easily hide at a moment's whim. With biters, hiding's not even an option. No hiding from them. They detect the living. He hopes this guy's too absorbed with the abuse of these women to notice him skulking haphazardly through the field, and he hopes there are no friends.

He should have an idea of their location inside before he kicks open the door. The windows on the same side as the springhouse are high enough to stand under without him having to duck.

Plugging his ears from the noises emanating inside would quell his anger. He draws his Beretta, raises his right leg to kick the front door open, and thinks better. He reaches for the door knob. It's not locked. A few seconds added to surprise this guy. He steps inside. He takes in the room, across from the modest living room is the kitchen.

The brunette, Elle, bent over the table receives blow after blow from a conductor's wand. Forced to feed the other two girls, like toddlers in a high chair, the woman allowed to keep her hands drops her eyes to avoid witnessing the beating.

No warning shot.

No chance at redemption.

He just raises the Beretta and squeezes the trigger. The bullet smashes into the man's skull, spraying blood as it exits.

Screams.

Elle refuses to move. He holds up the gun in a non-threatening manner. "Consider this a rescue. Who else is in the house?"

Blank faces recoil from him, unsure what to make of a new man. Finally, the woman with her hands intact speaks. "He was alone." She breaks down in tears.

"I won't even begin to pretend to understand the trauma you've all gone through. I'm traveling to a safe camp. I've got people in the woods. If you get everyone dressed and fit for transit…I'll take you with me."

"Why would you help us?" she stammers.

"It's what I do," is the best answer he musters.

"We'll go. I'm Leah." The girl with her hands explains, "I don't move too fast. He made me care for everyone, but cut and burnt my feet so I couldn't run."

"When we get to my camp, you won't have to worry about running. Now I need to collect my people."

He reaches toward her. Leah recoils until he snaps the dog collar lock removing it from her neck. "Get everyone ready to travel."

"You'll come back for us?" Leah pleads. Fear clings to her from whatever torture was imposed on them.

"I'll be back and I'll make sure no one else hurts you." He picks up a semi-automatic AK-47 with the largest scope he's ever seen. He tries not to grin at being correct, because these poor women wouldn't understand his smile.

Ellsberg drops his pack into the hay wagon. "This thing will make a lot of noise."

"We've lost a couple of hours. I don't know how far we'll get into the woods on this thing, but any time we gain before the dark, I'll take."

"If this thing even starts." Brock places Olivia in the wagon.

"You're just going to add these people to the group. You know nothing about them. How do you know Olivia will be safe around them?" Karley stews.

"I guarantee they won't lay a finger on her." He kicks the trailer hitch to ensure a tight fit. "These poor women have been in a bad situation."

"We should be nice to them," Olivia volunteers.

"That'd be nice of you," he praises the girl.

Sarah stands at the end of the wagon contemplating how to get in. She's too short to jump and too heavy to pull herself up.

He pulls down a hay bale for her to use as a step. "I'm going to get our new companions. Prepare yourself."

The four women follow their rescuer to the hay wagon. Karley clamps her hand over her mouth to hide her shock. She knows whatever words fall from her mouth will be insensitive.

"Mommy, why don't those women have any hands?" Olivia asks with the innocence of a child.

He and Ellsberg pick up the chubby brunette and set her in the wagon. "This is Elle."

They help the next woman as well. "This is Bobbi."

They place the third woman on the wagon. "Meet Willie."

Leah crawls into the wagon herself, but needs a bit of a push due to her weakened legs. "I'm Leah."

"Olivia," the little girl blurts.

"Sarah," she introduces herself before Karley can scold her daughter.

Brock gives his new commander a glance expressing these women will put them in a great deal of danger due to their handicap and inability to care for themselves.

Elle lies on her stomach over a hay bale. Olivia stares at her missing hands. Self-conscious, Bobbi hides her hands behind her back. Tears just trickle down Willie's cheeks.

The consummate rescuer of the helpless climbs into the tractor seat and fires the behemoth up. The rust red monster roars to life, sending plumes of choking black smoke from the exhaust pipe as it lurches forward. He depresses the clutch in order to grind the gears into second and the fast pace fifteen miles an hour jolts them across the field. They roll over a wire fence and keep moving toward the tree line.

The cattle path leads through the woods constantly jolting everyone in the wagon. The three handless girls have to continuously shift their weight to keep from being bumped over.

The tractor sputters. A few more feet forward and it coughs the last of the black smoke before dying.

"Looks like no more gas." Despite a search of the farm he could find no more gas to add in the tank. He hops from the tractor. "We're walking." He pulls out a plastic sleeve containing a map.

Ellsberg helps all the women from the wagon. "You think we made up any time?"

Figuring they gained seven or eight miles, he says, "Some, but this trail leads farther south than I want to keep traveling."

"Are we lost?" Brock asks.

He stuffs the map back in his coat and slings the AK-47 over his shoulder. "How did the pioneers cross The Great Plains? I mean, the first groups. Later, people followed the wagon ruts, but the first group. How did they know how to go without a map?" He hikes into the woods up a small ridge. At the top he halts. "If we cut through this way we'll reach the blacktop before dark, but everyone's going to have to move." He won't show any favoritism toward the handicapped women. No matter what, in order for them to survive they have to be able to move.

Karley keeps Olivia close to her. The little girl keeps attempting to run and help the handless women or touch the stump. Elle requires assistance. Sarah acts as a crutch for Elle.

Elle won't admit to pain. She marches on, somehow she knows even these generous people might leave her. Why would anyone take the time to care for handless girls? She slips. Sarah steadies her.

"You'll make it." Sarah's voice gives no comfort.

The trees give no sign of turning back into pasture. He feels his own long wounded leg strain under the hike. The area has become rocky, hard to navigate under foot, but they have no time to rest, not yet. Dangerous to be here, in the trees, in the dark. A fire would attract unwanted attention. He would get no sleep and potentially the most dangerous part of the trek remains.

The climb up the steep incline reaches a pinnacle at a cliff edge. The fifty foot drop into a shallow spring-fed pool would have been a beautiful location for a picnic, but now it's one more obstacle before reaching a safer location.

"Head over this way. It drops off here." He warns moving away from the cliff. The landscape inclines, and through some trees: pasture. If he calculated correctly, they should be on the other side of the farm and near a gravel road leading to blacktop.

Screams break the quiet of the trees. He spins around, the AK unslung and ready to fire. Sarah, Leah and Ellsberg stand at the edge of the cliff. Karley hides Olivia's face by pressing the little girl into her stomach. Bobbi and Willie hug each other avoiding glances toward the cliff.

He guesses, but marches back anyway. Even knowing what's over the cliff, actually witnessing the poor woman's twisted mangled body as blood balloons into the shallow pool turns his resilient stomach.

"She broke free of my arms and just ran." Sarah breaks down. "She leaped off the cliff." Major Ellsberg nods in confirmation.

Does he say something? Will words make it worse for these people? Should they just move on? He thinks back to his psychology classes in college and even other work-related sensitivity training. Nothing has prepared him for this. No matter what he says it will be the wrong choice of words. “We need to keep moving.”

“You heartless bastard,” Karley screams at him. “That poor girl just died.”

“I can’t do anything for her. She made her choice.”

“You want us to live in your camp, and you show nothing toward the death of that poor woman,” Karley criticizes.

“What do you want to do, repel down there and give her a funeral?” He leans over the cliff and raises the AK. The thunder sends Olivia into tears. Everyone jumps. “I did what I could for her. Now we know she won’t come back. Her soul’s at rest.” He marches on, shouldering the Kalashnikov.

“You want to go live and work for someone like him?” Karley sneers at her husband.

“Karley, shut up.” Brock marches after his new boss.

“We should move, ladies,” Ellsberg herds them forward.

“Does no one care about her?” Karley pleads.

“She’s been through too much,” Leah says, feeling as broken as poor Elle. She takes one last look at the girl she has been feeding, cleaning and witnessing her abuse for months. She accepts there was only one choice Elle had in a world rejecting her condition. For just a second she contemplates joining Elle, but if nothing else, she couldn’t leave Bobbi and Willie to fend for themselves. Leah hikes over the ridge.

“Mommy, we should go with them,” Olivia pleads, pulling at her mother’s hand. “Mommy, he will keep us safe.” She points to the duster clad man.

“I don’t know of any place safe anymore, my darling,” Karley says.

Twilight befalls the group as his boot kicks over a rock on the gravel road. Major Ellsberg stands on one barbed wire strand and picks up the strand above it, opening a portal through the fence for the group to scurry through.

“We’re not as far as you wanted,” Brock observes.

"We're close. A few more miles."

"I can't walk anymore," Leah confesses.

"Mommy, carry me," Olivia begs.

He rubs the growing stubble on his chin. "Camping here in the middle of the road would invite dangers."

"They can't keep walking," Ellsberg slips through the fence. "So how do you want to handle this?" The major doesn't directly play against his authority, but he certainly brings it into question.

"I've never scouted this gravel road before." He glances at his map. "In a few miles is a blacktop road I've been on. I know several houses and barns where it's safe to sleep."

"Can we cut across the field to one of the houses?"

"In the dark with no lights we could walk right past it completely."

"We need to move," Brock insists.

"No, the woods aren't the answer," Ellsberg slips in his bid for command of the group. "I suggest you and I head down each direction of this road and find a house and return to get the group."

"Barns are better. Biters can't climb ladders into the hay lofts. Houses have dark corners where the biters hide." He's never found a biter in a barn loft—not yet. "How far do you suggest we walk?"

"Maybe a mile each. Should be a house by then."

"Out here homes tend to cluster or be extra far apart." He hands the AK to Brock. "All you have to do is pull the trigger. Just don't shoot one of us."

Ellsberg throws a log onto the fire burning in the fireplace.

Brock fumbles with a box of nails and a hammer. He secures the door.

Stoic, their rescuer stands guard as Karley rummages through a bedroom closet for blankets. The flashlight he holds gives her enough light to strip the bed of sheets.

"They smell."

"Like what?" he asks.

"Just unwashed. Can we check upstairs, get enough blankets for everyone?"

He nods, but in the fire light darkened shadows mask his face. "I check out the rooms first."

Karley dumps the blankets on the family room floor. "Olivia, Mommy's going to check upstairs. You stay here with Daddy."

"Okay, Mommy," she eats from an MRE.

The first bedroom they check upstairs has a closet full of blankets. He opens the door to a second bedroom and checks the closet, each corner, even under the bed before letting Karley strip the sheets and pull more blankets from the closet. When she does, a plastic case hits the floor popping open. She scoops it up. "It's empty." She hands him the gun case.

He fumbles holding the flashlight and checking the case. "Too bad. Always use another gun."

"I see what's on your list of priorities over some poor girl's life," Karley berates.

"Karley, you're going to have to accept there was nothing to do but move on. We could do nothing for her."

"You didn't even try."

"What would you have had me do?"

"Compassion."

"Overrated."

She gathers the blankets. "This should be enough."

"Go straight downstairs. I want to check the rest of the rooms."

Downstairs, Brock nails the door to the basement shut. Karley whispers to him, "Leaving the military base was a horrible idea. He will get us killed."

"The colonel trusts him, and he didn't have to help those poor women."

"What are you doing?" Karley asks.

"Making sure nothing gets upstairs from the basement. You've seen scary movies. It's way too dark to make sure nothing's down there."

"Don't let Olivia hear you talk. She needs to sleep."

Ellsberg takes one of the heavier blankets and tacks it up over the window.

"An extra blanket would keep us warm," Karley protests.

"It will keep anyone including the Infected from seeing the fire light," Ellsberg explains.

Karley realizes the major would not oppose the man leading them. She looks at their new leader resting on the top stair. He desires safety.

Sarah collapses onto the bench of the road side park. "How much farther is this camp?" she huffs.

Even Ellsberg, with his daily regimen of physical exercise, feels the ache of the hike.

"Seventy-five, eighty miles at most." He marches into the tree line. "Take a break. I want to check something."

"I want to come, too," Olivia begs fascinated by the big man.

"Honey, no, he might need a private moment." Brock says.

"No, I might be able to shorten our trip."

"Can I go, Mommy?" Olivia pleads.

"I won't be going far," he says, inviting the little girl.

"Stay with him." Karley plops on the bench. She has no idea how she'll find the energy to walk the rest of the day.

Leah pushes a straw into her canteen allowing Bobbi a drink. She feels obligated to help the two women. She had only been allowed to keep her hands due to her luck in being kidnapped last. She was his fourth victim. Before her, Elle had cared for the other two. Once he took Leah prisoner, her captor cut off Elle's hands to demonstrate his power over them. He burnt Leah's feet to keep her from running and said as long as they please him then he had no need to find a replacement. The things he did to pleasure himself. The things he made them do to each other she did willingly to keep her hands. She feels so guilty, but with Elle gone she feels a burden somewhat lifted. Difficult as it may be, two women will be easier to care for than three. She opens an MRE bag containing more food than the four of them used to get in a day, not because her torturer didn't have a reserve, but he kept them malnourished as a means of control.

The roar of motorcycles breaks the natural silence of the road. He spins around and grabs Olivia by clamping his hand over her mouth and ducks into the trees. "You have to stay quiet," he whispers to her. His duster shields them both in the shade. She nods. He releases her.

Seven hardcore biker men dismount and take over the camp as if they own it. Ellsberg surrenders his rifle, being outgunned and knowing Brock would be useless in a firefight. The bikers confiscate the weapons and ransack the backpacks.

"You're a well fed group." The biggest biker shoves Ellsberg to a bench seat. "And with plenty of ladies, too."

"Diesel, check this bitch out." He yanks Willie to her feet. "Bitch ain't got no hands," waving Willie's stump at his leader.

"The soldier's still playing protector of the weak." He shoves Brock next to Ellsberg, "And plenty of women to share."

One of the bikers grabs Sarah and bends her over the table. He slaps her ass cheek three times. "Soft. Plenty of cushion for the long ride." He runs his hand between her legs still on the outside of her jeans. The bikers laugh. Tears well in Sarah's eyes.

"You want one, Xeo? You can ride her. Hell, you'll never touch the bed." Diesel grabs Karley by her neck and hair. "This one doesn't look too well used." He mashes Karley's face against the table top. The metal groove pattern imprints into her skin.

Xeo plucks Sarah by her hair and unbuttons her pants. He reaches his hand into her panties and whispers, "You're going to like this."

Sarah feels tingles as much as she doesn't want the impending rape. What he does with his fingers feels pleasurable. She fights hard with herself. She tries to make the good feelings leave her mind.

She can't.

It feels too nice to be touched. She now has this new understanding for women not reporting a rape. No matter what has been forced upon her, no matter how bad she doesn't want this or this man, he makes it feel so good deep down she doesn't want him to stop. She understands why some women don't report it.

*No*. This is rape! She jerks away. He slams her down. No matter how it feels, she doesn't want this. Sarah struggles to break his grasp.

Diesel isn't so nice to Karley. He jerks and tears at her pants, shredding the fabric until he has exposed her ass. "She's a peach, boys."

With the same gentleness he saved Emily with, he wraps the duster coat around Olivia, keeping her from seeing the inflicted trauma on her mother. He takes the small gun from his boot.

*Click.*

He flicks the safety off.

"Anyone you don't know walks toward you, you just point and pull back on this trigger and no one will hurt you." He puts the gun into her hand wrapping her fingers around the handle.

Tears cover her face. She knows her mother's screams of protest and fear. "Will you save my mom?" she blubbers.

"I need you to be brave for me. And I'm going to save everyone." He switches his M&P to the Beretta holster. From the sound of the bikes, he'll need all sixteen shots. "You have to stay here."

Olivia nods yes.

"If you want to pleasure yourself then take me. I'll do whatever you want." Willie stands, presenting herself. Diesel shoves her to the ground. Willie lands on her arm nubs as if she were a dog.

Diesel yanks her back by her hair.

"I like it rough, but you're a little weak," she taunts the biker with an invitation. Willie has spent the last few months constantly being brutalized. She'll handle one more day of abuse if it prevents Karley from experiencing what she's been living.

Karley attempts to hoist what's left of her panties up with just one hand. Diesel yanks Willie's head hard enough he could have snapped her neck. "You look a bit used up, slut." He shoves her back to all fours. "You're the miserable house dog everyone kicks."

Diesel draws the pistol from his belt. "Only one thing to do for a mongrel like you."

*Bam.*

Bits of brain and blood splash onto Karley's face. Diesel kicks Willie's body over. "Girls with no hands are useless."

"She still had a mouth."

"Shut up, Steele. You going to wipe her ass for her?" Diesel asks. "She's still warm if you want to pump the two holes she's got left."

Bobbi jumps back in her seat, bumping into Leah. She wants to flee. Something holds her in place. Diesel grabs Karley's panties so hard he lifts her into the air and flings her into the dirt before they tear off. Her skin peels back from where the seam cut against her skin. Karley pleads not to be violated.

Turmoil consumes Brock's reasoning. Witnessing his love's assault demands retribution on her honor. Unable to curtail his emotions...

*Slam.*

Ellsberg's arm crashes across Brock's chest to prevent him from saving his wife.

"Well, this one's important to him." Diesel glares at Brock. "She your old lady?"

Brock stands. "She's my wife."

"She's a whore. She's going to moan for each of us."

Brock lunges at Diesel. Ellsberg grabs him before he gets two feet, slamming Brock into the dirt. "He'll kill you," the major warns. "And he'll still rape her."

"I'll rape her on top of your bloody corpse."

"I doubt it." In full gunslinger mode, Emily's savior calls from the middle of the highway ready to protect his group. "Why don't you face me?"

"What are you supposed to be, some kind of hero?" Diesel sneers.

"I think he fancies himself a cowboy. This ain't *High Noon*," Steele taunts.

"And I ain't your Huckleberry," Diesel spits.

"Cultural classic, but if you're making me out to be Earp, remember he was never wounded, not once in any gun battle he was ever in."

Diesel rubs his grizzled chin, having stepped onto the road. "You know, you seem intelligent, why don't you just walk away?"

Two bikers back Diesel up on the road.

"You're hurting the people I promised to protect." The morning sun hangs over his left shoulder.

"Then I did you a favor. Handless girls would only get you killed." Diesel snaps his fingers and Steele drags Bobbi to the road. "This girl needs constant care. Maybe one handed she'll do all right, but she's just a walking corpse who hasn't died yet."

He wonders if Brock and Ellsberg are capable of handling the three men watching over them. Xeo keeps his hands on Sarah so they have to dispatch two quickly. Now Bobbi has become a makeshift shield between him and his quarry.

"How about I just kill this one, have my way with the white bitch and you all go on your way. Hell, I'll even leave your weapons. I wouldn't leave any able bodied person defenseless out here."

How much time does it take to weigh major decisions? It should take more than the hundredth of a tenth of a second it took to make up his mind of what to do let alone how he will handle it. In his mind, it goes down. The M&P discharges in rapid succession. Short of the time between controlled trigger squeezes reverberates like full-auto machine gun burst. He shreds Diesel with the first four shots. Each bullet strikes his body missing Bobbi completely. The next four bullets are shared by the two men on either side. The next shot splinters Steele's skull. He hits two more guarding his group, leaving only the one holding Sarah for Ellsberg to deal with. He puts a bullet into each dead man's skull.

But in his mind and the reality of his decision to draw doesn't take into account the poor thought processes of everyone else involved. His M&P flashes with the first shot before Diesel's weapon clears his holster, but not before he jerks Bobbi into a human shield. With his skill the first bullet shatters the brain pan of the biker on Diesel's right. Bobbi faints. Her now dead weight shifts Diesel off kilter sending his first shot wide. Giving Ellsberg the two seconds needed for two bullets to kill the biker on the left. Military training has educated him to people surviving one round. Steele has his pistol out. He pauses for an order to fire.

Ellsberg dives low for the biker nearest him. Brock makes a mad dash for Karley. Leah drops to the ground covering her face.

Sarah stomps on the foot of her captor with all her weight, breaking one of his toes.

Diesel fires.

Miss.

Struggling to hold the unconscious Bobbi keeps Diesel off balance unable to shoot straight. He releases the handless girl.

Poor choice number one.

Bobbi may be falling through the air to the ground alive, but she still acts as a shield. Emily's savior aims and shoots the biker nearest to Karley putting a slug into Steele's arm and not his gun one. Diesel's next slug impacts the black vest he wears under his duster.

*How many miles per hour does a bullet travel? At about twenty feet has to mean the velocity...* Understanding the math has little to do with the rib shattering pain the .45 brings to him. The movies would show him flying about twelve feet backward but in reality bullets don't blow people back. He actually takes the full impact and remains standing. However, his ability to return fire becomes impossibly impaired. His arms flail and the next shot misses Steele completely.

Brock scoops Karley into his arms. She struggles to yank her shredded panties over her bottom. Ellsberg struggles for the gun. Sarah yanks the weapon from her molester who is hopping around on one foot. Knowing enough to aim, she jerks the trigger until it dry fires.

Dead. Dead. Dead.

He should be dead. Outgunned by the last two bikers.

He fires.

Diesel fires.

Steele fires.

# CHAPTER TWENTY-FOUR

THE ABILITY TO track game is the new important learned life skill since the fall of civilization. Danziger tracked dozens of criminals, but not in the manner a hunter tracks a deer. Now he must learn the latter and quickly.

Millions of dead are easy to follow. Many drag limbs or shuffle-step as they gait forward. They make no effort to cover their footprints or snapping of plant life leaving behind trails of rotten blood. The dead stink—mixtures of road kill skunk, rotten meat and shit.

There might be other defecating smells, but rot overwhelms them all.

People, on the other hand, backtrack over footsteps, taking care not to break off leaves from trees and even avoid loose soil. Humans are cunning animals, capable of remaining hidden from those still alive. The growing army of walking corpses weed out the living, but they are unreliable, easily distracted bloodhounds. Better to search for clues a living person leaves behind.

Careless means dead.

It was careless to split from Tom two days ago. The man's walking straight toward the herd that decimated the caravan. Tom feels he must help retrieve survivors. Tom needs someone to help him until his arm heals. Tom believes Levin went south.

Statistically, Levin went in a southerly direction, but Danziger has to be sure. This trail could be gone by the time Tom finds any survivors from the caravan, if he does at all. And he knows which direction those people went even if their tracks get washed away. Not this set. One quick shower and he'll lose them. There's no BOLO warning on this guy. If he doesn't find him he'll be free to murder again and again.

Danziger kneels at the footprint of a small shoed person trailing into a makeshift campsite. Scattered among ravaged supplies these poor souls never expected danger would come from a fellow survivor. The detective rifles through the pockets of what used to be an old man. He yanks a cell phone from one of the pockets. Danziger holds the power button with no results, as he expected. Unzipping his vest pocket he slides out a portable quick phone charger.

Phones—the new wallet photos.

Danziger rolls the cylindrical charger in his hand. Glancing at the dead man's pictures could reveal if these dead were a part of his family. Maybe give the detective an idea of the girl with his own daughter's murderer. But the missing girl will look just like his own child. Serial killers tend to kill the same person again and again. So whatever his motivations, Levin extolls his reprisals on blonde fourteen-year-old girls.

They had been lucky enough to escape the herd, and their discovery of a good spot to rest should have kept all four alive. They had a tent and small campfire to cook with. Not enough to attract attention, but enough to have a warm meal.

Danziger chucks the uncharged phone against a tree. Plastic shrapnel rains on the scattered backpacks. He won't waste precious power. Knowing they were family won't help his pursuit. It won't change his next task. Scooping up a metal telescoping hiking pole, Danziger positions himself over a young girl – too young to have caught Levin's eyes – with a chest wound. He drives the pole into her forehead. Sparing her the return doesn't spare Danziger from the act. He kicks her backpack. Three *My Pretty Pony* DVDs scatter. The DVDs took up space where an extra can of beans should have been carried. He takes the stuffed bear from the pile of supplies and places it in the dead girl's arms.

Somehow preventing the rest of the family from becoming walking corpses weighs less on his conscience. Any useful supplies were picked over by Levin, including a fourteen-year-old, blonde, blue-eyed girl—his perfect target. Even with the world ending people cannot fight their nature, and the nature of a serial killer remains.

Danziger examines the ground around the campsite. Whoever killed them made no effort to hide the drag marks the girl made as he forced her to go with him. Her death has to be special to appease Levin's masochistic desires. This poor girl has to die in his ritual manner. The same way Danziger's daughter endured. Mom, Dad, Sis...they didn't matter. But this girl. This girl has to die like all the other girls. Like Danziger's own teenage daughter. What he did to her...

Danziger will visit upon the killer righteousness. No court and no jury, he will bring justice to a man the new world has forgotten about. Surviving the plague takes precedence over criminals of the old world. Not for him. His daughter will get the justice she deserves no matter what.

*Snap.*

Twigs crackle under movement. Danziger eases toward the noise. One of the family members might have returned from the dead. Near the camp a second girl more to Levin's taste crawls toward him. Red blood blossoms from her back signaling life remains in her.

Danziger futilely presses tattered clothes from the ransacked supplies against her back.

Mewing, she coughs. "He killed them."

The cop in him inquires, "Who?" The answer doesn't matter. Even if it's not Levin she won't live long enough to give him enough information about the killer. He squeezes her hand.

"Do you have a name?"

"Aleydis." She spits blood. "He took...my friend." Her face drops into the dirt.

He keeps his grip on her hand. Her warmth hastily ebbs away. Danziger drives the pole into Aleydis' skull before reanimation can occur.

With no one to cut the grass, the trail remains easy to follow. He sprints down the path. Stop.

The rules of the world have changed but not for Levin. Danziger asks himself, does he know he's being pursued by someone who knows who he really is? He left this trail. A wide, unquestionable trail. Running straight down it would be foolish. He pushes the hiking pole along the ground checking for trip wires.

It slows his progress. His prey has eluded capture for years. Seventeen girls before the apocalypse were credited to Levin's scoreboard. Eight or nine were dead before anyone recognized they had a serial killer, not that serial killers are as rare as believed. Police hide facts to prevent the press from connecting murder cases together and placing hundreds of people in panic mode. No police department wants scrutiny over serial killer investigations. Just like beachfront economies never want people to understand how many sharks actually swim along the beach. It's bad for tourist dollars.

Somehow in shadow of what was once accepted as civilization, Danziger doubts many serial killers perished. In fact, this brave new world has become a breeding ground for the depraved. He halts.

The patch of smashed grass catches his attention. The killer dropped the girl. He uses the hiking pole to pick a shoe out of the grass. He took off her shoes. Danziger wonders if she realized Levin was a danger to her and tried to run from him. Most people don't have the calluses built up on their feet to go without shoes. She wouldn't be able to run fast if she did break away again.

Shoes.

The parted grass trail leads on. The girl's barefoot. It will slow Levin and decrease their chance of running. The ground turns dry. In the dirt patches the girl's tracks reveal that they staggered. The kind of wobble a person has when they're handcuffed or their hands are bound behind them.

Forced to travel slow is better than Danziger could have hoped for. Levin needs a place to perform his lengthy depraved acts. He pushes the thoughts from his head. The idea that his own daughter screamed and called for him to come save her overwhelms him. His own baby girl, so small when she was born he could hold her in just one hand with only her legs hanging over the palm. His baby girl called and called for Daddy and he didn't save her. How betrayed she must have felt as she took her last breath, knowing Daddy had lied when he said he'd always protect her.

Not these two girls. These girls he will save. He will put a stop to this killing. No matter what else happens. No matter if a thousand dead mouths rip his flesh, he will end this. He will end the Blonde Teen Slasher.

The path extends into a field with a lone barn resting in the center. Danziger ducks back into the tree line. The building has one strategic advantage. It gives anyone inside clear sight of approaching visitors from all directions. The dilapidated structure looks to have more rotten boards than sound ones. It has long since outlived its usefulness as a storage facility. Still, it was built in the days when people took pride in what they constructed, and built to last.

Danziger doesn't question this location for Levin's hideout. He has to determine how to get to the barn unseen. If the floor loft remains intact then it would be perfect to hide and prevent the corpses from reaching Levin. People dare not stay too long in one location anymore. The buildup of the undead becomes overwhelming, but a few nights' sleep in a secure position would be welcome.

Darkness might be his best option. Risking crawling through the grass at turtle speed would be detrimental if a corpse were to stumble upon him. He'd have to shoot it giving away his location. With no electricity and a half moon, night provides cover. Danziger had no idea just how dark night really was until there were no more street lights, or even the ambient light provided by...well, even cell phones light up a room compared to no electric lights at all.

His mind slams with thoughts. Levin could have night vision goggles. Hell, he could have a fifty caliber with a heat sensitive power scope and kryptonite bullets, but nothing's going to prevent Danziger from saving those girls. He doubts Levin has night vision or many supplies with him. To escape the herd, he would have had to abandon much of his gear, and he left useful items at the campsite.

Other than survivalist nuts, most people didn't have an arsenal at their disposal when the deceased manifested. No one believed the dead walked and killed. Even the diehard of the apocalypse whackos weren't home locked away in their bomb shelters when it started. No matter how prepared people thought they were, the end of the world doesn't happen while one sits at home and waits for it.

He grabs the branch of a tree he thinks will support his weight. He climbs about seven feet where a forked branch works as a seat. It's not comfortable, but sleep exhaustion doesn't require comfort. He slips his belt off, loops it around himself and the branch before cinching it again. It should stop him from rolling. A seven-foot fall wouldn't kill him, but he won't save anyone with a broken leg and a rolled ankle.

Sleep hits him like a brick. He should plan his attack better while he watches the barn in the light, but it's been two, maybe three, days since he slept, and who knows how long before he only caught a catnap, and those didn't last long enough for REM sleep.

Life is full up with stuff making people question why they weren't taught it in school. Telling time with moonlight seems so antiquated based on the lack of need. Who needs that with watches and cell phones, televisions, DVRs, auto alarms? Nope. No need for any such skills with all those working devices at arm's reach. Map reading with GPS. Cooking by campfire. Hell, even beating your clothes on a rock to wash them.

Bathing.

A shower would be nice. He smells worse than the dead. No way, no matter how much education or training he had, nothing prepared him for this.

# CHAPTER TWENTY-FIVE

TWO...ONLY TWO.

Hollywood gunfights at high noon in the middle of the street actually occurred in the American West. He is unable to imagine Wild Bill or Wyatt Earp ever going through anything like this. He looks up. He knows his round went through Diesel. There was the rapid fire of a machine gun, and the impact of two more slugs into his vest.

He reaches up and fingers the two holes in his t-shirt. He feels the twisted metal slugs embedded there. He unzips the Kevlar vest.

"Ellsberg!" He coughs. The pain of what feels like three trucks running over him ripples through his chest. He should get up. He should force himself to at least get to a sitting position and make sure all the bikers are dead. He knows Diesel needs a head shot to make sure he stays dead. He listens to Karley's sobs and wonders how many biters will be attracted by the thunder the machine guns made. So much noise. He has left poor Olivia alone in the woods with a gun in her untrained hand. He has to protect her. He won't be the reason another little girl is discovered by a walking corpse.

Ellsberg offers him a hand. Emily's savior locks his hand around the major's wrist and lets himself be jerked up. The pain digs. He loses his breath and relaxes his grip. It hurts too much to move, so he uses all his strength to just lay there. He wheezes, "I...I left...Olivia…in the woods." Ellsberg vanishes from his view. "Wait!" He hears the major's boots scuff the pavement. "Gave her a gun," he warns.

"I'll use caution."

He just breathes.

Slow breaths.

Not too fast so as not to inflate too much lung.

He tries to make each one longer than the last, but still takes in the air slowly. His brain wants him to poke around the impact sights to examine the damage, but the pain won't let him. He can't stay like this. He has to lead these people. He keeps a grip on his M&P. Not all the dead bikers suffered head trauma. They will walk again. He has witnessed it happen. Whatever reanimates the dead brings them all back to life unless they have brain damage. No matter how much it hurts he has to at least get to his elbows.

He remembers the physical therapy to walk again after his incident. The struggle to walk wasn't impaired by lack of oxygen, or at least the inability to breathe without lung pain. He pushes off his elbows to a sitting position, finally brave enough to depress the bruising at the impact sight.

He pushes harder. Water clouds his vision. He forces his fingers to dig into the purple flesh. Nothing feels broken or cracked—grateful. Now if his legs work. Through watery eyes he spots Ellsberg carrying Olivia still wrapped in his duster coat. Leah comforts Sarah. Brock holds a sobbing Karley. Poor Bobbi has no one to attend to her. He gets to his feet to go comfort the handless woman.

"You gonna be okay?"

"What happened to the world? I never hurt anyone. I was always kind, and dropped all my change in the red bucket. I donated my old shoes. Why? Why do the ills of the world rain down upon me?" She holds out her stumps as she begs for answers.

"I don't have those kinds of answers."

"I love God and my mom. I never hurt anyone."

He has no choice but to plop down next to her. He wishes he had controlled his tumble better as the jarring to the ground reverberates through his bruises. He grabs escaping breath.

"The world has left little space for comfort, but you've survived, and are still a strong woman. There has to be a reason." He hopes he sounds sincere. He doesn't buy into a universal plan for anything. In reality, if there is a plan then all the doom visited upon people is deserved, and no baby born with cancer could deserves that. With the rise of the undead if any supreme being did exist he's long forsaken this rock.

Still, when faith is important to someone, it helps get them through the rough patches. If anything he needs to find a head-shrinker. Leah, Bobbi, Sarah, and even Karley all need someone to help them with the violations they've been put through.

"I've nothing to offer anyone except be a burden someone has to feed and clean. Those bikers didn't even want to use me for the one thing I'm still able to do." Bobbi's eyes glaze into a distant place only she sees.

He searches long and hard for correct words to comfort this fragile woman. Before he finds them, she turns from him.

Steele's leg twitches behind her. Attracted by the noise, Bobbi crawls to the dead biker. He realizes Bobbi has a solution to her pain. He raises his gun with a lackluster nowhere near his normal speed, but she's between him and Steele's skull. Huffing, he struggles to get to his hunches.

"Ellsberg," he calls.

The major bolts from the roadside park, but he won't make it. Ellsberg unslings his rifle at the sight of the rising corpse.

He gets to his feet, staggers back, but Bobbi, still in his line of fire, jabs her forearm into Steele's gaping mouth. The fresh corpse clamps down. She doesn't scream as the skin shreds.

Blood drips, exciting the undead.

He knocks her off the dead body finishing off Steele with a round to the head. Ellsberg halts before another dead biker and fires into his skull. He does the same to Diesel, before aiming at Bobbi's face.

"Just end it for me," she pleads. "There's nothing else for me now."

Ending for her quickly would be a mercy, no question. But no matter how many undead or vile humans he's had to end, somehow mercifully killing a helpless woman tears at him. He's not quite the cold-hearted bastard everyone seems to think him.

"The bikers have been eliminated," Ellsberg says, then offers, "You need me to?"

"Please just end it. I don't want to be one of those things."

"You turning into a biter would make this easier," he explains, "I've never killed anyone innocent. It's not the same."

"But I'll become one."

*Bam.*

Leah grips a smoking gun. "I've taken care of her for months, it's only right I..." She buries her face into Ellsberg's chest.

He holsters his M&P. Some part of him will forever be grateful he didn't have to kill the woman.

Brock asks, "Can we ride these motorcycles?"

"You ride?"

"No, but it's got to beat walking," Brock says.

"It's not so easy, and too dangerous to teach with someone riding pillion."

"But it's so far to walk, and the women..."

"First, we gather the bodies and start a pyre, make sure you check every pocket for anything useful. I've got a syphon pump in my pack. We drain all the bikes of gas, use some of it to burn the bodies."

"Look, I agreed to follow you, but I see no point in walking when we could at least ride these bikes until the gas runs out," Major Ellsberg argues.

"I brought us to this location because I've a vehicle stashed in those trees. I was interrupted in retrieving it. We fill the gas tank and burn the bodies.

He pulls back on the camouflaged tarp revealing a Cadillac Escalade.

"The apocalypse hasn't diminished your style," Brock about creams himself from the shiny luxury vehicle.

"This thing's built like a tank and gets great gas mileage. In case you hadn't noticed, there aren't going to be any more oil tankers from the Middle East. Plus we'll all fit inside because when it says it seats eight comfortably I bet this one car actually means it."

He loads pilfered supplies into the back. Brock wheels one of the bikes immediately behind the SUV. "You park here a lot?" He kicks at several dried tire tracks.

"Yeah. It's a good spot. No one has found it so far, and the gimps don't seem to come up here." He wheels a second bike next to Brock's. "I don't always get to leave vehicles, when I take one I've stashed." He checks for dry gas tanks before covering the Harleys with the tarp.

"How long have you been doing this?" Brock asks.

"Like a lot of people after the rise of the dead, I wandered and hid. I didn't want to be in a refugee facility, but there was no place else secure enough to get a good night's sleep."

"I understand," Sarah whimpers. She brings more equipment to haul with them.

"I found this place. I learned why it still had working lights, and ever since then I've figured out how to keep them turned on. See, I enjoy hot showers." Sarah almost smiles at what she figures is his attempt at humor.

"You need a pipe welder," Brock deduces.

"So everyone you stop and help you only help in order to make sure you have a hot shower?" Karley gives him the same look she had for the bikers.

"I keep my camp small. I do collect people to keep it secure." He won't bring himself to say 'safe.' He doesn't believe in safe anymore. "We've limited researches and, yeah, I am selective in who I rescue."

"I don't know if I can agree," Karley says.

"We saw what allowing everyone into the military base did," Brock adds.

"One day maybe we can afford to admit anyone. But not this week."

"You've turned people away from your sanctuary?" Ellsberg asks.

"Not so much. It's a little out of the way. People aren't rushing in the direction of a national forest for protection."

Wanikiya takes the gun belt through the metal window. "Glad you're back," he whispers. "We had an incident."

"I got banged up. People getting desperate out there."

"We'd a few try and get in here, and they spoke for God."

He slips his coat off. "Bring up a few female guards or some of the nurses. These women have been violated enough." He shoves his coat through the hole before explaining. "No one gets into our camp without being inspected and turning over everything on your person. I sent for some female guards for the women."

"Inspected for what?" Brock asks.

"Bites," Ellsberg answers. "All the way?" He asks, unbuckling his belt.

"Socks and underwear. No one infected gets in. Anything looking like a bite and the doctor inspects you while you stay in this cage." He pulls off his shirt.

Karley gasps at the three circular nearly black bruises on his chest. "My god that has to hurt." Karley knows her own backside is bruised from the jerking, but her discoloration won't be as dark as his.

"I'd say I've had worse, but this might actually be the worst." He hikes his leg onto the bench to unzip the side of his boot.

Wanikiya scratches on a clipboard getting back to the business of the camp. "What are the skill set of our new arrivals?"

"Major Ellsberg's an engineer. Brock is a welder."

"Good, I'll get Brock stowed away and show him where he'll start tomorrow."

"You got any more rules in this place we should know about before we commit to entering?" Ellsberg asks.

"Everyone works or they don't eat. We've been developing rules as situations arise. After you strip down, we'll tour the fence and get your expert opinion. The ladies can wait for female guards."

"I want to stay with my wife," Brock announces.

"What's his wife do?"

"What does she do?" *Besides be a tremendous nag?* He wants to say out loud, but thinks better of it.

"I was a stylist, and have been a waitress."

"Can you cook?" Wanikiya inquires.

"Some," she flounders.

"I'll try you out in the kitchen and we could set her up a shop in the common building. Some of the men would like a hairstyle more than a buzz cut."

"Sarah, what did you do?"

"I was a tax preparer."

"Not much call for that now. We'll find you something suitable." He leans toward Wanikiya and whispers, "Keep her inside the fence."

"Don't talk about me behind my back!" Sarah screeches. "I got enough of that at the military base. It was humiliating."

He turns, unclasping his belt the way an angry drunken father would right before nightly beating his children. "I told him to give you a job inside the fence."

"Leah, what was your career choice?"

"I worked in a daycare."

"We'll find them something." Wanikiya scribbles on the clipboard. "I've got trucks or horses ready."

He slips from his jeans. "I doubt I can handle the jarring canter of those quarter mares. We'll take the truck." He drops his underwear, before raising his arms and twirling. Plenty of bruises decorate his body but no bite marks.

"Along the main gate we have a dog run. I want to reinforce the inner fence."

"You're building twin fencing along your entire camp?" Ellsberg inquires.

"Along the front of the fence adjacent to the road."

"We patrol a few times an hour but at different intervals," Wanikiya adds, "preventing anyone from cutting their way in."

A cargo trailer interrupts the dog run with the ends cut open for access and the door side able to close and be locked. Two men stand guard on the top with high-powered rifles.

"They're certified crack shots."

"Certified?" Ellsberg inquires.

"Travis sent me a weapons expert, Chief Petty Officer Simon."

"I met him. He's a fine master of arms."

"Our biggest concern is fence security. I may have too many people assigned boundary patrol, but if a herd of those biters waltzes through, their combined weight could bring down the fence."

"You want me to reinforce the barriers. How much metal cable do you have access to?" Ellsberg asks.

"We'll make a run, get whatever we need. People did not pick over the hardware stores."

The dog run ends with an exit outside the chain link fences, keeping the two-story farmhouse completely isolated from the compound once the gate is secure.

"You keep all your homes fenced in like that? You're going to run out of chain link fast," Ellsberg points out.

"This was our original residence. I put up most of the fence, and since this place was up high on a hill it was a good place to start branching out to create this colony. Consider it my headquarters or executive offices." He leaves out that down the hill outside the fence is a growing collection of cargo trailers.

A young boy races from the house to greet the truck. Excited, Dartagnan babbles about too many cattle and the lack of grass land to feed them.

He slides from the backseat. "Dartagnan, settle. Sunday we'll expand the camp and you'll refigure the grass needed." He hands the young man a leather pouch. Excited, the kid unzips it. "Dartagnan, this is Major Ellsberg. He builds on a larger scale than your model."

"It's the wrong color. He holds up a yellow vial of model paint."

"All they had. Make it work."

Agitated, Dartagnan demands, "It's the wrong color."

"I know. Deal."

Dartagnan pouts.

"Calculate feeding the six new additions."

"Six. You said there would be two new."

"Things change. We have to learn to accept change."

"Takes care of some of the extra cattle. Lots to recalculate, but you need to expand more into grassland. More acres," Dartagnan insists.

"I'll make a run for more food."

"Find the correct yellow. Can't mix this. Wrong color. Calculate the new people. Wrong."

"I know, Dar, go finish your model."

Dartagnan races back to the house. The major waits until the truck travels again. "Boy's not firing on all thrusters," he observes. "What's wrong with him?"

"Asperger's, I think. It wasn't a well-known syndrome when I studied. I found him cooking in a camper. Mom was dead and he kept scrambling eggs for her. Must have been fifty uneaten plates. He's able to prepare great eggs. She never taught him how to cook anything else."

"You said everyone works, you make an exception for this kid?" Ellsberg asks, wondering now what they would have done if one of the handless girls survived. Wanikiya laughs a little as he pulls out from the farmhouse driveway.

"He works. He calculates the number of supplies we must have to sustain our community at its current population and what's necessary to retrieve for the camp when I go on runs. If he says five cans of peaches then you better fucking find five cans. It drives him crazy when I tell him I need a new member and I bring back more people than I said. We make it work, but his numbers are never wrong. Tomorrow, Wanikiya, we'd better figure out where to expand the fence to include more grazing land. It may be springtime, but we have to prepare for next winter."

"A lot of these older farms have the equipment to can homegrown vegetables. We should set aside a room in the community building to be a cannery. It would be a good job for some of the non-skilled weaker people you bring in." Wanikiya doesn't specify, but certainly teenagers like Emily who are unable to lift a hay bales will pickle cucumbers.

The truck jerks to a stop along a now single fence row. Wanikiya slams the gear shift into park. He opens the door. A solo biter mills around the wire. "I'll get it. You rest." Wanikiya draws a pistol.

"Not many make it along this fence line." Boom. The .45 shatters the undead.

"We've a special outside patrol scouring this fence line, freeing up the guards to patrol the other fences."

Wanikiya slides back inside. "That's the first one on this fence line in a week."

"Those boys do a good job."

The truck speeds between trees and the fence until reaching a rocky outcropping. Cargo crates butt against the edge of the rock wall, stacking like giant bricks of a castle.

"What's your brilliant plan here?" Ellsberg asks.

"We filled those containers with rock and eventually would like to stack enough that no biters or people get through without climbing over."

"Works better than chain link. It would take more than bolt cutters to get through."

"Save on guards and patrols, which would free up more people to expand the compound."

"Why not just bring in more people? You know there are thousands at Fort Wood."

"We won't stretch our supplies," he gives the simple answer. The truck follows the rock wall.

"Building a cargo container castle wall is not why I requested your help. We found giant dump trucks and some excavating equipment. Someone was digging in the limestone."

"Making a cave," Wanikiya adds.

"You want to continue?" Ellsberg asks.

"If we find enough qualified men to dig, we use the excavated rock to build up the outer walls and use the cave as a fallback shelter in case we're ever overrun. Maybe even a tornado bunker."

"You'd be trapped," Ellsberg says.

"At that point it's all about over but the crying. It would be our Helm's Deep."

Ellsberg nods in agreement. "A backup plan would give your people a secure feeling."

"Everyone already carries a gun. Makes me feel secure."

"I'm sure a lot more people have died in countries where there are no gun owners."

"Switzerland should be faring well," Wanikiya chimes in.

"Do you know absolutely?"

"No, but all adult men are required to own a rifle in Switzerland after mandatory conscription in the military."

"You took my gun," Major Ellsberg points out.

"Once my man-at-arms, Simon, certifies you, he'll issue you a gun. Camp law, everyone once trained is armed."

"Dartagnan wasn't."

"I said once cleared. He can't pass the test. He locks the gate in an emergency."

"Even little Olivia?" Ellsberg asks.

"Everyone. You're expected to defend this camp against all biters and others. You saw what was going on at the military base. I'll have none of that here. We meet every Sunday for a camp-wide meal. We discuss any problems and discuss new rules, and if they are effective, they become the law of the camp. The gun issue is law one. Once properly trained all citizens will carry."

"Other rules I need to know?"

"Everyone works. If you're not beneficial to the community, you don't eat."

"What would you have done with those poor handless girls?"

"I didn't have to cross that bridge. I haven't seen any handicapped people since the first month. Most people confined to a wheelchair or missing a leg didn't survive the initial outbreak. Dartagnan's the only special needs person I've encountered."

"There were a few in the refugee camp. The colonel had them evacuated," Ellsberg remarks.

Emily's savior knows the Fort will collapse soon. If the colonel had a place to evacuate people, he'd send his daughter there instead of preparing her to go with him. It doesn't take his elevated IQ to figure out where the infirmed were sent off base.

"How many people reside here?"

"About a hundred and fifty. There are bunk houses in the cantina where we have Sunday meal, and Dartagnan will assign you a home when a house becomes available."

"There are no single family dwellings anymore. If it has a bedroom, someone lives there," Wanikiya points out.

"We keep the big fields for cattle and crops. But we expand the west fence and the next expansion will take over several buildings. Moving the congregated people into homes was priority; next expansion will be more grazing land. I'll explain more when we reach there. The dam is the one area where I guess you could say you need security clearance." He points down the road they drive past. "We lose the power and we lose everything."

Ellsberg realizes how this Utopia functions. "So most everyone you've brought in here's skilled labor."

"Many of the fence guards are just people who survived and are great shots, but most people are here because they have a purpose. We're going to develop an apprenticeship for some so we don't lose our electricians, welders, and medical personnel, but rules for education have yet to be established."

"You really think that's necessary?"

"I don't see a rash of technical school graduates next semester. No matter what we do from now on life won't return to the way it was before. Too many have died."

"The military's working on restoring order," Ellsberg assures them.

"If anything, we'll return to a colonial lifestyle, only the Indians are relentless walking corpses. We'll salvage what we can, maybe even keep the electricity on, but trips to the moon are out. Advanced medicine, premature birth survival increases, and airplanes—all gone. Hell, bullets will soon become the best form of currency."

"Don't you have re-loaders?"

"For now. We've the ability to make some rounds, but eventually we'll need a lead mine. We should be rationing bullets, but I tell you, when attacked by the biters, I don't quibble. Shoot and shoot some more. I hope as we run low on shells we run low on undead. Unfortunately, they do reproduce. Eventually we'll all be walking undead or we will be able to drive back their numbers."

"We should head back to the community center," Wanikiya suggests.

"The government has fallen. People have to accept that, but when they cling to what they had before, it's a mistake. It causes death. I discovered an overturned armored car with people fighting over the bills inside. Killing each other for paper money that won't buy squat anymore."

"What did you do?"

"After they all killed each other I took two bags of coins and brought them to the weapons smith. He melts down the silver for ammo. If I could've carried more, I would have. Coins have value only in how many shells they make."

"People will want your electricity."

"The power plant's our life blood. It allows us to have amenities and keep surviving. We will eventually have to return to some pre-electric methods, but for now welding and other major food storage is preferable to housing goat's milk in a springhouse. We also have a small clinic and dentist office, all of which are much better visited with electricity. I don't know how they drilled a cavity before electricity and I don't want to experience it."

Wanikiya laughs. "Even in the apocalypse you try and avoid white people problems."

"Keep us away from the dam security. I haven't explored north much. I know the area south pretty well helping to quicken my travels. Along the river we've built up the fence to keep biters from washing ashore. We have to have a crew clean the fence line for river debris. We do try and clean up any corpses from the river. Keep contamination at a minimum. I really want your thoughts on those fences, but it's better to inspect them tomorrow."

"You've taken in a lot of woodland," Ellsberg notes.

"National forest area gives us some deer. No hunting for now. We want to let the population grow a bit and then we'll have a hunting season. Adding to our food supply."

"Those kinds of variables must drive Dartagnan crazy."

"It's good for him. He struggles with disorder, but in the end decoding it all calms his mind. He'll figure out how many deer we hunt and I trust his numbers."

Wanikiya explains, "We have several farms where we grow corn and soybeans and many small vegetable gardens. The other farms are cattle beef and dairy. We have some goats and keep horses to ride. Hogs are few, but finding more is our next task, along with more chickens. No one in this colony will go to bed hungry."

"As long as they work," Ellsberg ponders. "You haven't said what happens to someone who doesn't."

"Like a chicken that stops laying eggs, they will be dinner," Wanikiya assures.

"We haven't set up a social security plan, but I know we won't have welfare within these gates. I'll put a one-legged man in a tower. As long as he can shoot he's doing his part. Others weed the gardens or tend the cattle. Since I've a large number of guards, we are short on manual labor. But we are also short on room."

"It seems you've plenty of room to expand."

"As a student of history I was never a fan of the blitzkrieg strategy. We keep our expanding a slow process. We don't bite off more than we can handle. If we move too fast, complications arise. With this new gathering of land we'll get more cattle, be able to feed them and have room for more residence. I'll recruit more people."

"You hand select everyone?"

"I pick and choose most of those who have made it inside. I try to avoid the most unsavory of characters. And we've strict punishments for law breakers."

"Wanikiya, you weren't expectantly talkative to the major." He lies down on the examination table in the classroom converted into a hospital.

"I didn't want to discuss it in front of him, but while you were gone a group of refugees wanted to enter the camp."

"Did you give them separate jobs from each other?"

"They refused to turn over one of their number who had a bite."

"Turning them away was the right thing to do," he assures his second in command.

"They drew on us, leaving us no choice but to kill them. They wounded two guards."

Emily's savior rises up. Wanikiya pushes him back down, "Minor wounds, nothing critical." The doctor pulls open the curtain. He hangs an x-ray of a human chest on the light board. "You need to rest. Nothing's broken, but you need to lie down and give those deep tissue bruises time to heal."

"Doc, you're making me wish I hadn't liberated a portable x-ray machine. What day is it?" he asks.

"Friday," Wanikiya answers.

"I'll sleep tomorrow. Sunday, are we ready to expand the camp?"

"And we have our town hall meeting."

"I'll rest tomorrow, relax on Sunday, and Monday I got to head back out."

"I've no concept of anything outside the fence more important than you letting those bruises heal."

"Actually, doc, there is. I've brokered a deal for a convoy of supplies Dartagnan came up with."

"We got more cattle than needed and all those items from the distribution center."

"We've got that doctor/patient thing going, doc?"

"It goes beyond any law you decide to make."

"The military base will collapse soon. There will be no more government food shipment."

"Dear god. What will happen to all those people?"

"I don't want to be a heartless bastard, but consider what will keep our group alive. The military overstretched its resources and now they'll have to abandon thousands."

The whole of Acheron's citizens enjoy Sunday brunch together in the multipurpose room of the school. Emily's savior and Wanikiya sit at a head table near the stage.

"It's like a big family," Wanikiya muses as he stirs his eggs into his ketchup.

"You were a gourmet cook, and you put ketchup on your eggs." He shakes his head in disgust. "What a way to ruin perfectly good eggs."

"You were just shot, at close range, in a world populated with walking corpses, and you find it acceptable to criticize the way in which I eat my eggs?"

"The human race may be on the way out, but there's no reason to go out in such an uncivilized manner."

"Ketchup is a perfectly accepted condiment. Invented by a white man."

"Actually, it was a Chinese dude." He snatches the bottle from the table. "Who puts it on a breakfast food? I mean, how bad were the eggs the first person was eating they had to dump tons of processed tomatoes on it?"

"I prepare the food. You gather the supplies. I'll eat what I cook the way I feel it tastes best."

"First order of business today will be to ban the use of ketchup at the breakfast table."

"Then we will have to have eggs for dinner from now on." Wanikiya smiles.

He laughs, clapping Wanikiya on the shoulder as he rises. He staggers toward the podium, over exaggerating his limp slightly, a day of rest in bed stiffened his leg. Gazing at all the faces, Emily's smile catches his attention. He knows her look. He's witnessed it on a hundred teen girls before, just never for him. The two boys next to her take no notice of the way she looks at him. They are too busy trying to impress her for themselves. Men rarely understand a woman's desires, boys even less so.

Good for her. He's glad. Interacting with people her own age will make it easier for her to adjust to this new life. He glances toward lots of other faces. He knows them all even if their names leave him. He saved these people, and with their assistance they'll all continue to survive.

He taps the podium to draw their attention to him. "I'm glad our family enjoys Sunday brunch together. I know I've missed a few being on the road. I don't mind because all of you make this place safe for me to come home to." They cheer. "Now I'm back. Before we expand the fence line so we can start moving some of you into houses, we need to first welcome the new citizens to our community." The crowd claps. "I don't have much of an agenda today. So far the rules we've established are keeping us safe. We've plenty of food stores this week. So I open the floor to any discussion."

Several people stand and wait to be recognized. He knows what a few of them want to deliberate.

"Hadley, the gun issue's no longer open for debate. In order to survive the apocalypse, many of the rules and privileges of our old lives we can't hold onto."

"You've nine-year-olds packing heat."

"The dangers we face require gun-toting children. I know it's scary, but Simon won't certify anyone to carry who can't use the weapon responsibly. It saddens me, but childhood has been suspended for everyone to live. I suggest this, you accept everyone should carry, and after we are one hundred percent sure biters won't get inside our fence, we could look at raising the mandatory carry age. Especially when we start up schools again."

"You don't think the undead will ever stop," Hadley steams.

"From what I've seen outside our walls, it's not going away overnight. I won't lie to you. I think it will be years..." *maybe decades.*

"I just want our children to still be able to be children." She returns to her seat.

Many in the crowd murmur in agreement, but it's not a sticking point with too many. Even if they don't like it, these people realize the value of everyone being armed. Besides, since everyone must be trained it prevents some scared parent from just giving a kid a gun out of fear.

"Imagine in fifty years your grandchildren studying what we built here. We're in a transition society, much like the founding fathers of America were when they scrapped the Articles of Confederation and began building the American way of life. We face different challenges but we'll persevere just as they did."

He points at a man whose name he doesn't remember.

"We want to know what happened to Kyle."

"Evidence confirmed he was guilty of rape. Rape won't be tolerated. He was disciplined and banished. Only two choices for crimes in the community—death or banishment. I won't waste resources to keep a convicted criminal in a cage."

"Banishment is death." This murmur overcomes the entire assembly.

"Hawthorne wrote that all starting communities need to build two things: a cemetery and a jail. We still have need of a crematorium, but those of you who muck stalls, hoe corn, build the fence or stand guard in the rain, do you want to spend your hours toiling while a criminal sits in a dry, warm cell having three hot meals delivered to them?" The murmur shifts and the logic of what he said appeases the majority. He understands words win battles better than swords.

"Again, when we're secure, and don't need as many guards on the fence, we'll examine lesser penalty for minor crimes, but I won't debate rape." The cafeteria remains quiet. He nods at a standing woman, Annabelle.

"We understand you ordered the reverend not to marry us."

"I did." He waits for the shock of this murmur to spread across the cafeteria. "I need everyone to ask themselves. Why are we here? Is what we're doing here just surviving? Or is what we're doing preserving the human race? We aren't yet, but we could become one of the last strongholds of people left. Don't think I'm being dramatic. Refugee camps have fallen. The only successful groups out there surviving are road gangs, and they care nothing about families."

"We should be allowed to marry to preserve families," Annabelle says.

"This next part some of you aren't going to like. What we decide here will create the future for our children, and right now one hundred and fifty people won't genetically repopulate the planet."

"So you're saying we'll have to have children by several dads."

Laughter rumbles though the assembly. A lot of women did by choice before the end.

"At our current numbers, at least five children by five different fathers."

He almost doesn't recover the crowd. "Before everyone gets excited, we're a long way from crossing the baby bridge. We keep expanding and growing enough food we'll get more people. Realistically, and if possible, offspring aren't the best idea right now. If it happens, it happens, but protecting helpless babies...we're going to need more people first."

"Why can't we marry?"

"Because we will have to cross the 'having children' bridge eventually, so no marriages for a while until we do." He holds back his actual feelings and the most logical reason. People died because they couldn't shoot their bitten spouse.

A woman he remembers saving, but not her name, stands near the back. "What about opening a church?"

*Absolutely not!* He wants to scream, but not at the expense of sending this congregation into frenzy. "Most of you in the room belong to a Christian denomination, but we don't have the resources to operate fifteen churches. For now, I suggest you take up prayers in the privacy of your home." *Where they fucking belong.* "When we reach a point where we are stable in our community we'll open one of the churches and set off times for worship of denominations. I'd rather use building space for beds. There are a lot of people who have earned the right to not have to sleep in the community center. Your prayers don't need a building to be heard."

Another person rises. "You don't feel we are secure?"

"We have a long way to go before we move our resources away from so many guards being on duty. So as comfortable as I sleep at night in my bed, overall we've more work to do. Anyone else feel different?"

This soft murmur quells quickly.

"I remind you, supply requisitions need to go to Wanikiya. We'll prioritize them. If you need something we see as trivial, but isn't, make sure you explain what it's for. We've become good at adapting and many items have multiple uses. I do ask that requests remain reasonable. Jimmy, I'm not commandeering you a Lamborghini, and if I do, like I'm not going to keep it for myself."

The crowd laughs.

"Did you get hurt bad?" Emily asks her hobbling savior.

"Actually, it's stiff from sleeping so much. A rolling stone gathers no moss."

"What does that mean?"

"You need to read some of those books you're in charge of."

"Aren't there more important jobs than shelving books?"

"I heard you did real well at building the fence."

"Not funny."

"No. No, because these people need to feel some part of what used to be normal in their lives. I remember getting our first VCR, and since then renting movies became the normal thing to do. Throw a party, rent a movie, give movies as Christmas gifts. Miss a season of your favorite show—watch it whenever you want on tape. You're in charge of giving back some normal."

"Sounds good. But passing out books while others are shot at by raiders doesn't compare. I want to know that I'm useful," Emily says.

"Practice shooting and we'll assign you to guard duty."

He jumps backward onto the tailgate of a truck. Dartagnan lays out a legal pad of paper and five tape measures of various lengths."

"No measuring until the buildings are completely safe."

Dartagnan nods. A group of men cut the fence from the post, securing it to an inner fence along the dog run. They peel it back, allowing the majority of the camp's citizens to shuffle through.

Emily's savior climbs into the truck bed to address his group.

He announces to the camp crowd, "For those of you who are new, we've crews building a fence around the next section of land we want to appropriate. Then we open up a hole in the old fence as we just did. Before we take it down, we've got to make sure no biters are waiting for us. Everyone will line the inside of this fence. Spread out. No more than arm's length apart and we'll step forward kicking over every blade of grass to make sure no undead reside in our territory until we reach the new fence at the end."

"What happens when we run into a building?" someone calls out.

"The line halts at any structure and the commando squad," five men in somewhat mismatched full tactical gear uniforms march forward, "will clear the structure. No one else enters a building until they clear it. Some biters will just sit in a corner and wait. These men will clear them. Then the line moves on. We've got to be sure no biters are inside the fence." He must make sure everyone understands the importance of missing an undead. "Once clear, the homes will be emptied of everything. All supplies will be inventoried."

The crowd stirs at what they hope is his next proclamation.

"Tomorrow, these homes will be assigned based mostly on seniority. Beds and a lot of the furniture will be replaced in the homes. I remind you we assign based on space. If there's a bedroom, someone will get it."

Many stuck in the community center's makeshift sleeping quarters raise a cheer. Even those who won't get their own room realize fewer numbers in the center will make life better and give them longer in the showers."

"We need grazing land for the cattle. I encourage everyone to plant a garden. The more food we grow the better, but if you do tend a garden, request some fencing to keep the cattle out...and a shovel."

"Why a shovel?" someone asks.

"Every home should be issued shovels if cattle are going to roam free." He turns to Wanikiya. "We should drag in one of those dumpsters they rent out for moving. So we compost." He addresses the crowd, "If you thought your old neighbors who didn't curb their dogs were a nuisance, wait until you have cows fertilizing the lawn." That sends a laugh among them.

"Let's get this section cleared," Wanikiya howls.

The crowd disperses, assuming the line along the fence.

He drops back to the tailgate.

"Shouldn't I be in the line?" Emily asks. Some already think she's extended favoritism. She wants to prove she is like everyone else.

"I may need a runner, and I always keep someone to help watch Dartagnan if I have to check on something along the line."

Emily nods. "Once this area opens, what happens next?"

"We need more grassland, but we'll also expand into some more homes. Everyone has earned their own room. The fence team will get this inside fence down and then get a day off. Working outside the fence, they've earned it."

"Why didn't they fence in a few more houses?"

He shakes his head. "This needs to remain a slow process. Keep everyone safe. The guards protecting the construction workers have picked off more biters in the past week than in the last month. There seems to be a growing number of undead."

She notes troubled lines across his face and the white hairs peppering his sprouting beard. "That bothers you?"

"This part of the state wasn't heavily populated before. We don't keep a formal count of the undead. Those numbers would panic people, but we've eliminated more biters than there used to be people in this area."

"Someone at the military base said some of the soldiers would discuss how these things were drawn to where people were. Most figure it's the noise the living make, but what if something else attracts them?"

"Keep that theory to yourself," he orders. "But it may not be wrong."

"She's a smart one for being young," Wanikiya says.

A tarp covers the ground. People assigned to house cleaning crews carry out boxes of people's once prized possessions. Other people separate the items putting any food in one truck.

"It's redundant to move everything out to the canteen only to bring a lot of it back," Dartagnan comments as he sketches the house on the legal pad.

"Completely redundant, but we've reached a state of fairness. Food will be added to the supplies. Guns to the armory. Furniture will be reassigned based on need. This family had a baby. The crib will be given to a woman who needs it. If it stays in the house no one may remember it's there."

"You don't think someone would offer it if it's needed?"

"No. People hoard just to have something after so many have lost so much."

Emily chews her bottom lip. "I guess...makes sense."

The five men in tactical battle armor drag a dead biter from a house and toss it into a truck containing two other corpses.

"Finally, the last house." The tall one removes his helmet marching toward a white cargo van with the words 'tactical unit' spray painted on the side.

"Looks like everyone earned their meals today." He hobbles around to the cab of the truck.

"You're priority?" Emily wonders.

"There's no entitlement any longer. You work, you eat. You need something, you earn it. No one has more than they need to survive. No extras. No handouts."

"You didn't approve of the refugee camps," Emily realizes.

"The military should've handed out guns and sent every last person to take back their homes. Now when the base falls, we'll end up with a few renegades and more biters to deal with." He has to use his hands to pull his left leg into the truck cab. "They should've been training those people to defend themselves instead of coddling them."

"Were you always this rough before the world was destroyed?" She slams the passenger door.

He laughs. "That person died."

"I don't want the person I was to be gone."

"You're fifteen; you never developed into a person."

"You act like you know so much about teenagers. No kid in their right mind would hang out with you." Emily notes the pained look on his face and stops before she twists the proverbial knife she just thrust at him.

"The people who we keep encountering have lasted the last nine months because they are quite psychotic. It's the only way to survive in this new world."

"I didn't mean it that way. If you are crazy, I'm glad, because you saved me."

"People will just have to accept the new rules it takes to rebuild a life."

One of the men cleaning out the house carries out four DVD players.

"One reason I go on the supply runs alone. I won't have altercations over a useless item." He points to the DVD players.

"What if I brought some family heirloom with me?"

"I don't want to take away Grandma's china from you, but if you're carrying that garbage when you're fleeing the corpses, then you've proven my point in this redundant exercise. Those people had four DVD players. Who needs four DVD players?"

"You're asking a lot of people to change a mindset they think they were born with."

"Tell that to the biters."

He hobbles from the truck to his farmhouse. Dartagnan hops from the truck bed and races through the door, notebook in hand. Emily follows.

"You're going to have a long walk back to the community building."

"You wouldn't drive me?"

"Gas's a luxury."

"I'd more to talk to you about. And you've an empty bedroom. I could just stay here and you can take me to work in the morning."

"You just have it all figured out." He climbs the steps of the porch. "I doubt we've much to eat. I don't keep much food, and what's in the kitchen is Dartagnan's and I don't want to deal with his tantrum when a tin of Spam turns up empty."

"I understand."

He limps from the shower wrapping a towel around his waist.

"The water's so much hotter here."

Emily's unexpected voice sends his hand to reach for a gun currently not on his hip.

"We don't have to share the water with fifty other people, and you're not invited into my bedroom. I'm not dressed. It's a good way to get shot," he says.

"I saw you naked at the gate." Emily rubs the top of her right foot with the bottom of her left, failing to pretend she's not nervous standing before his bed.

"As far as I'm concerned that's different. I don't like the idea of you being in my bedroom alone."

"Do they hurt?" Emily points at the three bruises on his chest.

"Maybe a little more than I'll admit."

She takes a step toward him slipping the bathrobe loose on her shoulders. His chest tightens against the bruises. His blood pressure elevates, thumping in his neck. Her alabaster skin wrinkles of goose flesh from the impeding offer she's about to make. His breath quickens. He touches the purple marks.

"Too painful to..."

She lets the robe fall to the floor. Her supple soft virgin skin heaves with each breath. She swallows with nervous anticipation. She wants him. She knows what to expect. She knows what is supposed to happen, only she doesn't really know. No amount of slumber party gossip or even letting a boy feel her up through her shirt after she won harvest queen is like this moment.

He's a man.

Strong.

Experienced.

So strong.

Certainly he's made love to women before. She's barely kissed a boy, three, in fact, and one girl, Suzie Baker. It was a stupid truth or dare bet. Suzie used too much tongue.

Three quick breaths. Her chest heaves with her excitement, bouncing her breasts with each breath. She relishes his eyes never leaving her body. She never thought she would have it in her to just stand nude before a man. She fights the urge to run from the room and hide her body under a blanket. She wishes her B-cups were bigger. She knows he likes women with curves.

Funny.

She doesn't know. He barely glances at any of the women in the camp as far as she's noticed. He reaches out with his left arm. She touches it. Big, powerful, not pretty, but rock hard muscle. He grips her neck and the back of most of her head with his hand. He's got huge controlling hands. His rough touch dominates her and yet is so gentle. She feels her nipples constrict. They harden. No fantasy about some dreamy boy band member ever made them so firm. No fantasy has ever made her feel she has peed herself. Oh, god, she hopes her nervousness has not made her pee.

No. She knows girls get wet. She just didn't know this much. He pulls her closer cocking his head and pressing his lips on hers. It's forceful and yet not too rough. She closes her eyes. More wetness soaks her upper thighs. She opens her mouth and he pulls away, biting her bottom lip. Not a hard bite, a tease. He releases her and kisses her again. She opens her mouth inviting his tongue inside, but he just massages her lips with his. Impatient she rams her tongue into his mouth. He clamps down on it with his teeth just enough preventing her pulling back and yet not hurt.

He massages her trapped tongue. She flushes. Her eyes roll back into her skull. No boy kisses like this. To be with a man, she knows this is right. He uses his right arm to pull her lower body closer and twists her leg around his back. She wants to jerk away, embarrassed by her growing wetness against his leg.

He stops.

Now she knows she peed. No guy wants that.

"I can't do this." He keeps her close.

"What! Why...why not?" The last thing Emily wants is for him to stop.

"You're an amazing girl." He holds her at arm's length. "You're too young."

"I'm not."

"You're fifteen, a young fifteen." He shifts his eyes from admiring her bosom. "I'm a bastard, but not that kind of bastard."

"I want this. I want you. I want my first time to be with a man." Tears run from her eyes. She holds in the blubbering wail. Trying to convince him she's a woman would not be evident in near temper tantrum screams of protest. "Why don't you want me?"

Knowing full well he shouldn't, he continues to admire her soft breasts. The soft skin seems even more vibrant than any woman he's ever been with. It could be her young age or her desire or the length it's been since the last time he's held a woman. But it seems to be the softest, flawless most perfect skin. He rubs the back of his two fingers up and down her arm. "You need to be older."

"I may not get a chance to get older," Emily protests. "I may not get the chance to choose who gets to touch me. I don't want my first time to be a gang rape behind the pig barn. I want it to be my choice. To be special. To be where and when I say. I've met most of the women you've rescued and brought into our community. Not many of them haven't been assaulted or had the attempt made. Even if next week I am brutalized, at least I had this. I had a beautiful moment I asked for."

"You certainly behave older than just fifteen, but it doesn't feel right. I feel it isn't right."

"That's why I want it to be you. This will mean something to you, too. I won't be tail etched on your nightstand."

"It's not love." He speaks from experience.

Each breath makes her breasts rise. His eyes seem trained not to look away. "I will always love you for saving me, but no, this is not love, not like a husband and wife." She begins to shake. "I'll do whatever you ask, everyone behind this fence will. You saved us. You protect us. You keep us going. That's a love I can't explain. Grant me the right to choose who I give myself to."

"Behind this fence you will always have that right or I'll kill whoever touches you."

"I know, but you can't promise it won't happen, and strip me of my right to choose or I won't get bit. You can't promise in two years when I turn seventeen I'll still be pure, I'll still have a choice."

"It doesn't matter how attractive you are at this moment. It's just not appropriate." He scoops his towel up to cover his erection.

"You haven't taken your eyes off my tits. I'm old enough. Make me a woman. Make love to me."

"The offer's more than tempting." He leans in as if to kiss her. Their mouths hover close nearly touching but something avuncular in him won't bring his lips to hers.

He tosses his bag into the truck before swinging into the bed. Karen, geared for the road, leaps in next to him. He holds out his hand. She places the mini-rifle into his hand. He cocks the Winchester-style weapon. "A mare's-leg doesn't have much of a kick."

"It's for the dead, it's the .22 caliber version. Thirteen shots. Easy to control."

"Nice choice."

"I've a Beretta like yours." Karen grins.

"Keep your team safe. You must make it back over all else. The supplies are second."

"You're going to turn us loose on this run?"

"I work better alone, and I won't always be around to hold your hand."

"You sound like this high school teacher I had," she says.

"Sounds like a smart person. Where're the other two?"

Kalvin lays his rifle in the bed before climbing in. "Reporting, boss." The purple streaks in his hair have faded, but he still looks ready for a rave. Frank, still in his BDUs, hops in.

"You going to be able to forget your oath to help save people?"

"EMTs don't take such an oath." He pops the clip from his Glock to ensure it's loaded. "I never promised to do no harm."

He nods.

"Yeah, not a lot of call for emergency services inside the fence," Frank adds.

"You medics are adrenaline junkies anyway. Just keep your head out there."

"You three are young, fast, and good shots. You have skills to make a team. Medic, mechanic, and munificent."

"You forgot momentous, mollify and majestic."

"Malapropism," he says.

"What's that mean?" Karen asks.

"He's confusing words like 'motley' or 'morose.'"

"I only started mechanic training," Karen reminds them, "not a vocabulary lesson."

"No matter. Starting dead cars is one of life's new major skills."

"So what's your best pointer?"

"Trust no one. Even the most innocent child will shiv you for a stale crust of bread. I mean it."

They nod.

"The other thing I do is stash supplies over the countryside. I make myself my own waypoints. I have cars, guns, and food hidden in case I need them, and I don't head back to camp using the same trail. I know about seven ways to get back from a certain point. I don't want the wrong group to follow me back."

"What if we find survivors? Do we bring them back?"

"A tough call. We're not isolationists, but use judgment, and I'd stay away from large groups."

"But how do you know?"

"A lot of on-the-job training dealing with people before the world ended. You'll start to know people...and how they've changed. You want to bring people back who will help the colony."

The foursome marches on the blacktop, each with a hand on a weapon.

He quizzes his interns. "You've got a list of supplies the camp needs. Where do you start?"

"The mall or the superstore." Kalvin smirks.

"That's dumb," Karen scolds. "Malls are in cities with a lot of biters."

"Guns, food, ammo..."

"Have you ever even been to a mall?" Karen asks.

Kalvin continues his list, "Blankets, clothes, medicine."

"Let me tell you why it's the stupid choice. First, malls and superstores have multiple entrances, usually glass, tactically a poor choice, not to mention every fucking person thinks about running to the superstore to get a gun. Roads become congested. People fight each other over what, twenty or thirty guns, tops? People die, revive and now you have a few hundred undead."

"Hospitals?" he asks.

"More than likely a lot of undead and no supplies. People rushed there for help first," Karen adds.

Frank adds, "A lot of medical units were overrun as soon as people got bit."

"Could mean supplies are intact."

"It means a fuck-load of biters between you and *maybe* supplies."

"Now where should you go if you want a location with supplies and most likely little looting?" he asks.

"How do you know so much?" Kalvin asks.

"Life, experience, grew up before an app told me all the answers."

"You really harp on that app thing," Karen notes.

He rarely shares what he finds out on the road, but this group will learn soon enough. "I found this kid. A girl, about eleven or twelve, frozen this winter just staring into her iPhone."

"She could've been looking at her family pictures before the end."

"Of all the things to save, I understand photos, but she had nothing else to sustain her."

"Her supplies could have been stolen," Frank adds.

"Keep finding a million reasons to defend her keeping her phone. You're out here not just gathering supplies to keep yourself alive. There're one hundred and seventy-nine people back at Acheron depending on you." He mashes down barbed wire strands to make it easier to hop the fence.

"What are you doing?" Karen asks.

"That's one of those road historic markers." He points across the blacktop. "You each have a map, but you should never mark on it. If someone steals it," *or kills you and takes it,* he thinks, "you don't want anyone to find your stash." Kalvin snickers at the word 'stash.'

He ignores the kid. "So you have to come up with places to hide supplies and ways to remember where you did." He takes a folding shovel from his pack and a Tupperware container with a can of peaches sealed in it.

"You figure no one will care about those markers anymore."

"People don't have time to read about history when running from biters." Frank laughs.

He digs a hole. "So far people don't take the time to scavenge out in the open. Don't use homes to hide anything. I've seen homes where people have busted the walls."

"Why not just mark the road?"

"If I were to spray paint the road someone might figure out I hid something and look. Plus it's an old world marker no one cares about anymore." He twists the container into the dirt. Satisfied, he covers it.

"I said don't use homes, but I have a rifle hidden in a burnt out structure. It offers no shelter and no useful material. It's a gamble, but survivors have no reason to explore it."

"So even if they walk through it they won't mess with it."

"They shouldn't." He spreads the extra dirt around to make the freshly dug hole disappear. "Peaches are good to stash. The sugar water will keep you going if you get into trouble."

"How long before you turn south?" Frank asks.

"Many more miles. I've not traveled this far this way before."

"But there's a town."

"I don't head straight into towns. Towns mean biters, and worse, survivors."

"Both dangerous," Karen repeats.

"One more dangerous than the other," Kalvin adds.

"I find a lot of rural homes have canned goods. People who live far from the store tend to stock up. And not on the list, but note if you come across people who have home canned vegetables, take their supplies. We're going to make a cannery. If you find a town with a good number of useful supplies and you have no other pressing business then return to Acheron and organize the fence teams to recover it."

"Like you did with the distributing center?"

"I knew it was there, but I wouldn't risk all those people if it had been looted."

"We cut back the risk by going out alone." Prideful, Karen realizes her team's importance.

"We need more fence. So you run across a construction site, make sure you scout the road all the way back to camp to know if you have to clear it of anything. Abandoned cars aren't much, but if they have to remove a tree chainsaws are deafening."

"So much we used to take for granted."

"What I tell you seems so elementary, but..." he flares out his arms, "there's no racket, no cars, no lights. Makes what noise you do make echo even farther."

"Makes you not want to get out of bed," Frank adds.

"Sleep's important out here. You watch your fatigue level. Rest. Stay sharp. With three of you, plenty of safe sleep is possible."

"How far do you want us to go?"

"Your first trip out. I'd scout the edge of Paris. Find supplies you can stash and return to the camp. You're searching for fence building material. Look for signs of construction, maybe a lumber yard. But don't take unnecessary risks. Nothing on your list is life or death."

Frank folds his map and replaces it in a pouch on his pant leg. "Why haven't we explored the town surrounded by the lake?"

"Flooding," he answers without missing a beat. "On paper it looks good. Three sides surrounded by water, build a wall and be well protected. Biters can't swim, but some of the town's dozen or so homes are flooded. Most importantly, it was abandoned long before the apocalypse. Where you're heading had about twelve hundred people in it. The next biggest town had twelve thousand. So a lot of biters could be around."

"Why, didn't you explore this way?"

"No, just as many biters south and east of St. Louis with a million population."

"There's not a million people in St. Louis," Frank protests.

"You forget all the metro areas."

"I would hope a lot more people survived."

"I was telling you before where to hunt for supplies." He gestures at the building across the small valley. "I'm not sure what grade level it is, but schools are a great bet, and most people won't think they have anything worth looting. Nobody wants an algebra book."

"That's crazy," Karen says.

"Is it?" He glances through his binoculars. "The nurse's office is full of meds. All prescription and clearly labeled, plus a lot of First Aid boxes and at least an AED. Athletic offices have more First Aid and blankets. Law says they are to have a trauma bag. I've seen some of them rival what's on an ambulance."

Frank wonders how this man knows so much, forging the question of what he used to do before the apocalypse. Frank knows his leader has refused to tell anyone in the camp. Besides, to learn he was some lowly copy repairman would destroy the constructed image of his leader.

He spots a biter shambling through a field. A second uniformed biter patrolling the school parking lot. "If you take weapons and are unsure of their usability, don't fire them. Bring them to Simon. Even if they've rusted or are damaged, sometimes the internal parts are salvageable." He hands the binoculars to Karen. "That was a cop. His utility belt remains around his waist. Good stuff if the rotten flesh hasn't corroded it."

"I should be sick." Karen squints.

He continues with his supply lecture. "Food in the cafeteria, a lot of it's canned. Some schools have emergency supplies in case of a long-term lockdown. Vending machines with healthy snacks. Shop class has construction tools, maybe even acetylene torches, unused lumber. Home economics, sewing, cooking pots, and more food. Teachers also stash food and other goodies in their desks; same with kids in their lockers. It might be better than a superstore and less picked over."

"No guns," Kalvin observes.

"It's a public school, you might find a couple. Law or not, it's a rural school and some rednecks have them in their trucks. If the school has a resource officer there could be a patrol car or a lock box with some guns. The principal may have confiscated knives, cigarettes, a shitload of lighters."

"None of us smoke."

"Campfire, girl."

"I meant the cigs."

"I keep a pack," he explains. "A lot of people do. Trade them or give them to someone to help build trust, or see if you can trust them. People relax when they smoke. It reveals their intentions without them knowing."

Frank really has to know what this man did before the world ended.

"This's where I leave you. You check out the school and then continue on with your scout. I've an appointment at the military base."

Parked before a quaint farmhouse, the green camo military truck seems out of place. He knows the colonel put a stop to all patrols from his base. He could have stumbled over another military group from the Air Force base in the north. He doubts they would send just one truck. He figures some raiders took possession of this vehicle from a National Guard post. He confirms his suspicion when a man walks from the house to take a leak.

These people must be searching for supplies just like him. The truck provides near tank-like protection and would take a lot of biters to overrun it. It could even be a battering ram if necessary. Supply runs last for days, but the noise factor prevents it from being a useful tactic for scrounging in populated areas. He appreciates the advantage of being able to avoid undead.

He would never begrudge any well-meaning survivors a chance to exist, but they offer a new danger to his camp. If someone in their search team knows the area they may avoid the National Forest area. There aren't a lot of places to raid. Then again, they may be looking for more isolated homes to pillage. Plus they just acquired a cluster of homes.

At this distance, his binoculars give no clue as to what kind of people these are or even if they're part of a larger group. He has too many questions about them to just travel on and forget. He could circumvent the entire farm. They'd never know he watched them. Losing the people and supplies the colonel had prepared would be detrimental to his own group. It will be the last help anyone gets from Fort Leonard Wood. No longer will he be able to jet to the camp and acquire a skilled tradesman from the documented list of camp residents.

To keep his camp safe he has never refused entry to anyone, but he's avoided asking some survivors to return with him. His basis for admission is whether they would prevent or help him take hot showers. The dam engineer who keeps the power on declined to terminate the search for his family. Emily's savior found them. Once secure behind the fence, the daughter needed her braces removed. He found a dentist. Someone had to guard the dentist. Someone had to feed the guards. Someone had to train the guards. Everyone has a job and if they do their job they get to eat and he gets to take hot showers.

Too bad the government didn't operate on such principles. There may come a time when the government will get its shit together and restore some kind of order to the country. Having Travis's daughter would be to the camp's advantage.

Moving on would be advantageous to him keeping his hot showers, but if these people are a raider scouting party, knowing could save him. He could just kill them. Take their supplies removing any doubt in their motives.

*I'm a bastard, but not that kind of bastard.* The words he spoke to Emily echo in his ears. No, he hasn't succumbed to being a heartless bastard. He has no reason to kill and loot these people. Staying in the field and the trees growing along the fence row actually gives him a few hours if the overland terrain stays like this.

He pockets his binoculars and takes a sip from his canteen as he marches away from the house. A woman's screams scratch his ears. *Why can't one day just go by where things work out? Why don't the idiots of the universe just stay home one day?*

Through the binoculars he spots a woman being dragged from the house, bound at the hands in nothing but a poor fitting night shirt. The man who pissed beats a steel post into the ground with a hammer. The echoing ping provides noise cover for him to sneak closer without worrying about crunching twigs.

They tie her to the pole. Two more men stack split wood around as if building a bonfire. Four.

Hell, four's a slow day. The twinge of pain strikes him as his next breath presses his chest wall against his body armor vest and the new bullet proof plates he replaced. Three times his body reminds him with the next surge of pain. Don't get involved. The bruises remind him. Just sneak away. She could have tried to kill them for their food. Not everyone being executed is innocent.

He tells his wounds to shut up and executions for crimes has never been an issue he's opposed, but even child rapists need a quick bullet to the head. No one, no matter what they've done, should be burnt at the stake.

How should he approach this? Just march right in there and offer his services as executioner. Provided of course she committed a real crime. *See, there you go, going to get us shot again.* Can a lung really take on conscious thought?

*What if they shoot and don't kill you, but miss the vest. An arm wound would force you back to the colony. What used to be a few hours' drive remains a few days walk and you don't know how many days the colonel has before Fort Wood closes.*

The four men gather around the woman. One begins reading from a book. Another at his direction tears off her shirt. He slips off his belt and under the direction of the reader lacerates the girl's back with the stroke of the leather.

She howls.

Enough arguing. He marches toward the farmhouse.

# CHAPTER TWENTY-SIX

A TERRIFIED SCREAM jolts Danziger from his tree. If not for the belt securing him to a branch, he would have fallen to the ground. Not really a death fall but an ankle twisting one for sure. He had slept until the middle of the night. A few corpses have gathered around the fenced in livestock feeding pens surrounding the barn. They haven't figured out how to climb. Though Danziger did see one climb a chain link fence once, it was a newly dead and he'd had little muscle deterioration. These DKs look dead, long dead, even in the moonlight.

The detective in him ponders at how slowly these dead move. *I thought maybe the freshly converted could still move with speed, but there's no rhyme or reason to their movements.* The one who took out his partner moved so fast. The only one he ever saw move faster than living people. This unpredictable nature makes them more dangerous. If they ever move past the swarm mentality, they will be unstoppable.

Danziger leaps the stock pen fence and crouches low. Another piercing scream cuts through the night. Enticing more undead. Somehow he knows the pain the girl suffers lacks Levin's normal ritual. It seems to be an attractor. Either for him or the gimps. It must be to draw DKs. This maniac has no idea Danziger even found out who he was or that he's still chasing him.

He bolts through the opening of the feedlot into the barn. The quick tactic of rolling in and rising to a half crouch with gun drawn should have been effective, but Levin foresaw this approach. Danziger's ankle brings a tripwire taut, releasing a spring loaded two-by-four trap. Had he walked straight into the barn his stomach would be bruised. Instead his nose breaks open, not broken, but certainly smashed and bleeding.

Danziger feels the warm sun on his face as he rouses. Before he basks in the moment and recovers his bearings, he feels his full weight on his wrists. The pain jolts him into full awareness. He fumbles to get his footing and pushes up with his toes to take the weight and pain off his arms. A bear trap with some of the teeth removed clamps over his wrists. A swing set chain secured with a padlock keeps it in place.

"I had to improvise. I couldn't bring my entire workbench." The short muscularly built man spreads out his implements of torture on a makeshift table of hay bales covered in plastic.

Danziger darts his eyes around the loft. He doesn't dare move or the rig may slice his wrists. The teenage girl strapped to a particle board with belts has an S&M mouth ball gag between her teeth. Jammed into her left foot is a mortician's tool used to drain the body fluids of the dead. Jabbing it into her must have sent her into agony.

Levin takes shears from his tool selection, cutting off her pants. "I'm so nervous. I've never performed for an audience before."

"I'm going to kill you, Levin." Calling him by name causes pause, but Levin won't let anything distract him.

"Why must you insist on such idle threats? You'll not escape. If you pull on the teeth the bear trap will slit your wrists. It's not along the wrists, which is a quicker death, but you will cut deep enough to bleed out, and if you pull free at least one of your hands will be completely severed and there are no hospitals to sew it back on." He pronounced it like 'sue.' "And it doesn't matter...there are no more forensic scientists either. I think it will be much more enjoyable to work without worrying about the blood splatter." At this, the girl summons her last bit of strength, struggling to jerk free. "You ever watch *Dexter*? Now that man had talent. But you know I was always bothered by the sheer number of plastic rolls he used for each murder. Did he have stock in the plastic wrap company? Did he put it on his credit cards? He used a bulky amount of plastic." He cuts the material of her shirt.

"I never had time for Hollywood's version of cop life."

"No, detective, I'm sure you didn't. After all, had you spent a night at home watching television with your daughter she might not have been such an easy target. She told me you were never around. Always off chasing criminals."

"You fucking bastard!" The bear trap teeth draws blood as he struggles.

Levin makes each cut into the girl's shirt slow and laborious. Each small cut draws tears from the girl's eyes. "See. I figured someone would follow the girls I took. If their family survived the herd. I left one for dead when she wounded herself in the escape. I'd no idea you were still alive and tracking me."

Snip. He clips another inch of her shirt. "You're a little more beaten up than in all the newspaper photos I saw you in. You know there's no better way to disrupt a police case than to have the lead investigator dismissed and have someone new forced to take over. Too bad the next detective didn't have a blonde daughter."

Danziger controls his urge to jerk free. He can't kill this guy if he cuts off his own hands.

"So I'm sure your experts theorized exactly what I did to these girls and in what order. This one here's Kelly. She attends Greendale High, or did before. She played soccer. I bet they told you my victims mean nothing. No. I know Kelly's name. They are people to me. Breathing living works of art. And..." He runs his hand down her calf. The muscle tenses. "She's so athletic. There's no fatty tissue on these legs." He massages the skin the way a first-time lover would. "Great build for a girl and she still has hips." Tears roll from Kelly's eyes. "Your daughter didn't really have hips yet." He pulls off Kelly's ruined shirt. "Of course, I doubt she'll run again with a mortician's tube in her foot. Thing's sharp. It's amazing what you find in these abandoned homes. People didn't bother to pack their dirty little secrets when they fled for their lives." He taps the ball gag.

Danziger searches for his moment to escape.

"I miss my tools, but I'll make do. He cuts off her panties. "Looky there! You young girls today always staying so trim. Look, just a tuft of hair to tease." He grabs the pubes and tugs. "You ever let a boy see this?"

She shakes her head no.

"Why spend so much time grooming when no one sees this?"

The dam behind Kelly's eyes breaks.

Levin takes a bladed dagger and scrapes clean the hairs. With surgical precision he cleans all the hairs from her legs. "I bet you miss being freshly shaved."

Danziger knows he cleaned them of all body hair, except the head which he would curl into a wavy shape. Something he found attractive in the girls he took. He remembers spending hours thumbing through high school yearbooks looking for matching hairstyles. Whatever girl Levin idolizes had to have worn her hair like he gave the victims. FBI profilers insisted it could break the case.

Despite the razor edge flaking each hair just below the skin, not one single break occurs. Danziger forces his eyes to search for a way out. Every time he glances at the teen he sees his daughter's face. He knows she went through this. She felt this torture. She cried for her father, the cop, to come save her, and he didn't. She died believing Dad would save her. He failed. He won't fail this girl, too. He yanks full on at the bear trap, getting the chain secured to the beam to give a bit, but not enough for him to break free.

Levin unclasps the mouth gag. The girl screams. Aroused, the killer fondles the front of his pants. He takes a bag and dumps the contents on his tool table. A variety of makeup spills out. He rifles through, searching for the right colors before climbing on top of her. She struggles, whipping her head. The killer snags her jaw and pushes in his thumb until she stills. He paints her face, creating a pallet of what she should look like. Levin turns this poor girl into a duplicate model of his first victim. Whatever induced his need to murder must be replayed on the same girl over and over again. Kelly is now her in Levin's mind.

Levin climbs down and removes his clothes, folding each garment before placing them on the table. Never losing his raging hard-on, he climbs back on the table and works himself onto her. He fumbles himself, aligning with her hole. The first thrust sends a shooting pain into Danziger. He hears flesh tear. Screams. She keeps screaming. The thrusting becomes more violent with each wail she releases. Faster and faster until the screeching becomes constant. Blood pools under her legs.

Danziger read the medical reports on each victim. The irreparable damage or repeated violent attacks each girl experienced could have only been repaired through surgeries.

Each thrust barely keeps up with her shrieks. Blood splashes from between their groins. Her voice breaks. Her mouth remains locked open but no longer sounds. Levin halts his thrusts. With no squeals to excite him he goes limp. He slaps her. The makeup smears.

"Scream, you dirty cunt. Scream!"

Even if she wants to, her voice box fails to even let out a whimper. He slaps her face again leaving behind a handprint. He twists the blood drainer. The throbbing pain brings her to tears but no sound emanates from her.

Levin takes his razor tool, grabs Kelly's left breast, twists up on the nipple and pulls it up, lifting her up off the table. He draws the blade around the areola. "I'll cut it off."

Danziger realizes if she doesn't scream then she's useless to him.

"Scream!"

*Just scream, girl. Give me a little more time to rescue you. Scream!*

"You fuckin' bastard. She blew out her voice box. She may never talk again."

"Unlike your daughter. She screamed. She screamed for more. She liked it. She begged for more."

Danziger gives in to his anger and leaps toward the killer. The bear trap snags him and cuts his wrists enough to allow trickles of blood beads to flow. "I'll fucking kill you!"

"She said that, too." He shifts into a little girl voice. "My daddy will find you and kill you if you don't let me go." Levin's voice returns. "Well, you didn't find me. You failed. I enjoyed her. I made it last a long time. Like I'm going to do for this one." He slices into Kelly's flesh, breaking open the skin.

# CHAPTER TWENTY-SEVEN

"WELCOME, BROTHER." EXALTED at his appearance, the man with the Bible waves him in.

The one with the belt strikes the woman again.

Emily's savior balls his fists as if he were invisibly drawing his magnum. He imagines the pull and each shot he'll make. He plays the events about to transpire in his mind. He notes each man's position. All of the men have scars from a brand on their arms. He rolls his eyes back into his head at the thought of having to deal with a cult. Apocalyptic cults had popped up everywhere since the fall of civilization and these nuts had branded themselves with a flaming cross.

"What did this woman do?"

"She must be punished in accordance to His word."

"That would depend on what she did." He feels the other three men all shift their weight to an offensive posture.

"She is the worst, most offensive kind of whore."

"I didn't realize there were levels."

"Oh, yes, brother. Leviticus 21:9," he reads from the Bible, "'and the daughter of any priest, if she profane herself by playing the whore, she profaneth her father: she shall be burnt with fire.'"

"Well, that about covers it. I'll leave you to it." He turns away on his heel but pauses. "How do you know she's guilty of such a sin?"

"She told us and offered herself to us to spare her the rod."

"So she said she'd do anything you wanted if you didn't beat her, and you took that to mean sex, making her a whore?"

"We don't question what God wants us to do. We must purge the wicked from the world."

The chest bruises slow his draw by a mere two tenths of a second. In a gunfight it would be detrimental to his future existence, but these nuts don't see the danger until the second man falls. The third gets his shotgun strap hung up as he unslings it from his shoulder. The Bible wielder falls last.

He flips open his knife and cuts her free.

"Thank you." Two of the lashes on her back have broken through the skin.

"I wonder if they have a medical kit. I'll clean your wounds."

"I just want to go."

"I get it. You don't trust me either."

"No, my father. He's very sick."

He removes the guns from the fallen cultists. He twists the arm of one to inspect the brand. Flames surround a cross covered in unreadable symbols due to the burn. These marks must hold meaning to the men.

He realizes his rookie mistake. "Were there only four of them?"

She hunches over, still naked. "I only saw four."

"What's wrong with your dad?" He pulls a coat from the truck cab.

She takes the coat. "Pneumonia, I think. We have a small camp and we're running out of food. Dad's a preacher and thought he had left a few boxes of food in his office at the church from the food drive. I went to get them. I was hoping some steady food would help his condition."

He flips open the canvas tarp over the back of the truck. Nothing living. He climbs into the bed finding boxes of food and clothes.

He nearly falls out the back trying to climb down without landing on his left leg. "How far away is your group?"

"I can't bring you to them."

"Fine, take this." He holds out a medical bag. "It has some antibiotics in it. They've expired, but they could still help him."

"Why are you helping me?" she asks.

"It's what I do."

"Then you're the one sent by God." She smiles at him.

"Not quite. I should really clean those cuts on your back," he offers.

"I just want to get out of here."

"Let's find you some pants and you take this truck of supplies back to your group."

"I just want to keep my daughter safe." Travis paces behind his desk.

"As any father would," Emily's savior agrees.

"I prepared your list and I've a favor to insist upon you."

"A tall order, Colonel." There's a lot of people out there who will find a military convoy interesting.

"My daughter's obsessed with trying to save people. I put her on gathering your list of people with skills you needed. She'll pick the best. She also wanted to bring a few more people. I gave her a second personnel carrier to fill. I've a few seats left on it. Tell me if you need any others. I'll get them. I'll even send a M816 Wrecker crew to help move any abandoned vehicles off the road."

"Colonel, I taste the desperation in your voice, but I only have enough food to feed a certain amount of people. Doubling my order, and this is not extortion, will cut into my food supplies."

"I've trusted you. I've loaded the trucks with MREs. I'm assigning you troops and supplying you with equipment I've been ordered to destroy."

Now that catches his attention. Part of him figured he could always scrounge after the military abandoned the place. "They want you to blow up the base?"

"There'll be a final contingent of helicopters to evacuate remaining troops. I'm to blow the hospital, ammo depot, and motor pool. All military buildings."

"Our government actually willingly abandons its citizens."

"What did you think was going to happen?" The colonel seems shocked this warrior has had any doubt about what's going to happen.

"I assumed they'd just leave the Fort. Let the people fend for themselves."

"I've equipped your caravan with double the supplies you asked for."

"You want more than me protecting your daughter."

"I need you to wait two days to leave. I can't blow the buildings until the choppers arrive. Most people will think they bring food rations. I've a demolitions expert to destroy the base. I'll have to leave him and a small team at the main gate."

"You want me to take them with me."

"We don't leave anyone behind."

"I thought that was the Marines?"

"It's part of the Soldier's Creed. The commander-in-chief of this United States has forgotten. I will not let my soldiers be forgotten."

"Don't follow the order. Stay and protect the civilians."

"I've already followed worse orders. I can't protect civilians without food. Once they realize there's no more food they'll tear the base apart. Starting with the team I'm ordered to leave behind."

"One thing keeping us safe is being off the grid. My compound's secure. Thanks to the gun trainer you sent me, most of my people are crack shots. We're growing our own food and no one gets into the compound without a complete body search."

"We should've instituted such a policy. Some Infected have gotten in and turned others, costing me valuable soldiers." Travis drops his head in reflection of all the poor choices he'd made since assuming the base commander role.

"You've told all these people they'll have to work for their meals?"

"The mission has been conveyed to them. Those who accepted it have been isolated from the other campers. Those who said 'no' have been relocated to another part of the camp so no rumors of a safe haven could be started."

"What skills does your daughter have? She may be delegated to farm labor."

"Shoveling shit never hurt anyone. I want her safe."

"I'll keep her that way. Let me see who she's gathered."

Travis hands him a clipboard.

He flips through the papers. "Mechanics, carpenters, two nurses. She has made good choices. Maybe a few plumbers."

"You've flushing toilets?"

"The key to any great empire is proper sanitation."

"You know history."

"Reading was rather a requirement in my line of work before the world ended."

"You always struck me more of a Chaucer than a Clancy. When we meet again you'll have to tell me what you used to do."

"We meet again after this and I will." He hands the clipboard back. "I want a sniper."

"I assigned one to the gate team."

"A military ambulance and crew qualified to operate it, and another cargo truck full of heavy weapons."

"You expecting to fight a war?"

"I'm expecting one day the biters populating St. Louis will run out of food and move west or south since it's the only direction available if the bridges aren't maintained. A couple of hundred thousand corpses will have to be eliminated quickly."

"A sound argument."

"The majority of people to survive the apocalypse aren't exactly the kind you invite to Sunday brunch. Only the nut jobs seem capable of living in the Mad Max world."

"I've got a few of those types here. They're the reason to destroy the base."

"I want to meet the soldiers you want to hand over to me," he says.

"They've no families or we're certain everyone's gone, so you won't have any abandoning you. They know the alternative was to remain on base and assured death. They'll follow your orders."

"Remains to be seen."

"I wouldn't assign anyone who would endanger my little girl."

"Right now we've enough food to feed everyone. To take in too many more we'll have to expand our food production. Expanding too fast could lead to the biters getting inside."

"I've packed reserve supplies meant as backup for the soldiers for you. The rest will be handed out as a diversion while the troops load into the choppers. You should have enough MREs to last until you adjust your food budget."

He bets he could ask for a nuke and if the colonel thought it would keep his daughter safe it'd be loaded onto a truck.

"You seem to have covered three of the major problems we have with this base. You kept out Infected, you don't expand beyond your needs," the colonel pauses.

"You said three problems," he inquires.

"Well, you don't seem like the type of man to start a Thunderdome."

"We've cut rations for people who don't put in a full day's work. Cures problems quickly, and the only crime I've had to punish was a rape."

"How'd you deal with rape?"

"After examining all available evidence, it was clear he forced himself on the girl, so I cut his dick off in front of my people."

"Rather Old Testament of you."

"I can't handle rapists."

"A comfort, when you have a daughter," Travis says.

Kade squeezes and scrunches the breasts of the half-naked woman before him. "Nice and perky."

"Is this all I've got to do to earn some food?" Placid, she keeps her eyes away from his molestation.

"You think some tit squeezing gets me off? You're going to have to work that pretty mouth of yours."

"I heard about you, and your bottle fetish. I'll suck you, but my pants stay on."

"You want to eat, you'll do whatever I want." Kade smiles.

"I'm not that hungry."

"Not yet."

"What does that mean?" She knows Kade has insight into the base happenings and his food threat weakens her.

"You're a smart enough girl to realize food rations have dwindled."

"I know you've been doing more business." Her eyes admit why she's here.

"I've secured a little place outside the fence safer than this base's going to be when the food dwindles even more."

"So we all lose a little weight. The government's going to take care of us."

"You really believe that?"

She jerks away from his pawing hands. "You've fondled me enough. Without payment."

Kade grabs her, pinning her arm behind her back as he clamps his hand over her mouth. "Well, I see you're not a proper candidate for our new home. I'm sure there're plenty of other women who'll fornicate on command for food and safety."

He slides his hunting knife into her back, puncturing her lung. He bends her over the table as she gasps for breath, unable to scream.

"If I did it right I deflated your lung." He unclasps his belt, dropping his pants to his ankles. "You'll bleed out. Pretty quick." He scoops up her blood and rubs it on his cock. "I've never killed a person like this before." He slides his erection inside her. "You're pretty tight." His thrusts rattle the desk. "As you bleed out your muscles will contract and you'll get even tighter." With each thrust blood pours from the wound. "Feels so good, baby. Too bad you're just a one-night stand."

Her body collapses on the desk. She prays for this to end faster than it's going to. She feels her life slipping, but not as fast as each of his thrusts.

Travis escorts his daughter's future protector through the hangar bay devoid of any personnel. Helicopters in different states of disrepair line the floor.

"So if I wanted a gunship to protect your daughter..." He leans into a helicopter. It reminds him of the one used in the original

*Predator*. It destroys the illusion of two giant bodybuilders like Arnold and Ventura fitting inside along with the rest of the strike team who were all large, muscular men.

"One vehicle I'm unable to provide. They ordered all our choppers out months ago. We cobbled together a couple more from parts and shipped out all mechanics with them."

"I wouldn't want a copter anyway. Noise would attract all kinds of unwanted attention."

"They are loud."

"The crew needed to maintain a helicopter would send my food numbers into overload. Those extra people will cause my accountant a number of sleepless nights until I secure enough food for all of them."

"You have an accountant?"

"I've this autistic kid. Brilliant with figures. He calculates the number of people and how many cattle we need to feed them and how much grass the cattle need to eat. All in his head. He has fits when the numbers don't add up as fast as he thinks they should. I brought in too many cattle last time and now without enough grassland he's spazzing."

"These people will take care of extra cattle."

"Fresh beef keeps away the hunger."

"Tempting, almost enough to leave my command. I've not had a steak in months."

"Being the second largest beef-producing state in the country, when those city biters figure out there's a smorgasbord in the countryside..." He shakes his head, trying to avoid the thought of hundreds of thousands of fat biters climbing his fence. "No one in this camp's listed as a tanner, are they? Those cattle hides will eventually become a source of clothing and blankets."

"I think I'd remember seeing such a job. I'll have Hannah check around. There was a group of Civil War re-enactors. Sometimes those people take up the trades of the time period when they aren't being doctors and lawyers."

"We've become so reliant on technology and mall shopping we've forgotten how it used to be."

"People will survive this."

"The kind of people surviving aren't the kind you want to rebuild humanity."

"I take it you haven't run into a great deal of recyclers."

"Green Peace would be happy. We're relearning to reuse everything. Nothing's wasted anymore. We've started a junk pile for non-degradable items to find a use for it, and amazingly enough, the most reusable material's stuff we used to chuck in the landfill. Nothing is dreck anymore."

"So many people wanted us to become a nation of recyclers."

"I'd bet if you measured current greenhouse gas emissions they will have dropped to be the lowest rate in the last one hundred years."

"To fix the planet a few billion people have been reduced to DKs."

"We've still learned nothing. It's all gone and we still kill each other for the scraps of others. Do you know about the rest of the world?"

"Europe's about the same as we are. Great Britain is actually faring a little better since it's a giant island. Russia nuked a city. Destroyed a few million, but the radiation fallout created more undead spreading the radiation across the countryside. China claims nothing's wrong. They have no Infected. Other countries' communication fell apart so fast we don't know. Reconnaissance on the rest of the world isn't a priority. We've pulled back all our forces from around the globe to a staging point to retake the country."

"Comforting, but...we just took over a few houses. I had my men check each house room by room before we could use them. A good afternoon's work. This retake is a block-by-block, house-by-house, room-by-room war. That will take years if they are starting on the east coast."

"Now you understand why I'm entrusting you with my daughter's life." They reach a line of trucks and Jeeps.

"I can't give you tanks. The personnel carrier's armored. Your Humvee has a fifty cal. mounted to it and plenty of ammo." Travis opens the back and flips the latches of a plastic weapons case. "I almost drew the line at this." He opens the case. "Two LAW rocket launchers." He runs his hand over the metal tube. "They're not effective against the DKs," Travis points out. "Those not destroyed in the initial explosion are just crawling bags of flames. Fire doesn't stop them."

"I know, but I've always wanted to own a rocket launcher. This may be my only chance."

Travis smiles. He taps other boxes. "Food stuffs and extra automatic weapons."

"Not a big fan of the spray and pray method. I train my people to aim and shoot. Bullets are the new gold."

"I loaded the personnel carrier with more ammo. I've orders to destroy it to prevent it from being scattered among civilians."

"I don't want all these people to die, but can't feed them either."

"It's time to roll the hard six." Travis closes the cases. "The train wreck's coming and I can do nothing, but save my daughter."

"Nothing will happen to her as long as I breathe."

"I want to assign the base doctor to you, and his wife." Travis opens the back of the military ambulance. "Fully stocked."

"Fill it."

"All the bins are full."

"You're going to blow up the hospital. Fill it with medical supplies. Lots of antibiotics."

"You're correct. Shouldn't burn medicine. I'll get another truck."

"This caravan's going to draw some attention from the civilians, just fill the bay space, we'll unload when we get home."

"The exploding buildings will provide a distraction. They won't notice you."

"I'm going to have to re-plan my route home to prevent any followers. I need some maps."

Kade locks the metal collar around the neck of the dead girl. He pulls at the chain to ensure it's securely bolted to the ground.

"You sure about this?" Hale asks.

"When those people realize there's no food shipment they'll raid our tents. They'll find them empty, except for a few guard dogs." He pets her hair as if she were an animal.

"But won't they bite people."

"That's the point, Hale. The Infected will spread panic and send them running."

"Kade, if you're so sure the military's going to abandon the base, why don't you just take over when they leave?"

"Do you really think they are going to leave all those tanks lying around?"

"They can't fly them all out. I drove a forklift. How hard can a tank be to drive?"

"Hard enough, but not so hard they would just abandon them; you're such a dumb shit."

"Besides, to be in control here we'd need a steady source of food. There won't be any more food drops. That's why the soldiers are running."

The dead girl's eyes flash open with a milky white cataract glaze. She snaps her teeth and launches for Hale. The chain stops her just short of sinking an incisor into his leg.

"Kade, she's dangerous! What if she bites one of us?"

"She's on a chain, moron. Don't get close to her. Now, did you come in here for something important?"

"All the remaining trucks are the way you want them. We've moved everything else to the farm. Kale thinks you need to send a few more women."

"Little brother has to learn to share. We'll have to feed them."

"It's a farm. We'll grow food?"

Kade draws his knife from its sheath. He thinks better of stabbing his henchman and marches from the tent. A balding man whose comb over flaps in the breeze races toward him.

"Mr. Bowlin, I need food for my kids."

"Then go to the trading tent."

"The line's really long and I heard you're looking for very specific items." He unwraps the towel he carries.

Kade shakes the box of .22 shells. "It's about half full."

"It's still over two-hundred rounds. It's got to be worth a few cans of food."

"Hale, get this man three cans of food." *Fool. He should save those shells to protect his family. When they do abandon this base I want some of those fifty caliber machine guns. They will tear up the gimps like nobody's business.*

Before he ducks into another tent a dirt-covered pair of teens rush him.

"Kade."

"You two have nothing to trade." He notes the girl's shirt looks like a burlap sack.

"Please, Mr. Kade."

"What do you have to offer?"

"We heard you sometimes give food for information."

"I don't give anything," he snaps at the boy. "You've something valuable I might exchange it for some food."

"We were up by the motor pool, well my sister was. Sometimes if you look pathetic enough the soldiers will share some of their MREs."

"Explains the burlap sack." He runs the back of his hand over the material, making sure to brush against the girl's budding nipple. This agitates the boy. The girl doesn't jerk away.

"Don't waste my time, kid."

"Well, my sister saw..."

Kade cuts him off, "Then I should be making a deal with her. He shoves the boy back. The kid stumbles and prepares to bum rush Kade, but realizes he has no chance against such a well-fed, armed man.

"How old are you?"

"Fourteen," she stammers. Hunger prevents her from jerking away from his aggressive caresses.

"What did you see?"

"The motor pool's been locked down, and there are no troops except a couple of soldiers placing C4 bricks on each vehicle."

"How does a fourteen year old know what C4 looks like?"

"My brother loves action movies. They all use C4 in them."

"You wait in my tent. This turns out to be true, I'll make sure you get plenty of food." He jabs his shoulder into the boy shoving him back as a reminder who's in charge.

*All this to protect one little girl.* He understands why the world fell apart. People put too much importance and resources into a single individual and not enough into the group as a whole. *The good of the many outweigh the good of few,* he thinks, ignoring his own selfish need to have a hot shower.

He strides the length of the convoy he's about to take possession of. He slaps the green-camo tail vehicle, a Humvee with a fifty caliber machine gun and four soldiers. Next in the line are a cargo truck full of people and supplies. The ambulance and the armored personnel carrier precedes it. Another cargo truck full of the skilled people he requested. The military tow truck looks big enough to pull a jumbo jet and his sable Humvee leads the pack.

Once the choppers arrive they will drive over this hill to the main gate where the demolitions officer and the gate guards will fill in the blank seats of the convoy. All completed with military precision.

The soldiers will only add to his ability to guard the colony and maybe even allow Simon to train his guards better. A full staff of doctors to add to those he previously rescued, and now medicine. Weapons. Craftsmen. They'll have to acquire some more cattle and land to graze them, but his camp will have all the personnel it can handle for a while. Safe and secure.

His empty Humvee has one spot for the demolitions expert they will pick up on the way out the gate and two other spots for...

A Jeep pulls up with the colonel and his daughter. Corporal Jameson follows the colonel. Private Amie Sanchez hops from the driver's seat, grabbing her gear bag and rifle. She approaches the Humvee. "I'm your driver now, sir."

"Don't 'sir' me. I work for a living. Now store your gear." Emily's savior notices Private Sanchez's curves despite being clad in full BDUs.

Travis hugs his daughter before escorting her to the Humvee. "Hannah, this man will make sure you and all these other people will be safe."

"Dad, that's what you're supposed to do. Not some stranger."

"This is the only way. No civilians are to be evacuated."

"I don't want to go, Dad. You can't abandon all these people," she blubbers.

"We're saving who we can, and you saved a second truck load. It's going to make it harder on the people taking you in. So you must follow their rules."

"Corporal, put her in the Humvee," Travis snaps at Nick. He turns to Emily's savior. "Corporal Jameson has a crush on Hannah. He's not a bad kid."

"I couldn't save my daughter," Emily's savior admits, "but I'll protect yours."

"The choppers should be here within the hour. Sanchez's a skilled driver. She'll get you back to your home." Travis salutes the man given custody of his only child.

He climbs into the passenger seat of the Humvee. "They sure don't make these things with a tall person in mind."

Tears roll down Hannah's cheeks. "That's the last time I'll see my dad." Nick puts an arm around her to keep her in the seat. Sanchez assumes her position as driver.

"The world has become too harsh a place to say 'don't cry,' of course you will," Emily's savior says.

"You're not much on comforting anyone," Hannah snaps.

"There's nothing left to sugar coat. Not after I've lost count of the number of people I've had to kill to protect the people I care about."

"Have you had to kill a lot?" Corporal Jameson asks, having never fired his weapon off the range.

"More than I care to remember."

Hannah sucks in a blubbering wheeze. "So my dad gave you all this to protect me?"

"Yeah. I met him scouting the area and he paid me for information on the changes in the region when he had to stop sending out troop patrols. I've put together a compound of people. We've been able to keep the biters out."

"How's your place different from here?"

"I've running water and lights for one."

"Real electricity?" Sanchez and Hannah both squeal in unison.

"Isn't all electricity real?"

"Not solar-powered. Too many people try drawing off it and no one has any."

"The colonel should've turned people away."

"He couldn't," Hannah defends her father.

"I can, and I do. Everyone in my camp works, or they don't eat." He clears up any illusions they might have about their new home.

"Dad told me I might have to become a farm hand."

"Unless you're a crack shot. No matter what, we never seem to have enough guards."

"I shoot, but I'm no Annie Oakley."

"We'll find you an appropriate fit." He glances at his watch. Fifty some minutes until the fireworks.

"Kade!" Hale bursts into the tent.

"There better be a fire." Kade holds the young girl informing him about the C4 on his lap as if he were Santa Claus.

"The motor pool's been locked off, just like she said. I found C4 on two trucks." Hale sucks in a deep breath. "It also looks like every soldier is at the helicopter pads, and the choppers are approaching. They don't have no cargo containers."

Kade dumps the girl to the floor, scoops up his revolver, and flips the cylinder into place. "Get the boys and the trucks ready."

# CHAPTER TWENTY-EIGHT

BLOOD FLOWS FROM the cuts in Danziger's wrists. He rises up on his toes to put slack in the chain. The plasma coagulates as it covers the chain and bear trap. Danziger twists using his vital fluid to lubricate the makeshift shackle holding him in place. With enough work he slips his hand through without slicing open his radial artery. He could twist a bit more and maybe escape losing a meaty chunk of palm and his pinky finger.

Distracted by Kelly's failed screams to bring him to climax, Levin draws a knife blade across her skin. Even a cut produces no screams. Levin paces around the table. He punches her in the kidney. She contorts and convulses from the blow. Tears flow, but she's not able to cry out.

Levin's frustration allows Danziger to reach up and grab the chain. He pulls himself up, relieving the pressure on his wrists. He grips the chain with the other hand and lifts himself completely off the ground. Fist over fist, he climbs up the chain. The bear trap loosens. The drying blood greases the chain, forcing Danziger to squeeze tighter. A slip now would send him crashing down and likely sever his whole hand, not just a finger.

Danziger takes his eyes off Levin, whose anxiety of not finishing his brutal act reaches near volcanic levels. Within twelve inches Danziger will reach the beam securing the chain. If he grabs the beam, he can lift one hand out of the trap and be free.

Levin works the mortician's blood draining tube around in Kelly's foot. Blood spills onto the table. Her mouth opens, but she's physically unable to make noise. Too much for even her young body, the excruciating pain culminates in unconsciousness.

Danziger pushes the panic back down inside him. Five or six inches more to the beam. With the poor blonde girl comatose, Levin's now free to pay attention to him. The tip of his index finger touches the top corner of the beam. He stretches to get the whole fist knuckle of the digit over the wood. A second finger touches the beam. Danziger hand grips the beam. He lifts his weight off the trap allowing him to slip free.

Levin spins around. He bolts to prevent Danziger's escape. Danziger scissor kicks, sending Levin across a stack of hay bales. The serial killer rolls to his stomach, pushing himself to his feet, but is met with Danziger's shoe. He scampers under the makeshift table before a second boot lands. Without his body to stop Danziger's foot, his leg flies too high, scrapes the edge of the plywood table and sends Danziger stumbling off balance. Those seconds are all Levin needs to recover. He pops up on the opposite side of the table.

Danziger grabs his leg. The scraped skin under his pants stings more than the cuts in his wrist. Levin snags a knife. Danziger dives over the table in an attempt to prevent the puncture.

Levin doesn't bother with threatening, he simply stabs the blonde teen in her side. The thin blade perforates the bottom of her lung, deflating it. The sucking wound burbles with blood bubbles. A low gasp rolls from her lips marking Danziger's failure. He leaps from the plywood, tackling Levin. The much smaller man is quite stout; impacting him feels like being flung against a stone statue. They tumble across the floor. Levin has the reflexes to hold the blade. Danziger snags the killer's wrist before the blade pierces his shoulder blade. They struggle for the weapon, rolling across the floor. Like in a badly choreographed fight movie, one man rolls on top of the other and then they reverse. All the time Danziger keeps the knife at an arm's length.

The timeworn barn loft had been abandoned long before the apocalypse prevented any upkeep. The hay covered in the musk of rot leaves a film of dust in the air. The once sturdy floor built to withstand thousands of pounds of dried grass to feed livestock all winter now creeks with decay. The deterioration reaches a pinnacle when a board snaps. It flings upward, the board strikes Danziger's head. The impact barely costs him a second of his faculties, but it allows Levin to wrench free of the detective's grasp. He drives the knife hilt into the side of Danziger's cranium. Dizzy, Danziger rolls away to avoid a second blow.

Levin scampers to his feet. The floor collapses beneath him and he crashes into the stall below in a tangle of boards and loose straw.

The moan-howl of DKs waft through the new floor opening. Danziger, still wonky from the brain blow, crawls to the edge. The splintered boards form a windmill pattern around Levin, trapping him as well as protecting him from the growing number of undead gathering at the barn. Gray rotten fingers snake through the lumber, failing to reach him.

Danziger orders himself to move. He has to get to Levin before the man recovers from the impact. Blood rains on the floor from Kelly's wound. She's bleeding out. Torn between the two choices, Danziger reasons he can do little medically for the girl. He knows from her breathing that her lung's damaged. He has no skill or even the know-how to help someone with her kind of wound. But he does know how to stop this from ever happening to another girl again.

Part of him wants to leap into the hole ending Levin now, but if he's faking unconsciousness he could land on the knife. It will take longer, but he crawls toward the ladder, rising to his feet in order to climb down. His shoes kick up the hard dry earth. His mind clears enough from the blow. Danziger feels balanced enough to run. He pushes through the rubble to find Levin. He snatches up the knife. He holds the blade for a long second. He should end it. Something stopes him from just stabbing this man. Revenge would be assured, but Danziger wants more. He wants Levin to suffer the pain he feels for his dead daughter. He cuts into Levin's skin deep enough to send spasms of pain through him. Danziger cuts him again. Pleasure overwhelms him as he brings pain to the man who murdered his daughter. The knife speeds toward Levin's throat. This next cut will offers Danziger closure for the death of his only child.

# CHAPTER TWENTY-NINE

CORPORAL JAMESON GLANCES at his watch. "Eleven minutes until the choppers are due."

"The food rations will be handed out in one minute," Hannah adds.

Private Sanchez wrings her hands on the steering wheel as if waiting for the light to change to green so she can floor the accelerator.

"Won't people notice the lack of helicopters and the handing out of food?" he asks.

"Once the food lines start, a nuclear bomb could go off but people won't get out of line. The lack of soldiers to keep order could be an issue. If a shoving match starts, the soldiers normally put a stop to it, but not this time. I've worked the line a lot," Hannah explains. "I'm just glad Dad decided not to blow up the food with the weapons."

"The colonel has civilians handing out the food stuff he was to destroy," Sanchez chimes in.

"Food will keep some of these people alive."

"So would guns," Hannah snaps.

"They would just kill each other for the food," he remarks.

"Why can't you take in more of these people?"

*I can't take in the second truckload you filled but we'll make it work.* He considers blasting her with such information but thinks better of it.

Sanchez twists the key. "Choppers coming in."

"Drive us out slow," he orders.

Kade flips on the windshield wipers to disperse the shattered chunks of the undead person spattered over the hood of his truck. He races down a makeshift dirt road outside the fence line of the military base.

Every bump sends Hale floundering around the cab. The men in the bed barely hang on to the roll bar.

"Kade, you got to slow down." Hale slams against the door.

Kade mashes the gas petal, accelerating the truck ahead of the two vehicles chasing him.

"You said there was a convoy of trucks at the front gate."

Even with a seatbelt secured, Hale flails like a rag doll.

"I'll bet the farm the demolitions crew is in one of those trucks."

"I don't understand."

"They would have the detonators for the C4 on them. We stop them, we save all the tanks." Kade stomps on the pedal.

Before the transport helicopter lands, two soldiers leap from the landing ramp. They race through the platoon of men. Several soldiers point back at Colonel Travis.

"Sir, we've orders to load you first," the soldier yells over the helicopter noise.

"No. I'll see my men loaded first." Travis leers at the two men.

"We've our orders, sir."

"You're wasting time and fuel. Get my troops on the helicopter. I'm leaving enough behind not to leave any of them."

"Then we will stay with you till you're securely on board, sir."

The colonel flies the 'move out' hand sign and the first round of troops are sent to the chopper. Once full it takes off and a second lands.

Travis glances at his watch. The choppers are seven minutes early. The civilians won't be anywhere near any of the military buildings set to explode when the demolitions officer follows his orders in six minutes.

The once civilian-friendly entrance with the open tollgate style barriers and friendly officers, who only checked identifications to allow people on the base, have been replaced with sniper towers, concertina wire, chain link fencing, and tank stopping dragon's teeth obstacles in order to keep the undead out.

In the two seconds before impact, Kade prays the reinforced steel battering ram style front section of the truck meant to help move abandoned cars functions.

The chain link fence buckles and the truck slides through. The other two trucks of his henchmen ram the second gate, preventing anyone from escaping.

As the next chopper lifts off, Colonel Travis swears he hears the faint whisper of gunfire. Impossible with the noise from the whirling blades and the distance these landing pads are from the rest of the base. Still, once a soldier has faced enemy fire in combat he never forgets—bullets and the death following.

Travis fears for his daughter's life.

"Brakes!" he orders Private Amie Sanchez. The Humvee skids to a halt. Trucks shatter the front gates. Civilian men engage in a firefight with the troops in the watch towers.

"That's going to attract a shit-ton of biters," Sanchez says.

"That's Kade and his men." Hannah panics. "He runs the black market and forces women to trade their bodies for extra food."

"You want me to man the fifty cal.?" Jameson asks.

"No. We won't risk you hitting whatever they are using to set off the explosions. Hopefully your demolitions officer's still breathing in the tower."

"How are you going to stop them if you don't shoot them?" Sanchez asks.

"I didn't say I wasn't going to shoot them." He checks each of his pistols. All fully loaded. "Stay here. That's an order."

"You can't just walk down there," Hannah protests.

Jameson starts at this man in black, "Who do you think you are, John Wayne?"

"More like Han Solo. I'm going to shoot first." He clicks the door handle.

"If they kill you, where am I supposed to take her?" Corporal Jameson follows his first duty to his commander.

"You can't just go out there like this is *High Noon* or something," Hannah protests.

"Hard to believe a girl of your age even knows of Jimmy Stuart in *High Noon*."

"It was Gary Cooper, and my dad made me watch all those Westerns with him." She quickly adds, "I know who John Wayne was, too."

"Well, my cultured friends, 'I thoroughly disapprove of duels. If a man should challenge me, I would take him kindly and forgivingly by the hand and lead him to a quiet place and kill him.'"

Confident, Hannah barks at him, "That's not from the movie."

"Correct. It's a quote, and your only clue to where you need to go."

"Who are you?" Sanchez asks.

"What's in a name?" He contemplates for seconds before giving her an answer, "Ethan, Ethan Edwards."

"They'll kill you," Sanchez protests.

He taps his black vest. "Kevlar." He quick-marches from the Humvee.

"Clue? Clue to what? I'm confused." Hannah grabs the door handle.

Jameson climbs over the seat to prevent Hannah from exiting. "You got to stay here."

"He seems a bit too old to be an Ethan." Sanchez inquires, "Do you know what his clue means?"

"Not off hand. I figure it's simple, whoever said the phrase or whatever movie it's in is where we'll need to go."

"So if it's from *Juno* then we have to go to Minnesota," Hannah says.

"Something like that," Jameson releases her. The thundering boom of a .357 jolts Corporal Jameson back into his seat.

Ethan holsters his magnum, seven shots still unspent. Kade and his fellow renegades cease fire on the tower and turn their weapons on him.

*Maybe I should have just had the corporal use the fifty cal. on these assholes.* He raises his arms in a non-threatening manner before stepping closer.

"You hold it right there!"

"Kade?" he calls out. He doesn't need much confirmation. He will never forget the face of the man inside the farmhouse or what he did to Emily's companion. It is the same face standing before him now. He knows the offender's dead. He saw to that, but this one could be his twin, if not, certainly his brother.

"Who the fuck are you?" Kade waves to one of his men to keep guns on the tower.

"I hear you're the kind of man to make a deal with."

"I'm in a bit of a negotiation right now." Kade's curiosity peeks at the non-military man placed in charge of a military convoy.

"I think you want to hear my offer."

Jameson tucks Hannah onto the backseat floorboards in order to give her maximum protection from any stray bullets. He crouches, his boots in her seat ready to pop out the top hatch. He may be ordered not to engage with the fifty cal., but no order was issued about his rifle.

"What kind of deal do you have to offer me?" Kade waves Hale and LJ to accompany him as he steps toward this man in black. "Do I know you?"

"We've never met, Kade, even if you do resemble the fuck face I beat to death for raping a couple of girls he took from this base."

"You mother fucker. You took another group out of this base, with some fat chick. My brother went after you. He never made it back."

"Add that to the negotiation. I'll tell you his current location."

"None of you fuckers shoot. This bastard's mine." In a rage, Kade marches toward the man in black.

Ethan flips his shoulders back sending his duster from his huge frame. The .357 magnum shines through the holster holes even with the sun behind him.

Jameson watches Kade and his two henchmen stomp toward his new commanding officer. With the black coat crumpled on the ground, Jameson spots guns Kade doesn't.

"Does Ethan think he's some kind of one-man army?" Sanchez asks.

Hannah attempts to rise up to witness what's about to happen. Sanchez shoves her back to the floor.

"No matter what, don't shoot this guy. I need to know what happened to Kani," Kade orders.

"How do you know this guy knows?" Hale asks.

"Where's my brother?" Kade demands.

"You need to move one of your trucks and let my convoy leave the base, and I'll tell you where he is."

"You're not rolling out of here until I know where he is."

"Fine. I'll stand right here, but the convoy moves outside the fence." He uses the proclamation to rotate his body sideways to provide less of a target, keeping the shiny magnum facing them. An old revolutionary war duelist trick he remembers reading about.

"I don't know who you're used to dealing with."

The longer their banter takes the more relaxed Kade's men become on the trucks and turn their attention away from the soldiers trapped in the tower to this man in black resisting their boss.

"You're going to tell me right now," Kade demands.

"Like hell I will."

Explosions tear through the base behind him. He should have jumped like a jackrabbit, but he knew it was going to happen. He was hoping he could stall long enough to surprise Kade's men.

Jumping jackrabbits wouldn't begin to describe the men as several scatter behind the trucks for cover. Kade doesn't move even while Hale and LJ step back. They shift their eyes to the growing clouds of black smoke covering the military base. Kade never takes his eyes off the silver magnum.

The plumes of smoke remove his advantage of sunlight in Kade's eyes, and with this element of surprise he must take advantage of being so exposed in the center of the road with no cover. The M&P leaps into his hand. LJ gets no chance to raise his weapon as two rounds shatter his sternum. A stray round flies between the falling LJ and Kade.

Kade gets a wild shot off. Chunks of asphalt splinter before Ethan. A single round punctures Kade's right lung. A fifth and sixth round flies between Kade and Hale. Ethan loses track of one round, the other strikes a man in the leg. Before he howls, Hale gets a bullet in the kidney from behind. His instinct once the gun fire started was to turn and run, but he didn't get far.

His shotgun discharges. Lead balls pelt one of the trucks sending the men in it scrambling.

The soldiers within the guard tower find their opportunity to join the fray. They rain fire on the men in the trucks. This only assists Ethan in expending the remaining nine rounds.

Jameson pops through the hatch. He takes careful aim between each shot, never wasting a bullet or giving his new CO a reason to duck.

A soldier climbs down from the guard tower. He fires on the last remaining men in a truck.

Kade sucks in frantic gasps of air but not enough to fill his lungs. His gun slides with a kick from his hand. A shot rings out. His men, dead or not, are being put to death.

Ethan towers over Kade, slamming a fresh clip into his M&P. "I'm going to move your trucks now."

Kade hacks blood. "My..."

"Your brother. Me having to move the trucks myself sort of ends the deal. You've nothing to offer."

Blood spills from the chest wound. Ethan leans close to Kade. "You know I don't want to turn into your kind. So before you expire I'll tell you. I killed the one brother you sent after Sarah. I also killed another one who was into raping little girls."

Kade forces himself to rise up. He can't get enough air to curse this man or even get to his elbows. A hollow point slug imbeds itself in his skull.

"Jameson! Have the wrecker get up and clear the road," Ethan howls at the corporal. Four soldiers climb down from the guard tower.

The shortest one runs up to him, saluting. "I appreciate the help, sir."

"Your explosions helped a lot."

The helicopter lifts off. Colonel Travis steps onto the cargo ramp, being the last of his men to evacuate Fort Leonard Wood. The helicopter races through the black smoke. Travis views what's left of his base as it burns.

People scatter from the food distribution area. The explosions have sent them into a riotous panic. Many race for the tents of the Bowlin brothers.

"Sir, you need to take your seat in order to close the ramp," one of soldiers sent to escort him explains.

Thick smoke engulfs much of the base. Through the plumes, he spots the convoy speeding from the front gate. He counts the vehicles. All of them made it out. Knowing his daughter will remain safe allows him to take his seat. Knowing thousands will die because of his cowardly flight will cause countless sleepless nights.

# CHAPTER THIRTY

"I DON'T KNOW if I can do this," Hannah squats behind a tree, her panties around her ankles.

"You said you had to go." Corporal Jameson, poised on the other side of the tree, keeps his rifle at the ready.

"I do. It's bad enough I have to use a tree, but I can't go if you're watching."

"I'm not going to watch you poop. I'm just going to stand guard." Jameson keeps his back to Hannah and the tree. "I can go get Private Sanchez if you want."

"I'm a girl. I don't want you to know I poop."

"I can't leave you alone, especially squatting in a forest full of lame brains..."

"I wish you wouldn't call them that."

"What do you want me to call them?"

"They were people. Someone's mom, uncle, teacher."

"They're the enemy. An enemy we've not been trained how to fight." He raises his weapon. A squirrel races from some grass up a tree. The startling noise draws her attention away from him allowing him to peek at her naked rump.

"Turn around!" she snaps. "I don't know if I can go with you standing there, but I certainly can't go with you watching."

"I'll stay turned around, but you're going to have to get used to someone watching. I guess that's about one of the first things you learn in basic without realizing it."

"How to poop?"

"There're no stalls. You've ten minutes to be ready once the Drill Sergeant calls Reveille. You ain't ready, your unit suffers and you don't want that."

"Keep talking, it helps me to relax." She chews her bottom lip to disguise a small grunt. "You ever cause your unit to be late?"

"I don't think we were ever late. But we had to do extra pushups for this one guy who wouldn't shower."

"Why wouldn't he shower?"

Jameson forgets for a moment he's talking with a fifteen-year-old girl. "He'd the tiniest dick I've ever seen. Like the size of your thumb to the first knuckle.

She looks at her thumb. She bends the knuckle and flexes it a few times. Even having never been with a man she knows that won't do much for a girl. "Not even an inch." *Poor guy*, she thinks.

"I guess his embarrassment was too much. He'd rather stink, so he refused to shower in front of us. The drill sergeant would march past him during inspection and about puke from the odor. Said if one of us was going to stink we'd all stink so we did pushups."

"'Til you stank?"

"'Til there was so much sweat pouring off us. A lot of guys wanted to beat him up, but we just let him shower alone that night. The drill sergeant found out. Said we were a unit. We work as a unit. Drill sergeant set a time for the water to turn on and be turned off. The kid didn't shower. We did pushups until two men collapsed from dehydration."

She pulls up her pants. "Well, I guess I'm a big girl. I went potty." She bounces with a smirk toward the trucks. "So he just showered?"

"We helped him. We got some scouring brushes with the hard bristles like for cleaning burnt-on grease. We drug him into the shower and cleaned him. Told him if he didn't shower we'd scrub him like that every day."

"Did it work?"

"I never saw a person with such raw red skin. He showered from then on."

"Bet he wished he'd just have been laughed at for a small dick."

The laugh of a teenage girl bites at him. "I guess." He glances at his own lack of a bulge in his pants. They head back to the circle of trucks parked so not one blocks another but provides cover. The people she helped rescue are tightly packed inside the circle. The soldiers take up defensive positions to protect the civilians eating from brown MRE packages.

The men, now deemed her protectors by her father, hand out MREs to each person.

"Can we set up a tent?" Hannah asks.

"No. No comfort."

"It's going to be chilly tonight. If you don't want to travel at night, can't we build a fire?"

"Jameson, do you know how to construct a Dakota Fire Hole?"

"Never heard of it."

Ethan explains, "You dig a fire pit in the center. You can hid more fire the deeper you dig. Don't build it too high above ground. It will attract biters. Dig a second pit next to the one for the fire and then make a tunnel to connect the two. It will provide air for the fire and hide smoke and flames."

"If you say it works, sir."

"It will. Just do it."

Jameson snaps to the task.

"We've headlights. Why not travel at night?" Hannah asks.

"You've been in the compound for nine months. I've spent a great deal of time exploring the new world. The road clear for a dozen trips has a stalled truck not there yesterday. I can't explain it. It seems the evidence of people having been around grows but people themselves can't be found, and I've already crashed once in the last week." He hands her a brown packet. "Eat half the MRE and save the other half for breakfast."

"My father sent plenty of food," Hannah protests.

"How do you know?"

"He told me."

"I'm telling you how to eat it. My promise of safekeeping will be performed how I see fit," Ethan says.

"Don't think you can speak to me like that."

Jameson slides his finger over the trigger of his rifle at the angry father tone being blasted at Hannah. Ethan notices the finger shift, causing him to flex his own gun hand. Jameson knows this man's faster than he will ever be even with his rifle already drawn.

"And that food has to sustain you and these people for more than just while we travel. Safe doesn't mean you get to be a spoiled princess. It's time to grow up and work for your survival. You brought along more people than I'm able to feed until I get more cattle. We ration the MREs."

She looks to the soldiers, but none of them—even Nick—seem to disagree with this man. He's been outside the fence more than all of them put together and lived for all this time, and they respect he knows how to survive. Colonel Travis would never have put anyone else in charge of them.

"I'm not a spoiled princess." Hannah turns away. She doesn't want to cry, cry like the little girl this man thinks she is. Her tears are for a father she won't see again.

Ethan slams on the brakes. The bleeding man falls over the Humvee hood. Hannah's protector jumps out, drawing his M&P and placing his left hand over the right hand. Jameson mans the fifty caliber. *Ker-chunk.* The mechanism to make it fire clicks into place.

"Don't fire," Ethan orders.

*Bam. Bam.*

Two biters fall from his pistol.

"It's bad enough my gun shots will attract more. That thing will bring half the country." Ethan waves for the soldier in the passenger seat to follow him.

Demolitions specialist Cromwell slides from the Humvee and side steps to the front of the vehicle, weapon drawn. "Is he dead?"

The fallen bloodied man heaves for breath from running to escape the now growing number of undead emerging from the forest.

Jameson swings the fifty cal. toward the emerging corpses. "I can clean them all out."

"Not yet." He points for Cromwell to keep his pistol on the man while he rips open the shirt.

"No bites," Ethan says.

"Someone's beat the hell out of him."

"Or abused him for fun." Ethan follows a line of cuts in the chest with his finger inches above it. "He was running from whoever did this, not those corpses." He handcuffs the man's wrists together. "Grab the doc," he orders Cromwell.

"Why?" Stammers Levin, holding up his cuffed hands. He barely escaped Danziger's death blow.

"You want my help. I don't know you, and someone beat you up. Until I decide you're not going to harm my group, you stay cuffed or I leave you to the biters."

"Please help me, he's after me."

"Who?"

Levin passes out.

He keeps his gun pointed at the bloody man's head while he feels for a pulse.

The doctor jogs from the personnel carrier. Cromwell pops an approaching biter.

"What happened?"

"He flew over the hood."

"These wounds aren't from a car impact. He's been worked over." The doctor examines the wounds.

"You find a bite. I end him and we go."

"I understand." The doctor nods.

"You better, because your Hippocratic Oath no longer applies to those that have been bitten."

The doctor nods. "Someone's cut a chunk of hide out about the size of a pork chop." He places four gauze pads over a wound where chunks of skin have been carved from his flesh. "This man's been tortured not bitten."

"The cuffs stay on. It's non-negotiable."

"Can I speak to you privately?" The doctor jerks his head, motioning him away from the Humvee.

"You'll find, doc, if I think a situation will cost me my life I won't stand for any negotiations." Three thunderous booms rattle the air. He spins around. Three corpses fall. Private Sanchez blows the smoke away from her sidearm.

"Anyone bitten has to be put down." The doctor agrees. "This looks more like someone tried to filet him."

"Cannibals. I've seen evidence," Ethan says.

"Why would anyone reduce themselves to that?" Cromwell asks.

"If you don't know how to hunt or fish and the food mart has been emptied, what do you do to quell the rumble in your stomach?"

"You ask a lot of questions," Cromwell observes.

"Used to be my job."

"But the answers..."

"I don't like them, but 'once you eliminate the impossible, whatever remains, no matter how improbable, must be the truth,' Sir Arthur Conan Doyle once wrote."

"I'm not smart enough to understand what you mean," Cromwell admits

"If it walks like a duck and quacks like a duck..." the doctor explains.

Cromwell completes the idiom, "Then it must be a duck."

If we helped someone's lunch get away, they're going to come after him. And until we know more about this, we keep this fucker handcuffed."

"Help me," Levin regains consciousness for a moment to plead.

Cromwell slings his M16, loops his arms under Levin's armpits in order to pull him to his feet. The doctor takes an arm to act as a crutch and they move the wounded man to one of the cargo trucks.

As they pass the side of the Humvee, Levin trips and slams against the window. Blood smears across the surface. Levin eyes the colonel's daughter.

Surprised by the man's appearance, Hannah jerks away. Her blonde hair falls into her face. The doctor half drags Levin to the truck. Jameson pops another Infected.

"You're only drawing their attention to you," Ethan warns. "Noise attracts them." He backs away from the convoy so he can see the back of the cargo truck.

"But they ain't damn fast."

"Not as individuals, but even two or three turn into formidable enemies." He witnesses them secure the wounded man in the truck.

Cromwell races back to the Humvee. "Want me to drive?"

"I've got it." he pops another corpse and climbs into the driver's seat.

Danziger smashes a DK in the face with a two-by-four. Other undead near him are drawn away at the thunder booms of a machine gun.

He speculates about Levin finding a gun. *Would someone be helping him? What kind of person would help him?* On the other hand he appears to be some kind of victim of a brutal assault. Running after and screaming Levin's some kind of killer would more than likely get him shot, not Levin.

Danziger stays hidden in the tree line. He counts the military vehicles as they drive away and ponders, *at least they won't have a young girl in their unit.*

The corpses shamble to the road after the trucks. Danziger knows he can't catch the trucks, and with the DKs distracted, he races back to the barn.

The poor girl. It's too late for her. Danziger climbs the ladder to the loft.

Kelly's ankle remains trapped in restraints. She claws at the floor, attempting to drag herself toward him. Her teeth snap at him.

Danziger grabs a crowbar. The perfect instrument of courage for what he has to do. He drives the metal wedge into the top of her skull. She makes a last desperate grab for his legs as her teeth chomp at him for the last time.

Black blood pools on the floor. He drags a sheet over her body, covering all of her. He hovers over her for a moment of prayer, not so much for this girl but for his own. The goodbye he never got to say to his own child he gives to her. Then the promise he made to his daughter he swears to this girl. He will end this serial killer. As long as he draws breath, he will never stop chasing Levin.

He rummages through the gear, rifling through duffel bags Levin collected, dumping containers. The man must have found a few homes nearby to get all this stuff in such a short amount of time. Danziger gathers anything he feels will be of use to survive and stuffs everything into one backpack. With the number of roaming biters, he cannot bury this girl as she deserves. She should be buried. But it's a risk he can't take. He dumps bottles of chemical and motor oil onto the wood. The dry tinder soaks in the fluids. He cuts open the hay bales and scatters the dead grass over the loft. He covers the girl with an entire bale. The last bale he drops from the loft and jumps down.

A few biters mill around the barn. Danziger empties an oil bottle into the straw and lights a match. The bale ignites. The flames lap at the dry boards. They burst into flames much faster than he expected. The straw and chemicals he dumped catch in a flash of flames.

The crackling fire attracts the milling biters. He grabs the splitting maul from the chopping stump and strolls from the barn. The heavier-than-a-hatchet weapon swings off balance but still shatters the cranium of a DK. Danziger moves toward the road. Roads are dangerous but the military convoy had enough firepower to stay on them with little risk. It will make it easier for him to follow them in order to put an end to Levin.

# ABOUT THE AUTHOR

William Schlichter has a Bachelor of Science in Education emphasizing English from Southeast Missouri State and a Masters of Arts in Theater from Missouri State University. With fifteen years of teaching English/Speech/Theater, he has returned to making writing his priority. Recent successes with scriptwriting earned him third place in the 2013 Broadcast Education Association National Festival of Media Arts for writing a TV Spec Script episode of The Walking Dead.

His full-length feature script, *Incinta*, was an officially selected finalist in the 2014 New Orleans Horror Film Festival. *Incinta* received recognition again by being selected as a finalist at the 2015 Beverly Hills Film Festival for a full-length feature. *Incinta* has advanced in several other script contests, including most recently being an Official Selected finalist in The 2016 Irvine Film Festival. His next life goal would be to see his film transferred from the pages to the screen.

Writing has always been his passion even through traveling, raising twin children, and educating teenagers. While he specializes in the phantasmagorical world of the undead and science fiction fantasy stories, William continues to teach acting, composition, and creative writing.

CPSIA information can be obtained
at www.ICGtesting.com
Printed in the USA
FFHW020025250719
53859348-59557FF

9 781946 006516